THE EVOLUTION OF JEREMY WARSH

Jess Moore

A NineStar Press Publication

Published by NineStar Press
P.O. Box 91792,
Albuquerque, New Mexico, 87199 USA.
www.ninestarpress.com

The Evolution of Jeremy Warsh

Printed in the USA
First Edition
November, 2018

Print ISBN: 978-1-949909-55-5

Also available in eBook, ISBN: 978-1-949909-48-7

Jeremy Warsh has been in off-mode ever since his grandpa's death a couple years ago. He set aside their shared passion, comic art, and hasn't looked back. As an introvert from the other side of town, he fully expects to spend his boring life bagging groceries until, maybe one day, he's promoted to store manager.

Yet, his two best friends, Kasey and Stuart, are different. They're not afraid to demand more out of everyone. When Kasey comes out, Jeremy's inspired. He picks up his colored pencils and starts drawing comics again, creating a no-nonsense, truth-talking character named Penny Kind. Who speaks to him. Literally.

The friend-group sets in motion Stuart's plans for a huge Homecoming prank, and if they can get Penny's comic trending, they might be able to pull it off. Could this be a stepping-stone to a future Jeremy's only dreamed of? And after he kisses a boy at a college party, will Jeremy finally face what he's been hiding from?

To Fluff E.

Chapter One

CHILLY IN THE underground basement, one of my best friends and I spent the final hours of summer's freedom on opposite sides of the couch. Kasey's head poked out from under an orange-and-black chevron afghan. Her arm snaked out from under the blanket as she reached for the bowl of potato chips between us. In fact, we had moved only for snack and/or bathroom breaks since setting up camp earlier in the day. The last of August's to-do list was to listen to Nirvana's entire library.

"Did you catch this live when it came out on MTV?" I asked, as the first few notes of "Lake of Fire" sounded. Cobain's scratchy prophet-like lilt emanated from a set of waist-high speakers next to the fireplace.

"In middle school? I don't know. They re-air it every now and then though." She licked the BBQ-flavored spices from a potato chip.

"It wasn't long after that he was gone, and we were all down here drinking our first beers in his honor." I gave my can of Mountain Dew a little shake, empty.

"I remember." Kasey leaned her head back against the pillow. "This is too depressing for words." She popped the rest of the chip in her mouth and jumped up from the couch to switch off the stereo.

"Hey! I love that one!"

"Come on, Jeremy. You need to practice." She grabbed my hand and tried to pull me from the couch.

"Seriously?"

"Yes! School starts tomorrow." She gave up and walked toward her bedroom. Kasey's basement was hardly that. Basically it was its own two-bedroom apartment with a TV room, kitchen, and dining space. The lower level of her house cut into the hill and opened to a brick patio overlooking a pool and woods beyond. She'd lived down there with her older brother until he left for college. Now, it was just Kasey; her parents lived upstairs.

"Fine!" I called after her. Our senior year was less than twenty-four hours away; she was probably right. My distorted reflection peered back at me from the TV's black glass as I forced myself out of the sunken cushions.

Kasey's bedroom walls were sponge-painted with textured splats in varying shades of flamingo pink. It was dizzying and the opposite of subtle, but the same went for her.

"Jeez, you've grown, like, a foot in the last month. You could've played football this year." She reached for my shoulders and positioned me in front of her closet mirrors.

"That would mean more time around Russ. Plus, Mom would never let me."

Kasey stepped back, assessing my reflection. "Now, say it."

"Suck it, Russ." The words rolled clumsily off my tongue. I rushed through the line because I hated every minute of it.

Russ Landry had been making my life miserable forever. Kasey was convinced if I stood up to him, he'd leave me alone. I figured it would likely get me punched. But ignoring the bastard, which I'd been trying to do for years, proved an unsuccessful strategy.

She shoved me forward and flopped onto her bed. "You'll get nowhere if you say it like that. This needs flair, Jeremy. Again."

I repeated the line with some sass that I would never replicate in real life.

"Grasshopper, you must deliver a blow of such magnitude that thine enemy is left stunned." Kasey flipped through the latest issue of a teen fashion magazine. She hadn't even seen my sashay.

"Is that why you tell people to suck your dick?" I cleared my throat, a little embarrassed.

"I only tell misogynists that, and yyyyep." Kasey unwrapped a sucker and stuck it in her mouth. "Wah-wa?" she asked, her speech hindered by the candy.

"I'm good." I sat next to her. The magazine contained musky perfume samples. Kasey found one and rubbed the paper on both her wrists and neck.

"Yuck, that smells awful," I said.

"You're crazy. Everyone loves CK One." She flipped through the special back-to-school edition. "Wanna read your horoscope? Cancer, right?"

"Yeah."

"So obvious."

She read my crab-shelled future.

KIDS PACKED THE halls, most of them showing off stiff new clothes and kicks. My sneakers were the same ones from last year, and these new jeans were already creating itchy red impressions on my gut. Mom had spent most of her last paycheck getting new school clothes for me. So, I wasn't about to tell her. I'd wash them less and hope for some stretching. Maybe try to lose a couple pounds. Or not.

Overweight, with kinky hair and sweat permanently lining the sides of my face, I was boundaries upon borders.

As I mixed with the herd, it hit me how this would be the last time I'd cross the threshold of these halls with a whole 182 days of lectures and homework in front of me. The last time I'd find my new locker and get all sweaty when the combination didn't work the first, second, or...third time. *Damn it!* I slammed my palm into the area above the lock, and the door opened with a *clang*. I stacked a fat binder and a package of loose-leaf paper on the top shelf but kept a few pencils and spiral-bound notebooks in my backpack for later.

"Wat up, beeyotch?"

The last year I'd have to deal with Russ Landry.

The jerk rounded the corner, high-fiving one of his lackeys. "Boo-yah!" The two bumped chests and foot traffic came to a standstill as they hashed out how their summers had gone.

I kept my head down and decided on going the long way.

My first two classes, World History and Classic Lit, went off without a hitch. I kept to myself in the back of each room. Nobody I hung out with on the reg were in those classes, but neither was my archnemesis.

My two best friends were supposed to be in Physics with me though. I weaved through mazes of people the whole way. The district had approved the transformation of the smoker's courtyard a decade ago. Filled in with cinder blocks and fluorescent lights, the once green space had become three climate-controlled classrooms and a computer lab. Stuart and Kasey both waved as I walked in, and Stuart removed his backpack from the empty chair next to him.

"How goes it?" he asked. We'd been bros since we were a couple of twerps in elementary school.

"I'm here, ain't I?"

The bell rang, and everyone hustled to find a seat. Kasey sat across the aisle, and I leaned over and whispered, "Hey" before the teacher introduced herself and started taking attendance.

"Warsh?" Mrs. Paisley had frizzy sand-colored hair and wore a pair of lavender-framed glasses that kept sliding down her nose. Her long skirt had a swirling purple-and-red-violet paisley pattern, and I figured that was a purposeful choice. "Jeremy Warsh?"

People said my full name, and their mouths sounded full, as if they'd tucked two midsized sacks of marbles into their cheek pockets.

"Here," I murmured.

"All righty, then. That's all of us. Welcome, Class of '99; this is Physics!" Mrs. Paisley motioned to the room. She went right into a lecture on potential versus kinetic energy, not wasting a second of time with introductions and getting-to-know-you posters. I hard-core respected this decision. As she turned to write on the whiteboard, the classroom erupted with shuffling and zipping noises.

"I love that sound!" Mrs. Paisley chimed with her back still toward us. "It means you are invested in your futures! Your mission, if you choose to accept it, and you must..." Mrs. Paisley paused. Thirty adolescent groans tolled. "...is to build a mousetrap powered car by the end of this week." She straightened a stack of papers at her lab table. A couple hands shot up. Mrs. Paisley carried the bundle to the front of her desk and handed them to me.

"Jeremy will pass out the instruction sheets, which I expect will answer many of your questions. But, yes, you there. In the back, mm-hmm." Mrs. Paisley pointed to the back of the room. "I don't know your name yet. What's your question?"

The legs of my seat grated against the freshly polished linoleum floor. I counted two papers for each table. Russ Landry sat in the last row, smirking in his letterman jacket. Why the winter coat? It was ninety degrees outside. Even the AC struggled to keep up with the heavy August heat. Passing out the papers caused a line of perspiration to form under my pits. I tossed the handouts at him. Of course, he let them float to the floor.

"Hey, p-p-porky." He talked loud enough for the kids around him to hear, but not Mrs. Paisley. Hardly ever did a teacher catch this guy in prick-mode. "You better p-p-pick those up."

I'd stuttered one time in eighth grade during an oral presentation on Aztec culture—or maybe the Mayans? I couldn't remember. Point was, Russ did. Assholes must be born with an extra memory sector. Within the additional brain fold existed embarrassing details from every weirdo's tiny life.

"You wanna suck it, Russ?" My voice wavered, registering higher at the end of the sentence. *Damn it*. That wasn't what I'd practiced all summer with Kasey. She'd made it sound hard and offensive. I sounded as if I'd just offered my junk on a serving platter. People snorted with laughter. My heart raced. Sprouting legs and wearing knee socks, shoes, and a sweatband, the little organ sprinted inside my chest.

"You think you're funny now?" Russ leaned over the desk looking up at me, a coiled snake shaking its rattle.

"No." I backed away.

"Nobody talks to me like that." His cheeks flushed with excitement, anger, or his own body heat trapped in that ridiculous puffy coat. He wouldn't make a scene now, would he? I walked away totally aware a beating could be on my horizon.

"Are you okay?" Stuart asked. "You gonna hurl, Warshman?"

"Possibly." I patted my clammy face and sat back down.

"That sucks. I hoped to hit up Hefties for lunch."

The burger joint down the street permeated a constant smoky smell, bringing even the crunchiest of health nuts to their knees. "I'm in."

The bell rang—although more accurately, it chirped, signaling the end of class. Stuart promised to meet me at the restaurant and left. I'd shoved the new textbook and notepad into my bag when a meaty hand slammed all my stuff back down on the table.

"Leave him alone, Russ." Kasey stood at the lab station next to mine, fitting her arms through the straps of her bedazzled backpack. Boys loved Kasey. She made out with a few but typically moved on after a couple weeks, claiming an overall dullness contaminated our species.

A creepy smile surfaced on Russ's face as he sauntered toward her. "Looking good this year, Kasey." He adjusted his crotch and waited for the usual coo he got from most girls when he handed out compliments. Kasey ignored him.

"What, you're not gonna acknowledge me now? You had something to say when I was tryna chat with your boyfriend over there." Russ placed both his palms on the table, claiming territory wherever he could get it. His stubbled jaw, level with Kasey's chest, flexed as he chewed a wad of fluorescent green gum between his front teeth. "Least you can do is give me a smile, girl."

Kasey tilted her head to the side and batted her lashes at Russ. Extending both middle fingers, she said, "See you around, pig."

"You can count on it." Russ pushed away from the table, watching her leave. He adjusted himself again.

I grabbed my things and hurried out of the room behind her. Russ feigned a pounce at me.

"She won't always be around to protect you, dork!" he threatened.

Bodies shuffled through the two-lane hall. I trotted after Kasey. An easy trail to follow, her fake raspberry body spray overpowered the surrounding scents with its sweet-and-sour candyness.

"Wait up!" I panted.

"Do me a favor, Jeremy." She stopped short, turning to point her finger in my face. "Don't you ever pull that shit, okay?"

"I would never..." When her signature cat-eye outline around her eyes disappeared in a squinty glare, I knew to agree with whatever she said. "Um, okay..."

"Never tell a girl to smile for you." Her lips were stained the same color as her cuffed maroon minidress. Stomping down the hall, she came up to my shoulders in her chunky Mary Janes. "You know why?"

I leaned against the wall of lockers and looked around. Kasey's loudness and spasmodic movements were garnering attention.

"I'll tell you why." She wrenched her padlock down and banged open the metal door. "Because it's not a woman's job to look cute for you. That's why." Kasey dumped the textbooks from her morning classes in the bottom of her locker. She grabbed a fresh folder and zipped up her backpack. "Got it?" Hives were forming on her neck.

"Kase, it's me," I whispered. "You're more than how you look." That got her attention, and her shoulders relaxed. "We all are, right?"

"Right." She rolled her lips. "Ready for lunch?"

"Sure. Stu said he'd meet us at Hefties."

"Cool." Her purse hit me in the stomach as she flung it over her shoulder. "Let's get the hell out of here."

We stepped across the school building's threshold, and my lungs pitched back against the glass doors—the southern Ohio air so thick with moisture, it was near solid. Throughout the neighborhood, the steady whir of AC units hummed, an orchestra of heavy machinery tuning relentlessly but never playing their own song. They had a job to do. Cool the people. This town could stifle anything.

Chapter Two

PACKED WITH A mix of upperclassmen, construction workers, office temps, and people dressed in scrubs, Hefties was the only fast-food joint in town. The walls were decorated with framed newspaper clippings—colorless pictures of sharply dressed men shaking hands and clapping each other on the back. Rumor had it Hefties was the inspiration for one of the major burger chains found in every city across America.

Stuart was queued up at the front, near the registers. Adults grumbled when Kasey and I scooted in next to him.

"Welcome to Hefties. May I take your order?" The middle-aged woman behind the counter had dark bags under her eyes and oily skin, but that could have been from all the kitchen grease. She wore her hair pinned back in a tight bun and didn't make eye contact.

Stuart and Kasey hurried off to claim our seat while I ordered smiley meals for all of us and paid with the cash Kasey slipped me. After the waitress piled a tray with three colorful sacks of food, I carried it through the crowded dining room to our usual table next to the plate glass window. A pony wall topped with dusty fake plants offered up some privacy and blocked the stinking trash can from view. I passed my friends their meals, while Stuart chatted about new music. He worked a couple shifts each week at Spinz, the only record store within a twenty-mile radius of our town. A dream job if ever there was one. The manager paid under the table, and most of our acquaintances creamed themselves over Stuart's ever-growing pop-punk vinyl collection.

I never told anyone I had applied at Spinz. But the shopgirl, with her purple hair and multiple face piercings, crumpled up my application before the bells jangled above the exit door. Stuart got the job a week later. I didn't understand what made him more desirable as an employee. He was thinner, but ghastly so, with thick, wiry black hair that took on a mushroom formation if he went too long between haircuts. Along his temples, faint blue curving veins were always visible. Maybe shopgirl had mistaken his pallor for drug addiction, speed being way cooler than emo chub. I picked up work as a bagger at Bern's, an independent grocery store right next to my apartment building, and have been there ever since. It would never be as glamorous as all those records, but it paid for the insurance I needed to drive.

Spinz would not have been a good match. Any time conversations veered toward the verbal pissing contest over what indie band would sell out next, I clammed up. *Spoiler alert!* Anyone with the chance of signing with a major label took the money. So really, the debate boiled down to a bunch of pimply kids gabbing themselves into circles and dropping band names. Anyone who thought punks couldn't be pretentious was a damn idiot.

The other little nugget in play here was that I was awful at remembering the names of groups. They were all too random to stay in my brain. Lyrics got stuck in my head, and there were bands I enjoyed more than others. But conversations tended toward this...

"Have you heard the new so-and-so?"
"I don't know, maybe."

End of story, because I never could recall who was who; I didn't have the knack for it. The clerk at Spinz had done me a big favor. When she crumpled my application, she single-handedly prevented hundreds of awkward exchanges with customers.

"What do you guys think of our classes so far?" I interrupted Stuart. Dude needed to pipe down and eat something before he forgot.

"That's what you wanna talk about?" Stuart gulped down a bite and took a sip of pop. "For six hours a day, we listen to what *they* want us to. Out here, we don't. Jeremy Warsh, this is freedom lunch. Act accordingly, man."

"It's the first day of our senior year." I shrugged and dumped my fries onto the tray. "Maybe this year will be different."

Kasey tore open a pack of honey mustard sauce for her nuggets. "Nothing ever changes in there, Jeremy."

"I don't know, you guys."

"Don't kid yourself, Warsh." Bits of Stuart's chewed burger bun hit the table.

"The end is in sight though, right? It's almost over. We made it through all in one piece." Arguably.

Pieces of ourselves had surely been chipped away by the years of harassment we'd lived through. But nobody disagreed—out loud anyway. We munched quietly until Desiree and Danielle joined us. I scooted around to make room for an extra chair.

Des and Dani were advanced students. They spent their mornings at the community college campus and joined the rest of us for the afternoon. Fraternal twins, they both had dark brown eyes and skin. They looked more like sisters, rather than twins. Same height, similar coloring, but Dani's facial features were rounder, and she had a cute dusting of freckles covering her nose and the tops of her cheeks. Their family had moved to Ohio our sophomore year. Between drama and band, they'd fallen in with our crew.

"How goes it in the world of collegiate academia?" Stuart added a snooty accent to his speech. His chin disappeared in a weird approximation of a royal pout.

"Shut up, Stuart." Dani rolled her eyes and handed Des a burger.

"To be honest, college courses are equally mind-numbing. Only, the professors don't care if you show up, so nobody's ever there." Des unwrapped her sandwich and folded her hands in her lap. She lowered her head in silent prayer. Their dad had taken a position as a leader at one of the big churches in the city.

"Except for us." Dani dug into her lunch sans pious ritual. She'd explained once how she didn't feel the need to make a whole public thing over praying. I only half understood because Mom and I went to church for the occasional holiday, and that was it. My theological life lacked depth.

"What do you mean they don't care if you're there?" I asked.

"They don't take attendance. It's all on you, the student," Des explained.

"So, you guys could show up whenever you want? Nobody's keeping track?" Stuart looked intrigued, one eyebrow cocked so high it got lost among his unfortunate bangs. If I didn't know better, I'd bet on him using a curling iron.

"Yeah, but we still have to pass," Dani stated. The sisters shared a look. They'd known Stuart long enough to recognize a bad-idea-face when they saw one.

"So, we have to go," Des clarified slowly.

I wasn't really paying attention. Instead, I was focusing on whether I'd need a third mini-cup of ketchup when Kasey elbowed me.

"Did you see this?" She dangled the plastic toy she'd gotten in her smiley meal.

"What is it?" I asked.

"Look." Kasey ripped open the packaging and pulled out a cheap knockoff of Scooby-Doo's Mystery Machine. A shade of country blue, the van contained four passable characters piled on the seats next to a big spotted dog—a Scooby stranger. Kasey set it on the table, pulled it back a bit, and let go. The van took off over the smooth surface and crashed into Des's cup.

"Hey! Watch it!"

Retrieving the toy, Kasey smiled. Her teeth flashed perfect, almost blue-white against her reddish-brown lipstick. "I just figured out how to ace the physics homework!"

"You mean you're gonna cheat?" I asked. This stopped the chitchat around us. Des and Dani, gifted pupils that they were, took offense at the prospect.

"What's the assignment?" Des asked.

Stuart explained the energy transfer lecture from the morning.

"You don't even need to cheat, Kasey." Dani finished off the rest of her soft-serve ice cream. "Trust science. It will do the job."

Kasey rolled her eyes and sucked in her cheeks, looking pissed. "Consider it insurance then." She grabbed the toy and walked out of the eatery.

"What's her problem?" Stuart asked. We all turned toward the window and watched Kasey wobble in her heels on her way back to school.

"I don't know." I shrugged. "Back to school blues? Is that really a thing?"

"Maybe," Dani said.

I popped the lid off my drink and shook the ice around. "We had a run-in with Russ today."

"That could ruin anyone's day," said Des.

I agreed, but we'd been handling Landry for a long time. Kasey was kind of a master at shaking things off. A little *ping* in my brain signaled something else might be up with my friend. Getting her to open up though—now there was a hurdle measuring five and a half feet without heels.

Chapter Three

MOM AND I lived in a small apartment complex near an area referred to as Frog's Landing, so-called for the side streets that were named after thirteen different species of the amphibian. I tossed my keys into the wooden bowl on the counter next to the front door. Mom stood in front of the stove top stirring a sizzling pan of ground meat. A box of Hamburger Helper lay torn open next to the sink.

"How was your day?" Mom asked without looking at me. She'd tied an apron over her secretary's uniform—an A-line skirt, blazer, and flimsy blouse. "Damn it!" She jumped back from the stove. Her fingers tested a grease splatter near the jacket's lapel. "I knew I should have changed." She frowned while dabbing dish soap on the fabric.

"Fine," I said, picking up the wooden spoon where she'd left it.

"Hmm?" She turned around, still scratching at the stain on her work clothes.

"My day was fine."

"Good, glad to hear it."

"You asked."

For as long as I could remember, Mom had held two jobs. After her secretarial gig ended, she'd rush home and whip up a dinner for me, though it was often cold and gummy by suppertime. Then she'd change clothes and work as a night clerk at the gas station a few blocks away. Three jobs between us afforded all this luxury.

"Listen, dear, once you pour the seasoning in, let that simmer for a few more minutes, and it will be ready."

"It's only four o'clock, Mom."

She took a deep breath. Her eyes closed for a beat. "It's all I can do, Jeremy." She kissed me on the cheek and walked down the hall leading toward the two bedrooms. From her room, she called out, "Your father called!"

"Awesome," I mumbled.

The douchier parent by miles, Dad flitted around the parameters of my life. I'd go months without hearing from him, and then in a fit of parental guilt, he'd start calling again. No doubt, he wanted to meet for a meal and catch up.

I gave up trying to make these interactions comfortable in middle school, which was about the time a burning seed of anger took root in my chest. The mad sapling grew in his absence. And when we finally would meet up, I'd sit under the shade of its thick ropy branches while he squirmed. When sweat broke out over the thin line of Dad's well-trimmed mustache, I'd get a winning jolt from my rage tree.

At the end of each visit, after reaching his father-son time quota, he'd ask if I needed anything. I'd say money, and he'd dole out the bills. I dreamed of shredding it in front of him often enough. But, Mom always needed that extra bump in cash flow. We counted on those quarterly supplements. So, I'd call him back and run through the routine again because Mom deserved the break.

"I'll call him later, Mom. Once the first week of school is over," I yelled after her. The lid clanged shut over the soupy meat-noodle mixture, and I turned the heat to simmer.

"You working tonight?" Mom asked as she emerged from the hallway in a pair of too-tight black jeans and a royal-blue polo shirt. She absently tied a matching scrunchie around her black hair.

"Yeah, actually. Bern asked me to help after close a couple days."

"That late!" Mom made a clicking noise with her tongue. "I don't like it."

"I told Bern you wouldn't. He told me to tell you it's temporary. He had to fire somebody last week and hasn't found a replacement."

"What for?" She asked.

"Rumor was stealing." I shrugged. "I think the guy had kids though."

"Oh." Mom sighed. "That's sad."

"Guess so." We'd had our own hard months when I was too young to help out. Mom scraped together every penny to make sure I was fed. I don't think she had to steal; Grandpa was still around to lean on then. But I do know if she needed to, she would have.

"Don't forget to lock up." Mom grabbed her purse and keys from the coatrack. "And make sure you call your father," she nagged with a quick squeeze of a hug.

I cracked open a can of generic purple pop labeled GRAPE in bold font and headed to my bedroom. Kasey always begged to come here, but in this, I'd kept her at arm's length. She lived up the hill in one of the designer mansions. My plain navy bedspread over plaid sheets, chipped bedside table, and thrifted desk wouldn't live up to her polished bedroom set. A layer of mold growing in a half-empty glass on the nightstand reminded me to clean soon.

My most prized possessions sat in four plastic crates on the floor. Each dusty crate was full of gritty punk zines Stuart had brought over from the record store and my comics collection. Once every month, Grandpa would drive down from the farm and take me to Nati's Comics just north of Cincy. He'd arrive in a haze of diesel stink in his fat blue pickup truck. It had the longest gear stick I've ever seen with a shiny knob at the top.

Grandpa had been an old retired farmer, a regular Jonathan Kent. The kind of guy who would adopt an orphan child from another planet without second-guessing the circumstance. He was what people referred to when they said things like "salt of the earth"—a man who only saw a million ways to sprinkle goodness.

The cellophane-wrapped magazines went mostly unread now. I hadn't been back to Nati's since Grandpa passed away. These days, the only person rifling through my alphabetically organized stacks was Stuart.

I sat at my desk and unzipped my backpack. Carbonation bubbles fizzed in the pop can. I took a big gulp, my tongue shocked by sugar and effervescence. In my agenda, I penciled in stuff I'd need to do for upcoming assignments. The mousetrap car was due Friday. Great. I scribbled a list of supplies on a corner of paper and then ripped the mini-list from the header and tucked it in my wallet. Most of what I needed could be found at the grocery store and wouldn't cost too much money. I thought of Kasey and her plan to cheat with the pull-back van. I'd had one in my smiley meal too. I removed the toy from my backpack and set it front and center on my desk. Kasey would cheat because she was lazy. I might cheat because we needed the five bucks spent on supplies. We were worlds apart in some ways.

The phone's ring startled me. I shot up from my desk, and my knee knocked the ledge, making the pop can teeter. I quickly topped off the rest of the drink before crumpling the aluminum and tossing it in the wastebasket beside the desk. I picked up the phone.

"Yeah?"

"Hey, Warsh—"

My mother's voice kicked in: *You've reached the Warsh residence. We are not available...*

"Hold on, dude." I hurried down the hallway. In the living room, the answering machine blinked a red number two. I clicked the off button, and the miniature cassette tape stopped recording.

"Sorry, 'bout that. Mom's got it set to go off way too soon. What's up, Stu?"

"What are you doing right now?"

"Getting ready to eat before I have to work tonight. You?"

"I finished the last *Preacher* I borrowed and was wondering if you had the next one."

"Of course I do. Come on over." I clicked the phone back onto its base.

It was unspoken between Stuart and me, but I knew his home life sucked. Mom and I fretted over money, for sure, but at least we had quiet. Stuart lived in a two-bedroom with two younger siblings. His mom made lousy choices with men and alcohol. Therefore, he came over whenever he wanted.

A few minutes later, he pounded on the front door, and I went to the kitchen to let him in. I realized I still had the toy van in my hand, so I set it on the counter and pulled it back. The wheels raced until there was no more counter. It flew over the edge, right into the trash can's swinging lid.

"Amigo!" Stuart knocked more urgently. "I know you're in there! I can hear you breathing heavy."

"Shut up! The neighbors will hear you."

"Jeremy, the neighbors already know." Stuart sauntered into the apartment sniffing the air. "Ahhh! Is that the sweet smell of cheesy mac?"

"Help me set the table." I grabbed two forks from the silverware drawer.

Stuart held up the borrowed comic book. "I'ma just put this back and grab the next one."

"'Kay." I gathered plates from the cabinet.

"Duuuude!" Stuart called from my bedroom. "What is this?"

I set the stack of plates on the table and shuffled back to my bedroom. *No, no, no, no, no. God, no. Please, I did not want to talk about—*

He'd found it. Stuart sat on the floor with Grandpa's leather folio in his lap. Hundreds of Gramps's drawings were now at Stuart's fingertips. He wiped his hands on his jeans and picked them up carefully, one after another. A dreamy smile crept over his face.

"Did you do these?"

"No. They were my grandpa's."

"He was really talented, Warsh."

"I know." My chest tightened, watching Stuart regard Grandpa's artwork. "Can you put them away?"

Stuart's face went from wide-eyed wonder to concern when he noticed me at the doorway. "Sure, man." He gathered the drawings. "These are just so good. He could have been a pro, dude." Stuart admired a sketch of my grandma sipping a milkshake at one of those old-timey counter shops. She was young and pretty with tanned skin and a mischievous gleam in her eyes. The coloring was bold and cartoonish, the classic comic style Grandpa and I loved. I never met Grandma. These snippets, her through his eyes, were all I knew of the two of them.

"Yeah, well, he was just a farmer." I kneeled next to my crates and quickly scanned through the files. "Here's what you're looking for." I pitched the last issue I had of *Preacher* onto the bed. "Put the rest away."

Chapter Four

THE FAKE CHEESE smell wafted up from the bottom of the skillet. Behind me, Stuart's borrowed comic smacked the tabletop. He pulled out one of the chairs and sat down. The cracked vinyl upholstery emitted a puff of air when anyone sat on it, a noise that always left me wondering how whoopee cushions were invented.

Like most items in our apartment, the dining set was vintage, but not because my mom had spent hours deciding on the perfect decor. Everything had its own origin story regarding where she found it. These were picked up for free back in the early eighties. Mom took many drives through the countryside when I was a wailing thing of a baby, or at least that was how she told it. On one such drive, she passed a woman rolling the circular table out to the side of the road. Mom stopped, and they got to talking. The woman had tried to have a yard sale, but being so far out in the country, not a lot of people had come. Mom picked through her stuff and, whammo, we ended up with new-to-us furniture.

Stuart cleared his throat. "I didn't mean to upset you back there, Warsh."

I could tell by the way he mumbled that Stuart was chewing on the skin inside his cheek. A habit since grade school, he did it when he was nervous or thinking hard.

"Forget it, okay? I don't wanna talk about it."

"Nuff said. I can respect that."

I ladled food onto our plates and a bowl for my mom when she got home. At the sink, I squirted dish soap over the hot pan's surface. A couple of tiny bubbles escaped before the spray of water sizzled. I carried the plates to the table and sat across from my friend.

"Hey, Warsh, it's...well, you used to draw like that." Stuart got up and reached for the loaf of bread on top of the fridge. He untwisted the tie and set a slice on each of our plates.

At first, I didn't look at him. I held up my hand until he was silent. I took a heaping bite and sipped from my milk. Eyeing my friend over my cup, I silently dared him to say another word.

"Fine, dude. Be that way. I'm just gonna go on record and say you have the same talent, and you're throwing it away by not using it." He grabbed the yellow tub of margarine and spread a thick layer over his white bread.

I had no retort. I stuffed my face, stuffed the feelings with each forkful.

"People kill to be able to do what you and your grandpa could do—"

I tossed my fork down, and it rang against my plate. "Shut up, Stuart."

"Whatever, man." Stuart poked around noodles and bits of browned beef. "I'll change the subject then." He crammed his mouth full and barely swallowed before starting his next sentence. "So, I've been thinking. You know how Des and Dani said they don't have to go to their classes? I think we need to take serious advantage of that situation." When Stuart swallowed, I could see his neck working to get food down.

"What do you mean?"

"A prank." His eyes sort of twinkled whenever he got one of his big ideas. "Of epic proportions."

"You think it's worth it? Mr. Beeman hands out stiff punishments for pranks these days."

Our freshman year, a couple seniors had defiled the wrecked car that was used to teach us all a lesson on the dangers of drinking and driving. They spray-painted boobs all over the prop. The school-wide assembly was canceled, and everything. Since then, our principal, Mr. Beeman, would attack even the hint of a prank with fervor.

"That was three years ago!" Stuart dismissed my concerns with a wave and a snort. "Nobody's even tried anything big since then."

"For good reason, Stu. Those kids weren't allowed to go to prom or graduation. They were mailed their diplomas."

"Who cares? They still got them. Principal Beeman can't stop anyone from graduating once you've done the coursework. Whaddya think? You in?"

"I don't know. What do you have in mind?"

"Nothing yet. Except I want it to be a multitiered prank."

"Multitiered?"

"Yeah—like a prank that has scattered initial elements, culminating in one glorious moment that brings everything together. Way I figure, we have three chances—homecoming, prom, and graduation." Stuart's fingers counted off the events. "The trifecta of what seniors care about."

"Not all of us. And that sounds...lofty."

"Hey, who's got two thumbs and big dreams?" Stuart didn't wait for a response; both his thumbs pointed to his head, and with a big grin, he drew out the words, "Thissss guyyyy."

Stuart's heavy emphasis on "this guy" jokes always did me in. I chuckled into my glass of milk and laugh-coughed over my half-empty plate. "Okay, okay. I'll help you. But how are you gonna get Dani and Des in on it?"

"By sheer masculine prowess, my friend." He flexed his biceps, imitating a bodybuilder. "You laugh now, Warsh. But just you wait."

"Okay, buddy. We'll see."

THE FLUORESCENT LIGHTS inside the grocery store lit up the parking lot area in front of the doors. As I approached the entrance, a few daytimers were leaving with various parts of their uniform discarded or crumpled into a ball. Maroon apron strings dangled over their shoulders. Two sisters, each in their late thirties, treated me as if I was a long-lost nephew. They wore icy-pink lipstick and had matching bleach-blonde bangs, resembling a sculpted tidal wave.

As they headed toward the car, one of them yelled about there being a plate of marshmallow crispy treats in the break room.

"Thanks!" I called after them.

"Have a good night, hon!"

The automatic doors whooshed open. An ambush of easy listening music and air conditioning assaulted me. Bern Stevens, the store's proprietor for over thirty years, bent over and locked the doors behind me with an Allen wrench. Afterward, he tucked it into his shirt pocket and gave it a little pat. Bern was a kind man with a huge pot belly that hung over an invariable pair of black slacks. I only saw him dressed differently when he played Santa Claus for two weeks before Christmas. Customers would bring their hopeful kids to take pictures with Santa Bern for free. Most of our senior class had, at some point, sat on this man's lap and told him what we dreamed for most.

"Any registers still open, Bern?" I asked as we walked toward the back of the store.

"Nope. I've already logged them all out. Why? You need something?"

"Stuff for a school project is all."

"What stuff?"

"A mousetrap, toy car, rubber bands...and duct tape."

"That's a life rule, Jeremy." Bern held the break room door open for me.

"What?"

"Always have duct tape."

"Uh, okay."

"Gather what you need and put it on my desk in the back. I'll write it up and ring it in first thing tomorrow morning."

"Thanks, sir."

"No problem, young man."

The break room boasted no windows and a pale green set of lockers. Bern updated the store's tech system last spring but refused to let go of the old punch clock. At the staff meeting, he explained, "There's something satisfying about that mechanism stamping your card. It sets your mind to work. No beep can replace it."

I understood what he meant, but then, every time I punched in, I thought of Pavlov's dogs.

The crispy treats were in the center of the table, under a dome of plastic wrap, right where one of the pseudo-aunties said they'd be. I unwrapped them and took two for myself. Bern helped himself too.

"Thanks for covering this week, Jeremy. I know you started school."

"Mom's not too happy about it." I polished off the marshmallowy goodness and leaned against my cubby. "But it's no problem. If I'm outta here by midnight, I'll be fine for school tomorrow." I enjoyed working this shift. Bern closed the store a little early three times a week to do a light restock and full cleaning. I found the store's emptiness comforting. An ordinary place turned extraordinary by quieting down.

Tim strolled in behind Bern and punched his card. He pulled out a chair and sat his lanky ass in one of the metal folding chairs. Tim graduated two years ago but was headed nowhere fast. Kasey told me he still showed up at high school parties, and she overwhelmingly regarded him as a creep.

Bern stood in front of the bulletin board littered with flyers. He read from a clipboard. According to the shift plan, I'd replenish home goods while Tim took care of the freezer section.

"Come on, Bern! Make *him* do the cold stuff." Tim snatched one of the snacks from under the plastic wrap. "He's got an extra layer to keep him warm."

I held up a middle finger.

"Now, now. Let's not get all riled up. Once you get the little bit of stocking done, we can start the cleaning, and you guys will be outta here in no time." Bern went back to listing the night chores.

Tim had a joint propped behind his ear. I tried to make eye contact with him. Cleared my throat, but Tim was deeply involved with deconstructing dessert. Bern rambled on about the cleaning schedule—stuff both Tim and I already knew. When I kicked the metal chair leg in front of me, both Tim and Bern looked up for a second.

"Sorry, spasm."

Bern went back to his clipboard, but I finally caught Tim's eye and pointed to my ear. His furry eyebrows shot halfway up his forehead as he realized what he carried in plain sight. Tim leaned forward in his seat. As nonchalantly as possible, he scratched the back of his head and palmed the marijuana. He kept it in his fist and mouthed *Thanks, man.*

I stared at my shoes, worn-out Vans that stunk in the rain. Why had I helped him? He'd insulted me minutes ago. Maybe I hoped he'd share it.

When Bern finished his speech, he went back to his adjoining office. His chair creaked and rolled when he sat down. I could hear his fingers tap-tapping on the keyboard of his big beige computer.

Tim and I went to the storeroom and found the wheelie carts already piled high with grocery items. Before heading to the freezer section, Tim said, "Props, dude. That was a cool thing to do." He had a strip of stringy shoulder-length hair combed to the side. The rest of his head was shaved, and the overall look made his face seem longer and more horse-like.

"It was nothing." I shrugged and headed off toward my section.

"At break, come find me out back."

"Yeah, okay." Score for the Warsh-man.

We took care of the shelves first. Then I scrubbed the big windows, while Tim squeegeed the suds away. Bern was a stickler about the floor. After I mopped each aisle, Tim came through with the auto scrubber. Halfway through, in the middle of the canned goods aisle, Bern waved us down for break time.

"Back door's unlocked if you boys want some fresh air." Bern unwrapped a Twinkie and tucked the cellophane into his pants pocket, biting into three-fourths of the cake as he walked away.

I grabbed a pop, a bag of Cheetos, and the stuff I needed for the physics assignment. I tossed cash on Bern's desk and headed outside to the strip of asphalt behind the building.

Evening had turned to night. Crickets chirped and silenced as I walked toward a puff of skunky smoke just outside the flood lamp's ring of yellow light. I couldn't see Tim but could hear him suck down the smoke and blow out a long, low exhale, Vader-style. A raspy cough came soon after. When my eyes adjusted to the change in light, I could make out Tim in front of me, reaching out to hand me the joint. His ratty Metallica T-shirt hung from his pointy collarbones, his chest a tad concaved. When I didn't see any obvious signs of herpes, I put my lips to the paper and inhaled. The smoke burned, but it would pass.

"No better way to get through a night shift." Tim coughed and snorted through the sentence.

I nodded along and handed him back his weed. He took another hit and passed it back to me.

"You're that kid Kasey Axton hangs with, aren't you?" My surprise at his knowledge of high school cliques must have shown because he held up his hands. "No worries, man. She talks 'bout you, is all."

Again, massive surprise. "Okaaaay." Even with the blanket of warm fuzzies starting to take over my brain, my heartbeat ticked up a notch. Whatever Kasey shared with this guy was probably not a good thing.

"At parties, dude. She chats you up, like you're her boyfriend or whatever."

At that, I doubled over in a cloud of smoke. I choked and stared at the crumbling edge of black asphalt.

"You okay, Warsh?" Tim pounded on my back. "Strong stuff, right? Don't worry though, man. I won't make a play for Kasey. She's hot, but I can respect boundaries and such."

I stood straight again. With my fist over my mouth, I suppressed another fit. My sight blurred as my eyes watered.

"I don't mean to be rude, but how'd a guy like you score a girl like Kasey? I should take lessons, pick up some pointers and what not."

Coughing fit subsided, I cleared my throat. "We're not together," I croaked.

"Dude." Tim snorted, and I could see a skeptical line of black form between his eyebrows. "She's been telling people this for months."

"As far as I know—" I shrugged. "—we're just friends. I've got zero pointers for you."

"Huh, that's weird." Tim prepped what was left of his joint for later, clipping it with something from his keychain. "Girls be trippin'."

Bern's silhouette filled the back doorway. Break time was over. The pop hissed when I twisted off the cap, and its heavenly sugar-rush drowned my taste buds. Walking back toward the building, I was totally perplexed. What the hell was Tim talking about?

Chapter Five

BERN LET US out of work early, as promised, and I got home around eleven. The last of Tim's weed buzzed pleasantly around in my head as I trudged up the concrete steps to my apartment, careful not to wake any neighbors. Bugs buzzed around the ceiling lamp, casting a dim kaleidoscope of shadows over our front door. I could've stared at that for hours. But when the bag of untapped Cheetos in my backpack whispered my name, I reached for my keys dangling from the long chain attached to my belt loop.

Back in my room, I licked the salty orange powder from my fingertips and changed into a pair of mesh gym shorts. Working nights always kept me up later than usual. Even half-baked, my brain wasn't ready to settle. Cocooned in this space, every little thing represented parts of me. The full trash can with balled up tissues scattered around the perimeter said, here's a lazy-ass dude. A scuffed dresser told the story of a guy not concerned with pristine conditions. And finally, all those dusty comics lined up against the wall spoke of Jeremy, king of blocking loved things.

Grandpa's portfolio stuck out of its crate at a diagonal, jutting above rows of alphabetized order. I'd put money on Stuart clumsily putting it away like that. He knew I'd notice and straighten it into place. My friend was a pusher. I slid Grandpa's art from the crate, and the rest of the comics whooshed into a deeper lean. At my desk, I stuffed the empty bag of Cheetos into the trash.

After Grandpa died, I researched people who continued to feel their loved one's presence. The described encounters gave those folks an overwhelming sense of everything being as it should. Others told of dreams where the deceased appeared, giving a proverbial thumbs-up. *It's all good on the other side, man. So-and-so leveled up!* As for me, I'd experienced nothing. After Grandpa passed, there was absence. Nonexistence.

The art case's black leather cover was buttery soft, and it made a sound somewhere between a purr and a clack, as I unzipped the slider down its chain of metal teeth. One side had pockets containing rainbows of colored pencils, a small sharpener, and an X-Acto knife. Sketchbooks filled the rest of the folio. I flipped open the collection of drawings and admired snippets from Grandpa's farm life—an orange and red sunrise, dandelion seeds, a lamb sleeping on one corner of the page. Grandpa used every inch of paper, filling the pages with prominent flashes from each day, a collage of memories mixed in with everyday stuff.

I came to a whole page devoted to me. The first time I saw it, a couple days after his funeral, I closed everything and never looked back. In the page's center, an image of Mom in a rocking chair admired my bald baby head. In the upper left corner stood toddler-me, wearing nothing but a diaper. Wads of lined yellow tissue paper lay crumpled around my tiny feet. In the lower right corner, I looked around age five in a set of denim overalls, my whole body suspended mid-jump over a pond on my Grandpa's property. Then I was ten, sitting in a corner reading a book, my eyebrows wrinkled in a thinking-face and my hair puffy as Mom had just allowed me to let it grow out. In the last image, I sat in the passenger seat of Grandpa's truck, flipping through a stack of comics he'd bought for me.

Seeing myself the way he saw me was weird. In that handful of drawings, he'd captured something important about me, something I hardly knew about myself. The way I figured, no one would ever see me the way Grandpa had, and that was what was really sad about losing people.

This time, even though it hurt, I turned pages. A lump in my throat, nearly the size of a golf ball, grew. When I got to Grandpa's self-portrait, I blotted tears from the corners of my eyes. He stared back at me with wispy gray hair sticking out from under his green tractor hat. He looked ornery, like always. The laugh lines mapping his face hinted at secrets the rest of us weren't in on. In this moment, if his image winked, I wouldn't have been surprised. At the bottom of the page, in his neat all-caps printing were the words, "This next one's for you." His scratchy, cigarette-stained voice rang true in my ears.

I turned to the sketchbook's back cover expecting to see some amazing final depiction that would lead to all of Grandpa's answers. But it was just a stack of blank white pages.

Plink! I startled in my seat and looked around. The apartment was still empty. Mom wouldn't be home for another half hour or so. *Plink!* It came from my window. I unlocked the latch and slid the window open. Through the screen, a hazy version of Kasey stood on the lawn in front of the complex. At the street corner, a traffic light flashed, changing her skin color from green to red.

"What are you doing out there?"

"Nothing. I saw your light when I was walking by and thought I'd say hey."

"Why didn't you come to the door like a regular person?"

"Didn't want your mom to freak."

"She's still at work. Seriously though, it's late. What are you doing out?"

"You worry too much." Kasey scratched the base of her neck, a little tic I'd noticed way back when we first started hanging out. "Nothing's gonna happen to me in this tiny-ass town. The pigs have been domesticated, friend."

"Fine, don't tell me. I'm going to bed."

"Wait! Can I have a drink?"

My shoulders drooped. "Yeah, hold on. I'll bring down a pop." I sighed. All we had was the cheap stuff. It would have to do.

"No, water."

"Okay, fine." I grabbed a hoodie from the closet floor and zipped it up to my chin. Kasey had always been this unpredictable—a trait I both loved and was wildly annoyed by. I'd be laser-focused on one thing, and Kasey would come along and change everything. After an evening with this girl, my head would spin like a street sign next to the roadrunner post-takeoff.

In the kitchen, I checked a glass for cleanliness under the spotlight above the sink. Tap water spewed from the faucet before evening into a steady stream. The clock on the microwave blinked 11:43, plenty of time to figure out this most recent Kasey situation.

With Cincy summers, relief didn't come in the form of night air. Stepping out of air conditioning and into humidity was equal parts suffocating and satisfying. The cement steps scratched the bottoms of my bare feet as I pounded down. I scanned the front lawn for Kasey, who seemed to have disappeared.

"Kase?" I stage-whispered, not wanting to wake Ms. V, who's living room window I was standing in front of.

"Over here!" Kasey's voice boomed near the large bush next to our apartment building sign, Pickerel's Place. She jumped into the sign's spotlight, which cast her giant-sized girl shadow. Based on the speed with which her forearms covered her eyes, she regretted the sudden move.

"Get away from there, dummy!" I kind of ran toward her. My legs pumped, but my upper body hunched over, until we met on the grass. "Are you drunk?" I could smell beer but couldn't tell if she'd drunk it or dipped herself in it.

Kasey stumbled toward me. "A little. I had to pee." She motioned toward the bush with her thumb out. The movement seemed to be too much for her, and she started to topple but got a platform heel down in time. "I thought I'd come say hi-ee!"

"Okay, um...we've got to get you home."

"Water." She nodded once, but seemingly involuntarily, her head kept bobbing.

I handed over the glass, which was nowhere near the amount of H_2O Kasey needed to sober up. She downed it and hiccupped. Her hand flew to her lipstick-smeared mouth. Ringed around her middle finger was her set of clacking keys. The collection of plastic key rings with snarky taglines were all remnants of a younger Kasey, one who saved any key chain until she could connect them into one massive hunk, representing her freedom.

"My car's in the grocery lot."

"You are so not driving," I said with a tinge of snark.

"Fine." She handed me her bundle.

"I'm not either, Kase. I got high at work."

Kasey doubled over with laughter and defeat. She nearly fell, and I started laughing too.

"Shhh, be quiet. We're gonna wake up the whole complex. Ms. V won't hesitate to call the cops."

"Where we gonna go, Jeremy?" She struggled to pronounce my name, the *r* elongating with the slur of alcohol. "You never let me hang at your place."

"Well, tonight's the exception. Come on." I took her fishnet-sleeved arm and draped it around my neck. My other arm went around her waist, and we hobbled back to my apartment, trying not to laugh the whole way.

The living room-kitchen area was dark except for the light above the sink. Mom and I used it as a nightlight for our late-night comings and goings. It filled the outer rooms of our apartment with enough brightness to get around without falling and, right now, turned the window behind the sink into a dark mirror. Kasey leaned against the back of our couch while I filled up the glass with more water for her. She examined the new environment, as though she might be collecting clues. I didn't think she was clearheaded enough to see the torn fabric on each couch corner, (thanks, old cat) but she would be in the morning.

"This way." I lead her back to my bedroom where she plopped facedown on the bed without so much as a thank-you. I burritoed my comforter around her as best as possible, then emptied the trash can and placed it next to the bed in case she puked.

I sank into the couch as Mom opened the front door. She startled upon seeing me, and her purse flew from her hands as she clutched at her heart.

"Jesus, Jeremy! You scared me half to death."

Mom grunted as she bent over to pick up her things, and then piled them on top of the counter. *Hot dogs and perfume.* Mom always came home from her second job smelling that way.

"Why aren't you in bed? You've got school tomorrow."

"Do you remember me telling you about my friend, Kasey?" I pulled a periwinkle afghan over my legs.

"She the one you won't bring over here?" The fridge sounded a suctioning release when Mom opened it to grab a can of beer. She popped the top, took a foamy slurp, and sat at the table.

"Yeah," I answered, watching her expression from the couch.

She sniffed and let down her frizzy hair—similar to mine, except jet-black. When she wore it down, it fell past her shoulders in a mass of static kink. Tonight, it crimped in all the wrong places from being up for so long. Mom took another sip of beer and scratched her scalp with what were always pearl-painted nails.

"She's here now," I said.

"Now wait just a minute, mister." Mom's elbow banged on the table. Her pointed finger slanted right at me. "We worked this out a long time ago. You know the only person allowed here while I'm at work is Stuart. We cannot have neighbors complaining about a bunch of teenage kids coming in and out of this place all night long."

"Mom, it's not what you think."

"Then what is it?"

"I was getting ready for bed, and she, Kasey…needed my help. So, I let her crash."

Mom opened her mouth to say something and then stopped herself. She rested her chin in her hands and then got up and—not very conspicuously—counted the beers in the fridge. With one hand on her hip and the other holding the refrigerator door open, she said, "So, no partying?"

"Promise, Mom."

"Is she having trouble at home?"

"I don't know." I shrugged and stifled a yawn. "She didn't say much. I just knew she needed a place to stay tonight."

"I suppose you are old enough to make these kinds of decisions without consulting me." Mom paused before saying this next part. "Jeremy, if you're able to see when your friends need help without them telling you, well, that's pretty special."

I only half dodged when Mom reached out to ruffle my hair. She kissed my forehead. Her breath smelled of beer and the microwaveable broccoli-cheese pita pockets she loved from the gas station.

"Night, Mom."

"G'night, baby."

I grabbed the other throw pillow and stuffed it under my head. Our couch wasn't sleep-level comfortable. If I turned onto my left side, I couldn't bend my knees without my ass spilling over. On my right side, it was the opposite problem. I flopped onto my back and stared up at the popcorn ceiling. Not only was it that awful texture, but someone also had the bright idea of mixing in glitter, because nothing says class like a little sparkle. Although, it was kind of nice.

Chapter Six

I WOKE TO the sound of silverware jangling around as a drawer slid open and slammed shut. Someone was in the kitchen making coffee. *Mom.* Utensils clanked together as she selected—best guess—a tablespoon. Running water splashed into the glass carafe. She popped the lid from the can, and the spoon *shushed* through the grounds.

"Mornin', Ms. Warsh."

My eyes blinked open at the sound of Kasey's scratchy hangover voice. I stared at the scruffy beige couch cushion in my face. It took me a minute to remember what had happened and why I was scrunched up on the sofa.

"Shhh." I imagined Mom placing a finger near her lips and motioning my way. "So, you're the elusive Kasey." Mom's hushed tones melded over the percolating sounds.

"That would be me." The hallway light brightened the room, and I pictured Kasey stepping forward to shake my mother's hand. "Sorry 'bout last night."

"No worries. But I do expect you to call your parents before leaving for school and tell them where you are."

"They won't care, Ms. Warsh."

"You can call me Connie. And I don't know where you teenagers get the crazy idea that us parents stop caring. Let me tell you a little secret, girly, we're dying to know ya."

Kasey sniffled. I heard a *thunk* and chair legs dragging on the linoleum.

"Come here now." Mom must have rushed to comfort my friend. A little *meep* escaped from Kasey, and I imagined Mom's blazer stretched to the max as she wrapped her arms around Kasey's shoulders. "I didn't mean to upset you, dear."

"I'm okay. I'll be okay, Ms. Warsh. I don't know why I'm crying."

"Of course, you'll be fine. You've had a long night, that's all. You are always welcome here, and don't let my son talk you out of coming, got it?"

"Yes, ma'am."

"Oof, that's worse. Call me Connie, please."

"Yes, Connie."

"Now, I don't know what you want to do for school today. I have some clothes from my hippie days that might fit you."

"Oh, no, I couldn't. Can I take a shower? Then Jeremy can drive me back to my house for a change of clothes, or something."

"Well, if that's your plan, you better get a move on. I'll show you where the towels are."

When they were gone, I stretched my legs the length of the couch. After a few more tired minutes, I convinced myself to get up so I'd have time for coffee. Mom strolled back into the kitchen as I filled two mugs. She liked hers black; I preferred loads of milk.

"He lives!" Mom reached peak level of cheeriness in the morning. I don't know how she managed it. This time of day, my tongue mastered taste, not word formation. I grunted when she hugged me.

"Love you, my beautiful boy!"

I pointed at her cup.

"Thanks." She scooped it up by the handle and blew ripples over the steamy surface.

Her round blue eyes were highlighted with thick black mascara. For her secretarial day job, she styled her hair with heated rollers and clamped the sides back with tortoiseshell combs. Compared to her gas station uniform, she looked downright fancy.

"I met your Kasey. She's nice."

"Mm-hmm." I nodded, sipping away at the soothing bitterness of caffeine.

"You know, she's welcome here whenever."

"I know, Mom."

"You two will have to hurry if you're going to make it to school on time." Mom stepped around me and retrieved a travel mug from the cabinet.

"I expect we won't." I rubbed crusty sleep from the corners of my eyes.

"It's only the second day! You can't be tardy, Jeremy."

"I'll do what I can." I repeated the line I'd heard often enough from her.

"Okay, okay." The lid on her travel mug let out a squelching pop as she forced it closed. "I won't harp on you. I know you're practically an adult." She grabbed her purse from the counter. "Don't let senioritis settle in too early though, okay?"

"Whatever."

"Bye, hun. Have a good day!" She reached for the doorknob.

"Hey, wait!" I set my drink aside and turned toward her. "Thanks for being cool about Kasey." I hugged her. "I love you, Mom."

"For you, anything." Mom teared up at my show of affection, which happened way less than she deserved. "Now

I'm getting all misty." Her eyelids fluttered as she looked to the ceiling and blotted away any runny mascara. She kissed my cheek and made her way to the stairwell. Her anti-flowery perfume—she preferred hints of musk—lingered near the door as I repositioned the dead bolt.

"She's really great." Kasey stood in the kitchen dressed in what she wore last night, minus tights and platforms. Those were bundled up under her arm. Strands of wet hair saturated her baby tee, creating little pools on her chest. "Do you think you can take me back home? My clothes kind of reek."

"I gotta get ready for school. You can drive yourself."

"Too hungover." Kasey's hand trembled as she held it in front of her face. "See, I'm still shaky from last night."

"Fine. Let me shower real quick." Back in my bedroom, I checked out the alarm clock. It wasn't set to go off for another thirty minutes. We probably had enough time, if Kasey stayed focused. "Eat something!" I yelled before slipping into the bathroom with my own bundle of clothes. No chance I'd let Kasey catch me walking back to my room with only a towel wrapped around my waist.

In the bathroom, the fuzzy pale blue rug lay trodden with soggy footprints. Beads of condensation covered the walls while the rickety fan whirred overtime. I wiped down the mirror with my forearm, checking for any ready-to-be-popped zits. *All clear, systems go.* I stepped into the shower's hot running water.

When I came out, Kasey was in my room, flipping through my comics. She was crouched in front of the crates, one hand hovering over them, holding a half-full glass of water.

"Be careful." I finished drying my hair and hung the towel over the back of my desk chair. Kasey looked up at me, confused. "With your drink."

"Oh." She stood up. "Quite a collection."

"I've been out of the scene for a while." I bent over to lace up my Vans. Kasey's presence made things weird, and my takeaway lingered somewhere between an invasion of privacy and/or feeling manipulated. Either way, exposing how Mom and I lived didn't make me want to chat up comic books. "We've got time, but you have to hurry. Mom doesn't want me to be late the second day of school."

"I will not make you tardy, Mr. Warsh." Kasey held up her three fingers in a famous salute. "Scout's honor."

"You were a Girl Scout? I can't picture that."

"I made it to Brownie status, thank you very much."

"What's that? First grade?" I tried to hide a smile, but Kasey caught it and swatted at me.

"Don't be a jerk!"

"I'm not!" I dodged her smack, laughing harder. "Come on, let's go."

My backpack leaned against the wall next to my desk. When I bent over to grab it, I noticed Grandpa's portfolio still out from last night. Only, now, it was zipped up. I hadn't time to put it away last night; I'd been too occupied getting Kasey settled. Great, I anticipated another scene similar to the one with Stuart. But, Kasey hadn't known me back then. She hadn't been friends with the little kid who doodled through every class.

After the first time Grandpa took me to the comic book store, I was inspired to make my own. It starred two young boys who turned into dogs at night. Together, they fought crime and ate their own homework. Stuart loved it. *Pup Operatives*—that was what I named my first comic. Anyway, Kasey must have noticed me eyeing Grandpa's portfolio while I got lost in the memory because she held her hands up, as if she was under arrest.

"I barely looked."

"They were my Gramps's. I was checking them out right before you got here last night."

"The ones I did see were awesome."

"Thanks. He was gifted in that way." I blew out a big puff of air, letting my cheeks go slack.

"'Kay, let's go." Kasey grabbed her purse, a mini-transparent briefcase of a thing. I could see all her belongings—the mass of key rings, candy-flavored ChapStick, and a couple of tampons.

The morning air smacked damp against my bare arms and face. The high school was a few blocks from my house, but we plodded through wet grass toward the grocery store parking lot instead. Kasey's cherry-red Miata was the only car in the lot, except for Bern's. His boxy white Pontiac 6000 sat parked under a tree near the sidewalk along the main drag.

"Wanna drive?" Kasey unlatched her purse and dangled the keys in front of my nose.

"Isn't that what I'm here for?" I grabbed for the set. "I thought you couldn't."

"Meh, by now I'd be okay. I really need you to be my buffer."

"Buffer?"

"If my parents are still home. They won't tear me a new one if someone else is around."

"Fine." Like I'd turn down driving her sporty car anyway. I unlocked the doors, got in, and repositioned the driver's seat and mirrors to fit me. Kasey hopped in the passenger seat and flipped open the sun visor. She patted the dark space under her eyes with the pads of her fingertips and made a disappointed murmur.

The car zipped out of the parking lot. I took the one and only exit off Main Street, onto a rural highway that led up to the nicer homes in Ekkehard Hills. The swanky subdivision, located two miles from the bustling streets of Frog's Landing, was positioned to look down on the town. Kasey's modest house, compared to her neighbors, sat on a four-acre corner lot. From the outside, it looked similar to any other ranch-style brick home, albeit on the larger side. The lawn—treated like the putting greens my dad always chattered on about—was clearly manicured, and there was a heated in-ground pool around back. But the inside, the *inside*, really boasted her family's wealth.

Through the garage, a side entrance opened right smack in the middle of a gourmet kitchen, with copper pots hanging over an island of shiny white stone countertop. Everything sparkled with a professional level of cleanliness. I had no idea who cooked. The handful of times I'd been present for meals, they were all takeout.

Kasey held a finger over her lips and tiptoed under the living room's cathedral-beamed ceilings. She steered us toward the door leading downstairs to her space. I could hear running water, probably a shower. We crept down the stairs without anyone noticing.

The first time I came over, Kasey explained how the house was originally built with two separate living spaces. The previous owner designed the upstairs for her paraplegic son, while she resided in the basement.

"Together, but separate. My family's motto!" Kasey had chirped that day.

I sat on the couch in the living room while she bustled around her bedroom. Hangers scraped along the closet rod as she picked out today's outfit—a few fantastic articles of clothing that would somehow represent everything she wanted the world to think about her on a Tuesday. Through the den's French doors, I could see the top of someone's bright red swim-cap bobbing around in the pool outside.

"I'm dressed! You can come in now!" Kasey sat at her vanity in a fluffy short-sleeved ivory sweater. She brushed her hair into a high ponytail, pulling the sweater up and exposing the lean curve of her stomach. "Almost ready! I just have to put a little makeup on."

"It's cool." I walked to her closet, mentally poking through all the things—piles of purses, belts, scarves, and so many chunky-heeled shoes. "I need to ask you something." I turned to catch Kasey tugging on her eyelid, applying a thin smudge of eyeliner on the lower lid. She used a brush and swiped on a charcoal shadow, making her eyes look smoky and effortless at the same time.

"What?" She chose a lipstick, popped off the lid, and applied the frosty-brown shade to her lips.

"Last night, one of the guys at work told me you've been telling people we're together."

"We are."

"No, like, together-together."

Kasey rolled her lips and pouted, an appraising look on her face. I couldn't tell if it was for me or her makeup choices.

"Don't you have anything to say?"

"Not really."

"You owe me an explanation, at least."

"I don't owe anyone anything, Jeremy Warsh." Kasey stood too fast. The vanity stool toppled behind her. "Excuse me."

I stepped away from the closet, out of her way. She scanned her varied selection and finally settled on a cropped maroon jacket and clogs.

"Yeah, you do. What the hell is going on, Kase? I'm not your boyfriend."

"We don't have time to get into this now, Jeremy. We're gonna be late for school." Her eyes, under all the shadow, were Hershey brown and melty. "I'll tell you everything, but you have to let me do it my way. Not in some hurried conversation right before the bell rings."

"Fine. Today, after school, we talk."

"Deal." She held out her pinky finger, and I curled mine around hers. We promised.

Chapter Seven

KASEY DIDN'T SAY a word the whole way to school. From the passenger seat, she popped open the glove compartment and grabbed a hidden pack of Kamel Red Lights. She jabbed the car lighter. When heated, the button popped up, and Kasey held the burning orange coils to her cigarette. Smoke filled the car before she cracked the window. She stared at the passing farmland. I clicked on the radio and last year's chart-topper from Green Day, "Good Riddance," played for the millionth time.

"Thanks for the ride," Kasey muttered when we went our separate ways before first bell.

"Anytime." I hadn't meant to piss her off. In fact, her attitude over this whole thing was beyond irritating. She'd given me boyfriend status without clueing me in! It wasn't as though I hadn't thought about that possibility over the years.

In middle school A.C. (After Cobain), Kasey had inserted herself into my friend group. Stuart was convinced she like-liked me and talked me into asking her out. I tried. I failed in spectacular fashion. Kasey placed me deep in the friend zone, and I'd stayed there ever since. It suited me fine. No pressure in being pals. As a friend, Kasey's fun spontaneity had coaxed stuff out of my personality that never would have seen daylight. As a girlfriend, I probably would have invested way too much time in figuring out how to make her happy. So, whatever. Best of both worlds kind of deal.

Stuart was waiting for me at my locker. His face lit up when he saw me.

"Warsh!" He handed me the comic he'd borrowed yesterday evening. "You look like hell, dude. You getting sick?"

"It was a long night. I had to sleep on the couch."

"Why?"

"Kasey showed up too drunk to drive herself home."

"She stayed at your place!" Stuart's eyes bugged out. "Whoa."

"And I found out she's been telling people I'm her boyfriend."

"Wait. What? Are you?"

"Decidedly not boyfriend material." I pinched the shoulders of my T-shirt and lifted it from my frame.

"Then what's the deal?"

"I don't know. I tried talking to her this morning, but she shut down. Said she needed more time." I rooted around the shelf of my locker for a sharpened pencil.

"Sounds like one for the *X-Files*." Stuart stood with his back against the locker next to mine, people watching. Suddenly, he whistled a whispery high-pitched warning.

"What?"

Nudging me with his elbow, Stuart mumbled, "Landry, six o'clock. There's a bug up that arse."

I turned in time to get a glimpse of Russ Landry's heavy hand before it banged the side of my head into a locker door.

"That's for your lip yesterday." Russ came up close behind me, his wet whispered threat right in my ear. "Talk to me that way again, and your pretty girlfriend won't be able to protect you."

Russ pressed my face against the cold metal, and the best I could do was give a slight nod of comprehension. He let go and knocked into Stuart with his elbow before grunting a stereotypical, "What are you looking at, loser?"

Stuart and I started toward homeroom. As we swerved through and around different cliques, Stuart said, "That could have been a whole lot worse."

"You're right." Still, I rubbed the spot where my head had banged into the locker.

"So, I know Kase was kind of instructing you on how to handle those guys, but I think you gotta back off." Stuart played with the strings of his hoodie, stretching them to the limits. The navy-blue hood formed a crinkly frame around his face.

I agreed with Stuart because I didn't have anything else to say. The combination of work, lack of sleep, and just an overall crappiness settled over my brain in a haze.

"There are better ways to get back at people like Russ Landry."

"What do you mean?"

"The pranks!" Stuart whispered too loudly, not wanting anyone to overhear him but also unable to contain himself. "I've been thinking about the first one."

"Got some ideas, do ya?"

"Always, Warsh. Always." Stuart tapped his forehead. He handed me a folded piece of graph paper. "So, don't look at that until you know you won't be caught with it. That's stage-one planning right there. A first draft if you will, and I'll need you to tell me what you think."

"Will do, buddy." I instinctively placed the note in my back pocket. A headache formed along my temples. Today would be a wash. I already knew I'd drift in and out of listening to my teachers, who would go full throttle on the academia front now that the first day was behind us.

KASEY LINGERED IN the hall before Physics. She looked as distracted and upset as she had that morning. In class, she spent the whole time taking notes on Mrs. Paisley's energy lecture and never made eye contact with me. When the bell rang, Kasey gathered her stuff without a word and walked away.

"No word on what gives, huh?" Stuart patted me on the back.

"Not a one."

"Let's grab lunch and eat outside today. Just you and me."

"Okay."

Stuart and I stood next to the rectangular windows of the cafeteria. They were open, and whiffs of freshly mowed grass mixed with baked french fries. The noise of the lunchroom was overwhelming. Everyone talked all at once, competing for loudest alpha. Over the drone of constant chatter came an occasional shout of hilarity, or panic, or a peal of laughter—all of it blended together in a giant dodgeball game of sound. I didn't even try to speak with Stuart until we'd gathered our Styrofoam trays and made our way outside.

A group of nouveau hippies with a boom box gathered under the big tree on the front lawn. Dave Matthews' violin-and-sax combo wound itself around the tree's sprawling limbs. Stuart and I carried our lunches to the track behind the school. We climbed the bleachers, the aluminum banging with our every move, until deciding on a random spot to sit. I split open packets of ketchup and slathered it all over my maybe-meat burger while Stuart rearranged soggy pickle slices in the half-melted cheese.

"Did you get a chance to check out my plan?" he asked.

"Nah, I haven't been alone all day."

"Do it, dude."

I pulled out and unfolded his note. The graph paper was filled with a disorderly brainstorm, clouds of thoughts and ideas cluttering the page. This was a rare glimpse into the inner workings of Stuart's racing thought tank.

"Whaddya think?"

"Honestly, I don't know what to make of it."

In the middle of the paper, the underlined word—PRANKS—jumped off the page. Webbing off of it were three circled words: Homecoming, Prom, and Graduation. At the top, Stuart had written MAIN THEME: ZOMBIES in bold red lettering. "You're gonna have to explain this to me."

"It came to me last night. Homecoming is around Halloween-time, so I started thinking of costumes. And well, that led to zombies, of course."

"'Course," I said, not withholding that wisp of sarcasm.

"Then, I thought it would be funny to, like, secretly turn Homecoming into a dance for zombies without the administration, or even the cool kids, knowing. Picture it—Russ Landry crowned king in front of a sea of the living dead. Funny, right?"

"Absurd, dude."

"But then my mind kept cranking, and I thought, this could be bigger than Homecoming. We're seniors, they're getting ready to unleash us into the adult population, and what is that, really?"

I shrugged, dipping a wad of fries into a puddle of ketchup.

"Just a bunch of people, barely alive. Grown-ups are already zombies."

"So, what? You're making a political statement? I'm not sure I see the connection. Not sure anyone else will either."

"It's just an idea." Stuart snapped the plans from my hand, his mouth pinched in a disenchanted way.

"I like it. I need time to think it through that's all." I took the paper back from him. "I'll take a closer look tonight and see if I can organize what you're thinking here."

"Thanks, Warsh." Stuart's face lit up. He was so skinny his smile already etched deep lines into his cheeks. "That's your copy. I drew up one for each of us last night." He sat back against the bleachers, looked out at the field, and started eating. "Can you imagine what it must feel like to play out there and have a whole town cheering you on?"

"No, I can't."

"Me either. Does a real number on the ol' ego, I bet."

"You think that's why Landry's such a douche?"

"Probably not the only reason, but it might add up to something."

The football field was groomed with new lines painted on after each mowing. The custodian reworked them every week. Come Friday night, the bleachers would be packed with generations of alumnae. People said Texans went crazy over football, but I'd put money on Ohioans as a close second. Fall weekends were nothing but football at every level.

A thin line of woods spanned the other side of the field. Salacious rumors existed concerning that forest. In my opinion, the actual frequency of kids skipping class to have sex had to be low, but what did I know about it? As I looked out at the scene before me, a stray butterfly fluttered over a wildflower patch near the shed closest to the wood. And then, there was Kasey, stomping through the grass toward the tree line. I stuffed the last of the burger in my mouth and swallowed.

"There's Kase. I'm gonna try and talk to her now."

"Luck, my dude." Stuart and I slapped hands, ending the secret handshake with a snap.

The track's black pea gravel popped as I jogged toward the other side of the field. My lungs burned through unfamiliar wheezes of breath, and the backpack bounced heavily on my lower back. Upon entering the wood's shade, evidence supporting all the gossip of the place was scattered along the ground. A filthy unzipped sleeping bag lay rumpled among the litter, one of the corners was torn open revealing stained stuffing, flecked with dirt and twigs. A lucky family of animals must've found a well-insulated home for the winter. The idea of Russ leading an eager lady friend here, only to be pelted with mice as he straightened the sleeping bag made me laugh out loud. I kicked a couple of empty cans—mostly beer, some pop—along the trodden path toward the trickling creek that divided the wood. The banks had flooded during heavy spring storms. But now, near the end of summer, there was only an ashtray of a beach, each smooshed cigarette butt representing a future regret.

Kasey and I had come out here a few times. We'd stare through the branches above to either a brilliant blue or ominous gray sky. She stood in our usual spot now. Propped up against a tree trunk, she buried bits of beach trash with her shoe.

"Hey there." I stood on my side of the creek with my hands deep in my pockets. She'd been crying, her usual bright eyes bloodshot and puffy.

"I tried writing you a letter explaining everything." Her ponytail was loose, wilting with wear. "I don't know how."

"Kasey, I'm gonna be your friend no matter what."

She looked at me for the first time since I'd confronted her and tried a smile; her forehead wrinkled and her eyes welled up.

"I'm not even mad, okay?" I stepped toward the creek. "I'm just...you know, kind of disappointed. There are no perks in being a fake boyfriend."

That made her laugh. It was musical, floating through the woods, halfway between a sob. When she stopped laughing, she met me at the edge of the creek. We stood opposite each other. She bit the inside of her cheek and said, "I have a girlfriend."

Chapter Eight

WATCHING PEOPLE SCAN tabloid magazines while they waited to check out was the most fun part of my job, until last year, when a comedienne from TV came out as gay. Mom loved her and cried watching the televised interview. The resulting media frenzy brought a change in the store. Angry snippets of conversation wound around lanes one and two. I bagged groceries for pearl-clutching customers releasing long pent-up sighs. *What a scary new world we lived in!* They all agreed: end-times were upon us.

"It's a sin!" came a snooty hiss from an ancient one decked out in seafoam green polyester. So, was that pantsuit, but I kept my mouth shut.

Hype continued through the summer months. Some people seemed to enjoy the spectacle. Not allowed to be authentic in this world, the star fell, and the audience from our part of town could barely contain their glee.

"I'm gay, Jeremy." Kasey twisted a spare hair tie around her wrist. In the woods behind school, she confided in me, extending her true self to an onlooker. My reaction had to be perfect.

"So?" I shrugged, tucking my hands in my front pockets. Nonchalance, the key to success.

"Lesbian, dyke, queer. All of those." The sparkle returned to Kasey's eyes when she reiterated herself. "That's why I told everyone you were my boyfriend."

"Does that make me a fag hag?"

"No." She laughed and then tugged on the hem of her shirt so it covered her exposed navel. "More like a beard."

"I've never heard that one." I shook off a backpack strap and retrieved a pack of gum from the front pocket. "Want some?"

"Oh, it's a thing. And, yes, thank you." She slid the silver slip off the chewing gum and, after sitting through a million of my lectures on littering, pocketed the trash.

"So, what now?"

"I don't know." Kasey reached a hand out for me. I mirrored her action and helped her across the watery divide. Rocks wobbled as she stepped over the trickling creek.

"I got World History. You?" Kasey asked.

"Art."

"See you after school then?"

"Sure. I'm just gonna chill out here for a minute." The last twenty-four had been a whirlwind. I needed a few minutes apart from the cyclone of noise.

"Don't be too long." Kasey looked sideways, her eyes squinty. "The bell rings in..." She checked her watch. "...ten minutes."

"Don't worry."

She turned and walked away. I watched her leave. Speckled sunbeams, the lucky ones, cut through the canopy, highlighting her movements. When she got to the crumpled sleeping bag, she kicked it.

"This is disgusting!" she yelled. "You should pee on it on your way out, Jeremy!"

"Can do, friend!" And, I did.

WE DIDN'T TALK about it again. Kasey met me at my locker at the end of the day, and as we turned down the corridor, I took her hand in mine. Soft and dry, like powdered silk. If she needed a beard, I'd be it.

We strolled past Des and Dani, who exchanged looks with matching furrowed brows. Stuart walked toward the twins, probably getting ready to present zombie-fest to them. He did a double take and lost his footing, stumbling into a wall instead. As we passed through the lobby, popular kids offered no such reaction. They were all under the impression we'd been together long term.

"I'm gonna walk home, Kase." My eyes adjusted to the natural light as we left the school building.

"Really? I can take you. It's not that far."

"Exactly. I'm taking one for the environment."

"Way to make the rest of us look like slackers, Jeremy." She unlocked the driver's side of her car.

"I do what I can." I leaned against the side of the Miata and whispered this next part. "Hey, I don't care, okay. You're you, my friend. That's all that matters."

"Thank you." She threw her arms around my neck. One of her signature moves. Another body pressed up against my chest kind of destroyed me. I'd pretend for her though, fighting the urge to push her back into her personal space.

BYPASSING THE GROCERY store, I walked near the curb on the other side of the street, kicking up dust and rocks along the way. My cushy bed sang to me. Through poorly paned window glass, it hummed a steady classic. After a night on the couch, partnered with Kasey's emotional reveal, I was done being around other people. It might put Bern in a tight spot, but Mom could call in sick for me. Not the most mature way to handle things, but hey, technically, still a kid. So, whatever.

The apartment hinted of its emptiness. Filled with late-afternoon light and a blank TV screen, I knew Mom was still at work. In my bedroom, I dumped my backpack on the floor and tacoed myself into the comforter.

"Jeremy?! You home?"

I snapped awake and checked the clock. I'd been asleep for over an hour.

"Honey?" Mom's head poked around the doorframe. "Feeling okay?"

"Not really."

Mom walked in and pressed the back of her hand to my forehead. "No fever. You're probably overtired."

"Can you call in to work for me?" I'd forgotten to take off my shoes. With muffled thunks, they hit the floor.

"Excuse me?"

"Please, Mom."

"No, sir. If you're not going to work, you call your boss and explain."

I buried my head under the covers, all tantrum-esque. "I can't do it."

"Then you'll be a no-show, and Bern should write you up." Mom smacked my leg. "It's your choice, but this isn't something I'll do for you." She shuffled around my room, collecting laundry, I guessed.

Damn. I pinched the bridge of my nose. The room grew quiet. I peeked out from under the blanket. Mom had left, clearing the week-old path of dirty clothes. I kicked the blanket back and opened the curtains, letting the orange evening sun fill up my bedroom. Thinking about going to work tonight made my stomach somersault, but so did phone talk. A plastic bag of project supplies cluttered my desk. I hadn't started my mousetrap car assignment for Physics, and it was due by the end of the week. An excuse formed, and I made the call.

Mom banged around the kitchen. She tossed a frozen tray of brown food in the oven. Covering a glass dish of mashed potatoes, she yanked open the microwave and left them there to keep warm. Her Midwestern work ethic coiled up like a rattlesnake. Calling in sick was for the bleeding and/or dying, not the tired and/or emotional.

"Tonight's ruling—if you cannot work, you cannot have friends over. Got it?"

"I wanna be alone anyway. I've got tons of homework." I leaned on the kitchen counter.

"Maybe you *are* coming down with something." She stood on her tiptoes, and I lowered my head so she could kiss my forehead. "Kind of clammy, but not hot."

"I'll be fine. Don't worry."

"Okay."

After she left for her night job, the quiet filled me up. I closed my eyes and listened to the lack of human voice. Cars whizzed by outside, a door slammed in the apartment below, and the faucet dripped into the big pot Mom had used to boil potatoes.

When the oven timer rang out, I removed tonight's dinner—Salisbury steak. I piled three patties onto a plate and spooned gravy over a mound of potatoes. The kitchen smelled of onions and mushrooms, but actual pieces of those things hadn't made it to the final product. At least the mashed potatoes were real.

I portioned the leftovers into containers for Mom's lunch tomorrow and started the dishes. The water ran hot, and with a magnificent bottle fart, the last of the electric-blue soap drizzled into the stream.

Afterward, I set the supplies for my physics assignment on the table. Ripping the packaging from the race car, I drove it along the counter's edge. Duct tape squawked as it unrolled. I cut it into smaller strips and affixed the mousetrap to the hood of the Hot Wheel. The project turned out to be easier than expected. I tested it three times, measuring to make sure it traveled the required inches with each snap. Totally did, science win!

I flipped through the rest of my homework and grabbed Shakespeare's play for English class. Propped up by couch pillows, I read up to the ghost entrance and decided not to crack Hamlet tonight. All the TV channels showed simultaneous commercials. Bored, I went back to my room.

Grandpa's portfolio remained on my desk, his self-portrait, still there, egging me to do what I loved. Truth to self, I was being a pussy about the whole thing. If Kasey could come out in a world that would turn on her because of it, I could sit down and draw.

I took the colored pencils out one by one, sharpening the dull ones. The razor blade scratched along the pencil surfaces as I stalled. I hadn't created anything in a long time. Had I lost my touch? Maybe I should start with something simple, familiar even. I'd had tons of practice drawing dogs in my *Pup Operative* days.

When the oil-based tip touched the thick sketch paper, everything in me rekindled. My cheeks and ears flushed. My hand moved too slowly at first. Inside my head, flames burned, converting lines and shading into actual form. *Remember where the light comes from.* Grandpa's only advice for drawing. *If you can see where light shines, you can portray anything.*

My room darkened. I squinted to focus on the sketch without realizing the evening had scorched away. I flicked on the light switch. The big-hipped girl on the page wore a pair of baggy jeans, a lavender T-shirt, and a pair of brown chucks. She had two dimples, one always prominent in her chin, and the other indented her right cheek when she smirked, which she did now. The dents kept her face asymmetrical. Her eyes were a mix of green and brown, muddy waters one minute, a sparkling clear mountain lake the next. Along the tops of her round cheeks and nose were a speckling of red-orange freckles. She had auburn hair tied in a high messy bun. Unruly wisps framed her face. Next to her head, a talk bubble framed the words:

WHAT TOOK YOU SO LONG, FOOL?

Chapter Nine

PERCHED ON A high stool, Mrs. Paisley sat next to the sink at her science instructor's desk. A miniature drag-race track ran the length of the tabletop, but nobody could see the action from their seats. Each student fell somewhere on the spectrum of boredom, ranging anywhere from twitchy to asleep. Stuart picked at his cuticles, while across the aisle, a kid massaged the back of his newly shaved head in slow circles.

"Whenever you're ready, Ms. Axton." Mrs. Paisley made a note on the clipboard in front of her.

Kasey set the mousetrap attached to her toy vehicle on the track. She had three tries to get the bogus Mystery Machine to the finish line. But Kasey had purchased insurance on this assignment. Her van was a pull-back model. Inch that thing backward, and it bypassed the finish line, no matter what. I'd explained twice this week she wouldn't need to cheat. When the trap snapped, science took over.

Kasey looked right at me and smirked. She'd gone with neutral makeup today, except for her lips. They were painted a deep red, punctuating her smugness. In fractions of centimeters, I shook my head with one last warning. Cheating wasn't necessary. She winked, and with a sleight of hand, inched the automobile a smidge backward before letting go. At the mousetrap's crack, the van careened forward, zooming past the checkered stripe with ease.

That girl...man. I laughed under my breath. She got away with everything.

"Hey, wait a minute!" Russ Landry, of all people, spoke up. "That's one of those pull-and-go cars from Hefties! My little brother's collecting them." Russ's leg bounced under the table, as though he couldn't sit still much longer.

"As if!" Kasey whined. "I would never..." She faced Mrs. Paisley with an unnatural, guilty-looking smile.

"Hand me your project, Ms. Axton." Mrs. Paisley inspected the plastic toy. The teacher did what any kid would do and pulled back. The van sped toward the edge of the desk and tumbled over the side without any energy transfer from the mousetrap. The contraption clattered to the floor.

"See me after class." Mrs. Paisley showed no emotion and called the next name on the roster.

Kasey scuttled to her seat, her cheeks flaring pink. I stared at Russ until he noticed and gave me the finger. What was the point of ratting Kasey out? He'd never had a problem with her before, in fact, the opposite. Most of the time, he seemed only too ready to jump her bones if she ever gave him the go ahead.

"Why would he do that?" I whispered.

"Beats me," Kasey said.

A couple more kids completed their projects in front of the class before the bell rang. The room erupted with scooting chairs, shuffling backpacks, and Mrs. Paisley yelling instructions for chapter readings we were supposed to do over the weekend.

"I'll wait for you by the drinking fountain." I left Kasey to deal with whatever lecture was sure to come.

In the hall, people bumped into me. I leaned up against the wall, trying to both get out of the way and catch morsels of Kasey's scolding. But endless waves of chattering voices drowned out Mrs. Paisley's stern tone.

On her way out of class, Kasey tossed her project in the trash can, her shoulders more slumped than they were after her presentation.

"What did she say?" I asked.

Kasey bent and took a sip from the fountain. She blotted water from her chin. "She's giving me a redo and tacked on a bunch of busywork. She actually used the word, 'hoodwinked' in her spiel." Kasey cut a path through the flock. People moved out of her way automatically, making space for both of us without a fuss.

"Bummer. I—"

"Don't say 'I told you so,'" Kasey warned.

"I was going to say 'I wonder what's up Landry's butt.'"

"Who knows?"

"He's not usually a tattletale, is what I mean."

"I really don't want to ponder Russ Landry's anus or his sudden burst of conscience, 'kay?"

"Maybe you should." Guys like Russ, the perpetual bully, didn't rat people out for cheating. He lived and died by the code of teenage silence. We stopped at my locker, and I changed out the books I'd need for the afternoon.

"What are you two lovebirds doing this joyous weekend?" Stuart joined us as we walked to the cafeteria. We made our way past the trophy cases in the lobby and met up with Des and Dani holding brown-bag lunches, back from their morning at the community college.

"Top o' the mornin' to ya!" Stuart belted, mimicking a cartoon leprechaun.

"It's noon," said Dani.

"Rest of the day to ya, Stuart." Des curtsied, and Stuart bowed his head. They maintained eye contact and dreamy smiles until Dani interrupted.

"Come on. We have to check in at the office." Dani grabbed her twin by the arm. "What's with you?" She demanded as she dragged her sister away.

"Looks like you've got some 'splainin' to do, my friend." I put my arm around Stuart's neck and attempted a noogie.

"I don't know what happened, Warsh. We were talking about the zombie stuff the other day, and suddenly, she noticed me. Like, started smiling a ton and laughing at all my jokes. I mean, I'm a guy—not noticing how hot the twins are would go against the very grain of my dudehood. But Des...oh my god, Warsh! She smells like vanilla, man."

"Love is in the air, I guess." I bro-hugged Stuart and nudged him playfully. "Good for you. It couldn't have happened to a better guy."

"We're meeting at the mall tonight to work on the plans and catch a movie. You workin'?"

"Not tonight." Bern always gave me Fridays off, explaining all kids needed one weekend night to blow off steam.

"Has your ol' ball-and-chain here filled you in on the plans, Kasey?"

Kasey ignored him. She'd been super quiet through the whole Des/Stuart revelation, which was unusual for her. Kasey loved love. She usually savored every gossipy crumb regarding who was going out with whom.

"Kase, you there?" I asked, waving a hand in her sight line.

"What? Oh, nothing. No, I'm not up to speed."

"Fill her in before tonight, Warsh. It's your duty." Stuart fist-bumped me and ran off, presumably to find Des.

Kasey gazed through the lobby glass doors at a circle of boys playing hacky sack. Her thin brows pinched together right above the bridge of her nose.

"Funny about Stu and Des, huh?" We walked toward the cafeteria.

"Not really." She wore her hair down today, a long sheet of coppery brown that covered most of her back. "It's natural. The way it's supposed to be."

I laughed, but uneasiness tinged my thoughts. "Ooo-kay. You wanna meet up with them at the mall tonight? You can come over early, and I'll show you what Stuart's working on. It's kind of brilliant, really."

"I can't."

"Oh, big plans? Got a date?" I elbowed her arm in a jokey way.

The corners of her mouth turned down. "Yeah."

"Oh."

We came upon the end of the food line. Pizza day! I always marveled at the little cup filled with corn, such an odd choice for an accompaniment. But then again, pizza was such a star. When it took the stage, side dishes were damned.

Kasey looked down at her shoes, her arms crossed.

"When did you meet her?" I asked.

"A while ago, over the summer. Before I told you."

Now it was my turn to act weird. A rush of mixed-up feelings flooded up from the depths. I didn't have time to peel them apart. Instead, I struggled for logic. Kasey was gay. I'd known for a couple days now, plenty of time to wander through my minimal emotions. But why was it burning like a knee to the nuts?

"Who is it?"

"No one you know."

"Yeah, but like, like..." I sputtered, running out of questions too soon.

"Look." Kasey wrenched around. She placed her hand in the center of my chest. "She is nothing you need to concern yourself with, okay?"

"'Nothing to concern myself with'? Oh, that's rich." I stepped away from her touch, stung by her words. "How could you even say that? You make sure you're all I'm ever concerned with." A couple of kids sitting at the table next to us turned around. "I'm outta here."

"Jeremy, wait!"

I didn't face her. I couldn't explain what I'd said, or even why. No longer hungry, I left the celestial gods of pizza for another day.

THE MALL AT Pinewood Expo was never a true success, but with big name stores on rotation, there were always new places to wander. It was my shopping center of choice because of the discount movie theater.

"Where's Kasey?" Stuart sat at a booth in the near-empty food court, slurping an Orange Julius. In the middle of the table was a plain manila envelope that I assumed contained the prank plans.

"She had stuff to do tonight." I scooted myself over on the bench. My stomach dragged across the table's edge.

"What's up with you two? You never told me why she was telling people you were her boyfriend. The past few days, I've seen you guys holding hands like you're really a thing."

"I can't talk about it."

"That's not how things work between us, buddy." Stuart chewed on the straw of his drink as he talked.

"Look, if it were my thing, I'd tell you. It's hers, man."

"What is she, a lesbo or something?" Stuart's heh-heh of a laugh, the kind he reserved for pervy thoughts, echoed through the food court.

As an incompetent liar, I knew to stay silent. I shook my head. Avoiding eye contact, I checked out Spencer's storefront, its window jam-packed with cheesy T-shirts, lava lamps, and sperm-shaped plushies.

"Whoa. Wait." Stuart's eyes got big and round. "Am I right?"

"Just shut up, okay?"

"Are you serious?" Stuart reclined against the fake leather seat as he looked up toward the glowing blue skylights. The skin around his Adam's apple was red and irritated from shaving. "Man, that's some sexy shit."

"You're an idiot."

I spotted Des and Dani across the food court. Des bounced a little while she searched for our table. Her sister shook her head and headed toward the vendors.

"Hey, don't say anything to them about this, okay?"

"No worries."

"I mean it, Stuart. This is Kasey's thing. A bunch of rumors flying around the school would not be fair."

"I won't say a word." The lines around Stuart's eyes relaxed in one of the rare occasions he showed his serious side.

"Not even to your new girlfriend?"

"Warsh-man, I have more important things to do with Des Fields." Stuart winked at me and folded a piece of gum into his mouth.

Dani waited in line at a burger joint, but Des rushed toward the table once she spotted us. Stuart scooted, but not too far. A rush of electric current passed over their faces every time their forearms brushed. Stuart's ears flushed red, and they smiled at each other as if no one else existed.

"Jesus Christ," I muttered to myself.

"Disgusting, isn't it?" Dani banged a tray down with four orders of fries and drinks. "Help yourself, Jeremy."

I reached for a couple fries. The salt-laden, golden potatoes sent all the right signals through my brain. While I tossed napkins around the table, Dani passed out the rest of the food. Stuart and Des were still too entranced with each other to notice.

"Please, tell me you'll be here all night," Dani said as she sat next to me. "I can't be the sole witness to all this." She waved her hand at her sister and Stuart.

"Whaddya got against us, Dani?" Stuart finally broke eye contact with Des. He folded his gum into a napkin and munched on the fries.

"Nothing. I'm not into having all this mushy stuff in my face, that's all."

"Shut up, Dani," Des said through clenched teeth.

"Fine, whatever. I'm just asking Jeremy not to make me a third wheel."

"I got your back, Dani." And I meant it. Stuart and Des's display was set to topple into a full-on make-out session at any moment. I could spare Dani the awkwardness, especially since she'd backed up her request with treats. "Thanks for the fries, by the way."

"Anytime." She flashed a grateful smile.

I wondered what she thought of Des and Stuart and bet on cautious support with a twinge of jealousy. And there, at the heart of insight, were my own serving-size feelings about Kasey and whomever she was spending time with tonight. I was alone and had kept myself that way for a long time.

"Let's see this grand scheme of yours," Dani said.

"Yes! The moment we've all been waiting for." Stuart drum rolled his fingers on the tabletop while Des uncoiled the red string on the envelope. She placed five sheets of graph paper on the table. One, I'd already seen—the brainstorm; the other four were blank.

"You haven't gotten any further?" I asked.

"Have you?"

"I've been busy." I'd forgotten to organize what he'd come up with.

"Busy doing what?" Stuart made a pumping jerk-off motion with his fist.

"Drawing, sicko." The back of my neck prickled with embarrassment. I tossed a ketchup packet at him.

He dodged. "For that, I'll forgive you. But only if you show me what you're working on."

"I will when it's finished." The image of the girl I'd drawn waved at me from inside my head. I wondered about her name.

"So, this is it." Stuart straightened up and tousled his thick hair. It barely moved. "The big idea."

Dani and Des took the brainstorm sheet and read through Stuart's scheme. Both girls pinched their bottom lips when they concentrated.

"I told you I loved it the other day," Des said, her gaze set at goo-goo for my friend.

"It is interesting," Dani added.

"I'm the vision guy. You—all of you—have to help me with the details."

"How, Stu? How do we get most of the school to dress like zombies for Homecoming without everyone finding out we're behind it?" I asked. "We live in a small town."

"Write that down!" Stuart tossed me a little pencil, the kind used for minigolf.

"To piggyback on what Jeremy said—" (Dani never called me Warsh, and I liked her more for it.) "—because of the small-town thing, I think it's a mistake not involving the popular kids."

"No, look right here." Stuart pointed out a scene inside a thought bubble. A hand-drawn stick man stood on a boxy stage wearing a pointed crown. The overextended frowny face and single tear showed stick man's dejection. Stuart had taken the time to color the headpiece yellow and the tear a royal blue. "That's Russ Landry. He's accepting his reign as Homecoming King before a sea of living dead. See all the little green heads standing around him. They're zombies."

"Landry is such an ass." Des laughed.

"Maybe—"

"Totally," I interrupted.

"Maybe he is," Dani continued. "But we should ask ourselves—what's the end goal in a zombie-themed homecoming dance? Is it to prank the other kids? Making them appear as excluded and foolish as they've so often done with us..."

"Yes, that!" Stuart called out.

"Or, are we rebelling against the establishment?" Des finished her sister's sentence.

"Oh, that too!" Stuart chimed in.

"Big picture, in my opinion, is that this has the potential to be something our whole class could come together on." Dani nodded at her twin. "An uprising against the institution that's herded us toward graduation, as if it's some gleaming treasure on a hill. When really, it's one more item to tick off a to-do list."

"Another burning hoop to jump through before we settle into mind-numbing desk jobs, and our brains really do melt," Des added.

"I'm surprised you guys think this way." I dipped the last of my fries into the ketchup pile. "I mean, yeah, the rest of us will easily fall into whatever boring jobs pay the bills. But you guys are gifted; you've got way more options."

Dani laughed out loud, her thumb pointed at me. "Listen to this white boy tell me we've got more options than he does." She addressed her sister with her head low to the table, like she was telling a secret. Des huffed and rolled her eyes.

"I didn't mean it that way! Just that you're both so smart, and—"

"Relax, Jeremy. You're fine." Dani's smile reached her eyes. "Anyway, back to what we were talking about. I think most kids suspect the real world is a trap, even those of us you consider charmed." The last of Dani's pop rattled as she sucked it through the straw. "Isn't there a nasty history between you and Landry though?"

"He's been a dick to me since kindergarten, like he was birthed to be my archrival. 'Dickborn,' if you will."

"Good one!" Stuart laughed and high-fived me over the table. "I'm calling him that for the rest of the year. It's gonna stick, wait and see." Stuart scribbled the nickname into its own thought cloud.

"What do you think happens to people like Landry in the long run?" Dani asked.

"I don't know. Pretty wife, two and a half kids, decent work, more or less."

"How boring," Des observed.

"Ding, ding, ding!" Dani chimed.

"Well, maybe that's why Landry's such a jerk. He sees a future coming at him and recognizes the last four years are doomed to be the best of his life. Maybe that's why he acts out. He knows—"

"Nah, I'm sticking with Dickborn," I interrupted.

Chapter Ten

IN THE END, we accomplished nothing on the zombie-event front that evening. On a good day, Stuart's attention span could be compared to that of a puppy. Sit him next to a pretty girl, who kept finding reasons to touch him, and he was in heat. Eventually, he agreed to consider bringing the entire class into the prank, but as we stood in line for the movies, I told Dani not to count on Stuart changing his mind.

"It'll never work without the whole class in on it." Dani fiddled with the ends of her braids. "Ugh, I should do something new with my hair. I've had this style for too long."

"What makes you say that?" At the booth, I paid for two tickets for the eight o'clock showing of *Starship Troopers*. "And I like your hair."

"Thanks." Dani accepted the stub, and we moseyed toward concessions. Stuart and Des were already through the line. They carried their bags of candy and drinks toward theater two.

"There's too many loose ends. For the prank, I mean. Someone not involved will find out, and when they do, they are sure to rat us out."

Dani made a decent point regarding the plan. In our town, gossip counted as a hobby. It would be damn near impossible to keep a secret this big until mid-October. And even if, by some miracle of sealed lips, everything stayed under wraps for Homecoming, the cover would be blown with Stuart's prom and graduation prank plans. If those ever materialized.

"You're probably right. I'll talk to him," I offered.

"Of course, I'm right." She picked up a box of chocolate-covered mints and shook it, rattling the candy inside. "Plus, if all the seniors are involved, none get caught."

"Ah, I see. Smart thinkin'. That's why they've got you in the gifted classes." I counted out some cash, ready to order.

"Now, back to hair, Jeremy. You're due for a change too." Dani marveled at the mass of frizz framing my face.

"No way! This is my natural state."

"How does a white boy end up with such a glorious 'fro?"

"Good genes, I guess."

In front of us, an elderly couple huffed over something that was lost. Finally, the woman waved two Golden Buckeye cards in the air. A bored clerk applied the price reduction to their snack order. The man paid, all the while mumbling over the size of his wife's purse.

"Medium popcorn, please. And a large Mountain Dew."

"You can upgrade to a large for only another dollar." The kid behind the register had blotchy skin and didn't make eye contact. Behind him, a couple of his coworkers buzzed around, prefilling bags of popcorn and pumping extra butter after every couple of scoops.

"Uh, sure." Who was I kidding? I never resisted movie butter.

We rejoined Des and Stuart, who were waiting for us near the bathrooms. In the theater, the four of us picked seats near the top. The lights dimmed, and the screen lit up. The surround sound boomed with the explosions of a bug war and the love triangle of one Johnny Rico. I ignored the slurping kissing noises coming from the seats next to me.

But when Des sat on Stuart's lap, Dani changed seats. She moved a few rows below and jumped when one of the main characters lost a leg. So, I joined her.

"I don't know which is more grotesque," I whispered, motioning at the conjoined couple behind us.

"Definitely them." Dani laughed.

When the credits ran and the lights came up, I stretched, looking around the mostly empty theater. Stuart came up for air with flushed cheeks and a lipstick-smeared mouth, seeming confused. I balled up my popcorn bag and tossed it at him. It bounced off his forehead.

"There you guys are! I thought you left without us."

"We should have!" Dani finished the last of her candy, and her breath smelled peppermint sweet. "Thanks for sitting with me, Jeremy."

"Anytime. In fact, I think we better get used to it."

Des waited for her sister at the end of the aisle. "Ready?" She straightened her button-down shirt and radiated contentment.

"Coming!" Dani patted my shoulder awkwardly. "See ya around!" She stood and side-shuffled out of our row.

"Nothing says friend zone like a shoulder pat," Stuart whispered in my ear, his gangly frame balanced on the seat behind me.

"You don't have to tell me." I slurped the last of my pop as we walked together toward the red exit sign. Rekindling old basketball player dreams, I lobbed my cup at the giant trash can near the door. It swished!

Outside, the evening had shifted toward night. I checked my watch—10:15, still early by most standards.

"What're you doing with the rest of this beautiful night, Warsh?"

"Nothing. I'm scheduled to open tomorrow."

"Boo! Hiss!" Stuart balanced on the curb. With his arms outstretched, he concentrated on each step.

"I figured you'd be needing a cold shower anyway, buddy."

Stuart laughed and toppled to the right, joining me on the blacktop. "Can you believe it?"

No, but I didn't say that. Instead, I clouted my friend on the back and told him he deserved it. Before we parted ways, I asked him if he'd given any thought to what the twins said.

"I promise you, I did not think about Russ Landry whilst making out with Desiree Fields."

"Right," I snickered. "Well, I talked with Dani, and I think we should consider it."

"What? Humiliating Landry should be on the top of your to-do list!"

"True. But I can't see us getting this thing off the ground without the popular kids."

"Then let me ask you this." Stuart sat on the bumper of Mom's sedan, crossing his arms. "How do we convince the high school elite to go along with an idea two dorks from Frog's Landing came up with?"

"That..." I unlocked the Taurus and maneuvered myself behind the wheel. "...I don't know." With the door open, I yelled to Stuart as he walked toward his family's beat-up station wagon. "Yet!"

Stuart didn't look back. Under the streetlight's yellow glow, his arm shot up and two slender fingers gave me the international sign of peace. He stopped at his car to stare at the night sky with a dreamy smile on his face. When we were little, Stuart was obsessed with that wishing star, the one from the Jiminy Cricket song. He told me he looked for the first star every night and made a wish. At sleepovers, I caught him peeking out my bedroom window more than once. I wondered if he made a wish tonight. Maybe he didn't need to since he was in love. Maybe he just said thanks.

I waited for Stuart's unreliable car to start. He'd been stranded a couple times, and I didn't want to abandon him out here. I tried finding something good on the radio, clicking through Mom's saved stations. They were all either shouting RV salesmen trying to master the right kind of wacky tone, or classic rock. "Hotel California" droned. I turned it down low. Every Midwesterner was born knowing the words to that song. A grumbling engine pulled up next to me; Stuart's family car idled. He rolled down the passenger side window, and the overhead light came on.

"Everything okay?" I asked.

"You didn't have to wait on me, Warsh."

"I'm not. I'm trying to find acceptable driving music. See?" I turned up the smooth, velvety texture of The Eagles for Stuart's benefit.

"Oiy. Here, take this." Stuart pressed a button on the dash, and a tape slid out of the deck. "Shannon-from-the-record-store made it."

"What is it?"

"Not. *That.*" Stuart gestured at my radio and covered his ears. "Call me after work tomorrow?"

"Sure."

His car rumbled off with the sounds of this week's coolest punk band rioting around its bench seats. I turned over the cassette tape. Shannon-from-the-record-store had printed and taped a color-copy photo of a puppet shooting up with a hypodermic needle. Typed on the inside cover were a bunch of different songs by a bunch of different bands—a compilation. A couple of drama kids were obsessed with making the perfect comp, putting the right songs together in a certain way. Seemed to me that was what the bands were trying to do in the first place. Anyway, Shannon kicked off her comp with some blaring horns from an under-the-radar ska band.

As I picked up speed, the wind whipped around the front seat, and some loose papers fluttered, attempting flight. The dewy night air smelled like rain was in the forecast. I cranked the music, and frantic horns blasted my eardrums. They were young eardrums; they could handle it. My left foot stomped out the beat, and I didn't think about anyone.

AT HOME, MOM was camped out in the living room. All the lights were switched off, except for the TV's ever-changing glow. She sat on the couch in her Friday night sweats with her usual giant bowl of ranch-dusted popcorn.

"How was the movie?" She didn't look away from her show.

"Fine." I tossed my keys on the counter and headed for my room.

"Did you fill up the tank?" Mom hollered.

"Sorry!" I whined the syllables together, expressing true remorse. "I can do it tomorrow after work. It's not on E."

"No worries, hon. I'll take care of it. I've got a list on the table I'll need you to bring home from the store tomorrow, 'kay?"

"Got it. Night, Mom."

"Night, Jeremy."

Tooth brushing drowned out the canned TV audience laughter. I splashed cold water on my face and flicked off the bathroom light. My dresser sat in the corner of my bedroom near the windows with a boom box my dad had gotten me three birthdays ago on top of it. I hit eject and popped in the cassette Stuart gave me. Keeping the volume low, I remembered I still needed to call Dad. But the clock read near eleven, so, too late for a father-son talk. I changed into pj's, drew back the comforter, and lay under the thin sheet. Rusty brown water in the shape of Italy stained my ceiling. A ballad about wasting life softly screamed through my stereo speakers. A few seconds after the song's finale, a heavy click signaled an end to the B side. My eyes were still wide open. At five a.m. tomorrow, I would regret this, but not now. I got back up and kicked dirty laundry out of my path. The desk lamp flooded the work surface in white light, and I flipped my sketch pad open to her.

Chapter Eleven

AFTER THE FUNERAL, Mom organized most of Grandpa's stuff for auction. His papers contained a note granting me the art portfolio and comics collection. When we hauled everything away from the old farmhouse, I took the lamp Grandpa used to draw by as well. It stood on a short brass pedestal, complete with a green glass shade—an all-business lamp.

By that light, I sat at my desk and filled in the panel background from yesterday's drawing. My girl's bedroom had a full-length mirror, its shiny surface reflecting a fragment of her curves. A jumbled rainbow of Mardi Gras beads hung from the canopy of an extravagant four-poster bed.

"Now, what's your name?" I sat back in my chair, taking in the whole picture. Her smirk from yesterday merged into a complete frown. Words flew into my head. I penned them at a furious pace.

I'M PENNY KIND, AND YOU'RE NUTS IF YOU THINK I'D KEEP STRANDS OF CLACKING BEADS HANGING AROUND MY BED. HOW'S A GIRL SUPPOSED TO SLEEP?

In a new frame, Penny parted the beads down the middle and tied them back with a big red bow. Above her head, a thought cloud stated, *NOT A SOLUTION.*

In the top panel, I wrote, ANNOYED WITH HER ARTIST'S SENSIBILITIES, OUR HERO, PENNY KIND,

GOT OVER IT. Closing the caption box could have been a good place to call it a night, but Penny wasn't finished.

IS THAT HOW YOU SEE THIS WORKING? YOU, BOSSING ME AROUND?

"Well, I am the one drawing you."

I PROPOSE A TRADE. Penny stood with her fists at her waist.

Who was this girl that showed up on paper and doled out sass like it was her job?

I'LL LIVE WITH THE BEADS IF YOU CAN ANSWER ONE QUESTION.

"Sure, whatever." I pressed my fingertips to my temples. One question, then sleep.

YOU WERE COMFORTABLE WITH STUART AND HIS GIRL TONIGHT. BUT WHEN KASEY MENTIONED GOING OUT WITH HER GIRLFRIEND, YOU GOT ALL MAD. WHY?

In my blurry late-night thoughts, Penny's eyelids fluttered the same way Kasey's did when she already knew something I didn't. I clicked off Grandpa's light and left her waiting for an answer I didn't have. But a deal was a deal. Tomorrow, I would redraw her panels with breezy white fabric, wilting from her canopy posts.

Sprawled out over the covers, I saw way more than my room's boundaries. An image of Stuart and Des fawning all over each other projected itself onto my dark ceiling. If I could congratulate and support Stuart, why hadn't I done the same for Kasey? Both my best friends deserved happiness.

I heaved myself up out of bed again and tugged the pull chain on Grandpa's lamp once more. No more deflecting; I spoke to a blank page.

"Short answer, I love her. Long answer... She's not afraid to be with somebody, not scared to be who she is, and

I'm jealous of that. I'm tired of seeing this plain-faced kid in the mirror and wondering why he's allowed to take up so much space. I want to recognize what makes me, *me*."

Lungs fit to burst, I let out a deep breath and my shoulders slumped back against the chair. But again, Penny wasn't done. Her coming reply singed my fingertips until I finished penciling in the top half of her face. She peeked up from the bottom of the page. Trim brows arched upward creating rows of crinkling lines along her forehead.

Near her knotted mound of hair, a speech bubble appeared.

IF YOU THINK YOU'RE THE ONLY PERSON AFRAID OF NOT KNOWING WHO THEY ARE, YOU'RE AN IDIOT.

"Okay, but now you're the one that has to live with the beads."

Penny's middle finger crept up from the page's lower limits, and I laughed.

Knock-knock-knock! I startled at the sound.

"Jeremy, hon?" Mom said from the other side of the door.

"What is it, Mom?" I'd perfected the don't-open-the-door tone in middle school.

"Are you on the phone? It's getting late."

"Yeah." I checked the clock—a little after one a.m. Oof, the alarm would hurt in the morning. "I'm heading to bed right now." As I stood, there was a springiness in my step, as though I'd shed the twenty pounds my pediatrician confronted me with at my last physical.

REPETITIVE SCREECHING STARTLED me awake. Hitting snooze, I buried myself under both pillows for another ten minutes. Dreamy sleep drew me back in.

The grocery store was filled with water. I placed a box of sugary cereal on the shelf, and it floated away. Surrounded by buoyant blue boxes with grinning tigers, I swam toward one, snatched it, and put it back on the shelf. But it was an exercise in futility.

My coworker, Tim, drifted down the aisle. He carried a mop and was going through the motions of cleaning, except he glided three feet above the floor. Hovering nearby, he tried to talk, but his voice was nothing more than a swarm of garbled bubbles. Something tightened around my neck. I tugged and pulled away a clerical collar. It slipped from my grasp, sinking to the floor below us. I reeled for the break room, inexplicably embarrassed.

EEE, EEE, EEE!

The alarm again. This time I got up. My ears were still pressurized, as if the flooded work dream were real. I shook it off, going through all the motions of getting ready for work—shower, then my uniform, the fake flower smell of laundry detergent lingering around the collar. Sweat lines formed on my shirt, right under my pecs, so I applied an extra layer of deodorant.

In front of the kitchen sink, I sipped some sweet, beautiful coffee and stared outside. There wasn't much of a view, only our neighbor's dented front door and the stairwell. What would it feel like to run those steps? The blue digits on the microwave clock blinked twenty minutes before work. I went outside.

Our gray-green apartment building had two levels. Standing there on the sidewalk, all those failed presidential physical fitness tests flashed before my eyes. Chubby kid-version of me still clung to the pull-up bar, my hairless arms straining. The PE teacher counted time with tobacco spits in his trusty plastic cup. Once he got to ten, he'd let me jump down, until then, I hung there. But this was just taking the stairs; I could do this. It might hurt, but what doesn't?

I picked up my feet as fast as I could. My heart pounded in my ears, and my cheeks were hot when I reached the top. I caught my breath walking back down. As soon as my shoes touched the sidewalk, I turned around and went back up, a little slower than before. Controlling my breath—in through the nose, out through the mouth—I skipped stairs and lunged upward a third time. At the top, sweat dripped down my face and stained under my pits.

I cooled down on the park bench in the front lawn. My heart rate slowed, and breath steadied. The birds were already awake, chirping and pecking at the ground around two big maple trees in the yard. Mr. Feeney, the middle-aged neighbor across the stairwell, drove his pickup truck into the complex parking lot. The truck's engine silenced, and Mr. Feeney got out, yawning and stretching. He unbuttoned the top buttons of his starched white factory shirt and nodded my direction when he noticed me. Reaching for something on the front seat, he emerged again with a lunch pail and slammed the truck door shut.

"Mornin', Mr. Feeney."

"Is it?" He plodded along the pavement, looking heavy and tired from the night shift. "Don't usually see you out here this time of day, Jeremy."

"Getting a little exercise before work, sir."

"Good for you, son. See ya 'round."

Traffic increased as the town woke up. It was time to get to the store. I'd called in sick last time and wanted to appear the model employee today. I waited for the walk sign before crossing; it beeped when the light turned red. The donut shop's neon open sign caught my attention. Inside the store, a couple people sat at tables reading their newspapers. My stomach lurched for the sugary goodness on their plates, but I kept walking. I'd decided it was time to tame the beast, and that was what I meant to do.

When I got to Bern's store, I noticed Kasey's cherry-red car right away. Jeez, I hoped she hadn't slept in her car. The driver's side door opened as I approached. She had to-go cups of coffee and held one out for me.

"Peace offering?" Her skin looked paler than usual. Black smudges of old mascara encircled her eyes.

"Thanks." I took the hot cup. "You didn't sleep here, did you?"

"Nope. I got up extra early because I knew you were working. Believe it or not, I'm always this glamorous in the morning, Jeremy." Kasey took the lid off her cup and blew over the steaming surface. "Can we talk?" Her forehead creased with concern.

"I don't know. I have to get inside." She joined me as I went around the side of the building to the back entrance. "What's up?"

"About yesterday…"

If intestines could twist into actual knots, mine would have. Without thinking, I gulped the too-hot coffee. It scolded my tongue, and I coughed it up onto the asphalt.

"Are you all right?" Kasey asked.

"I burned myself. Go on." The beginnings of a blister formed on the roof of my mouth.

"Um, okay. So, I've been thinking maybe it's not fair for me to have asked you to be my pretend boyfriend."

"I don't mind, Kase."

"Jeremy, you are the most loyal person I will probably ever know. But if we keep playacting at being together, it closes off any opportunity for you to be with someone else."

With a dollop of sarcasm, I said, "I am a huge catch."

"Don't do that."

"What?"

"Make fun of yourself. You are awesome, and it's not okay for me to be in the way of someone else finding that out."

"Fair enough." We were almost at the back door. It was propped open for morning deliveries, and fresh air. I turned to her with my hand outstretched. "So, should we shake on it?"

"You're a dork." Kasey laughed and shook my hand.

"It's official, then. We're broken up." I met her eyes and tried to communicate an ounce of the feelings inside me. She wouldn't detect them though. Hell, I couldn't even name them.

"Jeremy, if I were different..." She pulled her hand away.

"Don't go there. If you were different, I wouldn't even get to be your friend." I took a deep breath. "I gotta go."

"Ope, yeah. I don't wanna make you late." Kasey took a couple steps backward. "I'll see you later."

"When do I get to meet her?" What had I just said? That had fallen out of my mouth before I had time to weigh the repercussions.

"You wanna?" Kasey's smile was huge. Now, I had to.

"Of course."

"How late do you work?"

"It's the morning shift, so I'll be done early."

"Okay, I'll pick you up around five." She practically skipped around the side of the building. "Hey, Jeremy!"

"Yeah?" As I turned back before walking into the storeroom, Kasey's head and shoulder popped around the side of the building.

"Wear something trendy. We'll be heading to the city."

"You know, I don't know what that means."

"Four o'clock, then. I'll help you get dressed." And with that, she disappeared.

Great. A date. Of sorts.

Chapter Twelve

NO MATTER WHAT the time of day, the grocery storeroom was always filled with gray. Flickering tube lights did little to combat the dull cinder block walls and cement floors. Even the stockpiles of flashy boxed goods dimmed back here. Off to the right, a forklift's beeping signaled its reversal. I maneuvered around stacks of crackers and headed toward the break room. Bern sat in his water closet of an office hunting and pecking over a keyboard. I apologized for missing my last shift.

"No worriesh, shon!" He removed the pencil that was clenched between his teeth. "We all need a day every now and then."

Bern looked like he could use a day himself. His black-framed glasses held back a mop of disheveled gray curls, and his shirt had crept up to reveal a pink roll of back fat. Bern leaned forward and squinted at his computer. "Pur-int!" he commanded. His fingers danced in front of the screen before double-clicking the mouse, and the office filled with hesitant screeches as the printer sprang to life.

"That sound makes me wanna die." Bern tossed his pencil toward an inbox stacked with manila folders and spiral-bound notebooks. He rolled his chair around and raised his arms in a shotgun shoot-out fashion. "*Chsh! Chsh! Chsh!*" He pretended to reload. "One of these days..." He stood from his desk chair, and it made a grinding squeal as he checked the whiteboard. "Let's see... I've got you stocking aisle three and four this morning but keep an eye on checkouts. Doris is up front, and she'll need you bagging if it gets busy."

"No problem, sir." I clocked in. Back at my cubby, I put on the stiff red uniform vest and adjusted my name tag. Then, I greeted Doris and told her to make an announcement over the loudspeaker if she needed me.

The morning flew, carried away by a flock of needy customers and the helpless Doris. She couldn't handle ringing and bagging for customers at the same time and called for me every time there were more than two people in line. It didn't bother me though. Witnessing awkward small talk was a secret pleasure of mine. At one point during the day, Doris asked a customer to explain the difference between brown and red lentils.

"Uh...besides the color, I'm not sure, ma'am." The middle-aged lady rolled her mouth into a close-lipped smile.

"I don't know anything about ethnic food," Doris replied.

"It's just what the recipe calls for." The customer changed the subject. "Hot enough for ya?"

"Lord, have mercy, yes!"

It went back and forth like that all day. I kept my head down, appearing to focus on the best way to maximize space in a plastic bag. But mostly, I tried not to laugh out loud.

Walking home, I thought through Mom's plans for the day—work and then drinks with a friend. I didn't want her around when I called Dad. She hovered, and every few minutes pantomimed, *What is he saying?* It always ended with me swatting her away to hear him better. Then she acted huffy for an hour or so afterward.

Our assigned parking spot was vacant near the side of the apartment building. Inside, I balanced the phone receiver between my shoulder and ear. The dial tone droned, interrupted by the beeps of numbers as I punched them in. It rang once...twice...three times.

He answered in his Dad way, "Yellow!"

"Hey. It's me, Jeremy."

"I know it's you, champ. Caller ID said so. How ya doing?"

"Fine. Mom told me you called."

"That I did. Thought we might meet up for lunch sometime soon. You can tell me 'bout school. You're big man on campus now."

"Just a senior, Dad."

"And listen, I've got some news too."

A female voice drifted over the line. "Maa-ark! Can you lend me a hand?"

"In a minute, hon."

Hon? Dad dated lots of women, or so he said. Once I hit a certain age, he started talking about them. I hated every detail, but he'd never used a pet name for them.

"Whaddya say, champ? You free for lunch tomorrow?"

"Sure."

"Great! I'll swing by around noon, and we'll get Chinese."

"'Kay, see you then."

"Bye, Jeremy! Love y—"

Click. "Some news" combined with this "hon" woman probably meant Dad was getting married. What would that mean for the random money he gave Mom and me? If luck struck, I'd pocket a wad of cash tomorrow, hopefully enough to cover the bills on top of the fridge, and then that would be the last of it. I legit sighed thinking of Mom's face as she struggled to make our money stretch.

My palms were sweaty after talking to him. The lady's voice kept playing like a scratched CD. *Maa-Maa-Maa-rk!* I hoped for one of the better TV stepmoms—a kid-less version though, one interested in keeping it that way. Dad wasn't a bad guy; he just never placed full-time fatherhood on his to-do list. Whenever we spent time together, he reminded me of people who didn't know what to do with their hands when they talked. Keeping them either tucked away or flailing about, that was him. Only, with his heart instead. It was either totally hidden or uncomfortably exposed.

I fidgeted with the phone cord, wrapping it tight around my index finger until the color purpled. A lingering fried garlic smell turned my stomach. Our apartment walls closed in. At my last physical, I'd measured six feet tall, and, in this moment, my head grazed our textured ceilings.

I dropped the phone cord and paced to my bedroom, desperate to get out of there. Clean gym shorts and a T-shirt were folded neatly in my second drawer. I changed, leaving my work clothes in a balled-up heap.

Outside, the fresh end of summer air filled my lungs. I raced up and down the steps until my whole body burned. After five cycles, I doubled over at the bottom level, struggling to catch my breath. My cheeks burned, arms ached, legs rubberized.

"Mr. Warsh, will you kindly explain what the hell you're doing?" Our neighbor, Ms. V, stood in her doorway.

"Just..." In through the nose, out through the mouth. "...exercising, ma'am."

She studied me through glasses with large round lenses. "You're as red as a beet. Get in here and have some water before you pass out."

She turned away from the door, leaving it open for me. The air conditioning beckoned as much as the promise of water. Ms. V's apartment had a twin layout to ours, except for a pony wall separating the kitchen from the living room. She decorated with the flare of a woman from a fancier time. Two rose-colored high-back chairs garnished with white lace doilies flanked a glass-topped coffee table. Under the windows sat a floral-patterned couch outfitted with a clear plastic cover. Along the far wall, a curio cabinet sparkled with a collection of crystal figurines.

"Sit down, son."

"I'm all sweaty."

"I have had men in my apartment before, Mr. Warsh. My things will survive your perspiration. Actually, as red as your face is, you'll be camouflaged."

I laughed and took her up on the offer. Ms. V had lived here as far back as I could remember, but I'd never known her to be this feisty. "You're in good form today."

"I'll have you know I'm in the same form every day. Here." Her wrinkled hand held out a clear glass of water. "Now, sit. I was going to have afternoon tea. You can join me."

Ms. V's white hair was cut shoulder-length and curled in the same way Hollywood starlets styled theirs long ago. A diamond-and-ruby-studded barrette sparkled above her right ear. In one hand, she carried a teacup and saucer rimmed with silver. Ms. V maneuvered around her apartment using an institutional-looking cane with a tripod base. She came into the living area one step at a time. Cane thumped. Shuffled step. Cup clinked. Repeat.

"Let me help you," I offered.

"Nonsense. I do this every afternoon. Just takes me longer than the average bear." Ms. V tottered toward a side table. She settled the china before sitting, a measured process.

"Learned to slow down the hard way. Nothing like a steaming cup of tea in your lap to liven up an afternoon!" Ms. V removed an embroidered throw pillow from behind her back and relaxed into her seat. "Now, tell me about this exercise plan of yours." She reached for her teacup. "For heaven's sake, sit back, Jeremy. Make yourself comfortable."

I'd been perching on the edge of the seat, not wanting to dampen her nice furniture. But, as this was annoying her, I loosened up and sat back into the chair's soft fabric.

"It's just something I started today. Running up and down the stairs. I needed to move."

"You'll ruin your knees that way." She brought the steaming tea to her lips. "Did you know I used to teach physical education?"

"No." And I never would have guessed it either. The extravagant elderly woman didn't match up with any PE teacher I'd ever had.

"I know what you're thinking. But let me tell you, sonny, it takes all kinds." Ms. V pointed to a stack of photo albums on the bottom shelf of the coffee table. "Pass me the yellow one, will you?"

I did as she asked, handing over her memories. Ms. V sniffed as she flipped through the first pages. "Here I am. This was my first year teaching." She turned the book toward me and tapped the picture of a vibrant young woman in a crisp knee-length uniform. A basketball rested in the curve of her thin waist and hip. I imagined that, in color, the dark gray stain on young Ms. V's smiling lips would match the bold red fabric of her chairs. "It was an all-girls school in Cincinnati proper."

"You're wearing your barrette."

"Oh, yes." Her old fingers touched it gracefully. "I've had it since I was a girl."

"Cool."

"I think that's a compliment, so, thank you. Now, about your workout routine. You're young, so you can do almost anything, including pounding up and down those stairs. But if you'd like to spare both your neighbors and your joints, you should start running and not on the pavement. Doesn't the high school have a track you could use?"

"Yeah. I'll keep that in mind." I finished my glass of water, and her grandfather clock struck three-thirty. "I don't mean to be rude, but I gotta go. A friend will be over soon. Should I put this in the sink?"

"No, leave it." She studied me for what seemed longer than necessary. "I hope you don't mind if you see yourself out, Jeremy."

"No problem. Thanks for the water!" I took my glass to the sink anyway and left Ms. V studying her photo album.

Making my way back up the stairs, I considered Ms. V's advice. I'd love to run at the track, but then every lookie-loo in the school would check out the big kid running at a walker's pace. I didn't want to bother anyone in the apartment complex though. Maybe I should resign, call it a day. A life, even.

I made a beeline for the bathroom and turned on the shower. As I waited for the water to warm, I checked my closet for something trendy to wear tonight. All I had were jeans and T-shirts. A teal bow tie Mom forced me to wear at a cousin's wedding dangled from a hanger. I tossed it on my bed. The studded belt from an old Halloween costume was curled up under my bed. I bet Kasey could work a little fairy tale magic on those items.

I hopped in the shower, cleaned up, and turned the water off to someone banging on the front door.

"Jeremy Warsh, I know you're in there. You're not backing out on me!" There was a bite of real irritation in Kasey's tone.

"Hold on! Let me get dressed!"

"Don't bother! Nothing you pick out will work anyway!"

"Well, I'm not answering the door in a towel, so, chill!" In my room, I threw on clothes. It was 3:45; Kasey had arrived early. That never happened.

I opened the front door with a butler's flourish. "Madam..."

"Thank you, kind sir. It's not proper keeping a lady in the heat." Kasey fanned herself in the way a southern belle might. Hooked over her forearm, she carried two grocery bags filled with clothes.

"You are fifteen minutes ahead of shh-edule, Madam."

"Ew, stop! I hate it when you pronounce ske-dule that way. Gives me the heebie-jeebs." She set the bags on the kitchen table. "I went thrifting today!" she sang. "Look what I got for you!"

"Good. I went through my closet and found an old bow tie and a studded belt."

"Oooh, those might actually work."

"Where're we going anyway?" The fridge opened with sticky protest, and I reached for a pop. "Want one?"

"You got red?"

I rummaged around the grape and saw one last can of red in the back. "Yeah."

"Then, yes. And to answer your question, Clifton. There's a poetry reading tonight, and then, if you're up for it, clubbing afterward."

"Any good bands playing?"

"I don't know. Mostly locals, I think." Kasey popped the tab. "What are we gonna do with your hair?"

"Nothing to do. It is what it is." I'd had time to run a towel over it before answering the door, but that was all.

"It's just so..."

"Big? Fluffy? Fresh as hell?"

"All of the above." Kasey started taking clothes from the bags and hanging them over the couch. "I think this will be your best bet." She handed me a vintage shirt with pearly snap buttons and a silver thread running through the striped pattern.

"No way, I'll sweat through this in seconds."

"It's short-sleeved. Look." Kasey snatched it back and held it up for me to inspect. "You can wear a T-shirt underneath, and that studded belt.

"I don't know." I rubbed the lightweight fabric between my fingers.

"Try it."

"What else did you get?"

"Couple T-shirts for me, and this..." The second bag contained one item—a red leather trench coat. "Isn't it magnificent?" Kasey slipped it over her shoulders. "Look at the lining." She flashed open the jacket, showing cheetah print silk.

"Wow!" It was as if it had been constructed with her figure in mind; it fit her frame so perfectly. "It's so you."

"I know! I'm in love!" Kasey tied the leather belt around her waist and twirled. "I'm wearing it tonight, and every night after. It's my official going-places coat."

"It's awesome," I agreed. "I'm gonna go try this on."

Kasey hummed a chirpy tune in the kitchen while I searched my dresser for my favorite black T-shirt. The coolest band shirts were emblazoned with a Ramones logo, and to be saved for special occasions. So, I pulled out the wrinkled mass of fabric and smoothed it over the bed.

Kasey broke into song in the other room. I recognized the catchy chimney sweep tune.

"Are you singing *Mary Poppins*?"

"I can't get it out of my head! It's been droning around in there all day."

"That's unfortunate."

"I love that movie."

I did too. Mom taped it on VHS when I was a kid, and I memorized the whole thing. She read me the chapter book as well. A smaller version of myself rested his head in Mom's lap, while magical images of Mary painting stars in the sky played.

I came out of my room modeling the outfit for Kasey. Her nose crinkled as if she smelled something gross.

"I'm not sold on the black under the white..." She circled me, making inspection noises as she went. "Or it could be the shoes..."

"I have a different pair."

"What style?"

"Doc Martin's, low-rise."

"Yes! Wear those; your Vans have about had it anyway."

I grabbed the pair of shoes from the back of my closet. A layer of dust coated the black leather, and I wiped it off with a dry edge of the towel. The Doc's were the last Christmas present Grandpa ever got for me. I wanted them to last forever, so I almost never wore them.

Kasey, still wearing her new red trench, plopped onto my bed.

"So, what's her name?" I turned my desk chair toward her and kept polishing my shoes.

"Anita."

"What's she like?"

"I don't know if I can explain it right." Kasey sat up and stared out the window. She scratched at her neck.

"Try." I tossed the towel toward the laundry basket and slipped on my shoes.

"She's one of those people who's passionate about everything. She fills everyone up with excitement. You know what I mean? I'm not making much sense."

"Exhilarating," I muttered as I got busy tying my laces.

"Yeah, that's it!"

Chapter Thirteen

IF LIFE MIRRORED the movies, our night was set up to be the one epic night every teenager got. A super special twelve-hour time frame filled with quick-paced dancing montages, good vibes, and loads of laughter. All leading to those gray morning hours, when a mishmash of characters from all the different cliques unpacked their key life events, transforming everyone involved. Should I put a mental pin here now, marking a personal epicenter of change? I didn't know, wouldn't know, until hindsight came into play.

Before we left, I scrawled a note for Mom, letting her know where I'd be and not to wait up. Kasey and I pounded down the stairs to the parking lot behind my building. She started the engine of her cool red car, and Courtney Love blared through the speakers.

Kasey bit her cuticles—a habit when her anxiety shot through the roof. As she accelerated onto the highway, I turned down the music.

"What's up, Kase? You're bleeding."

"What? Oh, crap." Kasey inserted her thumb between her lips.

Her intense nerves didn't put me at ease. On any given day, meeting new people made me want to die. This situation was different, delicate even. The thought of engaging in stupid small talk all night made me tired already.

"You want to cancel?" I'd be so fine with spending the night in my bedroom, drawing.

"No." Kasey punched the car's lighter. "It'll be great. Anita wants to meet you too." She positioned a cigarette between her fingers.

"She knows about me?"

"You're my best friend, Jeremy. Of course, she knows. In fact, it was her idea we drop the whole boyfriend-girlfriend routine." The lighter popped, coiled heat ready to burn anything.

"Not yours?"

"No. She said it wasn't healthy for either of us. After thinking it over, I agreed."

As we drove past the surrounding farmland, wind blew through the open window. Hitting me full force in the face was the sickly-sweet smell of manure—heaps of processed shit. I closed my eyes. Of course, it wasn't Kasey's idea. I laughed.

"What's so funny?"

Should I go to the place where I told Kasey how selfish she'd been throughout our friendship? That it had been nice thinking she'd considered my feelings first. I looked at her as she sucked the blood from her thumb. "Nothing."

"Damn, this won't stop bleeding."

Nope, not tonight. She had good reason for focusing on herself, like anybody did. I popped open the glove compartment and handed her a packet of tissues. She wrapped up her thumb, said thanks, and cranked up the music, singing along with Love's abrasive tone.

In the city, Kasey parallel parked near a dive coffee shop on Vine Street. A folding sidewalk sign advertised "Open Mic Night" in yellow chalk. Artist-types with beat-up guitar cases filled most tables. Christmas lights framed a handwritten menu behind the bar, and the coffee smell was intoxicating.

"You want anything?" I yelled over the crowd noise.

"Nah." Kasey scanned the mass of people. She stood on her tiptoes for a heightened advantage. "I don't see her."

"I'm gonna order. I didn't eat anything."

"Let's stick together." Kasey looped her arm around my elbow.

I excused our way to the counter and ordered a sticky bun and bottled water. The cashier, in crayon-red pigtails, handed over the goods and my change. Finding a place to sit seemed impossible. A narrow shelf ran along the room's perimeter, and I shoved through the crowd, claiming the standing-room-only spot.

"Crazy turnout for an amateur night, right?" I shouted.

"All the students are back. Maybe that's it." Kasey shrugged. Her neck extended as she searched for Anita.

"Wanna piece?" I offered her the pastry. Kasey tore a piece off and stuffed it into her mouth.

On stage, someone tapped a microphone. The knocking reverberated through the crowded room. A tall girl in a thin-strapped camisole bent over the mic, and the room hushed for her announcement.

"Hello, everyone." Her alto voice flowed like maple syrup. "Welcome to Larey's Open Mic night. If you wish to perform, put your name in the fishbowl on the counter. We draw randomly throughout the evening..." The girl's wavy dark hair was long on top and buzzed on the sides. She cupped her palm around her mouth as if she had a secret to share. "...because it keeps you here longer," she whispered. "Don't let management know I told you."

Onlookers responded with light laughter. The girl reached into her pocket. Turning slightly, she showed off a graphic shaved into both sides of her hair. I couldn't make out the design from the back of the room but awarded cool points.

"First, a little spoken word for your pleasure..." The mic picked up notepaper crinkling as she unfolded it. "...or not. I work here, so I get to go whenever I want." More laughter. Her demeanor touched on cheesy, but the kind people enjoyed. She cleared her throat and rolled her lips together before reading, appearing nervous for the first time since she stepped onto the platform.

"This doesn't have a title yet. It's still unfinished. Oh, maybe that's the title!" She pushed the long section of her hair away from her face and took a beat.

> "Tangled in the late night
> Tracing the line of your heart
> You ask me, is this right?
> And I misquote that song of songs
> No.
> That's not it.
> Try again.
> Tell me, it's okay.
> Your path intersected mine while we walked among the stars.
> We were meant to be together, no matter how they pray."

Her poem read like an eighth-grade journal entry. The girl folded the paper and tucked it in her back pocket, and a guy wearing a newsie cap whistled. As people clapped, her dark eyes penetrated the crowd, right to me. My heart skipped in her gaze, but I'd been wrong. The girl was staring at Kasey, whose cheeks turned pink and splotchy.

A man in cutoff shorts and a backward ball cap joined the girl on stage. He clapped as he walked toward her, and grabbing the mic, he spoke into it, "Anita Georgiou, everyone."

Anita curtsied. She started to leave the stage but turned and took back the mic. "Leave good tips, you guys!"

The crowd parted for Anita as she strolled through the room. Her hooded eyes met Kasey's, and they stared at each other, having secret conversations with their body language. Both girls smiled. Anita reached for Kasey's hand and brought it to her mouth, kissing it, as though Kasey was royalty.

"What on earth are you wearing?" Anita asked. "It's like 500 degrees in here."

I snorted but covered my mouth as I was still chewing up the last of the sticky bun.

"I got it today. You better get used to it, because I'm wearing it everywhere."

"Okay, okay."

Behind Anita, a tan-skinned man took the stage. He sat on a stool and serenaded the packed room in Spanish. His singing was average, but his guitar playing was from another planet.

"Jeremy! Hello? Are you there?" Kasey waved her hand in front of my eyes.

"Oh, sorry. That guy is really good," I added.

"That's Juan; he's a regular. And you're right—he's awesome." Anita held out her hand for a shake. "So, you're the famed Jeremy. I'm Anita. It's really nice to finally meet you."

Two shaved lines intersected in various locations, creating a zigzagged row of triangles over both of Anita's ears. Her smile captivated me with its dazzling straight rows of teeth. Simultaneously, she made me feel important. I could tell her my whole life story in one sitting.

"Same." I tried emulating her sincerity.

"Listen, you guys enjoy the talent. I'm working the upper deck tonight. After a while, it'll clear out, and we can chat." Anita pointed to an actual porch built within the building, a loft space. She pecked Kasey on the cheek and disappeared within the packed room.

"So?" Kasey asked.

"Seems nice."

"That's all you have to say!" She backhanded my shoulder.

"I barely got to talk to her!" I held up my hands in defense. "I mean, she's great, Kasey."

Kasey rolled her eyes and crossed her arms.

"She seemed candid, totally beautiful, and she, like, glowed during her poem." I nudged Kasey. "A poem about you, I might add."

"I love her," she admitted with a blush.

"Well, from what I can tell, the feeling is mutual."

The shop window became a hazy mirror as, outside, the sky turned indigo-blue. The audience thinned as the night wore on. A comedian told a few raunchy jokes, and people booed. He stammered as he walked off stage, flipping everyone off. I was embarrassed for him. Kasey ordered two soy lattes and handed me an oversized ceramic cup.

"These are the best." She blew over the steaming foam. As the crowd quieted, the manager walked on stage and pulled the next name from the fishbowl. Anita waved her arms from the upper deck, catching our attention.

"I think someone wants you," I told Kasey, nodding at the second story.

Kasey looked up and smiled at her girlfriend, who motioned again for us to come on up.

"They must be closing up the second tier. Let's go."

We walked around the tables to a hidden staircase next to the bathrooms. Tabloid clippings plastered the walls, announcing weird stuff from alien probes to a tiger's spontaneous combustion at the zoo. At the top of the stairs, the lights were turned low. Anita was wiping tables with a rag.

"That one's dry," she said, pointing toward a booth in the back corner.

I was ready to go home. I'd been up since five, and the thought of making conversation sucked. It was quieter up here though, the climbing notes of a saxophone made more pleasant with distance. Anita sat next to Kasey and unscrewed a bottled juice with a picture of New England shores on the wrapper.

"So, Jeremy, tell me about yourself." Anita kept her spine pin straight, without ever leaning back into the seat. She projected regality.

"Not much to tell, really." I lifted the coffee cup to my mouth and sipped the steaming latte. "I'm into comic books, get decent grades, work at a grocery store." I listed all the superficial stuff that somehow represented a whole person. "You?"

Anita made a humming noise as she thought over what to tell me. "Well, I graduated last spring. Decided to stay close to home and attend UC. So, that just started, and I moved onto campus last week."

"Your family's here?" I asked.

"Oh yeah, generations of us are scattered throughout the city. For a long time, I thought I wanted to get away, ya know? Head up to OSU, at least." Anita shrugged, her cupid-bow lips curled into a smirk. "But I love it here."

"That doesn't make any sense to me," Kasey chimed in. "I'd be outta here so fast."

"We don't live in the city though." I added, "Our town isn't really an equal comparison."

"Thank you! That's exactly what I said." Anita elbowed Kasey, who rolled her eyes. "It's a whole different world down here, Jeremy. Have you been to the Omnimax at Union Terminal?"

"Once, on a field trip."

"It's so cool. And my dad, he performs for the opera. So, that's always fun."

"Your dad's an opera singer?"

"Oh, no. He's a tax attorney. He plays an extra."

"That's...really cool."

"I know, right? My grandma volunteers as a docent at the art museum. I'm rambling though. There's so much to do here."

"I guess cities are like that. Have you decided what you're going to school for?"

"No. My parents insist I have plenty of time. I'd love to get into a dance program, but wrong body type." She modeled her athletic, solid-looking frame, her sinewy arms more muscular than my own.

"Don't let her downplay. Anita's an amazing dancer," Kasey declared.

"Pssh..." Anita waved her hand. "I'll audition, for sure. But if it doesn't work out, which I'm almost positive it won't, I'll get an undergrad in political science or something. I know dad wouldn't mind me getting a law degree either. What are your plans after high school, Jeremy?"

"I don't know." I—literally—scratched my head. "I guess I would need to talk to my advisor. Not sure what steps are available for me. Money's pretty tight for us." I don't know why I said the last part, except that Anita seemed to be one of those people you could say any old thing to.

"Definitely talk with your school counselor." Anita's half smile highlighted a dimple in her cheek. "Oh! Plus, I know someone who might help you. Kasey said you're an artist, right?"

"I'm not trained or anything."

"Duh! That's what college is for! There's a professor from the art academy that comes in here all the time. I could totally introduce you!"

My heart skipped a beat. I wanted that. I'd never put college on the table. My future had a prepaid stamp to minimum wage work at the grocery store, and maybe middle management when Bern retired.

"You should do it, Jeremy," Kasey added.

"You've never seen my work."

"Yes, I have. Stu showed me all the *Pup Operative* comics you drew. You have real talent."

"You think?" My cheeks were hot.

"I do."

"That's it. It's settled." Anita jumped up at the sound of applause from downstairs. "I'll talk to him next time he comes in." She walked over to the railing and peeked over. "They're all done. You guys ready to party?"

Chapter Fourteen

CLOSER TO THE city's heart, everything felt contrary to home. When I closed at the grocery store, I walked home with nature's brand of quiet. My town stopped functioning after nine o'clock, but Clifton was just getting started. The sidewalks were bright from a mix of street lamps and neon signage. Outside the historic music venue, fans waited in line for a show as awkward starts and stops of instrument tune-ups made it all the way to street level. A random drum roll ended with a cymbal crash. Through large shop windows, barkeeps glided behind the bar, hustling to serve demanding crowds. All around me, people talked, laughed, shoved, and played with the barely contained excitement of children tasting their independence. Giddiness dusted over their weekend rituals. It was infectious.

Anita led us up Vine Street, puffing on an American Spirit cigarette. Every so often, she checked over her shoulder, making sure Kasey and I kept pace. Bit by bit, the noise and light fell behind us.

"Hey, where are we going?" I asked after it became clear we weren't stopping at any of the local hot spots.

"A friend of mine is having a back-to-school party." Anita flicked the cigarette butt into the street with one last dramatic exhale. "He's a coffee shop regular."

"Not another frat party." Kasey stopped next to an orange Jeep parked on the street. "I'm not into it."

"What do you mean?" Anita turned around to face Kasey.

I tried to disappear. We'd left the business sector, and the shadows loomed longer in this neighborhood. I stepped out of the circle of yellow light cast from an overhead street lamp, preparing my passive stance.

A rowdy group whooped and hollered across the street. One boy leaped onto another for a piggyback ride, and they galloped off.

Kasey crossed her arms, the way she always did when she dug in for an argument. "The last time you brought me to a party, the guys treated us like some dyke freak show." She overenunciated the last three words.

Anita laughed. *Oof, wrong move.* I wished for one of her cigarettes. We were going to be here a while. I leaned against the Jeep, hoping (too late) it didn't have an alarm system. But to my surprise, neither an alarm nor Kasey ever sounded off. Anita's singsong manner diffused my friend. A miracle as such I'd never observed.

"Hon, it'll be okay." Anita tugged on the drawstring around Kasey's trench.

"Don't laugh at me." Kasey used her whiney voice.

"There will be minimal dude-bros at this party. Reggie is, like, head thespian." Anita pulled Kasey in for a quick kiss. "These are our people, okay?"

Kasey was stubborn though. Once she put her foot down, she'd need time to relent. I hoped Anita wouldn't drag me into it.

"Whaddya think, Jeremy?" Anita asked, her dark eyes sparkled over Kasey's shoulder.

Damn. "I'm just along for the ride tonight." I shoved my hands in my front pockets.

"It's like that, huh? Going Switzerland on me?" Anita joked.

I shrugged in response. Kasey would come to her own conclusion, with or without my input.

"Are you okay with this?" Kasey's highly manicured eyebrows wrinkled her forehead.

"Sure. I mean, we're here to have fun, right?" I'd never been to a college party. I was equal parts curious and terrified.

WE MADE A turn toward a dark section of row houses lining both sides of the street. Most were quiet, with television blues lighting up living room windows. But the corner townhouse overflowed with people and loud music. On the front lawn, a couple made out on a threadbare sofa while a troupe of swaying dancers twirled sparklers behind them.

We climbed the front steps and entered the house. In the living room, small groups clustered and bobbed to thumping techno music blaring through the speakers. I scanned the place for an acceptable place to stand, a spot out of everyone's way. Off to the left, a set of stairs led up to the second story. At the bottom of it was a decent-size landing. I elbowed Kasey and motioned that way, but a large cardboard cutout of Charlie the Tuna stood in the way. I flattened it against the wall, and we settled into the corner for the evening. Anita yelled something over the crowd, gesturing about drinks as she walked away.

"I hate this!" Kasey shouted as she side-eyed a long-haired hippie girl performing ballet moves in front of a row of bong-passing boys on the couch.

I leaned toward her ear. "Then why are you always at them?"

"Huh?" Her mouth screwed up in a pout.

"You're always hungover from some party," I yelled.

Kasey grabbed me by the shoulders. "Being hungover doesn't mean I was at a party. I do most my drinking alone, thank you very much."

"Tim told me he sees you at parties."

"Who the hell is Tim?"

"A guy from my work; he graduated a while back."

"Oh, right. I'll concede to always making an appearance, but I duck out before anything weird happens." Kasey let go. Conversation over, she scanned our new environment. "There's Anita with drinks.

"Party favors!" Anita reappeared, carrying two red plastic cups. She handed me one, and with an arm over Kasey's shoulders, presented the other. "We have to share. Two hands, two beers."

The beer barely registered as anything more than bread dipped in water, but I sipped on anyway. Not wanting to seem either immature, or pretentious, I focused on controlling my face after each taste. We were quiet. The music made conversation more of a screaming match. Awkwardness started to settle in as the three of us took turns swallowing, and before I knew it, the cup's bottom stared at me. Options now included twiddling thumbs or more alcohol consumption.

"I'm out." I shook my empty cup. "Is the keg that way?"

"Yeah, follow the flow of the rooms back toward the kitchen." Anita's head rocked along with the song's beat.

"'Kay, you guys need a refill?"

"Yeah, here." She handed me their cup. Daft Punk's robotic funk gained momentum over the speakers.

"Come dance with me? Pleeease…" Anita begged Kasey.

Kasey rolled her eyes. Anita loosely dragged her toward the area designated for dancing. They were oblivious to onlookers, only taking their eyes from each other when they twirled.

I watched from them the keg line. A tall guy dressed in baggy khaki shorts and flip-flops stood behind me. His head turned, following my sight line toward the girls.

"Girlfriend?" he asked.

His hair was longer on top, an indistinguishable color under the black lights, and parted off to the side. It held a perfect wave, which fell right into place even though he habitually ran his hands through it. Dressed in a plain collared tee, his demeanor indicated money, or at least a level of financial comfort I could easily spot, like a fortune-teller reading auras.

"No!" I leaned closer to him, so I didn't have to scream the next part. "One of them is a good friend. The other I met tonight. I'm Jeremy, by the way." I carried both cups and bit down on the lip of one to free up a hand, extending a shake.

"Matt."

"Nice to meet you!" I checked out the rest of the dining room. In one corner, a large computer desk housed an equally large computer. Wires sprouted from different angles, all leading to an overloaded power strip. A *Trainspotting* movie poster was tacked next to a window covered by an incongruous set of lace curtains. Everything glowed with a purple haze. I looked down at the thrift store shirt Kasey had bought me and noticed a bright blue spatter across my shoulder.

"Oh, shit!" I shouted and jumped away from the line.

"What's wrong?" Matt called out.

"Uh, can you hold these for a second?" I fumbled the cups at him before he could decline. Whipping the shirt off my shoulders, I tossed it across the room.

"Are you okay?" Matt stared at me, eyes wide and suspicious. He seemed to be making an important decision regarding my mental state.

"I am now." I straightened my trusty Ramones shirt. It hadn't let me down.

"What was that about?"

"I, uh, just got that shirt today. At a thrift store... Probably should have washed it first." I took back the cups. "Under the black light, there seemed to be—"

Matt's burst of laughter cut off my explanation. His head tilted back, and I watched his Adam's apple bob. When he finally caught his breath, he said, "I'm sorry, dude. That's..." Matt's face clenched up, and he covered his mouth, stifling another round of laughter. "...terrible."

"I guess I make one hell of a first impression."

The music stopped as two white girls argued over what CD to put in next, and I welcomed the debate because the room quieted. Now we wouldn't have to scream-chat.

"True." Matt rolled his lips with amusement. "Now I'll never forget you."

"Oh, yay!" I mimicked fanfare while a flash of this guy ten years from now flitted in my mind. His hair would be cropped shorter. Around his neck, a purple silk tie hung loose after a long day at the office. He sipped expensive wine with his wife and all their friends, and someone would beg Matt to tell the story about a pudgy kid showing up to a party with old splooge on his shoulder.

The line inched toward the kitchen, and the yeastiness of cheap beer filled the tightening space.

"So, do you go to school here?" Matt's voice still wavered with hilarity. His eyebrows stretched high, trying to keep a straight face.

"Nah, I'm still in high school. I live thirty minutes north of here. Near Hamiltucky."

"Come again? Ham-il-tucky?" Matt cocked his head.

"Oh, it's a nickname for the area. Small town. Pretty rural."

"Am I talking to an honest-to-goodness farm boy?"

"God, no. My gramps was the last farmer in our family. I live in an apartment with my mom." Handing out personal information upon meeting wasn't my usual style. My cheeks burned with embarrassment. "What about you? Are you not from the Midwest?"

"I am. Farther north is all. Ann Arbor."

"You'll want to be careful, telling Ohioans that."

"Trust me, I already know. If you'd said you were from Columbus, I would have announced that nefarious stain to the whole party."

"Lucky I'm not, then." I scratched the back of my neck, conceding defeat. Here came the only acceptable topic two dudes could always discuss. "You're a football fan, then?

"Nope. It's just one of those things you grow up with, you know?"

"Yeah, I do. It's in the Guidebook for Ohio Livelihood."

"There's a guidebook?"

"Mm-hm." I nodded. "It's in Chapter Seven—Small Talk for the Midwestern Male."

"You're funny." Matt flashed a smile. It shined a pale shade of blue under the black light.

Matt's hair lit up like the orange of an autumn leaf as we advanced into the flickering white light of the galley kitchen. I blinked at the breathtaking beauty of surprise color. Matt and I took turns filling our glasses amid the melting ice and spilled beer. He motioned toward the back door, and I followed.

The late night air washed over me as we stood on a small wooden porch. Matt hopped up and sat on the deck railing, and I found a seat in a lawn chair across from him. Music from the party floated through the open windows. Someone had opted for slow jams, and they were so much quieter than the techno, not a conversation block.

Matt lit up a skunky joint, and we passed it back and forth. He told me how he'd chosen UC for the architecture program when he was fifteen years old. But now, staring at age twenty, he'd been there a year and wasn't sure it was his life's calling. He also told me his older sister had gotten into Columbia's MFA program. I didn't know what that was but pretended I did. He confessed his dad always looked at him with thinly veiled disappointment.

"My dad's a ne'er-do-well." My tongue sat thick behind my teeth.

"That's a good word though. I mean, if one's going to be a ne'er-do-well, at least they get to be called a ne'er-do-well."

"Dads, who needs 'em?" I raised one of my empty cups in mock cheers.

"All of us." Matt hopped off the railing, swaying a little in the landing. "Woo, I'm trashed."

My eyelids drooped, narrowing my field of vision. The other red cup tipped over onto the glass side table when a breeze rushed through. "Oh, man. Me too. I drank both, plus the weed." I laughed. "How long have we been out here?"

"A while." Matt stretched his arms up over his head, exposing his flat stomach. A strip of darker hair led down toward his belted shorts.

I tried to get up. As I pushed up from the armrests, Matt was there, his hand on my chest, leaning in as he gently sat me back down.

"Are you into me, Jeremy from Near Hamiltucky?" His eyes scanned mine, looking for what, I wasn't sure.

"Uhhhh," I swallowed, my thoughts kinda swimmy from the booze/weed combo. "Idunnoknow...whachumean?"

Matt hadn't shaved. His whiskery jaw hinted at the possibility of a magnificent blond-and-orange beard, like fire. He came closer until his forehead touched mine. He smelled of the party—drinks and smokes, with hints of sandalwood and amber wafting up from underneath his shirt. His lips brushed over mine, daring me to reciprocate. I didn't, but I also felt as if I could explode, and not in a bad way. Our collective stale breath caught in my nose. Suddenly, he stood again, his arms crossed over his chest.

"Curiouser and curiouser."

I scooted back in my seat. "I should probably check on my friend."

"Fine." Matt's eyes narrowed.

I prided myself on being an observer, watching people to figure them out, but my tactics were not foolproof. Heck, they weren't even slightly dependable. I never knew anything about anyone, including myself.

I stood and made my way to the screen door. Under the porch light's bright glow, I stopped and turned back to Matt. He was a nice guy, and I liked talking to him. Funny how much we'd shared over the course of one night. "I'm sorry." I didn't know why I apologized, except it always seemed like the right thing to do.

Matt shook his head. "No worries. You shouldn't drive. You know that much, right?"

"I'll get a ride."

"I'm giving you my number, at least." He took a Sharpie from his pocket, uncapped it, and reached for my hand.

"I'm sweating—it won't stay on." Why had I said that?

"I bet…" Matt smiled. "…it's dry here." He touched the underside of my wrist and wrote his number there. "Call me next time you're in the city, Jeremy. Or, you know, when you figure everything out."

"Sure thing." I held my wrist as if it was wounded and stepped toward the kitchen. "Nice to meet you."

Matt put his hands in his pockets. His face tilted up at me. Between the black light and the dark outside, I never caught the true color of his eyes, but they bore into mine as if they knew everything I'd ever hidden. High cheekbones and a dimpled chin marked him as one of the pretty ones.

Chapter Fifteen

IN THE KITCHEN, the keg stood abandoned, left to an icy bath. Music still pumped, but people sounds had quieted to snores. In the dining room, couples shared beanbag chairs. A few kids were zonked out on the hardwood floors with hoodies balled up under their heads. Two people slept on the loveseat, practically on top of each other. I tiptoed around, checking for familiar faces or clothing, but no sign of Kasey. I made my way to the front door. They were either upstairs in a bedroom or at Anita's place. Either way, I'd lost my ride. The door clicked shut behind me.

The full moon shone a brilliant white in a perfect midnight-blue sky. Both colors, right out of a crayon box. Signs of the approaching dawn started popping up. As I passed the historic brick buildings, upstairs lights clicked on. A guy across the street started up his car, headlights blinding me for a sec.

Snippets of bird songs chirped from one tree to the next. Their morning calls were one of my favorite things—the idea of them trilling to each other, *Hey, it's me. I made it through the night*, would always be whimsical as hell.

At a crosswalk, the orange hand of delay flashed. I pressed the walk button and thought of the impossible color of Matt's hair. His lips in front of mine for the taking. It didn't count, right? I didn't kiss him back. But did I want to?

I checked out a flyer taped to a pole for a missing cat named Banjo. I sobered up a fraction; finding a way home was priority numero uno. Calling Stuart meant talking to either his mom or stepdad du jour, as Stuart had the uncanny ability to sleep through any alarm or ringing phone. Dani and Des might be up soon, but they'd be on their way to church. I'd never met their parents, but church leaders seemed to be the wrong move in my current predicament. That left either my dad (useless) or Mom (opposite of useless).

The bright white light of the man on the crosswalk sign appeared, and I stumbled across the street. What was that kid song? The one about the light shining? I remembered the first line, and then there was a bushel and Satan showed up. Where was my light? It had gone out with Gramps's. But twice in the last month, I'd felt it spark—once with Penny, and then back there with Matt.

Operating hours were hard to predict in this section of town. An undercurrent of independent spirit and a late-night drinking scene made everything flexible. Anita's coffee shop could be open. Luckily, bells rang out when I tried the door. At the counter, I ordered a fresher version of last night's sticky bun and a water. The barista wore thick black Buddy Holly frames. She flowed behind the counter, every task seeming second nature.

"Early riser, eh? I usually don't see campus kids in here this time of day."

"Late night, actually. Can I use your phone?"

"Sure thing."

She handed me a chunky portable and resumed wiping down the great hunk of a steaming, swishing, foaming machine. I took a seat at a nearby table and dialed my house number. Mom picked up on the first ring.

"Jeremy?"

"It's me."

She blew into the phone. I imagined her making the sign of the cross over her chest, even though I couldn't remember the last time we'd attended a church service.

"Can you come get me?"

"What's the address?" The phone made a rustling sound. "I've got pen and paper."

I told her where I was.

"Be there soon. Hang tight, okay?"

"Thanks, Mom."

I handed the phone back to the barista. Before eating, I licked my thumb and tried to smear Matt's phone number from my skin. It didn't work, just got blurrier.

As promised, thirty-eight minutes later, my mom walked in. She looked at me before ordering for herself. I wondered what she saw. Did she know I was still buzzed? Yes, definitely. Did she know I'd spent the night talking to a boy who'd hit on me? Nope, no way. Did she know how I felt about it? Maybe even before I did.

Mom pulled out the chair across the table and sat.

"Wanna talk?" she asked, crossing her arms over the giant purse in her lap.

"Sleep first?"

"A reasonable request."

The barista brought Mom's order to the table in a to-go cup, "Here you are, ma'am."

"Thanks, hon. Let's go, Jeremy."

I startled awake as Mom parked in the lot next to our building. Drool dripped from the corners of my mouth, and I wiped it away before unbuckling my seat belt. Ms. V's lights were already on as we trudged past her apartment. My leg muscles ached as I clomped up the stairs, either from yesterday's workout or dehydration; I wasn't sure. Mom's keys jangled together, and she tossed them on the counter after opening the front door.

"Home again, home again," she said, mostly to herself. Every time she walked in the door she said it, a personal mantra or good luck charm.

I started off toward my bedroom.

"Wait a minute, young man." Mom stood at the sink, filling up a glass with water. "Sit."

Water sloshed up the sides of the glass as she plunked it in front of an empty seat. My freshman year, we'd made a pact. If I were out and needed to get out of a situation, she'd come get me, no questions asked. I'd cashed in on the deal a handful of times, and she always let me sleep it off and talk when or if I wanted to. So, this took me off guard.

I sat, resting my clammy cheek in my hand. A dull headache pulsated right behind my nose, the inside my mouth tasted of chalk, and my breath probably stunk. Sans pen or paper, I doodled twirling spiral shapes on the tabletop with my finger.

"Drink up. You're dehydrated, and it will only get worse if you don't have any water." In the seat across the table, Mom folded her hands in her lap. "I know you probably don't want to talk..."

I gulped down the glass of water. Christ. No, I didn't want to talk, didn't even know what to say. I thought of Kasey, Anita, and Matt peacefully sleeping through hangovers. They'd all wake up whenever and head to some restaurant for a big greasy lunch, rehashing the night's fun. Still tipsy, they'd laugh too hard at stuff that wasn't all that funny. Meanwhile, I'd have to roll up all the feelings from one night into a nice little package that made sense for my mother, even though I couldn't even begin to put it together for myself.

"...but I need you to call your dad today."

"What?" My head shot up.

"I try not to press you on this, Jeremy. But the insurance bill came yesterday, and after that fender bender last spring, I can't keep up."

She meant the one time I drove to school last year. Russ Landry rammed into the back of my car and begged me not to tell anyone. And I didn't, until Russ's dad noticed the front of *his* car was all messed up. He ratted me out and sent the cops to my house. Fun little afternoon that was.

"I already called Dad. We're supposed to have lunch today." Tap water churned in my stomach. "So, can I get some sleep before he comes over?"

"Sure." Mom sat back in her chair. The worry lines dividing her forehead into sections lessened. "And Jeremy, thanks."

"No problem."

I desperately needed sleep. I brushed my teeth and stripped off last night's clothes before hitting the bed.

I dreamed of Penny Kind at a worn-down city park in the spring. White petals caught in the wind, like snow. At the swing set, she twirled until the chains were braided tightly around each other. She looked up and noticed me watching her. She lifted her feet and spun madly. Her wicked laugh drifted with the petals. Still twirling, she morphed into Kasey, then back to herself, and finally, she was me.

I woke to Mom knocking on my door.

"Jeremy? Wake up; your dad's here."

"Crap," I whispered to myself. The morning's dull headache roared, opening my eyes hurt. On top of everything else, I'd have to sit and listen to my turd of a Dad's big surprise, which would likely upset Mom in some way.

Last night's jeans lay puddled on the floor. I tugged them on, the fabric extra soft from wear. My T-shirt, on the other hand, reeked of burning skunk—classic Mary Jane. I hummed notes from Petty's song by the same name and sifted through my dresser for something clean.

In the front room, Mom and Dad ignored each other quietly. She sat on the couch flipping through an old *Better Homes and Garden*. Whenever she restocked the gas station shelves with newer issues, Mom kept some of the old magazines for herself. She called it salvaging, instead of stealing.

Dad hadn't strayed too far from the door. He sat on the edge of the couch, facing the kitchen, staring at the floor.

"There he is!" His big boom of a voice rang out. He moved in for an awkward half handshake, backslap of a hug. "Woo-eee! You're ripe, son. Big night, last night?"

"Something like that," I muttered.

"That's great!" he shouted and threw a few mock punches at my belly. "I bet the ladies go crazy for ya!" He reached for my hair, and I dodged him.

"Not really, Dad."

For a second, I saw the disappointment. Whatever he pretended I was in his head cracked under my lack of enthusiasm. Then it was gone. Plastered, sanded, and repainted with fresh delusion. He scratched his permed mullet and changed the subject.

"You ready to eat?"

"Yep." I kissed the top of Mom's head, which smelled of shampoo. She reached up and patted my cheek.

"I left something on the table for you."

Another glass of water and two little round pills sat next to a bottle of Excedrin. "Thanks, Mom."

"Have a good lunch!" She didn't look up from the recipe she was tearing from the magazine.

"Will try," I said as I closed the door.

ONE OF THE best parts of visiting with Dad was going to the Panda's Room. The décor was typical of a Chinese restaurant, including black lacquer with gold inlay tabletops, bamboo dividers, and watercolor paintings of cranes surrounded by thick black strokes forming foreign characters. The food consisted of lots of fried meat drenched in technicolor sauces.

Dad ordered pot stickers and wontons as an appetizer from a young waitress with a high ponytail and large hoop earrings. My stomach growled. The waitress quickly came back with the food and took the rest of our orders. She clicked the pen, tucked the notepad into her apron, and assured us our food would be right up. As she walked away, I dipped a pot sticker in duck sauce and didn't pull any punches.

"You said you had news?"

Dad shifted in his seat, looking unnerved.

"I was gonna save this for after lunch, but I've got a gift for you." Dad unfolded four checks in front of me, each written for an amount of five thousand dollars. "Happy birthday, son."

"It's not my birthday. What is this?"

"Your college fund."

Everything I thought I knew about my Dad came to the surface, making it hard to breathe. My eyes stung.

"It won't cover everything, but I've been saving since you were born."

"But..." Should I admit this next part? Tell him what a struggle money has been for Mom and me? "We could have used this."

Dad chewed his bottom lip. Our waitress brought two huge plates. She put them on the table and asked if we needed anything else. Dad said, "We're good."

"Thanks," I muttered and checked her name tag. "Ellie." She maneuvered my plate so the checks were visible. Her eyebrows shot up. There was twenty thousand dollars sitting on the table for Christ's sake! She hurried away.

"Look, I know money's been an issue with your mom for a long time." He dug around his sweet-and-sour chicken with his fork. It clanked against his plate as he reached across the table for my arm. "But this is a gift for your future." He let go of my arm and tapped the table with his finger. "My only stipulation is that's what you use it for."

Shocked, all I could manage was blinking. The person I blamed for everything just flipped the script.

"I gotta take a piss," I said.

In the bathroom, I splashed water over my face. The chemical tang from urinal cakes hung in the air. My total douche of a dad always let me down. He'd held us back with his lack of support. He faked everything except for his own self-interest. Now, he couldn't be described by any of those things.

And I could go to college.

I stared at myself in the mirror, all six feet of fluffy hair and dark circles under my eyes. Nope. I couldn't take his money. I'd spent years building up the perfect amount of loathing and apathy toward him. I would not be indebted to this man.

I went back to the table. Dad munched away as if those checks weren't still laid out in front of my plate. One for each year of college, ouch.

"Oh, and I'm moving," Dad said, his mouth still full of Chinese chicken.

"Where to?"

"California."

I hadn't even sat down yet. "Why?"

"Fiona's got family out there, and we're gonna make a go of it."

I looked at his signature, Mark Hopper, written in slanted, jagged lines. He hadn't even given me his last name. I swiped all four checks from the table and folded them into my wallet.

"It's a deal."

Chapter Sixteen

DAD WANTED TO help me set up an account for the college money. I worked at keeping my eyes from rolling back into the recesses of my brain when I reminded him I'd been working for two years, and already had one. Twenty grand in my pocket wouldn't change how distracted Dad was with his own life.

The undercarriage of Dad's car scraped along the pavement as he drove into my apartment complex. In the late afternoons, all the humidity from the day built up and had to be released somewhere. The clouds were a muddy brown, and the air smelled of rusty things.

"So, when do you leave for California?"

"Couple weeks." He unbuckled his seat belt and jabbed the radio power button off.

"Think you'll make it back for graduation?"

"Absolutely, champ! I wouldn't miss it."

This man disappointed me more than any man ever would. He'd forget, lose track of time, get stuck in traffic, inherit a sudden fear of flying, or get bitten by a rattlesnake.

"Well, thanks for the money, Dad. I really do appreciate it."

"You're welcome, son." Dad moved toward me, his arms outstretched in a semicircle.

Of all the goodbyes in the world, car goodbyes beat out the others in terms of supreme awkwardness. None of the angles worked. Dad ended up with his hand on my neck and the other clasping my bicep while I gripped his shoulders.

"See ya soon, bud!"

"Right."

But for a second, my eyes met his. That was where I resembled him most. He kept himself hidden behind pale lashes and irises the color of blue razzberry slushies, a profoundly fake flavor frozen around his cold stranger self.

"Love you, Dad." I hadn't said it since middle school but knew enough to say it now.

"I love you too, Jeremy." The ice in his eyes melted, and I could see him. The man I'd never known swam to the corn syrup surface, allowing me to glimpse his soul just once. Eyes weren't always the windows to a soul, but love was. I left his car thankful for the moment, at least.

The chill from air conditioning raised goose bumps along my arms when I entered our apartment. Ms. V and Mom sat in the living room chatting. Ms. V wore a crocheted shawl over her shoulders and lilac polyester dress pants. Officially in weekend wear, Mom had on sweatpants and a faded T-shirt.

"Hey, Ms. V! What are you doing up here?"

"I brought you these, dear." A cardboard box of VHS tapes with the word Simmons scrawled in red sat near her feet.

"You shouldn't be carrying a load that size up the stairs. I could have picked it up anytime."

"Nonsense. It's good for me to get out every now and then. And don't you worry; I came up here and had your mom collect the box."

"What is it?" I asked.

"Work out videos!"

I laughed. *Absurd!*

"I will help get you healthy if it's the last thing I do." Ms. V took a sip of water out of one of our commemorative

Burger King cups. "Three times a week, you and I have a date with one of these. How does that sound?"

It sounded like a pain in the ass. But Mom pleaded with her eyes. So, I nodded my consent and sat next to her on the couch catty-corner from Ms. V.

"Great. When you think of it, get me your work schedule, and we'll set a start date."

"Sure thing, Ms. V."

"Now, Connie, if you don't mind helping me back down the stairs. I'm afraid my vertigo might start acting up. And that would be the last of me!" Ms. V chuckled to herself.

"Absolutely, Olivia." Mom lifted herself from the couch and held out her elbow for Ms. V to grasp. Ms. V babbled about a couple new recipes she wanted us to try. Mom thanked her for the help.

The door closed, and I grabbed my wallet from my back pocket. Twenty thousand, still there. Carrying this much around made me sweaty. I'd get to the bank tomorrow, no matter what.

"Whew!" Mom busted into our apartment. "I might have to join you two. I am so out of shape." She panted like an asthmatic Kool-Aid man. "Thanks for doing that, Jeremy. I think it will be good for both of you." Mom opened the freezer. "How'd it go with your dad?"

I tucked my wallet away and couldn't look at her. Instead, I watched a squirrel balance on a tree limb outside the living room window. "Not good." I couldn't tell if my voice wavered in withholding the details.

"Why? What happened?" She stopped searching through the frozen goods.

"He's moving..." I rolled my lips together. "...to California."

"Well, that's just great." Mom dropped the box of whatever frostbitten stuff needed thawing.

I turned around, watching her, gauging the reaction. How bad would this be? She clenched both fists and held them against her forehead. She didn't see me observing. Then, she picked up the Stouffer's and slammed it on the counter.

"So great for him." She spoke through her teeth, her words lispy with rage.

"How much do we need?"

"Don't worry about it, Jeremy." She braced herself against the Formica.

"Mom, tell me how much. We've always been in this together."

She turned around, slumping down the hallway. Before she disappeared into her bedroom, she stood before her closed door and croaked, "Two hundred."

I preheated the stove. A string of beeps sounded up to 350 degrees. The boxed lasagna fell out of the container with a thud, and I peeled the plastic layer from the top. Two hundred dollars wasn't so much. If I deposited my checks tomorrow afternoon, the bill could be paid in no time. Or I could walk into her room and sign over all four checks right now. Then she'd stop crying. Dad wouldn't know who deposited the money, or what it was used for. But when would it end? Bills never stopped. Something was always broken. The gas tank never seemed full. We had to eat. My money would dwindle, bit by bit, until there was nothing left for me to go on.

I wanted the cash for myself, for a future.

In my bedroom, I yanked my drawings from the portfolio. The pencils I'd carefully tucked away flew around my desk. I grabbed the nearest two and drew the scene I'd dreamed earlier in the day. Penny Kind at an abandoned park sitting in a swing, spinning and spinning.

In the next frame, she swayed with dizziness, but the words in her speech bubble were clear.

KEEP IT.

"Mom needs it."

YOU DO, TOO. Penny walked around the vacant baseball field. She kicked dust around the swollen, cracked bases. The space above her head filled with orange-and-yellow-tinted clouds. In her world, it could be either dawn or dusk.

ARE WE PRETENDING THE KISS WITH THE COLLEGE BOY DIDN'T HAPPEN?

My answer was to fence the field in with hand-drawn rusted chain links.

YOU'RE SUCH A WUSS!

"Bite me!" I hissed.

WOULD IF I COULD! Penny chomped her front teeth together. **CLICK, CLACK**

I stopped doodling and flipped through the stuff cluttering my desk. A mini Post-It pack zipped as I repeatedly ran my thumb over its edges. A stray sticky note stuck to the upper left corner of my desk read, "Your best friend was here! Think zombies, loser."

Stuart must have stopped by while I had my lunch date with Dad. All the prank stuff had gone way back to the bottom of my brain. But when I looked down at Penny and her mildly vicious canines, I got an amazing idea.

On a clean sheet of paper, I sketched out a quick cartoon of Penny walking down a crowded school hallway. In the next frame, I zeroed in on her face. It demanded the viewer's attention with exposed teeth and an amused grimace.

I folded up the quick sketch and put her in my back pocket. With two quick knocks on Mom's door, I yelled, "I'm heading to Stu's for a sec. Putting dinner in the oven before I go!"

Sniffling and nose blows came from inside her room. "That's right. I forgot to tell you he stopped by." She sounded defeated.

"I'll be back for dinner, okay?"

"Sure."

I paused, nearly ready to say something. My mouth opened, waiting for words that weren't coming. I stepped away, whispering, "Sorry, Mom."

STUART'S PLACE WAS a couple blocks away on Mountain Chorus Road—fancy name, still a frog. Instead of the stackables, his family rented a ranch-style strip of apartments. There were lots of extra doors with lettered house numbers.

The typical large family noises drifted toward the sidewalk: a crying baby, the TV singing an alphabet song at a deafening level, and a small dog's yippy bark. The metal screen door slammed behind me. One of Stuart's sisters, Lil, dragged a naked doll by its bald head, and in difficult to understand toddler-speak, she asked if I'd help her dress it.

"Sure." I knelt and struggled to get the baby doll's stiff limbs through the armholes. "Is your brother around?"

Lil pointed to Stuart's room.

"Here ya go!" The doll's dress fit crookedly, the Velcro clasp fuzzy from overuse. A sticky purple stain decorated the skirt.

School portraits lined the dark hallway leading to the bedrooms. Images of kids with wild hair and loose collars smiled toothless grins at nothing.

"Hey, dude." I stood in the doorway of my buddy's messy room.

"Warsh-man! You got my note?" Stuart was sprawled out on the bottom bunk with his large feet propped up on the railing. He had headphones on and Hamlet on his chest.

"How do you read and listen to music at the same time?"

"I don't." He took off the headphones and hung them around one of the bedposts. "They buffer enough house noise, so I can concentrate. How was your weekend?"

"Fine. You and Des get together again?"

Stuart patted his chest where his heart should be, pantomiming a beat. "Not today. She had family stuff." He stopped and looked serious. "Where were you when I stopped by?"

"My dad paid a visit." Literally.

"Least you got a good lunch."

"Truth." I wasn't ready to tell him about the checks. Money changed relationships really fast in this part of town. "I had an idea for your prank."

"Oh yeah, what's that?"

"Well, you know how we didn't have a way to get people to listen to us?"

"Mm-hmm." Stuart turned over on his side, zipping Hamlet into his backpack.

"What if they don't listen to us at all?"

"That seems to be the main problem, Warsh."

"What if they listen to *her* instead?" I reached into my pocket and handed my friend Penny's cartoon.

He unfolded it and got a goofy smile on his face. "Warsh, you are one brilliant little dillweed."

Chapter Seventeen

IT'D TAKEN A couple weeks to produce a final draft of Penny's first cartoon, one ready for mass distribution anyway. Before the five of us could meet to approve the final copy, it was mid-September, an indecisive month with some days committed to autumn and others rooted in summer. I had handed over Penny's final draft to the twins, who took her to a Kinko's near the community college for two hundred copies.

My friends loved Penny, agreeing a more perfect vehicle for our message could not be made, but I couldn't stop burping up eggs from breakfast. She would go out into the world today. My whole class, and then some, would hold what I'd created in their hands. Would she get crumpled up? Tossed in wastebaskets? Would Penny be condemned to life in the footwell of someone's car? Would anyone notice the detail around her eyes? My heart was now a leaflet.

Stuart and I waited for the girls near the football field, loitering in front of the old concession stand, with its peeling royal-blue paint. Old grease from the weekend game spoiled the crisp fall air. The chain-link fence jangled and sagged under Stuart's leaning frame.

"You losing weight, Warshman?"

"Huh? Oh, I don't know." This morning, I'd tightened my belt to never-before-used holes.

"That cherubic baby face of yours looks different." Stuart patted my lower jaw, like those guys in aftershave commercials.

"Knock it off." I dodged and threw an elbow.

"Whoa, dude! Your jaw has, like, real definition."

I shoved him and laughed off his goofiness. He knew I'd be nervous and was distracting me on purpose.

Since dating Des, Stuart appeared edgier. He cuffed his jeans and smudged a bit of eyeliner around his eyes. He started combing his hair back, and I fully expected a rockabilly bouffant in the near future. It worked with his narrow facial features. Stuart straightened up, looked toward the parking lot, and checked his watch.

"They should have been here by now, right?" I asked.

"Yeah, no big deal. I can skip next period."

"Why would you risk that? We can wait until tomorrow."

"Nope, these go out today. No matter what." Stuart ran a hand through his thick hair. "There they are!"

Des and Dani emerged from rows of parked cars and ran toward us over the lawn. Dani clutched a gift box to her chest. They slowed down as they got closer, their Mary Janes now clip-clopping on the asphalt path leading to the janky refreshment stall. Dani held the box out for me and bent over panting.

"Sorry we're late. Genius over there decided it was a great time to haggle the clerk over the price of color copies, and then we had trouble finding a parking space." Dani had transformed her hair, the way she'd mentioned back in August. She'd lost the braids and cut it pixie short. She was getting all kinds of attention from dudes in our class, and rightfully so.

"We're planning on doing this a couple times, right? I thought I could get a bulk deal, but—"

"That's my girl." Stuart extended his arm around Des's waist and pulled her to him for a long kiss. When they finally separated, Des removed Stuart's spiked choker and put it around her own neck. Stuart beamed. He was mad about her.

Dani rolled her eyes and finished her sister's sentence. "There are no discounts on copies."

I set the box on the order shelf in front of the concession stand's roll-up door. My stomach dropped. I could either crap my pants or clench like a mofo and power through the moment. The lid slid off, and Penny stared up from the paper. It was a variation of the first drawing I'd made for Stuart as we'd all agreed that Penny Kind's introduction needed to be several frames long and folded into one brochure.

"I was able to talk the guy into folding them for us...this time," said Des.

"We may not want to cut our deadline so close for issue two," Dani added. "I don't think they'll do it again unless we pay them for it."

I picked one up. Even though I had the original in my portfolio at home, I wanted one run from my first publication. The story frames followed Penny through a series of mundane tasks—waking up, getting dressed, doing classwork. She never looked out from the page, until the last panel, which showed her facing the opposite direction as the crowd of students surrounding her. There, she connected directly with the reader and demanded their full attention. Penny stood with her back straight, chest out, palms flat against her hips. Her lips were parted, frozen in her time, as she spoke the words in her speech bubble.

We'd agonized over what she should say. It was damn near impossible to find words that meant "Be yourself," without sounding totally cliché. In my first draft, Penny said, *MAKE YOUR MARK*, which we were all unsure of. That soon became *BE YOURSELF*, which both Stuart and I vetoed as soon as I penciled it in. Dani suggested that what we really needed the audience to think about was FREEDOM! But her sister reminded her of a gruesome movie scene where an actor screamed that while his guts were removed. In the end, it was Kasey who came up with Penny Kind's first words to the public.

The previous week, Kasey and I had been doing homework out by her pool, when she dropped everything and walked toward the rock garden.

"What are you doing?" I asked.

"I just remembered something. Come here."

She trilled with excitement. So, I pinned my papers under the trig textbook and followed.

At the edge of the patio, a few shrubs were planted in a patch of pea gravel. Four irregularly shaped boulders were positioned around a sundial. I had no idea if the rock garden had a purpose, other than aesthetics.

"I used to play out here all the time. I'd ride the boulders like they were horses. Pretend I was a pioneer hero." She hopped on the biggest boulder and balanced there.

"A regular Calamity Jane, huh?"

"Something like that. Check out the sundial, Jeremy."

The front of Kasey's house absorbed all the end-of-day rays, placing the garden in shade. In the rockery's center, the sundial balanced on a stone pedestal with an ornate plate on top. The brass dial was lined with Roman numerals and dashes marking time as the earth rotated. Blooming flowers and a Latin phrase surrounded the shadow caster.

Kasey hopped down from the boulder and ran her fingers over the words. *Sic vita fluit, dum stare videtur*. She glanced at me. "I'm not sure of the pronunciation. Conversational Latin not being my forte and all. But I asked my parents what it meant when I was little. It's so perfect, Jeremy. I can't believe I didn't think of it until now!"

"What is it? What does it mean, Kase?"

"Life flows away as it seems to stay the same."

A hand touched my shoulder, bringing me right back to the present. I knew it was Kasey before I looked; her candy fog of perfume preceded her.

"Sorry I'm late," she said.

"No biggie." My voice came out in a hoarse whisper. We'd seen less of Kasey as she and Anita were building a whole new world for each other in the city. Nobody was upset or anything. But I'd be lying if I said it didn't make my moments with Kasey sweeter, more magical.

"Can I see?" she asked.

I handed her a copy.

She opened it and touched her fingers to her lips. "Jeremy, it's so good."

"Thanks."

"All right, all right. We don't need to weep over it," Stuart cut in, grabbing half the stack. "Let's distribute this bitch!"

Des and Dani took prints for themselves but then turned to go to class. They'd made their position very clear. Their portion of the prank would not include ditching school. That left the three of us for distribution.

We slinked toward the back of the school. I couldn't stop smiling, and Kasey kept giggling with excitement. I'm not usually a giggler, but she kept setting me off until Stuart reprimanded us both.

"Get it together, you two. If we're gonna hit up every car in the parking lot, we need stealth."

Kasey and I both snorted at "stealth," and the snorting set off another round of laughter. We crept along the building's shadow for a while. Unfortunately, the back door to the gym stood open, exposing us to kids running sprints inside, the squeaking of their sneakers and incessant whistle-blowing ringing true. Stuart froze and motioned for us to do the same.

"Keep your heads up, and make like you belong out here," Stuart commanded in profile.

"Hustle up!" The PE teacher's raspy version of cheerleading bounced right off my shoulders as we strolled past the door and around the corner.

The only part of the whole school with a view of the parking lot was the cafeteria. Luckily, the cooks didn't give a shit. They were too busy finishing up the last lunch period to notice anything beyond arrogant kids and mounds of trash.

Windshields gleamed in the sun. As we made our way among the rows, I noted a couple empty spots near the front of the lot. Without saying a word, Stuart pointed out the vacancies too. We kept an eye out for staff coming back from lunch. A car door slammed, and all three of us jumped behind the nearest pickup. From behind the mud-splattered rear tire, I peeked out to see Mrs. Paisley, our Physics teacher, rushing toward the school. Her heels clicked away from us.

"Let's start in the back. That way, by the time we get to the front row, most teacher breaks will be over." Stuart's movements were smooth and serious, not his usual jolts of spastic energy. "Okay, we work one row at a time, frog jumping to each car. We move fast, and no talking. Got it?"

Kasey and I nodded and went to work. Car after car, I popped up a windshield wiper and clamped down Penny's flyer. My heart pounded so hard it was all I could hear. Stuart's idea, my illustrations, out in the world.

The collar and pits of my T-shirt were damp with sweat, so my deodorant kicked into high gear. I wondered if ad agents had these kind of stunts in mind when they brainstormed brand names. I doubted it. Pure Sport and Mountain Air didn't quite match the nature of a senior class prank.

The last car in the line came into view, and I recognized it immediately. Russ Landry's silver Nissan with a black bra, which I never understood the purpose for, parked near the teacher spots. I weighed my options, checking out the back bumper while Stuart and Kasey caught up. I remembered two things—a conversation from a month ago when Stuart and I agreed upon a possible nickname for Landry, Dickborn, and the fat permanent marker I'd accidentally stolen from art class yesterday in my backpack.

"You've got a look in your eye, Warshman." Stuart had his own mischievous sparkle. "Whatever it is, I wholeheartedly support it."

I handed him my dwindling stack of papers. He went around to the front and put one under the wiper while I crouched with the magnum-sized marker in hand and the clean bumper in front of me. Uncapping the marker sent a blast of super-chemically unmistakable marker tang up my noise. I'd finished the last curly flourish of the letter *D* when one of the car doors popped open, sending me stumbling backward onto my butt.

"What the fuck are you doing?!"

Indisputably, that was Russ's voice. I scrambled up to see him facing Stuart. My shoes scuffed along the pavement, and Russ turned, his face streaked and red, as if he'd been out here crying or something. His eyes were murderous. I kept the marker behind my back.

"I said, what the fuck are you doing, ass wipe?" He lunged at me, and I instinctively jumped back.

"It's nothing, man," Stuart pleaded.

"You messin' with people's cars, Warsh?" He wiped a forearm across his wet eyes. "Because that is seriously screwed up."

"Nope, it's a handout! That's all, Russ." Kasey's lighthearted tone had an instant effect on the charging Landry. She stepped in and handed him her last flyer. His hackles deflated.

"What is this?" He scanned the pictures and tucked Penny into his back pocket.

"An art project we've been working on." Kasey hopped up on the hood of Russ's car and asked, "Why are you out here?"

"Nothing. Catching z's, that's all." Russ leaned against the hatchback next to him and crossed his arms. Even his forearms were well defined—and shaved?

"Nice." Kasey stretched with an over-the-top fake yawn. She jerked her thumb toward the school, signaling Stuart and me to get the hell out of there. We speed walked behind the rest of the staff cars, waiting until we reached the sidewalk before speaking.

"What did you draw?" Stuart whispered.

"I was going for Dickborn in fancy script. But I didn't have time to finish though, so it's just a pretty *D*."

Stuart laughed. "So, Landry has a curlicued *D* on his bumper?"

"Yep."

"Dang. That would have been a glorious thing to witness."

"You think she's okay out there?" We stopped at a bench facing the lot. A breeze picked up Kasey's hair while she and Landry talked about god knows what.

"Son, that girl can handle herself."

"I'm gonna keep an eye out for her anyway." I sat and pulled out my handwritten draft of a final essay on Hamlet, which had turned out to be one hell of a read.

"I'll wait with you." Stuart rested on the grass under the big tree the hippies always bogarted. "Man, this is a great spot. I'ma get me some of that patchouli oil, so I can hang here every day."

"You do that, and we'll no longer be friends."

"Oh yeah, why's that? I'll buy you a hacky sack and dread up all that hair of yours."

"Patchouli smells like a dead man's asshole."

Stuart snorted. "How do you know what a dead man's asshole smells like, Warsh? You got a weird side piece you're not telling me 'bout?"

"Shut up. I gotta get this done." But after all the excitement of the afternoon, there was no way to succeed at examining Hamlet's inner turmoil. So, I relaxed with my best friend. The breeze worked through the tree leaves, making that sweet rustling *swoosh*. I imagined ocean waves sounded similar.

Chapter Eighteen

"I SAID, LET'S get out of here."

I squinted to see Kasey standing over me, nudging me with her sneaker, the tree leaves rushing behind her. Next to me, Stuart had his arms crossed over his eyes, his mouth slack with sleep. I sat up and rubbed my neck where it felt stiff from sleeping on the ground.

"What time is it?" I asked.

"Final bell's going to ring."

"Jeez, you were gone a while."

Kasey ignored my statement and pulled out a set of keys from her pocket. "I thought you might want to watch Penny's launch from up on high?" She'd nicked the set from the drama teacher a few weeks ago. Kasey had paid for copies, and now we had roof access.

"Definitely!"

I shook Stuart awake. He moaned something about waiting for Des, so we left him on the lawn. As we walked along the sidewalk, the building felt heavy with an expectant quiet, the kind that couldn't last much longer. The bell would ring, and the noise of a thousand bodies would be delivered.

"What was up with Landry?" I asked. "He looked like his dog died."

"I don't know if I should tell you." Kasey gave me a serious look as she held open the main entrance door for me.

"Who would I ever tell?" We crossed the lobby, passed the rows of trophy cases toward the gym.

"It's his mom." Kasey lowered her voice. "She's not well...in the head."

"Really?"

My turn at chivalry, I held open the gym door, and we both trotted toward the stage. Kasey pulled the curtain aside and unlocked the attic/prop room door, and we climbed the stairs that led to the roof.

"She's been that way for as long as I remember. Roller coaster highs, really low lows." Kasey dropped her voice an octave or two.

"Like, manic?"

"Think so. Anyway, he found out Ohio State wants to recruit him for wrestling."

"That's a sweet deal. Why would he be so upset?"

"Because he can't go, Jeremy. He's got siblings. Two little brothers in fourth and fifth grade. He can't leave them to take care of themselves."

"Sure, he can. They've got their dad, right?" I assumed. "Or other family around."

"Nope. It all falls on him."

"Oh."

Russ Landry, the guy I thought had everything, was trapped here. And until my absentee father had presented a path to college, so was I. I thought this revelation would be like riding a monster wave of schadenfreude all the way to the shoreline of my own fortune. Instead, I felt bad for the guy. Even jerks deserved a way out.

"For the occasion..." Kasey unzipped her bag and pulled out a bottle of peach schnapps. "...how 'bout a drink? Or two?" The seal snapped as she twisted off the cap. "Or three?" She took a swig and handed over the bottle. "To your first exhibition, Mr. Warsh."

A line of school buses idled in the semicircular driveway. The bell rang, and the building rumbled with activity as swarms of students made their way outside. Some loitered in spots, but for the most part, everyone made a mad dash outta there.

I zeroed in on a band kid lugging a big black hard case. Based on the shape, he carried a percussion instrument. Other kids hurried past him, shooting dirty looks for taking up so much of the sidewalk, or for walking too slowly. He'd parked near the building though. After wedging the massive drum into the back seat, the kid hopped into the front and started up the engine. He drove off without noticing my comic fluttering under his wiper.

The syrupy schnapps burned going down my throat. The kind of burn only artificial sweetness mixed with alcohol delivered. My stomach warmed, even as I realized our plan had failed. More than half the kids had driven off without noticing Penny on their windshields.

"There goes that idea. Guess we won't have to pay for any more copies!" I said with fake cheeriness.

"Be patient." Kasey took the bottle back. "They'll find her."

Getting off campus before the buses was nigh impossible, and cars lined up in each parking row as the end of day cluster-F of a migration got underway. The band kid's red brake lights lit up. He opened the driver's side door and, with half his body out of the car, lifted the flyer from his windshield.

Kasey elbowed my side. She pointed out a few girls standing in a circle with the comic in their hands. We watched for any signs they'd taken notice of Penny. But, honestly, they could have been talking about Seth Tinkerman's unfortunate in-class boner, or Deb Shultz's constant state of nip slippage, or the weather. We couldn't hear their conversation from the roof.

"Have you worked out the next issue?" Kasey asked.

"Mostly."

"Hey, I saw Matt Brady the other day. He asked about you."

"Did he?" I kicked at the roof rocks. What were they up here for?

"He did. Said he really liked 'the talk' you two had." Kasey took another sip of alcohol and passed me the bottle. "Did something happen between you two?"

"No. He's a nice guy though."

"Because he got this look on his face when you came up."

"What kind of look?"

"Oh, I don't know. Something between star-crossed lover and worried."

"That's really specific and abstract at the same time." I stepped closer to the ledge. One of the girls from the gaggle below unfolded the comic. "We connected. You know, absent dad versus disappointed dad, that's all."

"'Cause it's fine if you're into him. We can all deal with it."

"Stop."

"Really, Jeremy. You can tell me."

"Aaaand, I'm leaving."

"Come on. Don't go."

Kasey's cheap liquor sloshed up the sides of the bottle as I handed it over. I stalked away from her. My cheeks burned with a mix of rage and embarrassment.

In the attic, moldy costumes stank with old stage sweat. Humidity and mildew filled the cluttered space. Standing atop a black prop box, I breathed it all in. Why did she have to go there? With Penny's cartoon going out today, I really could have skipped the interrogation.

I hopped down. My legs ached to run. Since exercise had become part of my routine, I'd found that it cleared my head in the way only drawing had ever done before. PE clothes were crumpled in my backpack, so, I made for the locker room.

The taste of body spray hit me as soon as I pushed the door open. I checked for people. An assistant coach talked on the phone in the back office, but other than that, the place was empty. I sat on a bench and untied my shoes. The gym shorts kind of reeked, but they'd have to do. My padlock clicked onto a locker with my belongings inside, and I went out back to the track.

Crap. I hadn't thought this through. Football players hustled and slammed into each other. Coach Bell blew a whistle every thirty seconds. Screw it. The team practiced in the grassy part of the field. They weren't using the track.

Each footstep crunched the sandy black gravel. I expected to get yelled at, but no one cared. With each stride, I propelled forward until the only focus was keeping my breath steady. My quads throbbed as my heartbeat thudded in my ears. When I finally slowed, I clasped my hands over my head, prompting my body to take in deeper pulls of oxygen. My limbs shook, but that tight panic in my chest was gone. Who cared about Penny's premiere? How could I be bothered by Kasey's snooping? Who says you can't run from your problems?

Back in the locker room, I tightened my belt as the football team started filing in from practice. A couple guys slapped me on the back.

"Lookin' good out there, Warsh," said the-nice-popular-Brandon-A. who lived a perpendicular existence to oily-haired-Brandon-F.

"Thanks." So, I hadn't gone unnoticed.

The guys peeled off sweaty practice jerseys and wrapped towels around their waists. Their confidence threw me off-balance. I could never drop trou like these guys. The locker room filled with steam and swagger. Russ opened a locker across the aisle.

"Hey, sorry 'bout the parking lot earlier," I said.

He nodded, acknowledging I'd spoken but nothing else. I buttoned my jeans. Russ tossed his practice jersey in a rolling hamper near Coach's office and came closer. He still had his pads on, so his shoulders took up a large amount of space, blocking my way out. I tried maneuvering around him, but he pinned me up against the lockers with both of his cartoonish bad-guy hands.

"Forget what you saw out there, aight?"

"Sure." I kept my head turned to the side, refusing to look this prick in the eye.

"Dumb faggot." Russ's stupid lips formed a sneer of disgust. He was every jock-bully cliché I'd ever read about. Not a single drop of sincerity existed in his whole person. He stalked away, stripping off the remaining layers of football as he turned the corner for the showers. And to think, I felt bad for him only a half hour ago. Well, fuck that.

I estimated it took twenty minutes, or so, for Russ to shower, get dressed, and goof off with the guys before making his way to the parking lot. Plenty of time, if I hurried.

In the gym, only the spotlight illuminated the stage for play practice. Mrs. Garfield, representing the entirety of the staff theater department, stopped me to ask about publicity posters. She never pulled her eyes away from the action playing out before her. Her pearly-edged glasses shone in the darkness, lenses reflecting the chosen actor's images. I hastily whispered I'd bring in what I had finished, and she dismissed me with a wave of her hand. *Tick-tock.*

The area outside the school was deserted. People were either finishing up after-school stuff inside the building or already home. That holy grail, a silver Nissan with its black bra, was parked before me. Angels sang. The hero's journey had come down to this. I walked up behind the car. Massaging my hands, I double, triple, and quadruple-checked for witnesses. Vindictiveness worked just fine served hot. I kneeled behind Russ's car, the afternoon's bit of graffiti completed in minutes.

*** DICKBORN ***

Chapter Nineteen

OPRAH WINFREY'S BOOMING laughter filled our apartment. Mom hit the mute button and turned around to greet me. Her forehead shined, and there were pink spots around her eyes and nose from scrubbing away her day-face.

"You're home! Ms. V called wondering where you were."

"Aw, man. I forgot." I opened the fridge and searched for something to eat. "Stuff came up at school."

"There's a letter for you on the table. It's from the bank."

I hadn't even considered the statements being sent to the house. I grabbed the milk jug and set it next to the envelope. The TV volume clicked back on, and our apartment was permeated with the overwhelming presence of a studio audience cheering for a celebrity.

I planned on telling Mom about the money. Every day, I woke up with those intentions. But then my brain to mouth connection failed and more time went by without doing it. At this point, she'd be equally hurt by how long I'd kept the truth from her. I picked up the unopened letter. I still had time to make sure the truth came from me and not some churned out banknote.

"What is it?" Mom asked.

I tore it open. "Credit card."

"Jeez, they don't waste any time, do they? You won't be eighteen until July."

Mom chuckled along with the studio audience. The camera panned over the toothy grin of today's guest. Her eyes searched the audience for their acceptance. She got it in spades, but I wondered if she knew it.

"I'll have dinner ready in an hour or so, 'kay?"

"Sure, Mom. Do we have anything to snack on?"

"Only apples and bananas. Maybe some nuts. Olivia forbade junk food, remember?"

Le sigh. Where for art thou, Doritos? I settled for a handful of almonds and a glass of milk.

Back in my bedroom, everything inside me yearned to throw my homework in the corner and draw. The feeling that came as I worked on Penny's cartoon could only be described as burning. All day long, there were these tingling embers where my fingerprints should be. When I could finally sit down and devote time to the artwork, my hands were nearly on fire.

But I made myself suffer through the backpack full of classwork first. With college as an option, I couldn't afford to lag behind now. Last week my guidance counselor, Mrs. Alfred, reminded me how important grades and extracurriculars were. According to my records, my grades were pretty meh. I'd been placed on a college track, based on who knows what, and had done okay. Extracurriculars were nonexistent though. In her closet of an office, I'd tried explaining.

"I work," I'd said to her.

"Lots of kids work and still make time to volunteer," Mrs. Alfred pointed out. Her desk dwarfed her tiny frame. Piles of rumpled tissues were strewn over the work surface. She called out, "Allergies!" at random as an excuse for the mess.

"Based on what you're telling me, I'm going to have you talk with the heads of the art and drama departments. They'll probably have opportunities for you to fill in these transcript holes." She sniffed and wiped at her nose.

"Great, thanks. Mrs. Alfred."

So, along with everything else, I'd been roped into drafting publicity materials for the fall production of *The Diaries of Adam and Eve*. However, the actors chosen for the roles were really flubbing it up. They couldn't remember their lines, and the show was a couple weeks away. But Mrs. Garfield promised I'd still get credit.

Finally, I unzipped my portfolio and set up my supplies. My colored pencils were all lined up. Warm colors on the left. Cool colors on the right. Neutrals near the top of the page. I checked for sharpness, and I thought about investing in a nice marker set, for the future. I popped each knuckle and then my neck.

"Jeremy! Dinner's ready!"

"Later, then." I left everything and joined Mom in the kitchen.

"Did you get your homework done?" she asked.

"Yes." I handed her a plate, and she scooped out a helping of a basic noodle casserole. "What's this?" The kitchen smelled of melted cheddar.

"Homemade mac-n-cheese. I shredded the cheddar and everything. There's some peas in there too."

"Cool. Thanks, Mom."

"Anytime. So, how was your day?"

How does one condense an entire day of high school into one grammatically correct sentence? I'd attended three different lectures, skipped afternoon classes, published my first comic, and taken shots of schnapps on the roof. A friend had made assumptions regarding my private life, I'd run a few miles, been called a fag, and vandalized a car.

Like this: "Fine. Yours?'"

Mom chattered about her boss's new baby, Phoebe. "Feefee" had come to the office today because the babysitter was sick. And she—the baby, not the sitter—had the fattest little chunk of cheeks. When Mom said the baby's head smelled like crack, which was totally weird, I tuned out.

After dinner, I loaded up the dishwasher. Mom opened the fridge and filled a tumbler with boxed blush wine. The wine was new, a step-up from her usual Milwaukie's Best.

"Jeremy, are you okay?" Mom leaned against the counter, sipping the light pink liquid.

"I am. Why?"

"You've been so quiet lately."

"Just, in my head." I could tell her about the money right now. She'd given me an opening and everything. But when I went to do it, the words "senior year is a lot of work" came out instead.

"Have you thought about what you're going to do after high school?"

"Uhhh…kind of." I let out a deep breath. "I met with the guidance counselor."

"That's great! I didn't know."

"She gave me info about the ACT. I should've taken it last spring, so I'll need to register for that right away for college."

"Where are you thinking of applying?"

"There's a couple art programs in Cincy. One of Kasey's friends offered to set up a meeting with a professor she knows."

"Wow! Jeremy, you really have thought this through. I had no idea." Mom sat at the table. Her eyebrows arched high, an excited smile on her face. She leaned in like this was going to turn into a lengthy talk.

"Thanks, Mom. So, speaking of, I better get back to the ol' grind."

"Oh. Right, right." Mom stood and planted herself back on the couch.

I wiped my hands dry on a dish towel and hung it over the lip of the sink.

"Honey, did the advisor talk to you about how to pay for college?"

"There's FAFSA, if that's what you mean."

"What's that?"

"Loans and stuff, from the government."

"Okay, I didn't want her getting your hopes up and then not showing you the financial side of it."

"Don't worry, Mom. It's covered." I walked away and left that half-truth hanging between us.

Back at my desk, under the light, Penny called me out.

IT'S COVERED. She finger quoted my lame words. *WHAT WAS THAT?*

"I don't know. Back off."

SEEMS TO ME, YOU LEAVE ALL THAT TRUTH HANGIN' IN THE AIR, EVENTUALLY, IT'LL START STORMIN' DOWN ON YOU, JEREMY. THAT SHIT DOESN'T JUST EVAPORATE.

"Fair enough. Now, can you hold still? I've gotta get your expression right. You're supposed to be filled with a sense of exploratory wonder after sneaking out of your house. Instead, your nose keeps doing something funny, like you smell dog crap nearby."

FINE. I WON'T SAY A WORD.

Penny let me fill in the rest of the scene in relative quiet. In her world, white sparkling stars pinpricked the purple-black sky. In the distance, the orange glow of a bonfire shone.

I'M JUST SAYING—YOU HAVEN'T DONE ANYTHING WRONG, JEREMY.

"You're biased. I created you. You have to say that."

OH YEAH, I SPEND TONS OF TIME STROKING YOUR EGO.

It was the least mature thing to do, but I couldn't help it. I stuck my tongue out at her and then smudged in a black smoke formation above the bonfire.

YOU NEED TO CUT THE PEOPLE WHO LOVE YOU SOME SLACK AND TELL THEM WHAT'S UP.

"I lied to my mom and withheld money from her when she needed it. She's gonna be überpissed."

JEREMY, FOR CHRIST SAKE, I'M NOT JUST TALKING ABOUT THE MONEY.

"What else, then?"

FAGGOT.

"Don't."

ARE YOU, OR AREN'T YOU?

...

ANSWER ME.

"Why?! Why do I need to answer?"

YOU DEFACED A GUY'S CAR TODAY BECAUSE HE HALFHEARTEDLY MUTTERED THE WORD AT YOU. A GUY, I MIGHT ADD, WHO WAS ALREADY HAVING A COLOSSALLY BAD DAY.

She had a point.

IN LIFE, YOU ONLY GET TO KNOW YOURSELF. THAT'S IT, JEREMY. SO, IT BETTER BE REAL. OTHERWISE, IT'S A HUGE WASTE OF TIME.

I stopped coloring and tossed the pencil among the others, the ordered sets now cluttered. There was a punk CD in the boombox from last night. I clicked it on and paced around the room to the thrashing beat. I had a nasty hangnail near my thumb. It already hurt, but I picked at it anyway.

Kasey always knew what to do. I needed to talk to her. It was early still, only a little after eight o'clock. So I didn't bother calling, just grabbed a flannel from my closet and left.

"Mom, I'll be back later. I need the car."

"'Kay, hun." Mom flipped through TV channels, trying to find one not airing a commercial. "I swear, if I owned a station I'd time it to be the one airing a program when everyone else is showing commercials..." She mentioned this a lot.

GONE WERE THE latest sunsets of summer. Navy blues already hung over the sun's streaks of candy-pink and orange.

As I merged onto the county road, I thought about authenticity. I tended to mentally harp on people for being fake. But was I? Should there be a check mark next to my heterosexual white male box? Everything felt so fluid all the time. And fluid didn't keep in paper boxes.

I felt something for Kasey. It wasn't by accident that I'd stayed this close to her since the first time she handed me a beer and mourned Kurt Cobain. But there was this giant emptiness every time I tried to name these feelings.

All the lights were on inside Kasey's home. They cast a fiery glow over the driveway and sidewalk leading to the front door. I rang the bell, and Kasey's mom answered. Jillian Axton had aged significantly since the last time I'd seen her. She'd gotten a rotten haircut, all short and spiky.

The cut left nowhere for her to hide her teary blue eyes and blotchy cheeks.

"Oh, hi Jeremy." Her voice warbled, and she kept sniffling.

"What can we help you with, son?" Mr. Axton came up behind Jillian and massaged his wife's shoulders. Their intimacy made me want to run or puke. It was a rarity for Mr. Axton to even be home. Kasey frequently mentioned his work travels kept him away Mondays through Thursdays.

"Is Kasey around?" I plunged my hands into my pockets. Otherwise, the only thing I could think to do with them was keep picking at that hangnail, which wasn't a great look.

Kasey's parents exchanged a nervous glance. Mrs. Axton whispered to her husband, "It might help."

"Sure, son. I think she's down by the pool."

They stepped out of the doorway to let me in. Something had electrified the air. Between Mrs. Axton's sniveling, and her husband comforting her, something big had happened here tonight. I could guess what it was too.

I followed teal carpeted stairs down to the converted basement. The double doors leading out to the pool were wide open. Two moths fluttered around the living room light fixture, and their confused little bodies clunked against the glass. They were frantic and relentless to be in the light—an instinct stronger than any fear of getting burned.

It was dark around the pool, except for a lone tiki torch. Hints of chlorine nipped my nose. Kasey sat in one of those long beach chairs used for sunbathing. She held her knees to her chest and curled her whole body around them except for her face. She was staring toward the stars.

"Hey," I murmured.

"They know." Kasey closed her eyes. "Anita called during dinner. I took the call in the office, but I guess Mom didn't hang up the other line." Kasey turned her face toward me, resting her cheek on the tops of her knees.

"She listened in? Why would she do that?" I squatted next to Kasey's side.

Kasey shook her head and shrugged her shoulders at the same time. "Anita and I talked about it bunches of times. She came out to her parents at sixteen, and they were fine with it. My situation..." She glanced at the deck. "...is different."

I made a half-whistling sound and rubbed the back of my neck. "I can't believe your mom would break your trust like that."

"Not all moms can be Connie Warsh, I guess." Kasey stretched her legs out. "And now, they're the ones up there acting all pious and heartbroken." She smiled the saddest smile I'd ever seen. The contradiction was so beautiful. I leaned in and kissed her because of that smile.

We both froze, our lips not doing anything except touching. I pulled away for a second. Checking if she was okay with this, checking if I was. We weren't.

There were tears instead, balanced right along the corners of her closed eyes. I let go of her and pushed my hair back with both hands. What an enormous misstep.

"Sorry." It was all I could think to say. Sorry, sorry, sorry...repeated itself in my head. I stared at the cement. When Kasey responded with something between a cry and a laugh, I stood up to leave.

"What did you come here for?" she asked.

"Answers, I guess."

"Did you find any?"

"At least one."

Chapter Twenty

SLEEP WOULDN'T COME. My pillow sagged with too much softness, and my neck started aching. Sweat collected on my upper lip, so I turned on the ceiling fan. I was thirsty, but that kept perpetuating the urge to pee. Finally, I clicked on my desk light and worked on finishing up Penny's next episode. Even that came out wrong. She wouldn't talk to me, and I couldn't keep her eyes from leering. I gave up and moved my desk chair near the window.

It was the time of year I always left my windows open because the nights were cooler. Autumn smelled like drying leaves, and I enjoyed the lingering process. Here and there, a patch of primary color popped in a section of the maple tree out front. But I couldn't see that now; it was still dark.

Town was quiet, except for a couple of bar stragglers stumbling home. Their shadows fell over each other. A slurry baritone broke into bouts of "The Piano Man," which sent the other two into hysterics until they were all yelling the chorus as they propped each other up for the trek home.

I told her I'd come for answers. Who was I kidding? There weren't any answers wrapped up in Kasey. I loved her the way I loved the sun. Because it was there, it was beautiful, and now and then, it did something spectacular, like rising. Kasey thrived whether I orbited or not. She was the heat I needed for survival, and from this distance, never threatened to burn me. I couldn't explain what had come over me last night, except to say I needed something. Yeah,

I'd asked her out. Yeah, I'd spent hours trying to make her laugh. Yeah, I knew she had a girlfriend. But I'd never kissed her. That kiss though, it death spiraled into its own black hole.

A gray wash fell over everything beyond the shadows of my propped-up feet. Things with Kasey were certain to be awkward now. I needed a relationship barometer measuring how bad tomorrow would be—survivable vs. melting into a pool of embarrassment. Here lay Puddle of Jeremy, est. September 1998.

I could sneak over to Stuart's place to revel in how badly I'd screwed things up. He'd crack a few good jokes about my lack of romantic skills. But I wasn't quite sure I wanted to share the humiliation yet. I thought of waking Mom up and unloading the truth. It kept getting tighter and tighter right where my heart beat. Just the idea of getting one thing off my chest brought some relief.

As dawn's yellow tint hit the leaves, I remembered the time my grandpa had me watch him sheer sheep when I was ten. He kept a flock on his property and called them, "the mowers." I climbed up on the roof of an outbuilding and watched as the hired men herded the sheep into a makeshift pen one by one. The young ones hated every minute of the act. They kicked and bleated something awful. Grandpa grabbed each sheep by the jaw and kept its head pointing up while the rest of the crew buzzed around the sheering table, completing the job in minutes.

After the work was done and Grandpa had handed out the cash, he came over to me. The outbuilding had a ladder on the side, and he stepped up on the lowest rungs, so his head popped up over the edge of the roof.

"What did ya think of that, m'boy?"

"They don't like it too much."

"It's for their own good though." Grandpa looked out over the field. The flock of shorn sheep milled together near the creek, their hides bright white once more, albeit wonky from the quickie haircut. "Keeps them from overheatin' and helps prevent fly-strike."

"What's fly-strike?"

"Type of fly, lays their eggs around damp wool." Grandpa spit tobacco juice through his teeth. "When the maggots hatch, they start feastin'."

"Ew, gross."

"Nature's way, son." Grandpa shrugged as he wiped brown spittle from his chin.

My alarm clicked onto the only alt radio station in the tri-state area, playing Nirvana's "Come As You Are." I got ready for school, still thinking about those exposed sheep and what happened to their skin if what grew around them kept weighing them down.

At the kitchen table, Mom fumbled with a grapefruit. "Hey, hon. There's coffee, if you want." Her spoon slipped, and she sprayed juice all over her blouse. "Awesome."

"I'm gonna head out, Mom."

"Take a granola bar. It's a long time 'til lunch."

She'd already set the box on the counter for me. I grabbed two and stuck one in my backpack.

"Hey, Mom."

"Yeah?" She glanced up from dabbing at her shirt, got one look at my face, and set the napkin aside. "What's wrong, Jeremy?"

"Nothing." I turned away from her. As I opened the door, I let in a big old housefly. Without looking back, I blurted, "Dad gave me twenty thousand dollars for college, and that's what I'm gonna use it for."

CAMPUS HUMMED WITH an excited energy, and I picked up bits of conversation as I strode through the halls.

"Who did it?" asked a curvy girl named Sam, her signature orange waves streaming down her back.

"Nobody knows," said Rosalyn—not so discreetly showing off her pierced navel. A metal barbell poked above and through the center of it, but still, belly buttons were disgusting caves of filth and dead skin.

I figured most of the talk concerned Russ Landry's car. Stuart was waiting at my locker with a big shit-eating grin on his face.

"Did you hear?" he asked.

"Hear what?"

"Everybody's talking about Penny, tryna figure out what it means." Stuart's whole body trembled. His words jumped on top of each other, and he struggled to keep his voice at a whisper. "I think we've gotta have the next one ready to go on Monday. Feed the curiosity of the masses and all that. Can you get it done?"

"Shouldn't be a problem. I'm almost finished already."

I spun the dial on the combination lock, and we set off toward homeroom. His was next door to mine, so, we lingered out front waiting for the first bell.

"Did you hear anything else..." I looked around, making sure no one was eavesdropping. "...Landry's car, remember?"

"You mean, the *D*? No." Stuart rotated his body at the waist, doing warm-up exercises for a long day sitting at a desk.

"Not just the *D*. I finished it before leaving school yesterday." I chewed on my bottom lip.

"You what?!" Stuart froze mid-twist.

"I finished it. His bumper says, 'Dickborn.'"

Stuart ducked his head in the classroom and told his teacher he needed to use the bathroom. She granted permission, and he took off.

"Where are you going?" I yelled after him.

Stuart turned and ran backward down the hall. "Are you kidding? I gotta see this!" He pumped his fist in the air and completed this crazy little hop-step, before colliding with Russ Landry.

"Watch it, punk." Russ shoved Stuart, who stumbled but managed to stay on his feet.

Russ's eyes were rimmed in red and bloodshot. Mine probably were too. I hadn't checked the mirror this morning, but after a sleepless night, I fully expected to look like crap.

Landry stepped up to me with a sickening amount of swagger punctuating each step. He knew it was me. I knew it was me. No point in backing down now.

"How's it going, Russ?"

"Just fine, Warsh." His crooked smile was tinged with maybe an ounce of respect?

He wouldn't call me out for writing Dickborn on his car. In the weird and wild world of high school politics, there was a 60-40 chance it might give me the upper hand. I was sick of this shit.

"How's your car?" I asked.

Without saying a word, Russ hit me. I saw his fist coming, but it was moving too fast for me to do anything other than absorb it. There wasn't any pain, at least not at first. I was just...confused. There was a thud at impact, a sickening click, the sensation of falling, and the blinking blurriness. I noticed the layer of dust on the baseboards and sneakers squeaking around me. Somebody sat me up, and people yelled.

"What happened?" asked a deep teacher voice, full of authority.

"Oh my god! That's, like, a lot of blood," squealed a high-pitched girl's voice.

The salty iron taste flooded my mouth. I touched my jaw and winced at the sting. My fingers came away wet with my own blood, and then I started gagging and trying not to dry heave because that was about the time the pain started registering.

"Give him some space! He needs room to breathe!" Somebody shouted at the gathering crowd. "You're gonna be fine, Jeremy. Do you think you can stand?"

I nodded. The teacher slipped his arms under mine and helped me to my feet. Russ's own people surrounded him, including the coach who seemed to be tearing him a new one.

I tried to say something smart, but a shock of pain shut me up. I flipped Russ off as the teacher and Stuart led me past him, toward the nurse's office.

The nurse had me lie down. She cleaned the cut delicately, pressing gauze over my cheek until the bleeding stopped. She was an older woman with chin whiskers. I counted them: one...two... Two dark hairs that grew out of nowhere. Non-conformists, those chin whiskers were. There was a shelf above the bed, and she reached for it. Make that four fuzzies; there were two more long ones on her neck.

"Was he wearing a ring, darlin'?" She had a tinge of a southern drawl.

I nodded my response. The big hurt had settled on my face. Four Whiskers handed me an ice pack and taped a covering over the wound.

"Can ya open it at all?"

I tried, but it hurt.

"Ooo, you might need stitches, hun. Here's some water." She handed me a plastic Dixie cup and a bottle of water. "I can't give ya any i-byou-profin. But I'll have your mama bring some. For now, keep the ice on it." She wheeled her rolley chair away from the side of the cot and pulled a curtain for privacy. I could hear her on the other side, flipping through papers and the pitter-patter of a phone number.

"Hi, is this Mrs. Warsh?" She tapped her pen on the desk. "Hi, darlin'. This is Nurse Lee from the school."

"Oh, yes, yes. Everything's okay, or it will be. Seems Jeremy got himself in a bit of a tussle."

Tussle? Who used the word tussle?

"You're gonna need to come on down and see for yourself, ma'am. It might be worth a trip to the doctor."

...

"Right along his jaw, ma'am."

...

"Okay, I'll let him know you're on your way." The phone receiver clicked into its base. Nurse Lee turned on an oldies radio station, and a bunch of crooners serenaded my aching face while I waited for my mom.

MOM'S HIGH-HEELED boots clicked in the hall. Her steps had an urgency—that worried parent-bouncing stride. Teachers didn't walk that way, unless something really bad happened.

Nurse Lee's chair screeched as she greeted my mother.

"How is he?" Mom sounded winded.

"He's all right." She pulled back the curtain. "Not talkin' too much obviously."

The two women stood at the foot of my cot in total contrast with one another. Nurse Lee, used to this kind of thing, had a relaxed little frown. Mom, though, was on the verge of tears. Which put me on the verge of tears. Actually, as soon as I saw her, I started crying. But it hurt like hell, so I squeezed my eyes shut.

"Oh, Jeremy. Come on; let's get you home."

"My official advice is to get him in to see a doctor. He might need stitching up, and you'll wanna make sure nothing's dislocated or broken. Urgent care if you have to."

"I called his doctor before I left my office, and they've got a slot for him later this morning."

"Keep ice on it. I 'magine he'll be wantin' some pain relief lickety-split!"

"Thank you, ma'am."

"You take it easy now, Jeremy," said Nurse Lee.

I tried to give back the ice pack.

"Oh, no, no. You keep that, son. You're gonna need it. I got a whole mini-fridge full of those."

I put the ice back up to my face and followed Mom out to the lobby. She held the door open, looking over the campus's green space. As I walked past her, she chimed in, "I know you can't tell me what happened right now, but I expect you to real soon."

Russ Landry's car sat in its usual spot in the parking lot. Only this time, his bumper was covered in silver duct tape. I might have ripped it all off, if Mom hadn't been with me.

Chapter Twenty-One

MOM THREW OPEN the door to our apartment and marched down the hall. She came back with a clacking bottle of extra-strength ibuprofen and handed me two along with a glass of water. I edged my jaw open just enough to fit the two pills behind my teeth. Sipping proved difficult; it sloshed out the sides of my mouth and dribbled down my shirt. But I managed to swallow without too much screaming pain.

"Finish the water. Did you get a chance to eat anything before this happened?" Mom asked as she rifled through her purse.

I grunted twice and dissolved into the couch. Mom tucked pillows behind my head. The sick bed, we'd called it for as long as I could remember—a most soothing combination of bed plus couch plus daytime TV.

"All right then. I'm gonna walk over to the store and get you some liquid stuff for food. Milkshake diet for today, I guess."

I looked up at her. We hadn't talked since I dropped that money bomb this morning. "I shorry," I managed with a heavy lisp.

"Shhh. It's fine. Your appointment with the doctor is in two hours. Rest, okay?"

She pushed my hair back from my face and handed me the remote before leaving. I clicked on a morning talk show, zoning out when the audience started chanting the host's name every few minutes.

AT THE PEDIATRICIAN'S office, sick and feverish little kids played with a collection of germ-ridden toys. A few of them were real curious about why the hurt giant showed up.

"What are you in for?" asked a little girl with super curly hair. As if we were all sitting around in a holding cell ready to swap sad stories.

I didn't want to scare her with my slurry, stunted speech, so I took the ice pack away from my cheek to show her. There wasn't much to see, what with the bandage and all. But, still, her eyes got all wide.

"Owie!" A snot bubble blew out of her nostril, and she started coughing. It was that rattly kind of cough, reserved for lifetime smokers and small children.

A nurse called my name from a clipboard. Her pale-yellow scrubs were covered in bunny rabbits. At the waiting room door, I waved goodbye to the girl.

"Good luck, mister!" she said.

I gave her a thumbs-up and followed Mom down the hallway to the exam rooms. A jungle-themed mural coated the walls. Playful monkeys swung from vines, while brightly colored insects crawled over giant tropical leaves. A basket of picture books sat near the tissue paper–lined examination table. I sat on the crinkly stuff, and Mom took the chair across from me while we waited. She picked up a back copy of *People* magazine and didn't talk.

When Doctor Chan arrived, he poked around inside my mouth—by then I could open it with only minor wincing. Final verdict: nothing was broken or dislocated. Since the bleeding had stopped, the gash from Landry's ring didn't need stitches.

"I'd say soft foods and pain management oughta do it."

The doc slapped his knees in his official end-of-appointment signal. I estimated four patients an hour for a whopping thirty-two leg slaps a day. Multiplied by five workdays for a grand total of one hundred sixty smacks a week! Were there permanent handprints above his knees?

"Thank you, doctor." Mom had her professional parent voice on.

"No problem, Ms. Warsh. Come back if it keeps giving him trouble."

"Come on, Jeremy. Let's go home."

MOM BLENDED A vanilla milkshake for me, but I skipped the straw and opted for tilting the thick mixture directly into my mouth. The sweetness shocked my tongue. After that high point, I went to bed and passed out.

Moments later, a light tapping woke me up. I blinked at the red numbers on my alarm clock: five o'clock. Hours had passed in a flash of deep sleep. The day had that late afternoon light to it, the sun burning more yellow right before Earth turned away.

"Hey, man." Stuart stood in my doorway twirling the spare key around his finger.

"Hey." My jaw lit up with pain. Talking hurt again. Mom had left the bottle of pills and a cup of water on my nightstand with a little note instructing me to take two more when I woke up. I followed her directions.

"Brought your homework." Stuart walked in and unpacked my books from his bag. A fresh hickey marooned his neck.

"Thanks." My voice was hoarse and whispery from not using it most of the day.

"Pretty wild what happened, huh?"

Mom had also left a four pack of pudding cups next to my bed. I opened one of them up and started eating, gingerly of course. Everything I did would have to be fucking gingerly for a while.

"I checked out Landry's car. The bumper's all taped up. Everybody's talkin' 'bout why he would've hit you, but nobody knows."

"He does."

"Duh." Stuart collapsed on the foot of my bed, spread out, and stared up at me. He pretended his fist was a microphone. "So, why'd you do it, Mr. Warsh?" He held the fake mic toward me in a mock interview. When I didn't answer, he dropped the act. "How the hell did he know it was you? We were the only ones that knew about Dickborn."

"Long stawhy."

"Give me the highlights."

"He stawted in on ee affa schoo. I coodit leh ih go" This conversation was pointless.

"Well, I'm sorry you got hurt, dude." Stuart sprang off the bed.

"Ee too." I laughed in my usual self-deprecating way but stopped because it ached.

I tried with the pudding again. Getting my mouth wide enough to fit the spoon hurt like a bitch, and licking it made me feel toddler-ish. So, I set it aside; I'd give it another try once the medicine kicked in.

Stuart poked around my room. We used to spend hours goofing around in here. Crazy ideas had bloomed in this ramshackle place, but he'd gotten real busy with his girlfriend as of late.

"I need to bring over those last comics I borrowed," he said.

An agreement grunt rolled from the back of my throat.

Stuart stopped at my desk. He picked up the latest Penny Kind. The one I'd been working on last night before taking off for Kasey's. The one where Penny spat Landry's accusation back at me. I held my breath. That conversation with Penny, actually any conversation with Penny, would seem crazy as hell. I should have stashed it.

"This isn't what we discussed for the next issue."

"'At's naw it. Ts ovah dere."

"But what is this, Jeremy?"

Between the swelling and the pain, it was ridiculous to try to speak right now. But I didn't even know what to say. There were loads of conversations between Penny and me hidden away in that portfolio, and to anyone else, they wouldn't make any sense.

"Nuffin. Is a dia-ee. 'Kay?"

"This is your diary?" A twinge of concern crossed Stuart's brow. He tried to hide it, but it flickered there like a candle flame reaching for enough oxygen. "Are you okay, buddy? You know you can tell me anything, right?"

If I owed anyone the truth, it would be Stuart. On top of being an awesome human, the sheer longevity of our friendship called for honesty. But I couldn't do it right now, not when it physically hurt to talk.

"All right, listen. Couple days from now. You and me, dude's night out."

"Shur."

He left soon after, but not without giving me several worried looks. My best friend legit thought I'd gone straight-up outta my head.

I STAYED HOME from school on Friday, because really what was the point? But by Saturday, Mom pushed me to move through the gears, as Ms. V would say, and I worked the morning shift at the grocery store.

Mom bought these extra-large bandages that covered my wounded face. In fact, they went from my cheek down to my jawline. Shaving was kind of weird though, 'cause I wasn't going near that gash with a razor. Given a choice between letting the beard grow in, or cultivating a patch around the spot where Landry had hit me, I chose beard mode. It grew in fast and didn't look half bad. The last time I'd attempted facial hair, it had been pretty pathetic— 'course that had been in ninth grade.

When I got to work, Tim was smoking a cigarette by the loading dock door. His head bobbed up and down underneath a set of headphones.

"Hey, Warsh! How goes it?"

"Been better." If I kept up with the pain meds every six hours, I could talk without the lisp from the last two days.

"Whoa! What happened to your face, man?"

"Oh—" I touched the bandage's smooth plastic. "—I got into it with Landry. You know him?"

"Shit, Warsh. I heard all about that. I meant the beard, dude." He laughed at his own joke.

"What are you listening to?" I changed the subject.

Tim popped open his Discman and showed me a Pearl Jam CD. I read the title out loud: "Vit-alogy."

"V-eye-tology, Warsh. It's been out forever."

And with that little exchange, I started my day feeling top-notch idiotic.

Bern told me what to stock, and I went to work. The minutes ticked into hours, and I lost my head in the music Bern played over the speakers.

I was humming along while stacking two liters on a wheel cart and nearly jumped out of my skin when Kasey tapped my shoulder.

"Hi!" she said as she chewed a wad of pink bubble gum and then blew a big bubble.

"Hey." It came out as a whisper. I had no plan for this. A lot had happened since that kiss in her backyard.

"That's the biggest bandage I've ever seen." Kasey held a grocery basket filled with chips and a loaf of bread. Her face skewed as she took in the damage on my face. I knew from the mirror everything was still pretty puffy.

"How bad is it?" she asked.

"Not too awful. I can talk again." I squeezed the back of my neck and stared at the floor. "Gotta chew stuff on the right side though."

"Makes sense. Are you coming back to school on Monday?"

"No reason to stay home, really." I glanced at her. "'Cept fear of being hit again."

"He won't. Coach will pull him from Friday's game if he does."

"Is that the rumor?"

"That's a fact. Rumor is..." Kasey's eyes grew wide. "Well, they're flying over why he attacked you in the first place. I mean, Russ has always been an asshole, but he's never sent anyone to the nurse's office before."

"What are they saying?"

"Umm, let's see..." Kasey readjusted her stance, moving the basket from one forearm to the other. "Some people say you must have been doing homework for him, and finally stood your ground." Kasey continued to report the gossip, recounting each story with her hands. "A whole camp speculated you were shit-talking his mom." She shook her head at that dumb theory. "But then, and this is the most interesting one, there's the saga linking Penny's release to the two of you."

"What? How?"

"I've heard a couple different versions, but the consensus seems to be you got ahold of Landry's artwork and distributed it as payback for how harsh he's always been with you."

"Landry's work! That doesn't even make sense. Landry wouldn't know art if it... if it punched him in the jaw!"

"I know. It's totally a bummer they're being connected."

"It's bullshit."

"I'm working on it." Kasey shrugged.

"How?"

"I have my ways." She twirled a piece of hair around her forefinger.

"What did you do, Kasey?"

"Nothing yet; it's only an idea." She stepped closer to me. Her lips glistened with shiny gloss. "No one would be talking about Penny being Russ's creation if someone dropped the idea that what happened the other day was a lover's spat."

I choked on my own spit. "What the fuck is wrong with you? Do. Not. Do. That." I gripped the two-liter in my hand, squeezing as hard as I could.

"Why not? It would totally work. Juicy chatter gets sprinkled over the fishbowl and *bam*! Feeding frenzy. Penny is yours again."

An elderly man smelling of pipe tobacco shuffled between us to ask me where he could find batteries. I directed him to the home goods aisle, and when he was nearly out of earshot, reengaged with Kasey.

"If you start that rumor, Landry actually murders me, and it won't matter who gets credit for Penny."

"Possibly." Kasey took out a fresh stick of gum and wadded the old one up in the wrapper. "Is there a trash can around here?"

"Here, I'll take it. Trash's in the back." I took her garbage and put it in my pocket. "Look, I mean it. This is not something I feel like risking, Kasey."

"Okay, okay." She scratched at her nose, "So, about the other night—"

"I'm sorry." I cut her off before she could tell me what an awful I kisser I was, and that she didn't see me in that way. "I misread the moment."

"No, Jeremy." She clicked her gum behind her front teeth. "Look, what happened...it's fine. I just want you to know that Anita and I are still together."

"Even after your parents found out?"

"I had to come out sometime." Kasey twisted the crescent moon stud earrings she always wore. "Mom's snooping saved me the trouble."

"How are your parents? They seemed really upset the other night."

"Mother of surprises, they want to meet her. They're planning a dinner and everything." Her eyes searched mine, and she blinked faster. I knew this look. She needed a favor.

"I want you to be there too, Jeremy."

I crossed my arms. "You come in here threatening to spread a rumor that might get me killed, and then invite me to dinner?"

"I was pulling your chain! I would never really do that."

"Why would you want me there?"

"I don't know." Her eyes got all puppy dog-ish, and she clasped her hands together. "I think it might soften everything if you were there. Anita can be...a little much. And my parents love you."

"No."

"Pleeee-ase."

"Yeah, no. I'm not doing it."

"Why not?" Her praying hands dropped to her sides. A dark line formed between her brows.

"I gotta get back to work." I turned around and finished putting the last couple bottles of pop on the shelf.

"I can talk you into this while you work."

"Not this time, Kase." I started rolling the empty cart back to the storeroom. "I don't want to go, okay."

"What the hell, Jeremy? It's one dinner."

"One incredibly awkward dinner that I don't wannabe a part of. You and Anita can handle it."

"I thought you were my friend."

I stopped the cart mid turn and faced her. "I am your friend. I've always been your friend. Your buddy. Your beard. Whatever you needed me to be, in whatever moment you were in, I was there. But this time, just this one time, I don't want to do this. So, I'm not going to. Later, Kase."

The cart's wheels squealed as I pushed around the corner of the aisle. Kasey stayed behind, probably too stunned to move. The swishing doors to the back room opened, and I rolled into the grayness. Maybe I was being brutal. Maybe she was.

Chapter Twenty-Two

I HEADED DOWN to Ms. V's place for another one of those workouts I'd promised her. She had a thing for Richard Simmons and always popped one of his videos into the VCR. It was so easy, practically a rest day for me. But I kept showing up and danced for a while with the old lady because, on the down low, it was fun.

Ms. V answered the door in a tangerine getup. Apparently, being a retired gym teacher came with a rainbow assortment of tracksuits. The nylon swooshed with her measured movements. Even for workouts, she still wore her ruby-studded barrette, and it sparkled near the brim of a white visor.

"Ready to get crackin', mister?" She had that old-person warble in her throat.

"You know it!"

Our video was all cued up—the TV screen paused on Simmons sitting at the counter in a diner. When she hit play, he'd pop a nickel into a table jukebox and get everyone dancing. Ms. V's glasses hung around her neck on a gold-and-pearl chain, and she brought them up to her eyes without putting them on to search the remote for the play button. She always did that with her glasses, never tucking the temple tips behind her ears.

"You need a monocle." I leaned toward her and pressed a triangle-shaped button on the remote.

"A monocle?" Her head tilted. Confusion transformed the wrinkles around her eyes and forehead. They moved like drawbridges creating new passageways along her face. "What the hell would I do with a monocle?"

"What you always do." I took the remote and glasses from her hands and showed her how she looked at things. Ms. V laughed with this infectious back-of-the-throat cackle.

The first tune on the tape played, and we followed Richard's lead and swayed our arms along to the beat of "The Loco-motion." Ms. V informed me that although it'd been redone a couple of times, the original song was performed by Little Eva in 1962, and no one ever sang it better. A big music buff, she knew stats on all the oldies.

Together, we lightly aerobicized. Toes tapped to the music as instructed. We galloped these strange little pony kicks around Ms. V's crowded living room, trotting in circles with Richard and his unlikely gang. He'd probably fought studio execs every step of the way to get a bunch of average people on-screen. They represented the total range in size, sex, race, and age. What they had in common were their comfortable clothes and smiles. Occasionally, I caught a glimpse of myself in the mirror over Ms. V's mantel. I wasn't drenched with sweat. My cheeks were not splotchy and red. But they were raised up, and I laughed most of the time.

Ms. V couldn't hang through the whole tape. Midway, she asked how I was doing. This was her signal that she needed a rest.

"I could use some water," I said.

She paused Richard mid-stretch, with his arms frozen wide open. Ms. V swooshed her way to the kitchen table and sat as I got us both a glass of water the way she preferred it served, with a fresh lemon slice. She always kept precut lemon wedges in the fridge, saying it was the single indulgence her mother had started post-Depression.

Ms. V squeezed the lemon slice over her glass and took a sip. She placed her visor on the table, and with one of her crisp linen dish towels, blotted her forehead.

"How's that jaw of yours?" she asked.

I downed half my drink in one gulp. "Almost back to normal now."

"It was wrong of that boy to hit you."

"One might say I deserved it."

"Well, go on. You can't leave an old lady hangin'. I'm minute to minute over here, Jeremy."

"He called me a faggot, so I tagged his car."

"Remind me what 'tagged' means."

"Vandalized."

At that, her eyebrows shot up. Her eyelids seemed papery thin. "Don't you know not to mess with a man's car?"

"Guess I do now."

We both laughed.

"Guess so," she said, giggling. "It's an ugly word though. What he called you."

Ice floated around the lemon in my water. I dipped in two fingers, pulled out a chunk, and cracked it between my back teeth. Little chunks sprayed around my mouth, and I swallowed the freezing pieces whole.

"You know, my daughter, Jaquelin—we called her Jackie—she was a lesbian."

"I did not know that, Ms. V." I glanced at the clock above the sink.

"It was different then."

"Probably not so different."

"Wanna bet? Jackie was born during the height of the McCarthy era and the Lavender Scare, Jeremy." Ms. V sipped her water, her glass tremoring in her shaky grasp. "Do you know what that meant?"

I shook my head.

"People were arrested, boy. Picked up from bars, their homes. Their names were put on lists, and they were fired from jobs." Ms. V's voice stilled with seriousness. "Jackie couldn't bear telling us face-to-face. If it weren't for the free love movement, I don't know if she would have ever told us. She sent us a letter after moving to New York."

"What did you do?"

"I called her up and told her I loved her. She was my girl. Mine. All I ever wanted for her was happiness." Ms. V's eyes filled with tears. She sniffed into a handkerchief kept in her sleeve.

"What happened to Jackie?" I hadn't noticed at first, but she'd been speaking in past tense.

"Car accident." Ms. V closed her eyes. "Even after telling us, she kept part of her life hidden away from us. Her father had a harder time with it. Wanted her to see a therapist and all that. I know she traveled the world. She'd send me pictures."

"I'm sorry."

"Thanks, Jeremy." Ms. V tried to get up. "Gosh, look at me. I'm a mess. I didn't mean to get all emotional on you."

"It's okay."

"You better get on home. I'm sure you have better things to do than listen to an old bag dither on about the past."

"Do you still have them?"

"What?"

"Jackie's pictures. Can I see?"

"Of course, I do!" Ms. V's eyes sparkled with tears and happiness. Each visit, she opened a part of her carefully wrapped past, gift boxes spanning her timeline. I usually made sure to let her talk. Her stories drifted around the kitchen, and I gathered them into the newer gold foil they deserved.

Ms. V carried a shoebox with "Jackie Marie" written in cursive on the side. It was stuffed with photographs, so the lid barely fit over the top.

"I never got around to putting these in an album. Don't know what to do with them now that she's gone." Ms. V filed through old Polaroid pictures. She picked out a few and dealt them on the table like playing cards. Seeing the standard-sized squares framed in white brought back the sound of a Polaroid camera. Point, click, whoosh, wave, wait.

Lots of the pictures were of typical tourist attractions. I recognized the Eiffel Tower and the Leaning Tower of Pisa. On the wide margin at the bottom, either Jackie or Ms. V had written the location and year.

"Here she is." Ms. V tapped the photo of a girl burned onto the film. "That's my Jackie." In the picture, Jackie clutched a wide-brimmed hat over her stomach, and her shoulders slumped forward. A big toothy grin indicated the photographer snapped this one right as something wildly funny had happened. I imagined the same deep-throated cackle Ms. V had, bursting from the girl right after the click. Her eyes were dark, matching her shoulder-length hair.

"She's beautiful."

"She was." Ms. V's lip quivered. She covered her mouth with her hands. "I'm sorry. I just haven't seen her in a long time now."

I got up and gave Ms. V a hug. The thin fabric of her tracksuit crinkled. She was frail, barely there in some ways, and hugging her too hard might cause something to crack.

"Should we leave her out then?" I attached the picture to the fridge with a magnet.

Ms. V turned and nodded at Jackie's placement. She meticulously picked out each picture and cradled it in her palm, seeming too overwhelmed to talk. I rinsed my glass and brought Ms. V a plate of the gingersnaps she liked.

"I'm gonna leave you to catch up. I'll see you later." I placed the small plate of cookies on the table and let myself out.

AT HOME, MOM was dressed up for what looked like a date.

"Go get yourself cleaned up. We're going out."

"What?"

"I'm taking my son out for a nice meal. Okay?"

"Sure."

I stripped off my gym shorts and got ready. As I showered, I figured this would be the dinner where we laid everything out on the table and mentally prepped myself. I needed well-thought-out responses as to why I'd kept the money from her. She deserved that much.

"Where are we going?"

"A little Italian place, next town over. It's really good."

"Oh yeah, you've been there?"

"Contrary to popular belief, Jeremy, I am datable."

This was the first I'd heard of any recent dates. She'd gone out here and there over the years, but nothing ever seemed to stick. At least, not long enough for her to feel the need to introduce me to anyone. Oh, jeez. My stomach dropped. Was that what this was?

The restaurant was in a strip mall being quietly overtaken by fast-food chains. The Spinning Fork had a cute three-dimensional sign with a fork that spun around in a pile of fake noodles. Inside, the tables were covered with red-and-white checkered vinyl tablecloths. Each table had a small vase filled with flowers—their real or fakeness yet to be determined—set next to glass jars of Parmesan cheese and red pepper flakes. But none of that mattered much, because the smell of roasted garlic and fresh basil enveloped me.

The hostess reminded me of Rizzo from the movie *Grease*—only if the movie never ended, and Rizz had aged fifty years with the crackling voice of a still heavy smoker.

"What can I do for you?"

"Table for two, please," Mom stated.

"Smoking or non?"

"Non."

Old Rizz grabbed two plastic-coated menus and marked off something in grease pencil on a chart at the podium. She led us through the empty restaurant. Mom always ate earlier than most because of her shifts at work, although there were a few people enjoying happy hour at the bar. As we both scooted our chairs under the table, a waitress asked if we wanted water and told us Fredo would be our waiter.

"So, what's good here?" I scanned the menu. Everything sounded awesome.

"I had eggplant parm with Michael."

"So, that's his name, huh?"

Without missing a beat, she said, "I don't think you're in the place to be coming down on me, mister." Mom blinked up from her menu. I looked away.

Fredo came with our waters, and Mom ordered for both of us. The meal selections seemed authentic, and she knew I'd be nervous about butchering pronunciations.

"Vino, no?" Fredo asked as he scribbled in his pad.

"You know what—? Yes, we'll split a bottle of your best merlot."

Fredo didn't seem to have a problem with that, with a simple nod he walked back toward the kitchen. I was surprised when he didn't ask for my ID.

"Isn't this place great?"

They served minors, so hell yeah. The Spinning Fork ticked off every idea of how an Italian eatery should appear. Except, now that I was up close, I touched a flower petal, and they were real. Red and pink carnations, nothing fancy, but the puff of silky fringed petals was the perfect amount of next-level authenticity.

"So." Mom pressed her palms together, and the little steeple she made with her fingers supported her chin. "We need to talk."

"I know." Despite my shower thoughts, I had zero logical responses. The only reason I kept the money from her was my own selfishness. "I got greedy. I'm sorry, Mom."

"En-joy." Fredo deposited a basket of bread and a plate of swirling balsamic vinegar in a sea of olive oil on the table. A visual representation of how my stomach felt.

"Jeremy, I would have never taken that money from you. I hope you know that."

"I do." I took a slice of warm bread and tore it up into little bits.

Fredo came back and presented a bottle of wine to us. He uncorked it at the table and handed me the maroon-stained topper. I had no idea what to do with it until Mom made obvious snuffling noises. I sniffed the cork, and it smelled of...wine. Fredo poured a tiny amount in a glass and offered it to me.

"Taste it, Jeremy."

I took a sip and swallowed. It tasted like...wine. I wasn't sure if I was supposed to spit it out. I'd seen people do that on TV. Fredo waited, the bottle of wine settled in the crook of his arm as if it were precious.

"It's good?" I offered.

Fredo sprang into action. He refilled my glass and poured Mom's. I imagined he went back to the kitchen to let everyone know what a "classy" fool I was.

"Mmmm, that's good." Mom savored the drink for a minute. "Jeremy, I'm happy your dad saved that money for you. And I want you to use it for your future."

"Okay." The wine burned my tongue a bit going down at first. There was a smoky sweetness to it. "I really am sorry."

"It's done, okay. I, as your mother, will never fault you putting yourself first." Mom brushed crumbs from the tablecloth. "Now, we really need to talk about what happened at school this week. I spoke with Michael, and he thinks we should talk to a lawyer."

"What? No."

"Honey, that boy assaulted you. I've had time to think it over, and I agree."

"You can't."

"Why? Tell me what I don't know."

So, I did. I recounted what Russ had called me in the locker room and my part in all of it.

"I see. So, if I contact a lawyer, they'll find you had culpability in all this."

"Yes, ma'am."

"And this is all because someone called you a name?"

I didn't answer. Just pinched my fingers around the stem of my wine glass. At the bar, a crummy guy in tan pants put his hands on the women's stool next to him. He rotated it until she was facing him, his legs spread wide apart, making room for her knees. He was even chewing gum.

Fredo interrupted our silence, presenting a long pepper mill while a younger kid carried our steaming plates. The boy deftly placed them in front of us, gave a curt nod, and walked away. He could've been Fredo's younger brother. They both had thick lips and a butt-dimpled chin.

"You want pepper?" Fredo asked.

Mom nodded.

"Say when." Fredo twisted the top of the mill and peppercorns scrunched through whatever grinding mechanism was inside the contraption.

Mom sipped her wine and then held up her hand. Fredo stopped and pointed the thing my way.

"No thanks," I said, twirling angel-hair noodles on my fork, as the sign out front advertised.

Mom sliced into her fried eggplant. With her first bite suspended in air, she finally said, "This is so out of character, Jeremy."

"I don't have anything to add, Mom. I did it. I got punched for it. And honestly, I don't feel bad about it."

"Okay, then. I guess we chalk this one up to natural consequences then." She put the fork into her mouth. "Oh my god, so good," she said while chewing.

Mom was right; the food was delicious. The sauce, both sweet and acidic, took my mind to a distant, faraway place. A place with golden grass and rows of vineyards where the air might smell of heat and dirt.

I hoped for the end of the conversation. The key to my teen-hood success was to know when to shut up. Let Mom come to her own conclusions, and subtly change the subject. I'd never gotten into too much trouble, but whenever I did, this strategy worked like aces.

"Where'd you meet, Michael?"

"Huh? Oh, the gas station."

Shit. The gas station guys were the worst. She never really discussed it or brought any of them home, but the cycle with the gas station guys was always the same. Week of glee, month of tears. They moved on quickly. My guess was that none of them were interested in that teenage boy at home. Although, now that I was halfway out the door maybe Mom would have a real chance. She'd obviously already told this Michael person about me.

"I know what you're thinking, but Michael's going to be different."

"I hope so, Mom. What's he do?"

"AC and Heating. I've known him for a while. He stops in for a fill-up after his Thursday shift."

"Sounds nice. I'm happy for you." I always said this, and for the most part, it was true. I still appreciated the hell out of her not bringing any of these losers around the house though.

"Oh, I meant to tell you. Kasey called to invite us to her place for brunch tomorrow." Mom scooped the last bit of sauce onto her remaining eggplant. "Brunch, so fancy."

I dropped my fork. "What did you tell her?"

"That we'd be there with bells on."

"No!"

"What? You always do stuff with Kasey. And frankly, I should've met her parents ages ago."

"But Maaawwm." The standard kid whine heard round the world over, suddenly mismatched my frame. And I knew it. Here I sat, sharing a bottle of wine with my mom at a fancy dinner place. That whine would never work for me again. Although, to be fair, it hardly worked even when I was little.

"We're going, mister. I'm dying to see that house on the hill."

Chapter Twenty-Three

KASEY GREETED MOM and me at her front door the next morning. Her red baby doll dress fell a few inches above her knees. Knowing her, the Doc Martin boots were a perfectly planned contrast.

"I'm so glad you came!" Kasey opened her arms and gave Mom a big hug.

Mom hugged her back and stepped past the entryway that smelled of bacon. Just bacon. Bacon smell ruled supreme.

"Hi, Jeremy."

"I told you I didn't want to do this," I deadpanned.

"You said you didn't want to come to dinner. This is brunch!" Kasey extended her arm imitating one of Barker's Beauties from *The Price is Right*.

"Brunch is different, how?"

"There's breakfast items in among the mix, and everyone is notably more chill at brunch. No one loses their shit at a brunch."

"Anyone can lose their shit anywhere, Kasey." I walked past her into the living room with its vaulted ceilings and stone fireplace. On both sides of the hearth, french doors lead out to a deck with views of the pool, surrounded by acres of ash trees atop rolling hills. Picture windows emphasized the room's height and shape. Someone had tuned the enormous TV to a classical music channel. Mom and I didn't get these channels.

My mom and Kasey's mom were already chatting things up in the kitchen. Mom offered to help, as every good Midwestern guest should, and Mrs. Axton declined, as every good Midwestern host did.

I looked for Anita, but she wasn't there yet. Neither was Kasey's brother—he'd shipped off for his second year at OSU in August. Atop the mantel sat his senior picture. It was standard issue: a suit and tie combo with hands clasped in the lap, subject instructed to lean forward, tilt head, and smile. *Click! Perfect!* It was impossible to appear non-douchey, striking that pose. *Here I am! Totally psyched for my future in car sales or real estate!* Kris wasn't an asshole though. He'd been a nice guy to everyone in high school. And I was pretty sure Kasey mentioned a biology degree in college, or it could have been paleontology. His masculine version of Kasey's face grinned back at me.

"It's still weird not having him around," Kasey said. She'd come up next to me and picked up her brother's framed photo. "The whole house is off...unbalanced, I mean."

"That makes sense." Although, I didn't know what she meant. Those were the perks of being an only child, I guessed. I could kind of connect what she said to how I felt about Gramps being gone. But he was dead, not getting tanked at frat parties or whatever it was guys like Kris did at college.

"Jillian, I can't get over this view..." My mom's voiced trailed in from the kitchen.

"Why did you have to invite my mom?" I asked.

"One, I knew she'd make you come." Kasey winked at me.

I hated when she winked at me, because, for real, it was my kryptonite. Those winks knighted me as her coconspirator. They gave off this "Us against the World" vibe.

"And two, my parents will remain cool if they know another parent is watching."

"Oh, you're good."

"*Tsk*. I know. Given time and much practice, you too may aspire toward manipulative greatness."

"I doubt it." I laughed at her though. She'd done it. With her wink and a stupid joke, my anger over being here dissipated.

"Let me get you a spritzer!" Kasey skipped to the kitchen and came back with a bubbly orange drink.

"I've never had a spritzer before." I took the crystal glass, filled to the brim with fizzing citrus juice. As I sipped, bubbles popped in my mustache—part of the beard combo I'd been rocking since the fight. "Fancy."

Kasey rolled her eyes. "Literally, it's lemonade, orange juice, and 7UP."

The doorbell rang. The flushed color drained from Kasey's cheeks, and her eyes got super wide, in that trapped, fight-or-flight predicament.

"It's gonna be okay. Go to the bathroom and splash water on your face or something. I'll get the door."

"Splash water?"

"I don't know! People are always doing that on TV, right?"

"I guess so."

"Go, do it. I'll let Anita in."

Kasey turned and walked toward the hall bathroom, her fists clenching and unclenching the entire way. The doorbell rang again, and Mrs. Axton yelled out, "Coming!"

"I got it, ma'am!" I called from the living room.

"Thanks, Jeremy!" Her voice was unwavering. I suspected either Valium or an adult version of the spritzer.

From this side of the sidelight, Anita looked no different than the first time I'd seen her. When she noticed me looking at her through the glass, she tucked her hair behind her ear, exposing the zigzagging shaved on the side. I waved and then remembered I was supposed to let her in.

"Hey," she said.

"Hey, yourself." Certainly, she knew that I knew why we were all assembled here today.

"How's it goin'?" Anita asked.

"Oh, you know, school, work, grindstone."

I hadn't let her in yet. She stood on the threshold waiting for a pass. She nodded, and her gaze dropped to the stoop where Mrs. Axton kept an arrangement of potted plants and the only piece of kitsch on the grounds—a painted gnome.

"Cute." Anita nudged him with her platform sandal.

"Come on in." I wasn't one of those guys who'd hold anyone's opinion of kitsch against them. It was cute; that was why it was mass-produced. People liked what they liked.

"She's in the bathroom." When I gave Anita the heads-up, she still looked unsure of what to do, where to go, and especially what to do with her hands. They finally ended up behind her back as she took in the grandness of the living room from her spot near the landing.

I moved past her and sat on a plush couch near the fireplace. Kasey came out a few minutes later. Her hair was wet around her face.

Anita's face lit up, the same way it had in the coffee shop. She stepped toward Kasey and tried to kiss her.

"Not here," Kasey muttered as she dodged backward. She cleared her throat. "Have a seat. I'll get you a drink."

Anita's jaw dropped, but she quickly recovered with a click of her teeth and a sigh. She primly sat on the loveseat, smoothed out her black-and-white striped skirt, then took off her miniature leather backpack and set it on the floor next to her feet. She crossed her legs at the ankle. Her toes were painted a metallic brown, and on one of them, she wore a toe ring.

My cheeks were hot, and I could've cried over how awkward the next two hours were bound to be.

Mr. Axton walked in the living room. Sweaty and pale, he looked as if he'd eaten something gone sour. But once he noticed Anita and me sitting there, he composed himself.

"You must be Anita. I've heard"—he floundered with the common greeting, and in this case, realized it would be totally and completely false— "nothing about you."

Anita stood, shook his hand, and looked him right in the eye. "It's nice to finally meet you, sir."

I couldn't help thinking that if she hadn't called, the Axton household would be blissful in ignorance right now. But then their daughter would be a stranger. I didn't know if it mattered to the Axton's. Ms. V sure seemed to have some regrets. Years from now, Kasey's parents may look back and realize Anita had done everyone a big favor.

After the initial meet and greet, Mrs. Axton announced the food was ready. I piled a plate with slices of bacon, quiche, and a sprig of grapes. The Axton table sat in its own room, separated from the kitchen, which seemed to be more of a hassle, but it was another mark of their wealth.

Mom folded the sage linen napkin in her lap and touched the silver. I could tell she was trying to hide the awestruck, and for that, I was thankful. I won't say I hadn't worried she'd embarrass me somehow.

Everyone ate. I had to slow myself down, because it didn't take that long for me to eat quiche. At the rate we were going, we'd be outta here in an hour, tops. And that was fine by me.

Mrs. Axton offered seconds, but only I took her up on it, and she brought me another slice of the egg pie.

Conversation moved to our future plans. I expected to be left out of the discussion completely—figured Mrs. and Mr. A would use the time to focus on getting to know their daughter's girlfriend. Alas...

Mrs. Axton had rolled a tray in with coffee and sweet bites of mini-muffins and chocolate-covered strawberries. Mom helped herself, and so did I.

Mid muffin bite, Mr. A asked me what I planned to do after high school. I swallowed.

"I'm looking at art programs in Cincy, Mr. Axton."

"Art programs? I had no idea."

"My Jeremy's quite talented." Mom patted my forearm.

"Sure, but art school costs so much. And comes with little payoff."

Mom bristled at the mention of how much college would cost. I'd overheard her talking to one of the other secretaries on the phone once: "Rich people are so rude!" There had been an office-wide kerfuffle over their boss's loud complaints regarding service at an all-inclusive resort in the Bahamas. Both secretaries had listened to her complaints, and then as soon as they got home, called to share their appall. Money talk always stayed in the family. No one ever discussed salaries, savings, or shortages outside of the people you trusted most. Any attempts otherwise came across as extreme rudeness.

"We're a hardworking family, Mr. Axton."

"I didn't imply you weren't—"

"If my son believes in his art, so do I."

"I only meant he could get all the way through art school, and then what jobs would he be eligible for? An art degree isn't a guarantee."

"A guarantee of what, Mr. Axton?" I asked.

"Well, for starters, a career. How does one make money with an art degree?" Mr. Axton's thick black-and-gray hair was slicked back in the way of every greedy '80s movie antagonist. He would never understand what I planned to say next.

"There's more important things in life than money."

Mom's eyes were, what she'd refer to as, misty. She rubbed my back in little circles between my shoulder blades. I knew she wouldn't say anything more. When she had that look, she never trusted her voice not to tremble.

Mr. Axton laughed a laugh that was either snide or nervous; I couldn't tell. But Mrs. Axton shot him a look that said shut up.

"Jeremy's right, Dad."

"Of course, he is," Mr. Axton patronized.

"No really, Dad. I've seen what his drawings can do. They move people to act, to feel, or to connect with something they never thought of before. That's so powerful. More powerful than any of this." She motioned at the exorbitant surroundings—the table with the glossy finish, temporarily covered in lace, the crystal glassware clinking with ice, the matching china plates with a single line of silver running the circumference. "None of this means anything."

Now it was Mr. Axton's turn to bristle. "You're being a brat," he muttered.

Kasey flushed as if she'd been slapped.

"Can we not do this with company present?" Mrs. Axton's lips pressed into a tight smile.

"Sure thing, dear." Mr. Axton rolled his shoulders. "I won't argue with the young minds of tomorrow. They obviously know more than me." He placed both hands on the table, and Mrs. Axton grabbed for one.

"Jeremy, since I'm here," Anita chimed in, "why don't you let me see your drawings? Remember that prof? I totally mentioned you, and he said to get a portfolio together and we could schedule a meetup."

Stringing these four sentences together was the most Anita had spoken all afternoon. Her eyes had grown bigger with that last exchange between Kasey and her dad, and I suspected she wanted to put Mr. Axton in his place. Thing was, he already was in his place, and apparently, she knew enough about family politics to go the indirect route.

"Okay, sure." What did I have to lose? Russ Landry might get the credit for the Penny comics in high school, but maybe she'd open doors for my future. That seemed to be a decent enough trade.

"So, Anita, Jeremy's never mentioned you before. How did you all meet?" Mom knew nothing about the relationship between Kasey and Anita. I'd never told her. I'd been too mad at Kasey for getting me here to warn Mom about the things we should steer clear of, conversationally.

Kasey coughed up a piece of muffin. "Wrong pipe," she choked.

"Actually, I've known Kasey for quite a while," Anita said. "We met at the coffee shop, where I work."

"You know the one you picked me up at a while back, Mom?" I interrupted, trying to give Anita an easy place to stop talking.

"Meeting Anita was straight out of a fairy tale," Kasey finished. She reached across the table, and Anita slipped her hand into Kasey's. Their gazes connected, and it was like watching two stars dance around each other, oblivious of the gravitational upheaval.

Mr. Axton threw his napkin on the table. When he stood, silverware clanked against plates, and what was left of my fizzy drink sloshed up the sides of the glass. He stomped off, playing the fool.

On the other hand, Mrs. Axton straightened her shoulders as she glanced at her daughter, then over to my mother, and then at her lap, in a continuous loop. Both her hands rested on the table, and she ran her manicured nails over the rim of her glass. With my mom there, I didn't think she expected Kasey to be so open.

"I'm sorry, Connie." Mrs. Axton turned to my mother. "I wasn't expecting this to turn into a whole...event."

"What were you expecting?" I mumbled. Mom smacked my leg under the table.

"Jillian, there is no reason to apologize." Mom scooted her chair closer to Mrs. Axton. "I remember being this age. Don't you?" She rested her elbows on the table and folded her hands under her chin. "Back then love could rip you open, remember?"

"I do." Mrs. Axton sniffed and blinked back tears. She brought her fingers to the corners of her eyes, blotting away smeared mascara.

Mom leaned in closer to her and whispered, "That's all this is, okay? Just love."

Mrs. Axton choked back a sob. She smoothed her terrible haircut across her forehead and addressed her daughter. "I'm happy if you're happy."

"Thanks, Mom." Kasey's face was hard to read. Her smile was crooked, and it touched her eyes, but not in the usual way. It was kind of droopy and sad. Maybe she thought her mom was saying all the right things because guests were around.

"How far do you live from here, Jeremy?" Anita asked.

"Um, not far." The abrupt change in subject was disconcerting, but I saw what it allowed for in Kasey. Her chest rose and fell with a few deep breaths. With a sip of her effervescent juice mix, sorrow dissipated from her eyes.

"A couple miles from here," I said.

"Can I follow you? I wanna see what I'm endorsing."

"Yeah, sure."

We left soon after, Mom and I in our car and Anita following behind in an older Mercedes. I thought it was, anyway. It was the kind of car with that peace sign hood ornament.

As Mom buckled herself in, she asked, "Why didn't you warn me?"

"I don't know."

"Christ, I don't even know why they invited us." Mom started up the car and shifted into reverse.

"Kasey wanted you there."

"Why on earth would she want me there? That was terribly awkward. I didn't even pick up on their relationship until she all but announced it. I'm such an idiot about these kinds of things."

"Mom, you were amazing."

"Puh-lease." She huffed and checked the rearview for Anita's forest-green dream car.

"No, really. You should have been a counselor."

"That's funny." She stopped, checking for oncoming traffic before turning onto the county road. "That's what I always wanted to be."

It had only happened a handful of times, hanging behind sentences spoken out loud. *But I got pregnant.* A statement never vocalized but earsplitting in its own right.

BACK IN OUR apartment, Anita examined the place—the shaggy brown carpet matted in the most used spots, the outdated fixtures, and, as part of the grand tour, I pointed out the water stain in the shape of Italy located in the northwest corner of my bedroom ceiling. Bonus points awarded to Anita, she didn't flinch, not even a nostril flare during my whole deprecating spiel. I handed her my Grandpa's portfolio.

"My work is near the back."

"Who's is in the front?"

"Those are my gramps's."

"Ohh, a dynasty, huh?"

"He was a farmer. Drawing was his hobby."

Anita turned the loose-leaf pages, carefully pinching the bottom of each sheet. "If you're even half as good as your grandpa, then I have no qualms recommending you."

That statement irked me. Like she was some gatekeeper for the arts. I stared out the window at an empty robin's nest. October was coming. The little bird family I'd watched throughout the spring and summer was long gone. The nest would start disintegrating with no one around to keep up appearances.

"I wasn't sure what to think of you, at first." I leaned against the window frame.

"Oh, I'm aware." Sitting on my bed, Anita turned to face me. I imagined mischief behind her elvish gray eyes. "You definitely gave off that vibe." She took a beat, flipping her hair back from her face. "I think you enjoy your role. You're the only one who understands her, right? But honestly, you've not been a model friend."

"What do you mean?"

"Don't act like pretending to be her boyfriend wasn't beneficial to you."

"Whatever, Anita. It barely lasted a day."

"Psh...she made it official for a short time, but you've been puppy-dogging her around for years."

"Shut up." I rolled my eyes and slouched my shoulders. "Why are you even helping me?"

"Mostly because I enjoy being in the middle of other people's stuff."

I put my hands in my pockets and watched as Anita arranged my drawings on the bed one by one. With each turn of a page, I caught a glimpse of Penny. She winked. She waved. She flipped me the bird.

"Who is this girl?" Anita asked.

"That's Penny Kind. Those are the gesture drawings I did for the comic. The finished copies are over here." I opened the top drawer of my desk, and a couple pencils rattled around with the swooshing movement. Penny's comics were stacked neatly to the right. I grabbed the originals and handed them to Anita.

Anita scooted back, leaning against my headboard.

"You want anything to drink?"

"Sure," she said without looking up. "Whatever you have is fine."

I retreated to the kitchen. Not even the core group had seen the final copy of the second comic yet...

Penny finds a flyer for a mysterious underground party and sneaks out at night to attend. The party's kind of lame, with just a bunch of kids from high school getting wasted around a bonfire. When a set of tricked-out speakers blare a thumping bass line from the back of someone's trunk, everyone starts dancing, grinding up against one another, the threat of an orgy pumping through the crowd.

Thunder rumbles in the distance. Silhouetted by stars, Penny sees the void: blackness speeding closer. But no one else notices the low-flying crop duster until it emerges in the firelight, spraying as it passes, flying so low they all look up as a fine mist covers their cheeks. To be continued...

It was set to go out Monday. Stuart and I planned to spend tomorrow copying, folding, and writing up the next episode.

"Crap, Jeremy." Anita stood at the hallway entrance to the kitchen. She had her purse and was shuffling through it.

"What's up?" I asked, handing her a bottled water.

"It's hard to explain." She stopped her rifling to crack open her water. "There's this feeling, it's like I'm being sucked in...by Penny."

"That's my girl. She really grabs ya by the—er—ovaries."

Anita waved away my attempt at a joke as she swallowed a drink of water. "So, what's the endgame for Penny?"

"Kasey didn't tell you?"

"No, we haven't talked about it."

"It's kind of dumb."

"Stop it. Tell me without all the qualifiers."

"Zombie Homecoming."

Anita coughed up water as she patted her sternum to finally croak out, "I did not see that coming. How?"

"Not exactly sure yet. The dusting will turn all the high schoolers into zombies, but I don't really see Penny as a zombie. Stuart and I disagree on that though."

"Stuart?"

"Oh, my friend. The whole zombie homecoming dance was his idea. I think we'll get two more comics out before homecoming themes are chosen and all that parade business starts."

"Wait a minute. You're planning to turn your actual homecoming dance into a zombie homecoming?"

"That's the goal."

She laughed, and I laughed with her.

"I love it," Anita said. "Make sure you include that in your interview." She gave me a business card. Next to a rough sketch of the human form and printed in raised black ink was the name Charlie Wyatt, Artist and Professor, along with his contact information. "He's expecting your call."

Chapter Twenty-Four

MOM HAD A shift at the gas station that evening, so she let me borrow the car for the morning. I set out to pick Stuart up early Sunday. We wanted to be the first ones in the place, to get the copying and folding portion of today's work done as quickly as possible. Then we could move on to writing the next episode. It was fun teaming up with him. His ideas bounced like bright blue racquetballs.

I pulled over to the curb in front of Stuart's house. He got up from his stoop as soon as he saw me and stretched and yawned his way over to the car. Stuart was so lanky the cartoon weasel on his shirt had deflated into his center.

"Hey, Warsh-man." His eyes were bloodshot, and his voice was thick from smoke. He always chain-smoked on party nights.

"Hey, man. You okay?"

"Get me food and beverage, and I'll be among the living for sure."

"What were you up to last night?" Checking my mirrors, I merged into the churchgoing traffic.

"Partied with Shannon from work. You know, the girl with the piercings."

"Sure, I remember her. She hates me."

"What do you mean? Shannon doesn't hate anybody, 'cept corporate scum."

"Nothing. Never mind." I clicked on my blinker and changed the subject. "How's Des handling your party lifestyle?"

"She doesn't."

"She seems pretty straight."

"Can't change me, man. Pull into Hefties. I need food, like, yesteryear."

Stuart ordered a huge breakfast, while I stuck with coffee.

"You're not eating?" He asked.

"I ate at home, is all."

"Yeah, right. You're dieting."

"Shut up, Stu."

He danced a hash brown around my mouth and laughed at my choices. "Why doesn't Jewemy want a wittle hash bwown?"

"Stop it. I'm trying to drive. You smell like you're still wasted."

"I probably am." Stuart unwrapped his cheesy egg biscuit, and I won't say it didn't smell heavenly.

There was a Kinko's over in Hamilton. A doorbell chimed as we walked in, and the clerk looked up from her reading. Everything gleamed in hues of gray, white, or beige, and Stuart shaded his eyes under the fluorescent lights.

"Need help?" the clerk asked, popping the gum in her mouth.

"Nah, just running color copies," I said.

The girl pointed to the rows of machines along the walls, and we picked one at random. In the center of the room stood platform desks decked out with grids, paper cutters, and cups full of pencils and scissors.

"I'll do a hundred, you do a hundred. 'Kay?" I fed the original into a Xerox, and it whirred out a copy. Stuart whistled at the price per double-sided color print. He took the copy and started cranking out duplicates on another copier.

"This is pricey." Stuart hopped on top of one of the centerpiece desks with his feet dangling over the side.

"I know."

"You think we can afford two more runs?" He asked.

"I sure as hell can't, but I think Kase can handle it."

"Pays to have a rich chick on the side."

I swiped at him. Got him in a headlock and dragged him down from his perch on the table. We danced around the store, play-fighting until Stuart got the upper hand by crouching down low and shoving me upward. Tangled up together, we toppled into the counter. With a crash, the desk organizers tipped over, scattering supplies over the tabletop and floor. The clerk gave us a knock-it-off look as we picked everything back up.

Both copiers came to a halt, and we checked on them. All finished. We took the vouchers to the clerk and paid. She put each stack in a foldable box and taped our receipt on top.

"Should we fold these here?" I asked.

"Nah, it's a beautiful day. Let's do this outside."

I knew what he meant. We had a special spot we'd found riding our bikes along the dry creek bed the summer I turned twelve. The same woods that edged the school's track extended behind my apartment complex. So, I drove us back to my place. We grabbed some supplies, mostly snacks, but also paper and pencils for planning the next comic, and then headed into the woods with our backpacks heavy. The asphalt turned to grass as we stomped toward the line of trees.

"It's been awhile," Stuart declared.

It had. I couldn't exactly remember the last time we'd been out here, but substantial drinking had been involved. I knew for a fact it was before Kasey came out and Stuart went and got himself a girlfriend. So, before school started.

September could still be hot in the tri-state area. People threw phrases around like, "dog days" or "Indian summer," but I didn't really know what those things meant and suspected neither did most people using them. Today was a reminder that fall was on its way though. There was a chill to the morning air. I assumed the cooler temp would be gone by noon, but it was still there, waiting, biding time until the earth's axis tilted and the angle of sunlight incidence shifted.

Under the ash trees, the light was all green and yellow. We hiked down to the creek and followed it north. The bugs were thicker down here. One buzzed around my ear, and Stuart slapped the back of his neck.

We'd tagged the turn out years ago. Every time I saw it, I was surprised it still existed—a stump, turned on its side, where we had taken turns spray-painting a Day-Glo orange smiley face with X's for eyes. Stuart veered to the right in front of our trail marker. From there, it was a five-minute hike to the makeshift fort, which really was three dilapidated walls with a piece of tin balanced over the top. It must have been an old shed, because along the back wall was a worktable with a rusty vise still attached to it.

Approaching the structure, we put the old stones back around the firepit. I kicked away the fallen leaves, and Stuart started wiping off the workspace with his hands.

"It's pretty dirty. Should we fold these up at your house instead?"

"Nah. Let's break apart the boxes. Lay them down flat on the table, and then work on those."

"'S up to you. I don't want to get dirt all over your masterpieces."

"It'll be fine."

After setting things up, we quietly folded each comic with precision. When we were done, we put the finished copies in the front pocket of his backpack and relaxed around the firepit.

"So how are you and Des?"

Stuart rubbed circles around his temples. He reached into his bag and pulled out two cans of beer and handed me one. "Hair of the dog," he said, popping the tab.

I opened mine, and as the beer foamed up, I hurried to slurp it before it spilled to the ground.

"Cheers, Warsh." Stuart held up his beer, and I tapped mine against it.

"You didn't answer my question."

"That's 'cuz I don't know."

"What happened?"

"Got weird."

"Your mom?" I guessed. "Got weird" was usually his code for my family screwed something up.

"She saw me and Des holding hands at the Dairy Barn and flipped about her being black."

"Whoa! In front of Des?"

"No, at home mostly."

"So, what? You're giving up because your mom's racist?"

"No, I am not giving up." Stuart took another sip. "But my mom introduced herself, and now Des thinks we should all have dinner together. And, Jesus, that seems like a clusterfuck of an idea."

"I hear ya. Did I tell you Kasey tricked me and my mom into showing up at her coming-out-to-my-parents brunch? It was awkward as hell."

He snorted. "I can imagine."

"Anita's not so bad though. She's hooking me up with this art professor down in Cincy."

"Oh yeah, what good will that do?"

Crap. Sometimes, I expected Stuart to just know things. I hadn't told him about the money though. I took a big gulp of beer, draining the last of it. After scrunching the can, I tossed it with our collection under the bench.

"Uh, apparently, my dad saved some money for me to go to college."

"No shit." Stuart wiggled a finger in his ear as though he hadn't quite heard me.

My cheeks flushed, probably a mix of chugging the beer and embarrassment. It felt real strange telling your best bro, the one you'd been on equal ground with your whole life, that you could level up without him.

"He gave it to me right before he left."

"So, a month ago? Why didn't you tell me?"

"I don't know. You've been busy with Des."

"Don't. I've known you too long for you to pull that crap with me." Stuart emptied his beer and let out a tremendous belch. "You didn't tell me because you were afraid."

"Afraid? No, that's not it. I didn't want—"

"To make me feel left behind. For whatever reason, you thought I'd be petty enough to make your opportunity about myself. Like I wouldn't congratulate my best friend and celebrate him getting a shot outta this town."

He grabbed a pack of smokes from his back pocket and lit one up. Nothing smelled quite so sweet as the first few seconds of a lit cigarette. Those whiffs were bliss, but after that, it reeked. Stuart handed me his cigarette. I took a hit and handed it back.

"I'm sorry, man. I've been trying to figure out all this stuff."

"You lowballed me, Warsh."

"I did."

"I'm gonna be real with you right now—this is a thing that you do. Underestimating people is your Achilles'."

"You think?"

"I know." Stuart side-eyed me through the haze of smoke. "I am happy for you though. When you're a famous artist, you have to come here and look up your old pal, Stu-Meat." He popped the cherry out of the cigarette butt and pressed dirt over it.

"'Stu-Meat'?"

"It's a nickname I'm trying out." He feigned a punch to my ribs, and everything went back to being copacetic. "What do you think?"

"I will never call you that."

"Nicknames never stick with me." He crossed his arms behind his head.

"So what do you want for Penny's next chapter?" I asked.

"You already know. The kids start changing into zombies. That leaves the final episode as just a bunch of zombies having fun at the homecoming dance."

I'd been mulling this over for a few days. We'd had this conversation a couple times, and it didn't sit right with me. Penny—a zombie? She was too tough.

"I don't know, man."

"I know you don't want to turn her into a flesh-eating monster. But dude, you have to think endgame. The goal is to get everyone to cosplay this B at our homecoming dance. Which means Penny has to turn."

"I have trouble believing she would though."

"Dude, she's not a superhero. She's a kid. There are lots of things out of anyone's control. And for Penny, being sprinkled with zombie dust is one of them."

"You don't think there's another way?"

"No. There are no work-arounds."

I'd keep thinking on it, but every time I came up with a different ending, one with Penny not changing, the result was a totally different message. We needed followers. People who'd see what happened to Penny and form a willingness to recreate it. In the end, we wanted performance art.

Stuart finished up and announced, "Snack break!"

I grabbed my backpack and tossed Stuart the bag of pretzels and crunched into an apple.

"Got anything to drink?" he asked.

"Water."

"I'll take it." Stuart ripped open the bag and ate as he leaned against a tree trunk, mindlessly staring into the bits of char and ash as if there were a fire burning.

I stretched and breathed in the pre-fall air.

"So, tell me about the drawings I saw the other day. The ones not for the comic."

I waited a beat, swallowing the juicy bite of apple I'd been chewing on. "I was kind of out of it when you came over. What did you see?"

"An interrogation sequence that ended with Penny calling you a fag."

"Knock it off, Stuart. I don't wanna talk about this."

"That's for sure. I've been waiting for you to bring it up all morning."

"I can't explain it. It's...we talk to each other. I know it looks crazy."

"Looks crazy?" Bits of pretzel sprayed onto Stuart's shirt. "You think that's why I'm worried?"

I took a final bite of the apple. Before tossing it into the woods, I picked out the seeds with my fingernail. Three brown specks in the palm of my hand. When I was a kid, I did that with fruit. Planted the seeds, I mean. Apples, peaches, plums—any kind—all buried in the front lawn of my complex. Nothing ever grew, but I wondered if they were all still there, lying dormant.

"Earth to Jeremy? Did you hear anything I just said?"

"No. I wasn't listening."

"Dude, what is with you?"

"I was thinking about these." I showed him the apple seeds. "How cool would it be if we planted these, and years later come out here to find a fucking apple tree, Stuart? It would be filled with birds, and squirrels, and bees. Its own little universe, right here in our spot."

Stuart's eyebrows came together. "We'd carve our names in it." His voice was softer. The bag of pretzels fell to the ground in a crinkly mass as he stood. With the toe of his shoe, he cleared away the ashes in the center of the firepit.

"Nah. We wouldn't need to claim it. It would be enough to know we started it." I found a stick and started digging in the spot Stuart had cleared away.

"Like gods, or something."

"Yeah...like gods." I dropped the seeds into the hole and patted down the dirt. Stuart sprinkled the rest of his water over the mound.

Chapter Twenty-Five

THIS IS RIDICULOUS.

"I'm aware."

I WOULD NEVER BE A ZOMBIE. I DON'T EVEN EAT MEAT!

"I don't know what to tell you. There is, literally, no other way to get the point across, and the vote for homecoming theme is this week."

I colored Penny's skin a faint green color. Her once vibrant eyes were dull and coppery-brown like overused pennies. The kids at the forest party had changed within minutes. Luckily, I got Penny out of there. But now, she stood in her pink-tiled bathroom, wrapped in a towel, hoping with all the hope in the world the steamy, hot shower had gotten whatever that dust was off of her. But when she saw her own eyes in the mirror, she knew.

I'M DEAD.

"Not really."

WHAT WOULD YOU CALL THIS? Penny pinched her forearm until a tiny piece of it ripped away.

"Ew, don't do that." I erased and replaced the pale skin of her forearm. "Technically, you're undead."

I CAN'T BELIEVE THAT'S HOW I DIED. ONE NIGHT OF PARTYING AND I'M OUT FOR THE COUNT.

"It's probably a trope."

DEFINITELY, TROPE-ISH. GOOD GIRL GETS HER PARTY ON OR DIES TRYING.

"Well, we weren't going for any literary awards or anything. And I'm not sure you're the good-girl type."

SUCK IT, JEREMY. NOW'S NOT THE TIME TO BE INSULTING ME. Penny readjusted her towel, making sure it was still clamped tightly. *SO WHAT'S NEXT?*

"You go to the dance. That's it."

I'M NOT EATING ANYONE.

"Deal."

The rest of September flew by. October was here, and the twins were hosting the first of the student council homecoming meetings on Wednesday. We decided on only one more comic run, making three issues total. Things with Kasey's parents were dicey, and we'd been counting on them as patrons.

This put a tad more pressure on me though. Condensing two issues into one meant loads of editing and weighing out the importance of every frame. I'd wanted to give Penny a breakfast scene where the smell makes her sick, but I didn't have time for it. I needed to fast-forward to the dance. But I still had to get her there; otherwise, the continuity would be off, and no one would understand the premise of the thing.

I could hear Michael and Mom making breakfast through the walls. Plates clanked, silverware clinked, and their laughter sang down the hallway. Turned out, Michael was a nice guy. I got zero gut vibes around him. He worked hard, stayed sober, and made Mom laugh more often. It was still very weird having him here in the mornings. But what's a guy to do about that? Especially when said guy's days were numbered.

It was Saturday, usually a workday for me, but I had my appointment in the city with Charlie Wyatt from the art academy downtown. I wanted to get this comic finished for my portfolio, expecting the dance scene to add the extra umph my body of work needed. But with Penny fighting the whole zombie thing, it wouldn't be done in time.

I packed a leather portfolio with the two finished Penny episodes, all her gesture drawings, and a few other sketches I'd put together, some for the theater productions, some landscape stuff. I had no idea what this guy needed to see.

Mom had bought me a new pair of dress pants and a red-and-navy-blue plaid shirt for the interview. No matter what happened today, the fact my mom picked out my clothes would be totally apparent. The pants were a little loose. All the exercising hadn't caused any major transformative weight loss, just an overall firming of my barrel-shaped midsection. I searched through my drawers for a belt.

"Mom!"

"Yeah, hon?" She poked her head into my doorway. She'd been letting her hair grow more than usual. For her, this meant out, widthwise, instead of down, lengthwise. "Oooh, look how handsome you are!" she crooned.

"I need a belt." I tugged at the waistband, showing her the extra inches of space around my belly.

"You've lost more weight than I thought."

"Mom, this is the only belt I have." I held up a black belt covered in silver spikes.

"Oh!" Mom covered her mouth, stifling a laugh. "You'll look more artsy." She giggled at her own joke.

I started threading the spiked belt through the loops.

"Hold on. There has to be another option in here somewhere."

Mom helped herself to my closet. That was where I kept all the clothes I never wore. Who wanted to go through the trouble of hanging them up each week after laundry day?

"Here you go. I thought I remembered buying you one." Half of her fuzzy-robed body disappeared as she reached to the back of the closet. She emerged with a plain brown fake leather belt. "This should do the trick."

"Thanks, Mom."

"No problem. Good luck today. I can't wait to hear how this goes."

"I don't know what to expect. He can't get me in."

"Jeremy, in this world, connections lead to opportunities."

"You gotta know the right people, huh?"

"Sometimes, that's all it takes."

I finished buckling the belt, and Mom took me by the shoulders, her eyes searching mine.

"You go into that interview proud of who you are and where you come from. Ya hear? Let your artwork speak for itself, and don't worry about one man's judgment."

"Okay," I barely whispered. There were times when making eye contact with her made me want to just cry. Ten-year-old Jeremy would've buried his face into the waist of her soft, fluffy robe. But I was taller than she was now.

"Everybody's gonna critique you, son. And it will feel like they are picking apart pieces of your own skin. But listen to me now, all those critiques point back to the person who said them. It's their perception, that's all."

She pulled me in, wrapping her arms around my neck. It wasn't the most motivating of pep talks, but I hugged her anyway. She'd always be rooting for me.

"I love you, and I'm proud of who you are." Mom let go first, dotting the corners of her eyes. "Now come on, your breakfast is getting cold."

Michael stood at the stove top, pouring batter into a frying pan. "Hey, big guy! Pancakes okay?" He was a short portly man with a bald head and laughing eyes.

"Sounds good, Mike." I don't know if he minded me calling him Mike. In fact, I counted it as my way of getting back at him for being here in the morning. If it bothered him, he never said anything though.

"Michael makes great pancakes!" Mom said as she scooted her chair under the table.

In the center of the table, a stack of them was piled on a plate, surrounded by cups of milk, a bell crock with a half-used stick of butter, and some off-brand maple syrup. I helped myself to two cakes and a slab of butter. I paused, letting the butter get soft before spreading it around. I didn't participate in any of Mom and Michael's breakfast banter. All I could think of was my meeting with Mr. Wyatt. He said he'd bring coffee down to Fountain Square, and to look for an old guy in kelly-green sneakers. My new dress shoes pinched my littlest toe, and they would definitely clip-clop on the cement pad around the fountain.

Mom patted my arm. "You're gonna do fine."

"You sure are, Jeremy." Michael added another pancake to Mom's plate. Steam rose from its surface.

"Thanks for the vote of confidence, Mike." There it was, the tiniest twitch of the nostril. It annoyed him. I poured syrup all over my breakfast and wolfed it. "Mom, you don't think I'm overdressed?"

"Not for an interview. I wish you would have let me get you a suit."

"No way."

"What time are you heading down?" asked Michael.

"Soon," I answered with my mouth full of the last bite.

"I thought your meeting was at ten. It's only eight o'clock." Mom cut into her breakfast.

"I wanna make sure I have time to park. I don't mind walking around a bit."

"Do you need any cash?"

Michael started to reach for his wallet. Thankfully, he always came to the table dressed for the day. Seeing him in his pajamas might have vaporized my eyeballs.

"I've got it covered, guys. Thanks." I helped Mom clean up breakfast while Michael finished eating. I couldn't stop checking the clock on the microwave.

"Go, hon." Mom touched my shoulder. "Maybe you'll relax once you're down there."

"'Kay. Love you." I kissed her on the cheek and left.

I was glad she hadn't wanted to drive me downtown or anything weird like that. This gave me thirty whole minutes in the car. I picked out Stuart's latest comp, willing myself to get pumped. Stuart was intrigued by an idea he'd concocted concerning the lead singer of Jawbreaker being a perfect match for the lead singer from The Muffs. He was slightly obsessed over the what-ifs. Like, if the two ever hooked up, it could create this musical master power, and their forces would combine for the greater good or some shit. This tape was nothing more than a back-and-forth between the two bands, one song from *24 Hour Revenge Therapy* followed by one from *Blonder and Blonder*. It actually kicked ass and gave some credence to Stuart's superpunk power theory.

Cincy was laid out in a grid. Fountain Square was located at the intersection of Fifth and Vine, but I decided earlier to pick the closest garage and shell out money instead of driving around in search of a meter I'd have to worry about the whole time. Emerging from the garage, I was washed by sunshine. It was probably the last of the warmish days. Summer held on for dear life, and so did I.

If I followed the sidewalk north, I'd end up back at Anita's workplace—a real-life version of connect the dots. Heading in the opposite direction, I strolled past thriving businesses and those that weren't. Cars honked their way up and down the crowded street. Buses created their own whooshing exhaust-filled breeze. Worn-out buildings were strewn with worn-out people.

Foot traffic picked up the closer I got to the center of the Queen City. Slow walkers were scorned by their busy, sharp-moving opposites. From the crosswalk, I could see the huge fountain. A towering woman's outstretched hands poured water over the people below her. A gift to the city way back in the 1800s, the massive bronze structure, named *Genius of Water*, was built over a butcher's market that had once been an Indian mound. It had been considered the center of the city ever since.

Near the edge of the platform, a haggard man in a trench coat stood on a plastic crate with a sandwich sign that read Hell is Real. I tried not to view it as a red flag.

I walked around the fountain, checking feet for rich green shoes. I had no idea what direction Charlie Wyatt would be coming from, and I didn't feel much like sitting. So, I walked in circles around the fountain, enjoying the misty spray. The cascading spumes of water splashed and rumbled together. My shoulders eased up. I hadn't realized they were up around my ears until then.

"Mr. Warsh?" A clear deep voice came from behind me.

I turned to find an older man with a squashed Popeye-looking face. His unshaven jaw was lush with silver whiskers. He wore a white button-down shirt with a bright blue bow tie. He straightened it, and I noticed tiny stars painted on the fabric.

"Charlie Wyatt." He held out his hand and sucked his teeth like there was food stuck in them.

"Jeremy, Mr. Wyatt." I shook his calloused hand. His fingernails were stained with what I guessed was faded paint, although I didn't know his medium.

"You can call me Charlie." He walked back to a metal table in the shade and indicated that we take a seat. Our coffee sat atop the table, still in its carrier. "I didn't know how you liked your coffee, so I got a bit of everything." Charlie grabbed for a paper sack set in between the cups and removed a handful of half-and-halfs.

"Black is fine." I wiggled my cup from the carrier.

"Really?" Charlie looked at me quizzically. He nudged the sack toward me. I saw lots of extra creams among a rainbow assortment of sweetener choices.

"Ok, I'll take some." I peeled back wrappers on four of my own tiny cups of cream.

"A man after my own heart. Servers always seem to judge how tan I like my coffee." Charlie stirred his concoction and sat, eyeing me while doing so.

"I'm not sure how this is supposed to go, sir. I brought my port—"

Charlie held up his hand, and I stopped talking.

Sweat broke out along my hairline. Once that happened, I knew I was a goner. For the rest of the interview, I'd keep wiping my forehead as we both pretended the amount of perspiration was normal. I rolled up the long-sleeves of the shirt Mom made me wear. The coffee wasn't helping though. I took off the lid so it would chill faster. Under Mr. Wyatt's grueling scrutiny, I picked at the table's chipped paint near the edges of grainy red rust spots.

Charlie cleared his throat. "Why are you here?"

"Because I wanna be an artist."

"You already are though."

"I don't understand."

"You already have a body of work in that little pouch of yours, yes?"

"Yeah."

"So, you're an artist."

"No, I'm not. This is..." Words were not succeeding, so I unzipped the portfolio and laid some of my work on the table. "...what I've been working on in high school."

Charlie bit his upper lip, exposing a crooked row of front teeth, and leaned forward in his seat. "Mr. Warsh, one could argue that the truest art anyone ever made was before they were influenced by any outside forces. That includes art school." He said these things while he casually flipped through my work. "It looks to me you have a talent for drawing, but honestly, I don't see anything unique here. Nothing that sets you apart." He stopped looking through my work before he even got to Penny Kind. "Why don't you tell me what you want out of this meeting?"

I swallowed. What did I want? I thought it was art school, but now, this guy was making it sound like it wasn't necessary and that my work was bland. "Just a chance, sir."

"A chance at what?"

"To get outta my town. Like, I always had a feeling my life was already plotted. Now, I see an opportunity to do something nobody expected."

"And what was it everyone expected?"

"Work through the ranks at the grocery store, get married, pop out kids. There's nothing wrong with that. It's just, I want more."

"So, you want to break out of your Mellencamp song of a life, and find where you belong?" This seemed to excite Charlie. His hands popped up like a jack-in-the-box.

"Yes, sir."

He tapped his fingers over his barely-there lips. "You know, John Mellencamp is quite popular in these parts."

"I know, sir."

"Two things. One, stop calling me sir. Two, I'll give you a month to create something that is only you. I'll be needing a new intern next summer, but first, I want to see your absolute truth. If you can work from that part of yourself at your age, art school may not turn you into a complete hack." Mr. Wyatt put his hands on the chair armrests to stand. That was it. He was leaving.

"Do you want to see my comics?"

He sat back in his seat. "Do you want me to see them?"

"I do." That was what I was here for. I moved the theater production pieces out of the way and shuffled through the gesture drawings I'd packed.

"The Evolution of Penny Kind." Charlie read the title out loud. "That's kind of catchy." He picked up the first one and scanned through it. "You did this alone? The writing too?"

I didn't know what he wanted to hear. Was it better if I'd written the dialogue? I had, for the most part, but both Stuart and Kasey had contributed as well. "Mostly, yeah. My friends and I planned out the story, and some of the dialogue was done by committee."

Charlie nodded and sipped at his coffee. "My offer stands. If you want my recommendation, make something original and get it to me by the end of October."

I thought I already had.

"My address is on my business card." He stood once more. "It was nice to meet you, Mr. Warsh."

I was in the middle of gathering up all my drawings, trying to get them to fit back into the portfolio when Charlie held his hand over the table.

Not one to leave anyone hovering, I stuffed the whole packet under my arm and shook his hand. "Thank you, sir."

"Good luck, son." He walked toward the fountain. When he got to the Hell is Real guy, he stopped, and they had a laugh together.

"He said—knock off the 'sir' shit!" The Hell is Real guy had his hands cupped around his mouth like a megaphone.

Charlie roared with laughter, his face upturned to the sky as he braced himself against the bedraggled man in a trench coat.

I saluted my apologies and left the plaza, my steps clip-clopping quickly against the pavement, as I'd imagined.

Chapter Twenty-Six

INTERVIEW OVER. ON the whole, it had taken a little over twenty minutes of my day. In terms of life span though, I may have lost a month or two. The car next to mine in the parking garage was a clunker. The smell of burnt oil lingered in the air as I unlocked my door. I tucked my portfolio under the passenger seat and buckled my seat belt. The steering wheel touched my knees; my hair flattened against the ceiling. Screw this. I got back out.

My steps once again clacked against the pavement. Mom would be anxious to hear how the meeting went, but I wasn't ready to tell her or anyone else about it. I guessed I hadn't blown it. The dude had given me a chance, and that was way more than most people got. It was up to me now. I had to find my "absolute truth" and wrangle it onto paper in the next few weeks. No big whoop.

Along the way, it registered I was heading north on Vine. I'd passed a little Greek place with a giant rotating lamb skewer in the front window, and my stomach bellowed for junk food. It was early for lunch but not elevenses, so I stopped for a gyro and pop. After weeks of eating healthy, all the grease and sodium brought my taste buds back from the dead. It was intoxicating.

As I tossed my trash, I felt the urge to explore more of the city, kill some time, and celebrate a little. It had taken massive balls to make the appointment with Charlie Wyatt, and I wasn't quite ready to put them away. I hadn't gone comic shopping since Grandpa died; it was time for a new series. There were only two other people I could think of who lived around here—Anita, who'd undoubtedly ask me one million questions regarding the interview, and Matt, the guy I'd met in August.

I'd pushed the kiss Matt and I shared way down to the bottom of my conscious thought, like any good Ohioan. It floated to the surface now, all stubbled chins and masculine pheromones. I checked my wallet for Matt's number. It was there. I'd transferred it to a napkin and tucked it away later. For safekeeping? I liked the guy, but had I liked the kiss? We were both pretty buzzed; maybe that was it.

I finished off my pop and asked the cashier where I could find the nearest payphone. She handed a man dressed in a business suit a handful of change and his slip of a receipt.

"Keep north. You see one a block up." She reminded me of Mom with her frizzy black hair and the tightened red hankie used as a headband.

The cook behind her stopped chopping the grill for a second and grabbed a wad of napkins. "Those things are disgusting. Wipe first."

"Thanks."

The blue-and-white pay phone booth soon came into view. Cincinnati Bell shined in white lettering across the top. The Greek guy was right; it was gross. I tried not to picture the mixture of oils, bacteria, and lice—please, let there not be lice—on the receiver as I wiped it clean. Next to the phone was a stinking city trash can. It reeked of spoiling food, and I hoped that was all. I tossed the bundle of used napkins from as far back as I could reasonably stand and made the shot. After feeding the machine a coin, I punched the silver buttons for Matt's dorm. It rang and rang, to the point I contemplated hanging up and getting my quarter back.

"Hullo?" A voice I didn't remember as Matt's answered. "Hullo?" Whoever this person was, it sounded like they had an air bubble stuck deep in their throat.

"Sorry. Hi. Is Matt there?"

"Just a sec." There was a *clunk*. I imagined air-bubble voice had set the phone on a desk or something. He yelled for Matt, and I heard a "Thanks, dude" on the other end and more shuffling.

"This is Matt."

"Hi, this is Jeremy." I suddenly panicked over whether he'd even remember who I was. "We met at a party a couple months back. Jeremy Warsh?"

"Big hair, dad problems?"

"That's me."

"What's up? I wasn't sure I'd hear from you again."

A wave of heat rushed up from my chest to my face. I hated being on the phone. "I'm in town today and felt like exploring. I figured you'd know where to go. Any comic stores nearby?"

"Where are you?"

"I'm at a pay phone on Vine Street and...hold on let me check...Eighth." A woman sighed heavily behind me.

"Okay, you're not that far from me. Keep heading north until you hit Twelfth Street, then make a left. Follow that to Elm—make a right. Wait, are you driving?"

"My car is parked back down by Fountain Square. I'll be okay though."

"There's bars and stuff, but I can't think of a single comic store."

"Oh. I guess I'll head home then."

"Or you could ask me to join you."

"You don't have plans or anything?"

"I don't. But I'm not moving until you ask me."

I looked around, unsure about my next step. Did I want company today? Particularly Matt's? The frowning lady behind me tapped the face of her wristwatch.

"You wanna hang out?" I asked.

"I can be there in fifteen. I have the perfect place in mind."

A few minutes later, Matt met me near the entrance of Washington Park. His emerald-green Jetta was double-parked.

"There you are! Hurry up!" he yelled from the front seat.

I trotted the rest of the way and slid in the passenger seat of his car. It smelled of cologne and smoke. The ashtray overflowed with stubbed-out cigarette butts.

"What have you been up to, Jeremy?" Matt rolled up his window and shifted into drive.

"Oh, nothing. Same old, same old." This was not a good idea. My insides felt like they were hurling themselves up against my abdominal wall. My mind was blank. I had nothing to say. I wanted a beer, which usually meant the level of discomfort had surpassed my mental limits. "You?"

"I'm flunking out of school." Matt braked as we approached a yellow stoplight. The car behind us honked.

I remembered Matt's directness from the party—he removed the small talk, and it was super refreshing. Grasping conversation was easy when one wasn't trying to dance around Midwestern niceties. "Why?" I asked.

"My dad won't let me switch majors. So, screw it."

"That's dumb."

Matt gave me a sidelong look as he clicked on his turn signal. "Hey, I just saved you and now you're calling me dumb?"

"I'm not calling you dumb, I'm calling purposefully failing to get back at your dad dumb. And saving me is a stretch."

Matt laughed. He had perfectly white, straight teeth. His parents must have spent thousands of dollars so that when he smiled people would notice. It worked.

"Following my dreams is stupid, huh?"

"That's not what you're doing though. If you don't want to be an architect, don't be an architect. Make the switch, with or without your dad's support. But don't blow college off because of his opinion. You'll screw up your whole life that way." My neck felt flushed, maybe even a little hive-y, but I had to say this next part. If Matt was okay cutting out the nice code, so was I. "And guess what, it's insulting to all the kids that would kill to be in your place."

"I hadn't thought of it that way."

"Of course not. You've never had to."

"I get it. I'm being a brat."

"Damn right, you are."

"Change of subject, I'm digging the beard."

"Thanks." I stroked the hair along my jaw and cocked an eyebrow, like a villain. Matt laughed again. His laugh was extra loud and continued way past what was even remotely funny. I liked hearing it. "Where are we headed?"

"You like art, right?"

"Yeeeeah." Had I told him that the night we hung out? If so, I was surprised he remembered.

"It's settled then. Instead of giving in to our capitalist underpinnings, we're hitting up Union Terminal for a little culture?"

I hadn't been there since a junior high field trip and said as much.

"It's settled then."

As we turned onto the next street, the museum's half dome appeared before us. Matt paid for parking, and in step, we walked toward the manicured stretch of lawn and hedgerows. Both of us hushed as we neared the fountain, its waters bursting into the air and cascading down an expansive set of aquamarine steps. Giant columns of windows lined the inner portion of the building's face. In its center, there was an enormous clock.

"I don't think I've ever used the word grand before, but I would for Union Terminal," I said.

"You know they turned it into a mall for a while?"

"I didn't." This was my city. How'd this kid from Michigan know that?

"Union Terminal is part of the reason I wanted to be an architect."

"Oh yeah. How'd you know about it way up in Ann Arbor?"

"Uh, hello! *Super Friends*? The cartoon."

"Oh my god! You're right! I totally forgot this was the inspiration for the Hall of Justice."

The doors were glass with a three-pronged metal railing that encircled the word "PUSH," and even the font was art deco. I was getting ready to ask Matt about the building's design features when we emerged under the rotunda.

If the outside of the building was considered grand, the inside was straight-up majestic. It was like walking into a citrus fruit, the ceiling ringed with stripes of orange and yellow, arching into a rainbow of warm color.

"Jesus," I whispered. My neck strained as I took it all in.

"I come here all the time, and it never stops being amazing," Matt said.

Running the circumference of the dome, a massive mosaic depicted a part of Cincinnati's industrial history. Tiny individual tiles morphed into vibrant portrayals of working men. The city, in varying shades of pale blue and silver, in the background. My throat tightened with all the work and fear—and, ultimately, love—that had created this place, and then saved it for history's sake. No, no, no, no. I would not cry in front of Matt over art. But then it hit me—*this* was what Charlie Wyatt wanted from me. In this room was truth, because it touched every soul that walked through those doors.

"Have you heard of the whispering fountains?" Matt asked, breaking my awestruck reverie.

"Sounds familiar."

"Okay, this is so great." Matt rubbed his hands together, so similar to all the eager little kids dragging their parents around the terminal I couldn't help but laugh. "See the water fountain over there?"

I followed the direction of his finger to a line of kids waiting for a drink. Matt pointed out a twin water fountain on the other side of the room.

"Because of the acoustics of this place, if one person stands at that fountain, and another person stands at the other, they can whisper back and forth to each other and still hear."

Once Matt explained it, a highlight reel of the tour I'd gone on in junior high came back to me: Stuart's scrawny eighth-grade-self galloping toward my chunky eighth-grade-self. "Did you hear me?" It had kind of worked. I'd heard something, but the rest of the noise in the room made it difficult to interpret. Stuart cupped his hand over my ear. "I said, you're a cocksucker!" We both burst over laughing. I remembered the old feeling of heat and excitement flaming up inside whenever Stuart used bad words and was terrified a teacher might ask us what was so funny.

"You wanna try it?" Matt asked. "I've never brought anyone here, so I don't know if it works."

I found that hard to believe. "Why haven't you brought anyone with you?"

"I guess, for me, coming here is like going to church."

"Why did you bring me here?"

"Because I thought you'd feel the same."

Matt walked over to the fountain on the right. He held up his hand, all five fingers splayed to show how many people were in front of him. I counted the kids already in my line. We were even.

What would I whisper? Going through this—waiting in line to whisper into a magical fountain—weighed on the words one chose. I would not be quoting Stuart. Maybe a song lyric? A few favorites ran through my head, but I couldn't grasp a single sentence that made sense in this setting. Poetry? Nope. I was not the type to memorize poems.

A girl in front of me, age seven or eight tops, hopped continuously. The beads at the ends of her braids clacked together with each landing. She put her palms on the fountain for her turn. After she stopped giggling, she whispered something. When she turned around, her eyes were big, as if she'd borne witness to her first miracle.

"It worked," she told me.

"Cool!" I said and held my hand up for a high five. She slapped it and ran off.

I stepped up to the fountain, not sure what to do.

"In the halls of the Justice League..." Matt picked the intro line for the cartoon.

"...a team of heroes gathered?" I quoted the cartoon's hook, pretty sure I'd fudged it up a bit. Matt's rolling laugh traveled through the enchanted acoustic tunnel. I smiled as we both moved toward the middle of the rotunda. Everything about Matt seemed easy. His relaxed-fit jeans hung loosely around his legs. The collar of his green polo shirt was crinkled. He walked with his hands in his pockets.

He wasn't a redhead, more like an orangehead, and he kept it long on top, with a wave that fell over his eye, so he was continually raking it back from his face like the star in a Pantene commercial.

"Wanna see the dinosaurs?" he asked.

On our junior high field trip, there'd only been enough time slated for the Omnimax, so I'd never seen big fossils. The creek bed Stuart and I had used to navigate to our spot was littered with rocks with tiny shell imprints. I checked my watch; it was close to noon. Mom would be pacing the apartment wondering how my interview had gone.

"I gotta make a phone call first." I scanned for payphones.

"Here, use mine." Matt produced a purple handheld flip phone.

"You carry a phone?"

"I know, I know. It makes my mom feel better since I'm so far away."

"Do I just dial my number?"

"Let me..." Matt came in close. He smelled like Dial soap, my second favorite soap behind Irish Spring. His forearm brushed against mine as he hit a button and asked me for my number. I gave it to him, and he keyed it in.

I mouthed thanks and turned around for a bit of privacy. Mom picked up at the first half of a ring.

"Jeremy, is that you? How did it go?"

"Hi, Mom. It went fine."

"I've been thinking about you all morning. What did he say? What was he like?"

I put my finger in my ear to block out the echoes from the crowded rotunda. "Hey, Mom—"

"I knew it would be fine. Didn't I tell you it would work out?"

"I know. Yes, you did—"

"So, what did he say about school? Will he give you a reference?"

"Listen, Mom. I'm at Union Terminal with a friend. I'll tell you all about the interview when I get home. Okay?"

"Oh, okay. Sure. I can't wait to hear all the details. Bye, now! Love you!"

"Bye, love you too."

I took the receiver from my ear and wiped it against my shirt. "I don't know how to turn this off." Matt pressed a button and pocketed the thing with an amused look on his face.

"Interview, huh?" He motioned toward the ticket booth for the natural history section of the museum.

"For an art thing."

"What kind of an art thing?"

"School, and maybe an internship." We passed the area sectioned off for eating. The aroma of french fries emanated from the cafeteria-style counter.

"That sounds promising."

"I have to create something that shows absolute truth."

"Jesus, no pressure."

"Right? I wasn't even sure what he meant until I walked into the rotunda."

"Well, lookee there. I'm a regular muse!" Matt joked.

There wasn't a line for tickets, and we both grabbed for our wallets. We each paid and meandered toward Dinosaur Hall. Away from the noise of the dome, the hall was hushed. People lowered their voices and slowed their strides. Complete models of the terrible lizards, with their armored plates and strange beaks, lurked around the corners.

"I always wondered how they chose the colors for these models," I said as we stopped in front of *Ankylosaurus*.

"Probably based on modern lizards."

"God, you're right." The thought had, literally, never occurred to me. I experienced my own little-big boom inside my head over life's interconnectivity. It sparked.

"You got a pen?" I asked.

"No, I don't think so." Matt patted his back pockets, coming up empty.

"Shoot."

"What is it?"

"An idea, or like the beginnings of one."

"Did you just figure out the meaning of life for your art project?"

"Something like that." My fingers itched to put the glimmer of an idea on paper before whatever had been sparked left me forever. Brochures for the exhibit were stacked on a table near the restrooms, and I grabbed one, hoping for a picture of *Ankylosaurus*. If I could associate the picture with that feeling, maybe I could piece together the track my brain had started putting together when Matt said what he did. I ripped along the edges of the brochure and tucked the picture of the dinosaur into my wallet.

"That'll have to do." I blew out a sigh.

"You're cute when you're inspired." Matt bumped into me with his shoulder in a jokey way, his hands in his pockets.

"Thanks?" I shoved back. My ears burned with the attention.

This section of the museum was lined with rock faces, revealing fossilized skulls and imprints of fern fronds. One of the highlights was the *Allosaurus*, which was twenty feet long, and from a non-paleontologist point of view, really similar to a *T. rex*. The bones were umber and shined under the spotlights. The kid next to me pressed his face against the glass surrounding the once ferocious beast. After a while, he puffed out his cheeks, mimicking a suckerfish in an aquarium. Matt and I walked once the kid's mom started scolding him for putting his mouth on everything.

"These are my favorite." Matt stopped in front of the cases of bones not fit together. They were creamier, rougher. He clasped his hands behind his back and bent over the fragments.

"Really? Most people go for the awe-factor of the whole skeletons."

"Oh, those are awesome! Very obvious though. These..." He ran his fingers along the wooden frame of the case. "...are still a puzzle with most of the parts missing."

I looked over the disjointed pieces. I couldn't make out where things fit. The bones were so huge, what I imagined as a femur could have been a humerus. And those were the only two bone names I could remember. A collection of six smaller bones set together could have been a hand. Or paw?

"What are dinosaur hands and feet called?" I asked.

"Manus in the front, pes in the back."

The clear love for this stuff brightened Matt's eyes. They danced over everything in the room.

"Oh, I get it," I offered, following Matt to the next length of casing. "This is what you want to change your major to, right?"

"I don't want to be an archeologist if that's what you mean."

Too bad. I found it very easy to picture Matt in an Indiana Jones–like setting.

"I'm thinking more along the lines of museum curator," Matt said. He walked over to a plastic spiral wishing well and dropped a coin into its funnel vortex.

"So, what would it take?" I searched my pockets for my own coin.

Matt licked his lips, not taking his eyes off the spinning coin until it dropped with a *clink* into the collection box. "I don't know. An extra year or two. Dad says no way. He thinks I should finish what I started."

"That's logical."

"But it's not my passion. I mean, it used to be my passion. I love buildings, but I don't know if I can do it my whole life."

"Yeah, but you haven't even tried. And flunking out certainly won't get you closer to a curator position."

Matt blew out an exasperated sigh. "So, you think I should do what my dad says?"

It was weird giving anyone advice that could potentially influence the rest of his or her life. Especially Matt—we'd only hung out twice. I scratched my head. "What year are you again?"

"Second year. Finishing up all the general ed classes by the end of this year."

"Meh, you could go either way."

Matt huffed. "Thanks for the sage guidance."

"Weigh it out, man." I shrugged and dropped my own coin into the vortex. "If your dad won't help you, then the curator road will be harder, but not impossible. Either way, it's only a choice. Stop being an ass over it."

"Jeez, don't beat around the bush much, do ya?"

"Not anymore, I guess."

"Well, if that's the case, then I think we should talk about that kiss." Matt stepped closer, brushing against me. I straightened and scanned the room. People were distracted, either by their wild kids or the skeletal beasts on display.

"Not here," I whispered, my voice thick and syrupy. My heart beat wildly. And for some stupid reason, I kept envisioning a cartoon bunny thumping its leg.

Matt's eyes were more than just blue. Up this close, they were the kind of blue that lends electricity to a summer sky. In a barely-there gesture, he tilted his head toward the exit and walked away. I let a little time pass before following him past all the displays, back to the rotunda, and out the front door.

The temperature had dropped while we were exploring the museum. A cold wind whooshed over my skin. Matt checked over his shoulder to see if I was still there, and we jogged down the stairs to the parking lot. We both got in after he unlocked the doors, and out of the corner of my eye, I could see him fiddling with the keys. I stared out the window at the van parked in front of us, a discolored D.A.R.E. sticker peeling off its bumper. Matt's breath was as erratic as mine. Finally, he tossed the keys on the dash, and we crashed into each other. There was grabbing and pulling and biting, and all I knew in that one moment was how I wanted every part of him mixed together with every part of me. If I kissed him hard enough, it would happen; we'd blend. Stars flashed, universes collided, all the clichés happened.

Chapter Twenty-Seven

WE SEPARATED AMID an audience of fogged glass. Rain spattered the windshield and pattered against the metal of the car. My whole body burned. If not for the roof, the downpour would have sizzled against my skin.

"Damn, Jeremy. I wasn't expecting that." Matt sat back in the driver's seat. He smoothed the legs of his jeans.

"Me neither." I rolled down the window and let the fresh wet air hit my face. "I didn't call you...for this." We'd toppled the cigarette butt mound and now they were littered over my seat and the floor. I brushed ash from my shirt.

"I'm sure." Matt lit a cigarette and blew smoke rings around the car. He winked at me. "These things just happen, right?"

"Actually, no." Incidents like this never happened to me. I could count on one hand the number of kisses I'd partaken in. Full-on gropey make-out sessions had stood firmly at zero until that afternoon.

"Want one?"

"Sure."

Matt selected a smoke from the pack. "Oh, the lucky one."

"What?" I put the cigarette to my lips.

"Nothing, it's dumb." Matt leaned in to light it for me.

I dragged in a breath, as he steadied the flame. "Tell me," I coughed.

"After you pack the cigarettes—" Matt grabbed a new pack from the glove box and tapped them against his palm. He unwound the cellophane strip and ripped away the foil. "You flick the bottom, like this." *Snap!* "And the one that shoots up the highest is the lucky cigarette. You turn it upside down and save it for last."

"That *is* dumb," I said, laughing. "It's like a reward for finishing each pack. I bet cigarette companies came up with it."

Matt shrugged, his head cocked to the one raised shoulder. "People search for good fortune everywhere. Take it where you can find it."

I thought of all the people I knew best. They all had their own good luck rituals. Every time Kasey saw a penny, heads up, she'd snatch it. Mom kept an upright horseshoe nailed above our front door. If Stuart saw a bright red cardinal, he'd swear his day would end up better than it started.

"I don't have one," I said.

"What?"

"A lucky thing, or habit. I don't have one."

"Maybe it's your hair. You know, like Samson."

The smoke swirling around inside the car caught in my laughing throat, which turned into a coughing fit. I wiped my eyes and cranked my window down farther. "You, literally, just damned me to a lifetime with this haircut."

"How do ya figure?"

"Samson and Delilah. I can't ever cut it now."

"Oh shit!" There was that super loud barking laugh again. "You're right; you can't." Matt stubbed out his cigarette. "Where to next?"

I blew the last of my smoke out the window and scrunched the butt into the overflowing ashtray. "I should probably head home."

"Ah, okay." Matt's jaw twitched. He started up the car.

I was afraid he thought I was bailing on him—on whatever this was. "I need to let my mom know how things went today."

"No problem." He shifted the car into reverse, then checked his mirrors and over both shoulders. He wouldn't look at me, and instead, turned on the wipers to clear the collected rain blurring the view out the windshield. They did the job and then screeched against the dry surface. He put them on low and asked, "Where are you parked?"

I gave him the address of the garage, and we drove the rest of the way in silence. We should have been talking— pretty soon, he'd pull over, and there would be a rushed goodbye to avoid holding up traffic. We'd leave things awkward. I didn't know what to say though. I liked Matt, a lot. He was funny and direct. There were no games. He was into me, and with that make-out session in the books, I shared his feelings.

As expected, Matt parked next to the curb. He turned his hazard lights on and looked at me.

"I'll call you?" Bravo, Warsh. Make it sound like a question.

Matt rolled his eyes and looked away. His upper teeth scratched over the surface of his lower lip. It highlighted the sharpness of his jawline.

"I mean it." I leaned forward, trying to catch those bright eyes one more time before I ran into the rain.

"We'll see." Matt gripped the steering wheel. He wanted definitive answers, but I had too many questions.

"Today was fun," I said.

"Catch you later, Samson." A car honked as it drove by, splashing a wave of water over the driver's side. "You better go."

I grabbed the front of his shirt. I made him see me, and then I kissed him. Slower than before—not a beer-buzzed accident like the first time, or a searing crash, like the second—a regular slow burn of a kiss.

"Has anyone ever told you, you look like Daredevil?"

"My whole life, no one has ever said that to me, Jeremy."

"Well, it's true. Look it up." I popped the car door open. "In the first comic, the reader sees Matt-slash-Daredevil without dark glasses, before the accident. And his eyes are the same color as yours."

"Where would I even find a copy?"

"I have one." I stood, bent over on the curb, leaning on the door. Cars honked and splashed through the wet streets. "I better go. I *will* call you."

Matt leaned over the console, smiling up at me. "All right then. We'll talk soon." He bit his lower lip as I reluctantly closed the door. I watched him drive off, red taillights flashing his destination back out onto the road. The sidewalks were less crowded than before, but people carried umbrellas now, and here and there, I got poked as they shuffled past me.

Scenes from the day flashed through my head the whole drive home. Matt's too-orange hair, his smile, his laugh, his Daredevil eyes, the highway of veins on the backs of his hands. Then came the labels, flashing neon thoughts. Gay. Fag. Nelly. Queer. Bi? I'd spent years convinced I wanted Kasey. Had I been fooling myself all along? Was she my cover? A safety net constructed of curvy lines and just enough emotional distance?

I pulled into my apartment complex and sat, staring at the woods. Mom would be desperate to talk about art school, but that seemed a million miles away. She'd know something was up. I couldn't hide it from her. My chest tightened, and I rubbed circles around the spot where my heart should be. I was vaguely nervous I was having a heart attack. A knock on my window sent me into V-fib, and I didn't even know what that meant.

Ms. V stood outside the car, the hood of a navy-and-white polka-dotted rain slicker pulled down over her forehead. I collected myself, ran my hands over my hair—making sure I wasn't crying—and rolled down the window.

"Hiya! Ms. V!" I was screaming at her. She took a step back from the car. "What are you doing out in the rain?!" Still shouting.

Ms. V's eyes narrowed, and she turned her reddened arthritic palms toward the sky. "It stopped a while ago, and there's nothing like after-storm air."

"I agree!" I could not get the correct messages from my brain to my vocal cords.

"Are you okay, dear?" She folded her fingers over the window's edge. Her nails were freshly painted red. "Oh, your interview was today!" She noted my portfolio in the passenger seat. "How did it go? That must be why it sounded like a herd of elephants were traipsing over my ceiling this morning."

"Mom paces when she's nervous." The distraction of Ms. V's everyday prattle took me further from what had happened with Matt. I was back to my little life in Frog's Landing. Here, people chitchatted in parking lots, instead of making out.

"What are you sitting out here for? Go tell her. Don't keep your poor mother in suspense, boy!"

"You're right." I turned off the ignition. Ms. V backed away as I opened my car door. I slammed it shut, then reopened it, pressed the locking mechanism down, and turned back toward the building.

"You sure are antsy." Ms. V took my arm at the elbow, and I walked her back to her place. Her hesitant steps helped me slow down. Along the way, she gossiped her suspicions regarding another neighbor harboring animals.

"I'm telling you I can hear them mewing away at all hours of the night. I have half a mind to report it to the landlord. But then, I don't want to make anyone homeless over a couple of cats. I'll never understand why people can't follow the rules."

"They probably didn't see it in the lease."

"Jeremy, it's right there in black-and-white!"

"Lots of things fall into gray areas, Ms. V."

"No shit, Sherlock. But I'm not talking about lots of things. I'm talking about this thing." At her front door, she fumbled with her key ring. The set jangled as they hit the pavement. "Oh, darn!"

"Here, let me." I picked them up and unlocked her door. A wave of flowery old lady perfume attacked my nostrils, and I tried not to sneeze, pinching my nose shut. "Did you spill something?"

Ms. V strolled in, flipping on her lights. "Of course not. I always give myself a little spritz before I meet my public."

"Do you need anything?" I helped her out of her raincoat and hung it on the coatrack.

"You're such a dear. I shouldn't keep you from your mama, but would you please pour me a glass of iced tea? The pitcher's in the fridge." Ms. V settled into her favorite chair, fanning herself with the *TV Guide*.

"Sure thing."

The refrigerator was visible from the living room. What was once shiny and bare was now covered with pictures of Jackie. In most of them, she was smiling, posing in front of various locations. In others, Jackie was looking away. The camera had captured the back of her head in one photo as she watched the sun setting over a shining orange and gray ocean. Another showed Jackie's profile, her long neck exposed as she looked to the heights of silver and turquoise skyscrapers.

"Been doing some redecorating?"

Ms. V giggled from her chair. "I was a fool not to be looking at that beautiful soul all these years."

I found the pitcher and poured her a glass of tea.

"Thank you, Jeremy." Ms. V took the cold glass from me. "Look what I found." She handed me a tattered envelope from the top of the stack on her side table.

"What's this?" The paper had yellowed over time, along with the blurred inky loops of someone's handwriting.

"An old address for Jackie's partner, Jean!"

"You think she still lives there?"

"I intend to find out."

"Good for you." I sat on the edge of the chair next to her. "Are you going to write to her?"

"That's my plan. I'm going to introduce myself and invite her out to lunch." Ms. V sniffed and wiped her upper lip with a crumpled tissue she usually kept in her sleeve. "Do you think she'll like the Olive Garden?"

"You can't go wrong with free breadsticks, Ms. V. What made you decide to do this now?"

"I want more of my daughter."

We both gave that sentence the moment of silence it deserved before Ms. V asked, "Now, I know it's not fair to your mother, but can you give me a hint. Wink if your interview went okay."

I indulged her with an overexaggerated wink.

"Aha! I knew it!" Ms. V slapped her knee. "Go, now! Go tell her."

I got up to leave.

"Oh, hand me the clicker before you go. I'm feeling a little dizzy."

"You need to take it easy, Ms. V." I checked the coffee table, but so many magazines littered it that I didn't see the television remote.

"It's behind you."

It must have gotten smashed between the cushion and the seat back when I sat down. I ran my fingers along the cushion's edge and pried it out. "Here you go." I held out the remote for her, but she didn't take it.

"Ms. V?" Her head tipped back against her chair and her mouth was slack. "Ms. V?" I gently shook her shoulder, but her head lolled to the side. "Damn it! No, please, wake up!"

A lump in my throat grew till I thought I might gag. I dropped the remote and ran to her kitchen phone and dialed 9-1-1. The responder fired off a load of questions, to which I answered as quickly as she asked them. The lady had a smooth even tone and wanted to keep me on the phone.

"I gotta go. I gotta go get my mom." I banged the receiver down so hard the base rang out. I raced up the stairs and pounded on our door.

"What the—" Mom's voice came through the door before she opened it. "Jeremy, what is it? You're crying, hon."

"Come with—" Panic closed off my voice. I grabbed her wrist and dragged her downstairs. Ms. V's apartment door was wide open. Mom walked in and immediately rushed to the elderly woman's side.

"Olivia?" she whispered. Mom took Ms. V's wrist in her hands and placed two fingers where a pulse should be.

In the distance, sirens rang out. Ambulance doors slammed. Two paramedics dressed in dark blue uniforms pushed past me and assessed the situation. Ms.V's mint-green tracksuit swished as they lowered her out of her chair. They placed my old friend on a stretcher. Mom stood next to me, her arms wrapped around my waist as the paramedics extended the gurney's legs with a clicking *clank* and rolled Ms. V from her home.

Mom followed them. I turned to leave, but a glitter in the carpet caught my eye. I knew what it was before I reached for it. Crouching on the floor, I picked up the ruby-and-diamond barrette. The stones gleamed as if nothing had happened, as if their owner wasn't fighting for her life in the back of some rig. I closed my fingers around them. I'd hold them for her.

Chapter Twenty-Eight

BIRDS CHIRPED FROM the tree out front, a couple of them dive-bombing all of the poor worms washed up from the afternoon storms. I squeezed Ms. V's barrette hard enough to make a mark in my hand. The pressure kept me there, kept me from disappearing too.

"What hospital?" Mom blurted out.

The paramedic slammed the ambulance doors. "Mercy." He gave the rig door two knocks. His partner, sitting next to the crumpled version of Ms. V, gave a thumbs-up sign. Did that mean she'd be okay? Or were they signaling the all clear for takeoff?

"Thank you, sir."

"No problem, ma'am."

Mom rushed back up the stairs to our apartment. Seconds later, she hurried down with her purse slung over her shoulder. Michael pounded down after her, his shoelaces still untied. I sat on the bench lining the sidewalk.

"Let me drive," he offered.

"I got it," she said.

"Connie, you're upset." Michael touched Mom's shoulder, and she froze. He moved in front of her, both hands on her shoulders, hunching to make eye contact. "She's your friend. Let me help."

Mom blinked as if she were waking up. She gripped Michael's forearms and nodded. He took the keys and looked to me.

"Coming?" Mom asked.

I didn't want to go. I hated hospitals. Time froze in all those waiting rooms. "No, I wanna stay home."

Mom bent over and wrapped her hand around my neck. She brought her forehead against mine. Her eyes were the safest brown, a mix of walnut with flecks of burnt sienna. "You did good, Jeremy. You did everything you could."

I nodded, and she walked away holding hands with Michael.

"We'll call you!" she yelled over her shoulder.

After they drove off, I checked the barrette. Shadow shapes of the stones had formed in my hand. Everything continued around me. The traffic light hummed from the corner. Chittering squirrels raced in spiral patters around the tree trunk. Gusts of wind brushed through hardening fall leaves. A stray cat tiptoed along the cement path, its steps weary and cautious. It stopped and lifted its orange-and-white back leg high in the air for an impromptu licking. Near the bushes sat a metal bowl heaped with brown bits of cat food. I'd have to let Ms. V know, before she called the landlord, that our neighbor was just feeding strays. I plodded up the stairs and into our apartment.

The microwave beeped its finish. I pressed a button, and a bag of buttery smelling popcorn greeted me. The TV was still on. A striped football field flashed across the screen. The camera panned over cheering faces and vibrating pom-poms. Brassy band sounds filled our apartment. I found the remote and clicked it off. Then I sank into the couch's cushiony forgiveness.

Ms. V's barrette was still in my hand along with our remote. *It's behind you.* Those were her last words to me. Maybe to anyone. *It's behind you.* Out of context, they had a profound ring to them.

She'd been fine. How was a person okay one minute, and snatched away, stolen, pocketed by life's biggest mystery, the next? Grandpa had gone in a similar way. He didn't wake up one morning. The doctors said his heart gave out in the night. I hated when people said that, "gave out." It made me think of car parts, or major kitchen appliances, rather than a person.

I clenched my teeth, and my breath came hard through my nose. My fingers involuntarily rounded into fists, ready for punching. My toes twitched for a run. I should cry. But I couldn't do anything. I was helpless here in my apartment, at the hospital, at school, working on my art. It made no difference where I was; the only truth was that I was totally out of control.

I melted into the fabric of the couch, succumbed to liquefying, my legs curled into a fetal position. I pictured myself as a kid, crying so hard that, after a while, grief subsided into hiccupping gasps. What had happened to that kid, whose feelings were right there, readily available for processing? Then came waves of exhaustion. My eyelids too heavy for lifting, I crashed.

"JEREMY?" MOM'S VOICE was little more than a whisper. She gently shook my shoulder.

I came awake with a gasp, spit trailing my cheek. I wiped it away and rolled onto my back, bringing my forearm over my eyes. "How is she?"

"She's gone, hon. The doctors suspect it was a massive stroke."

Sunlight filtered through the blinds, framing Mom in an array of tangerine hues. I rubbed sleep from the corners of my eyes. "What time is it?"

"Not that late. She was gone before we got to the hospital. They pronounced time of death as almost immediate." Mom swiped under her eyes. Dark smudges of mascara came off on her fingers. "God." She wiped them clean on her jeans. "Hungry?"

"I could eat." My stomach growled. Amid everything that happened today, my body still needed the routine of life.

Mom got up. The freezer's suction seal broke with a *schwuck*. It hummed as she rummaged through the crinkling packages. "Nuggets and fries okay?" Before I could answer, the oven beeped as she cranked up the heat. "Do you know if Olivia had any family?"

"She only talked about Jackie with me." I sat up and rested my chin on the back of the couch.

"Jackie?"

"Her daughter. She died in a car accident a long time ago."

Mom shook her head. "I didn't know she had a daughter. Her husband passed years ago. I don't think there's anyone to make arrangements for her. The hospital asked me before I left."

"Did she have any siblings?"

Mom dumped frozen fries and nuggets on a cookie sheet. Her shoulders arched up toward her ears. "I'll go through some of her things tomorrow and see what I can find." She popped the pan into the oven, and turned around, crossing her arms. Her brows were wrinkled with concern.

"Did Michael go home?" I asked.

"I dropped him off after we left the hospital." Mom stared at the linoleum floor. She massaged the flabby part of her arms, a deep-thinking tic of hers. "I suppose if there's no one to plan for the funeral, I'll have to do it."

"I bet Ms. V has it all set up."

The last funeral Mom planned was Grandpa's. Between the money, endless decisions, and the unshakable impression it was all a hustle, she came away resentful on top of her own sadness. Funeral planning was like the whipped cream and sprinkles on top of a heaping scoop of grief-flavored ice cream. The worst sundae in the world.

Mom pinched the bridge of her nose, her eyes closed with the pressure. "Jeremy!" Her eyes popped open. "How was your interview?!" She slapped her hands on her thighs.

I laughed because it seemed infinitesimal in the span of what had happened throughout the afternoon. "It was fine."

"More. Details." Mom reached for two glasses and filled them up with tap water.

"Mr. Wyatt seems kind of out there. But he offered me an internship and his recommendation if I can pull a piece together in the next few weeks." I came around the couch and sat at the kitchen table.

"What you had wasn't enough?"

"It's hard to explain. He looked at my stuff." I took the glass of water she offered and took a sip. "He thinks, or implied, it's too influenced by others. Like, it's not truly me, or something."

"Well, you can handle that."

"It has to represent my truth."

"That sounds lofty."

"That's art."

"What are you gonna make?"

"I have no idea."

The oven beeped again, announcing its preheating conclusion. Mom never waited for the alarm to put the food in. She said it was a waste of time.

I played with Ms. V's barrette, popping the clasp open with my thumbnail.

"What are you fiddling with?"

"I found it on the floor as the paramedics were taking her out." I held up the hair clip. "Figured I'd hold onto it for her until she..." I let my voice trail off. She wasn't coming back. "Do you have anything like this? Like, a charm?"

"A charm?"

"That's how I thought of Ms. V's barrette. She wore it every day. I figured she must have thought it brought her luck or something."

Mom tested the nuggets in the stove, pressing them with a hesitant touch. "Not crisp enough. Few more minutes." She turned around, licking crumbs from her finger. "I don't have anything I wear every single day. There's the horseshoe. I found that at a yard sale in my twenties. And, oh my gosh! I can't believe I haven't shown you this before. Hold on." Mom hurried to her room and came back with her saddlebag of a purse. Her arm disappeared inside as she rifled through her things.

"Aha!" She banged a rock on the table. "This. This is mine."

It looked like an ordinary gray rock pocked with miniature craters. One such dip was actually a hole bored from end to end. I instinctively held it up to my eye and peered through.

"It's called a hag stone. There's all kinds of folklore surrounding them. It's said they have healing powers, provide focus, or, when you hold it up to your eye like that, you can see into the fairy realm."

All I saw was the kitchen sink littered with dishes and damp hand towels. Still, it was a cool rock. I'd never seen one like it. "Where'd you find this?"

Mom's cheeks flushed. "Oregon coast. It was before you or your dad." She sat and rested her chin in her hand, staring into the invisible space of remembering. "I was so young. One morning, I woke up with an idea in my head; I needed to see the Pacific Ocean. I saved my money and bought a bus ticket. Rode out there all by myself." Mom snorted. "Didn't plan a thing. When I made it to the beach, I found the hag stone in the sand. I tucked it in my purse and kept it ever since."

The tip of my finger fit into each depression. The rock felt coarse, somehow sandy, its surface still reminiscent of the place it came from. Even tiny grains of sand had made their imprint. I placed the hag stone at the center of the table. "It's really cool, Mom."

"Your grandpa was furious." She took the rock and tucked it back into her purse. Her mouth tightened, visibly trying not to smile at her own insolence.

"I can imagine."

"I don't regret it though. Oh crap! I better get the food out before it burns." Mom jumped up. Luckily, nothing was charred or smoking. The food was crunchier than usual, but I didn't mind.

I WAS SCHEDULED for work in the morning, but I knew it would be a late night. I'd taken a nap for Pete's sake. I hated naps. Overall, they were a nuisance, messing with your entire routine.

The girls were set to pick up the last Penny cartoon and make final copies tomorrow. I sat at my desk to finish the last scene; it only needed coloring. Penny, herself, was still wildly upset about being cast as a zombie.

I HATE THIS.

"I am aware of your feelings."

I decided against an evening gown for Penny's homecoming dance. She wasn't the type. Instead, I fashioned her after a girl I'd seen at a punk show who wore a short red-and-black patterned kilt, complete with a giant safety pin and sporran. Her top half was covered in a tight black high-necked shirt with long sleeves.

THIS IS CUTE THOUGH.

"I saw a girl wearing it at a concert once. Would you like Doc Martens or heels?"

HEELS.

"Really?"

IT IS A FORMAL EVENT.

"Whatever you say, boss?"

DON'T BE A DICK. I'M NOT THE BOSS, AND YOU KNOW IT.

"What would you have me do here?" I set down my colored pencil to listen.

Penny crossed her arms and pouted. When she didn't respond, I colored gray tights and black Mary Janes over her bottom half. Her hair stayed down, wavy and naturally swooping over one eye. I gave her exposed skin a once-over with a hint of chartreuse. Tears welled up along the bottom edges of her eyelids.

"We've been over this. It's the last one, okay? We have to get the homecoming planning committee to choose a zombie theme. That's the whole point of you."

YOU'RE EXPLAINING THE REASON FOR MY EXISTENCE TO ME NOW?

I let out a sigh and colored in the rest of Penny's classmates around her. A girl in the background had a long red dress on, with a slit up the side, and matching lipstick. She clung to her date, who was in a pale blue tuxedo. The pair was frozen mid-celebration, his gaze stapled on the girl's ample cleavage, her face upturned toward the glittering disco ball. What showed of their skin shined with the same green as Penny's. Around the odd couple, the rest of the students contorted into odd dance poses. Arms up, elbows out, hips popped. I threw in some wounds for good measure. We couldn't all be the fresh-faced zombie youth of tomorrow.

"Can you look like you're having fun?"

DIDN'T YOU EVER LEARN NOT TO TELL A GIRL WHEN TO SMILE? Penny leaned toward the page's surface, the arch of her eyebrows raised high on her forehead and a massive crazed smile plastered across her face.

"Tone it down, will ya?"

WHAT HAPPENS TO ME WHEN THIS IS ALL OVER, JEREMY?

"The story ends. It doesn't matter."

IT MATTERS, YOU DOLT.

I put finishing touches on the gymnasium decorations. White and green streamers hung from the rafters, and music notes dotted the air.

AHEM. Penny cleared her throat. *AND I QUOTE— WE'RE SENIORS, ABOUT TO BE UNLEASHED INTO A WORLD OF ADULTS, ALL OF THEM MARCHING TO THE SAME BEAT, NONE OF THEM STEPPING OUT AGAINST THE GRAIN.*

"That was a conversation between Stu and me when this was only a fledgling idea. So what?"

SO WHAT! IF THE POINT WAS TO SHOW PEOPLE HOW TO BE THEMSELVES IN A SEA OF SAMENESS, THEN

I SHOULDN'T CHANGE. I ALREADY AM WHO I'M SUPPOSED TO BE. I ALL I HAVE TO DO IS TAKE OFF THIS MASK. Penny took her forefinger and scratched a line across her cheek. Underneath the sickly yellow-green color was her original self. *I SHOULD ALWAYS GET TO BE ME.*

I tapped my pencil against the drawing. We'd lost some of the prank's original meaning in translation. Originally, it was supposed to be a giant *screw you* to adulthood and the system churning us out. The zombie theme was our way of saying...what? I couldn't remember. Instead, the thing had quickly morphed into *let's see if we can get all these people to follow our lead.*

"I see what you're saying, Penny."

I smudged the zombie-green color back over the scratch on her cheek. A new idea sparked in my head—a protostar still gathering mass. All I needed to do was wait, let my brain do the heavy lifting. I packed away my utensils.

WAIT, I'M SUPPOSED TO GO OUT MONDAY! Penny held up her arms—a mime frozen in a transparent box.

"I can't change that part. It might not be your ending though."

I pulled the chain to my desk lamp.

Chapter Twenty-Nine

IN THE COMFORT of my bed, I crisscrossed my arms behind my head, and whatever remained of Pure Sport deodorant wafted around. I was mildly surprised I didn't reek after the long list of today's events. I stared up at the ceiling: white layers of popcorn texture blurred the borders of the brown water stain. Penny, Ms. V, Matt... Phantom words and expressions floated over me—a drizzling of sound bites and dreamy imaging.

My phone was right there on the bedside table. Mom had given it to me as a present for my fourteenth birthday, and Grandpa paid for the installation. The only person I'd ever needed privacy to call was Kasey, until now. For the first time, I dialed numbers without thinking through every word I might say. With each ring, I swallowed more anxiety. Oddly enough, it tasted like ketchup. There was a pause; the next ring didn't come. I heard his yuk-yuk of a laugh and then, "Yep, hello."

"Hey, it's me."

"Me who?"

"Jeremy."

"Hi there! Hold on a sec." The handset swished against fabric, I thought. "There's a bunch of people in my dorm room, so I moved to the hallway. I can't get you out of my head."

"Yeah?"

"Definitely."

"My neighbor died today."

"Oh shit." There was a clicking sound and a deep inhale. I pictured his long body propped up against a cinder block wall. "Did you know them?"

"We were close." I saw smoke encircling his bright orange hair. What was that thing Gramps used to say? Oh yeah, "smoke follows beauty." I foraged around in the side table drawer, knowing Stuart always stashed cigarettes back there. I didn't enjoy the act of smoking every day, per se, except I liked how it kept my hands and mouth busy. "I mean, she was old so..." I felt a deflated soft pack at the back of the drawer, but it was empty. The cellophane crackled in my fist as I tossed it toward the wastepaper basket. "I was with her though."

"Jesus, when she died?" His eyebrows would have risen, blue eyes lit with concern.

"It was weird." I lay back on my pillow and rubbed my forehead. Closing my eyes, I pretended Matt was in my room. I put him sitting next to me on the bed. He'd flick ash into an almost empty pop can, and every now and then, there'd be a sizzling.

"Tell me."

"We were just talking. Her daughter, my interview. She asked me for the remote, and when I turned around to hand it to her, she was gone." I closed my eyes and let tears run. I didn't want him to hear me crying.

"Are you okay?"

"I think so," I said, my voice heavy with sadness.

"When's the funeral?"

"I don't know yet."

"I can come with you, if you want."

"Okay." Everything was confusing, except for Matt. I wanted him with me. I could see our fingers interlaced through whatever ceremony my mom planned. The same steady feeling I had in the car with him, minus the raging hard-on, flooded my chest "I should let you get back to your friends."

"They're fine without me." Matt lit up another cigarette, mumbling, "What up" to somebody. I heard a clapping sound and imagined him high-fiving the person as they walked past.

A couple seconds passed without either of us saying anything. Even though we were miles apart, our breath magically mixed together through cords and wires.

"Do you want to keep talking about your neighbor?" he asked.

"Not really."

"All right, then. Tell me something else."

I told him the rest of Mr. Wyatt's internship requirements and how the search for a truth that had to be wrangled onto paper seemed impossible. The conversation meandered to talk of Penny and how the prank wasn't one hundred percent because the overall message seemed off. That lead me telling how Russ Landry was taking credit for my work at school.

Matt listened. He interjected at all the right times with a "shut the fuck up!" or an "oh my gawd!" Sometimes, he snorted at my jokes. I'd wound myself up in all these happenings, but gradually, the coil loosened, and I started getting sleepy.

"Roadblocks, man. Are they going to stop you?"

At the moment, things seemed insurmountable, but I wasn't going to walk away from anything. I loved it all too much. "No. I'll figure out a way to work through it."

"Good."

"Might not be pretty though."

"Then it will be interesting."

Eventually, I conked out. The next thing I knew, the phone was beeping incessantly near my pillow. I hung it up. My neck was stiff, probably from falling asleep with the handset nestled between my shoulder and ear. I kicked my shoes off and turned onto my side, facing the window. It was still dark outside. I rubbed sleep out of my eyes and wondered about Ms. V. Was her new sky black and blue? I hoped Jackie was with her to show her around. She could start a Richard Simmons class there too. I bet the bodiless still enjoyed dancing...

THE FOLLOWING DAYS were a whirlwind of work, funeral stuff, and school. It turned out Ms. V had no family members left alive. She'd prepared everything in advance though. Mom set it all in motion with a few phone calls, and we prepped for a Wednesday ceremony.

"What do you mean you can't make it? Wednesday is the homecoming meeting after school," Des whined.

We were at lunch in the cafeteria. The last Penny comic had gone out that morning. Des and Dani stuffed them through locker slats during first period. Around us, kids were pouring over their copies while they ate. Indifferent others tossed them in the trash along with their lunch trays.

Sitting opposite me were Dani, Stuart, and Des. Stuart and Des still appeared together, waiting for each other after class and holding hands in the hallway. But things had chilled noticeably since the date at the movie theater two months ago. I wasn't sure if it was the natural cooling that occurred after you made out with someone a certain number of times, or if Stuart had screwed up. Either way, he wasn't discussing it.

"Somebody died, Des." Dani nudged her sister. "He can't really help it."

"We wouldn't have gone anyway," Stuart chimed in.

"What? Why not? This was all your idea!" Des crossed her arms. "That's so typical. You don't want to see this through to the end."

"I am seeing it through." Stuart crunched into a taco, shredded lettuce and cheese sprinkling over his tray. He swallowed and said, "It would be more obvious if Warsh and I showed up at one of those things. Everyone in school knows we would never be part of a planning committee."

"Listen to the man." I reached up for a high five. Stuart obliged.

"But..." Dani leaned over the table and whispered, "People believe Russ did this." She picked up a corner of the comic. "Don't you want credit for your work?"

"It doesn't matter," I lied. It pissed me off Russ got the praise for Penny. No one had ever seen him draw anything except dicks on classroom whiteboards. But in the end, it was the real punishment for trashing the bumper of his car. He'd steered clear of me since the punch, though, so, it kind of had the feel of a stalemate. "Besides, it may even help the cause."

"How?" Des asked.

"He'll be there Wednesday, right? Isn't the float usually built at his house?"

"No, not his house. It's always at an ag kid's barn. But you're right, he always heads up the construction portion of our class's float entry."

"Since everyone thinks Penny was his idea, maybe he'll come armed with a certain dance theme as well." I polished off the last of my chocolate milk.

"With nary a Warsh-man nor a Stu-meat present. Nice!" Stuart and I fist-bumped.

"So, the whole thing rides on Russ Landry connecting some dots." Dani wiped the corners of her mouth with a napkin. "It's risky."

"You can help him see the way, babe." Stuart put his arm around Des, who shot him an annoyed look.

"Have any of you spoken with Kasey?" Dani asked. "She's been absent since last Friday."

"I can call her tonight if you want," I said.

Lately, Kasey reminded me of Bern and his orchids. He always kept a selection of these delicate orchids near the front door of the grocery store. They weren't really a quick ticket item, so every now and then, all the flower petals would fall off of one. In appearance only, the plant was dying. Bern said it was part of their life cycle, so he'd leave them in the back room, taking care of them until they bloomed again. Anyway, that was what being around Kasey made me think of—wilting flowers.

Meanwhile, my heart felt near ready to burst out of my chest—a sunrise of the bloodiest order. Matt and I had talked for hours on the phone for the past two nights. I hated that our second date would be at a funeral, but the thought of seeing him again set everything on fizz.

"Will you, please?" Dani asked. "I went over yesterday because she was supposed to help with the comic, but her mom wouldn't let me in to see her. That house has a weird vibe."

"No problem."

WHEN I GOT home from school, Mom was still at work, so, I used the kitchen phone to call Matt. His roommate said he wasn't back from class and took a message for me. I peeled a banana, eating most of it before dialing Kasey's number. It rang once before Kasey's mom answered.

"Hey, is Kasey around? It's Jeremy."

"Oh, Jeremy. She's sick, honey. You'll have to call back another time."

"I have her homework. Should I drop it off?"

"No, that's okay. She'll get it later. Bye, now." She hung up. Red warning lights flashed inside my head. Mrs. Axton was usually impossible to get off the phone. She'd talk anyone's ears off.

I unzipped my backpack and took out Kasey's assignments. They were starting to stack up. She hadn't been at school Friday, missed Penny's print over the weekend, was absent again today, and no one had seen her. I tried not to jump to conclusions, although I wasn't quite sure where my brain could leap.

Keys rattled in the deadbolt.

"Hey, hon." Mom's shoulders sank as soon as she saw me. "What's wrong?"

"Probably nothing." I bit the inside of my cheek.

"If you're making that face, I'd guess otherwise."

"Could I drop you off at the gas station today? I think I need the car."

"That's fine. I'll have Michael pick me up after my shift." Mom took off her suit jacket and hung it over one of the kitchen chairs. "Is everything all right?"

"I don't know yet."

"Okay." She squeezed my shoulder as she walked past me. Through a yawn, she added, "Let me get changed." Her bedroom door closed, and hangers screeched along the metal bar in her closet as she searched for a clean uniform.

"Hungry?" she asked, coming out a few minutes later in a purple polo and black jeans, her hair contained in a bunny tail at the base of her neck. She scratched her eyebrow and yawned again.

"No." The banana peel landed on the edge of the trash can. I stretched back in my chair to urge the rest of it in with my pencil. "Sleepy?"

"I am."

"Is it the funeral planning?"

"Oh, I don't know. Most of that was already taken care of. I think I'm just tired of working so much."

"Maybe you won't have to soon."

"I don't know how that would be possible."

"I'll be moving out next fall. You and Michael seem pretty solid."

Mom waved her hands around as if swatting gnats. "We don't need to go there." She opened the freezer and took out a microwave dinner. "I've never been married, and at my age, I'm not looking for it." She packed her frozen meal for one in her purse.

"You don't have to be married to live together, Mom."

"Blasphemy. Come on, let's go. I don't want to be late. You can handle getting dinner together on your own, right?"

"Gee, I hope so."

"Switch me, smart ass." She tossed me her keys. I caught them with a jangling smack against my palm and handed her my set.

I didn't have a fully formed plan for approaching Kasey's house. Dani had said Mrs. Axton wouldn't let her in. Considering our brief phone conversation, I figured it would be the same for me. Mrs. Axton was the gatekeeper. So, I needed to skip the gate.

Kasey's rectangular bedroom windows were long and human height, totally accessible and perfect for a breakout. All she had to do was pop out a screen and step through. But it was only a little after four o'clock, barely evening, and if anyone happened by the main floor's deck, they'd spot me creeping across the lawn.

I parked at the bottom of the hill, where the columns of blue ash trees on Kasey's property started. I slipped my backpack over my shoulders and bounded over the drainage ditch. The ground, saturated with runoff, gave beneath my feet and mosquitos buzzed around my ears. It was chilly at night, but the first frost hadn't come and killed them all off yet.

"Enjoy your last supper, ladies."

The leaves were every variation of gold this time of year. Words like butterscotch and honey flitted around in my mind as I hiked up the hill. High above, limbs swayed in a rush of breeze, sending a drizzling burst of yellow leaves in a final descent.

The property wasn't as big as it felt when you were up at the house, surveying the land. I checked my watch. It had only taken seven minutes to walk through the woods, and I'd even meandered. Kasey's home, with its Tudor-style dark beams and creamy color, was in view from where I stood at the edge of the woods. I scanned the lower-level windows, but they were dark. The pool was closed for the season, and all the long sunbathing chairs had been packed away. The only furniture left was a glass table with two cushioned chairs near it. One chair was pulled away from the table, and someone was sitting in it. I could only see the back of a head, their feet seemingly pulled up into the chair's seat. The person gathered their hair and let it fall over the back of the chair. It had to be Kasey sitting out there alone.

"Hey!" I stage-whispered, but she didn't flinch. "Kase!" Then I fake-coughed.

She looked up and then over to where I stood. I waved—a big swooping two-armed please-see-me kind of wave. She closed her book and after a seemingly long pause, walked over. I expected her to come into the woods with me, but she stopped a few feet away from the tree line.

"Are you sick?" I asked. "I brought your homework." I slid the bag from one shoulder and swung it around in front of me.

"Don't." Kasey shook her head. She wasn't wearing any makeup. Underneath her signature trench, she was dressed in a sweatshirt and baggy jeans. I hadn't seen her look this plain since elementary school, back when we were all swinging from monkey bars and folding paper into fortune-tellers.

"What's going on?" I asked.

"They're keeping me home." She cleared the raspiness from her throat.

"Why?"

"I'm scheduled to see a counselor tomorrow. They think it'll fix me."

"Kasey, you're not broken."

Raw pink lined her eyes as she blinked away tears. "Ugh, I can't stop with this crying." She dragged her knuckles under her eyes and sniffed. "Will you be around later this week?"

"Ms. V's funeral is Wednesday, but other than that, I'm free."

"Can you stay near your phone?"

"Absolutely."

"Okay, see you later, Jeremy." Kasey turned away, stepping back toward the paved patio.

"Wait..." But I didn't have anything to offer except, "...you could stay with me?"

She squeezed the back of her neck. "It would be the first place my parents would think to look. And then your mom would be right in the middle of everything. That's not fair."

"I think my mom would see it differently if I told her what was going on."

"Thanks, but no thanks. I'll be okay. It's just a therapist, right? I can handle talking to a stranger for a few hours. I'll let you know how everything goes."

As she walked away, I rushed out from the woods, not caring if anyone saw me from the house, and wrapped my arms around her, hugging her close. She smelled of strawberry shampoo. Under her coat, her frame seemed thinner, not her usual warrior-girl self.

"Get outta here, you big lug." Her laughter sounded like wind chimes echoing over the property. I hadn't heard it in weeks.

"Nobody says lug anymore."

"In your case, it's an accurate description. Seriously, I'll be fine. I'll come to your place if I'm not." She turned around and held out her finger. "Pinky promise."

I wrapped mine around hers and hoped to hell she meant it.

Chapter Thirty

"HAVE YOU TOLD your mom about me?" Matt asked.

I liked Matt's phone voice. Every one of his vocal tics was spotlighted, carried through bundles of wire. His deeper tones crackled more, and sometimes, the slightest intake of breath echoed. It was Tuesday night. The funeral was tomorrow, and Matt planned on meeting me there. I'd been rambling on about trigonometry and how it would serve no purpose in my life when he asked this question out of the blue.

"Uh, no," I responded.

"I think you need to."

"Why?" I thought of Kasey and how weird things were at her house.

"I'm not trying to prod you out of the closet, Jeremy."

"Good, because I hate labels." I liked my Switzerland status. I didn't feel entirely one way or another. Most of the time, I could be counted on to waver around eighty-five percent on anything. So, what would be the purpose of making some declaration?

Matt continued, "If I'm going to show up at the funeral tomorrow, you need to tell your mom who I am. It's not fair to blindside her."

"My mom's cool."

"Take it from me. I've been through this before. Even the coolest parents might need some processing time."

"That's bullshit. I'm a person. Nothing needs to be sorted, it just IS."

"I think you should give her a heads-up."

I popped my knuckles, listening as Matt shared his experience with his parents. He'd hinted at his dad's reaction back on the night we met. I pictured my own dad, settled somewhere in California. Our dinner at the Chinese restaurant had been goodbye. But when Matt described his mom's crying, my stomach tied itself up. I told him I'd think on it and said good night.

I wanted Matt with me tomorrow, which meant that if I waited too long to tell Mom, we'd be having that talk over breakfast. But I didn't know what time Michael was supposed to show up, and I was not having that conversation with him around. So, that only left the present.

TV sounds bled through the walls—a late-night talk show with lots of canned laughter and applause mixed with blares from a big band. If I told her now, would she be able to sleep? If I told her at breakfast, would it make tomorrow that much worse? The questions were my form of procrastination. It was time. Mom could never be like the Axtons. Connie Warsh was the best mom. She would not abandon me.

The matted hallway carpet cushioned each step until I stood at the entrance to the split kitchen, dinette, and living room. Sitting on the couch, Mom popped the top on a canned drink, and it hissed as the comedian host completed his intro-bit in the background.

"Hey, Mom, is it okay if a friend comes with me to the funeral tomorrow?"

"Sure." She slurped from the diet pop.

"His name is Matt. I met him a while back, and we've started talking. A lot."

She muted the TV and turned around to look at me. "Is this who you've been bogarting the phone for all hours of the night?"

"Yes."

She pressed her lips together. "Is there a reason you'd like him to come?"

"Moral support."

"Is he more than a friend?"

I stared at the floor, my vision glazed and blurry. I was ten again, copping to cheating on a math test. I'd been shown my wrongness over and over again with Russ Landry using "faggot" like a weapon, and Kasey's parents sending her to a therapist. Even Ms. V seemed to have regrets about how things had gone down with her daughter.

"Jeremy, you're doing that thing you do. You're not here with me right now. Come back and talk to me, son."

Shaking myself out of the procession in my head, I rejoined her in the living room. The oversized armchair catty-corner the couch enveloped even my large frame. It was a great and loved chair, pillowy and threadbare along the armrests. I rubbed my hands like an old person suffering from arthritis, the way my grandpa always used to when he started any serious conversation.

"Matt is more than a friend," I admitted.

Mom blew out a long breath and sat back against the couch. Her eyes were watery, and she dotted the inside corners with the collar of her shirt. "I'm not upset."

I wasn't so sure.

"I'm crying because you have the guts to tell me."

That took me off guard. "Did you know?"

"Jeremy, I've known you since you were a blob of cells. No one will ever know you like I do." Mom set her drink down on the end table.

I went to interrupt.

"Hold on, I'm not finished. When you were little, you weren't ever scared. I've watched you grow up in a world that makes us all afraid, including you. But now, it seems you've grown around it." Her eyes welled up again. "And for that, I deserve a big ol' pat on the back. Or ice cream? How 'bout a little ice cream?"

"Sounds good, Mom." I followed her into the kitchen.

"Have I ever told you about the curvy path?" She grabbed two spoons and bowls.

"No." I took the carton of Graeter's chocolate chip out of the freezer. No matter what, Mom always kept good ice cream in the house. She called it a catchall food, used for celebrations and defeats alike.

"It's something your Gramps said when you were little. Goodness, you couldn't have been more than five or so." She paused and pressed her fingers to her lips, her eyes glazing over into that faraway place of memories.

"Anyway, one of his ewes was expecting a lamb, and he wanted to show you. But when he tried to take you out there, every other thing caught your eye and you'd scamper off into the fields, coming back with your pockets full of rocks, flowers, snail shells— Gems!" She snapped her fingers. "That's what you used to call your collections. When I asked Dad what you thought of the lamb, he told me you two hadn't even gotten to the barn. He looked at me and said, and I'll never forget, 'the boy likes a curvy path.'"

Mom pried the lid off the ice cream carton. "Lord knows what Dad meant exactly, but it's true that you don't ever take the quickest way to get somewhere. But then, shortcuts weren't made for you."

"Mom, I have no idea what I'm doing."

Mom chuckled as she scooped from the carton. "Welcome to adulthood!"

"I always thought I had a good read on people. Knew what they were doing and why. Yet I'm still surprising myself most days, and so are they."

"Preach, son." Mom licked her fingers and put the top back on the container. "Realizing you don't know shit, that's the true mark of maturity." She handed me a serving. "Now tell me what this Matt person is like."

"Nice. Funny. No bull, ya know? Calls things like he sees them." I sat down and scooped a creamy bite. A rush of frozen sugar and bits of chocolate melted in my mouth.

"Thank god! Don't get me wrong; I like your friend Kasey Axton fine. But she is the queen of pulling your chain. I am happy to see you taking a step away from all those games."

I stirred my ice cream into soup, frowning at the bowl.

"I'm sorry, did I offend?"

"No. Something's up over at the Axton's place."

"What is it?"

"I'm not exactly sure. Kasey's parents are keeping her home from school. That's where I went yesterday when I borrowed the car. I wanted to drop off her classwork, and she said they were making her see a counselor."

"That's not necessarily a bad thing."

"I know. It just feels off."

"It could be nothing. They're probably concerned and want her to have someone neutral to talk to."

"You're probably right."

I finished the ice cream and rinsed out our bowls in the sink. Mom stretched her arms over her head.

"Time for this ol' bag-a-bones to hit the hay. It's going to be a long day tomorrow. Night, baby." Mom yawned and went to bed.

I switched off all the lights. The muted TV showed a strange infomercial—an unfortunate soul spray-painted his bald spot. I clicked the power button.

In my own bed, I compared Kasey and me. My coming out ended in acceptance ice cream. Hers, well, I wasn't quite sure how it ended yet. That got me thinking of how Stuart and I had forced Penny into the role of a zombie—a part she adamantly expressed she did not want to play. I couldn't do anything for Kasey at the moment, but I knew how to help Penny. So, I got back to work.

MY ALARM SCREECHED. *Rrrr! Rrrr! Rrrr!* I smacked it full force and burrowed back under the covers. Every now and then, instead of setting the alarm button to radio, I accidentally moved it over to pterodactyl scream, the worst sound to wake up to.

Even from under the covers I could see the edge of morning light filling my room. I tossed back the bedspread. The condensation on my windows signaled the change in season to the cool icy promise of winter. Mom's muffled voice traveled through the apartment walls, but I could only guess who she was talking to. Then came a gentle knock on my door.

"I'm up."

"I called the school to excuse your absence today. Would you like to go out for breakfast?"

"I'm not hungry."

"Okay, I'll have Michael pick up something on his way over. The bathroom's all yours."

I'd only been to one other funeral, and it sucked. I expected today to be no different. There would be an awkward hush over the whole day. A guarantee of tacky flower assortments with glittery sashes spelling out words like Mother or Wife. Although, with Ms. V being the last of her family, there might not be all the usual props. I wasn't sure which was sadder.

I showered and got dressed in the outfit I wore for my interview last Saturday—the same clothes Matt had seen me in. He'd know I only had one set of dressy clothes, but I pushed that thought back to the murky depths from which it came. Not today. Today was marked for Ms. V's final farewell, and any time spent worrying over stupid crap wasn't about to fly.

Michael showed up a little while later with a pink box of donuts, and the three of us stood around the table and ate.

"How many people will show, you think?" Michael asked between bites.

"Her invite list had about ten people on it. I called them all. We'll see." Mom wiped sprinkles from her blouse. "Jeremy's new friend Matt will be there, right honey?"

"He'll meet us at the funeral home."

Mom watched Michael carefully, almost daring a reaction from him. I wondered if she'd told him already.

"All right then, should we go?" Michael asked.

"I'll ride with you guys and then with Matt to the cemetery."

"It's settled. Let's go." Michael buttoned his suit coat before holding the door open for Mom and me. The two of them descended the steps while I locked up.

Michael's pickup wouldn't hold all three of us, so Mom tossed him her keys, and we piled into our sedan. Before he pulled out, Michael tuned the station to local talk radio. Sports opera and Bengal "Who Dey" yelps got fans through the workweek, but Mom clicked it off, and we rode the rest of the way in silence.

I closed my eyes and leaned against the cool glass window in the backseat. My heart kept rolling over itself, skipping beats altogether. I was excited to see Matt and trying not to feel guilty because of it.

The funeral home parking lot was almost empty, save for a sleek black Lexus parked in the row marked with staff signs. Matt's car was at the far end of the lot under a tree with monarch-orange leaves that matched his hair.

"He's here." My voice caught in a whisper.

I left Mom to fill her boyfriend in. If Michael was smart, he wouldn't let Mom see if it bothered him. If Michael was good, it wouldn't actually bother him.

Matt stepped out of his car as I approached. The tips of my nose and fingers tingled in the brisk autumn air, and in a walking contradiction, my ears burned with nerves. In sum, I was more alive than I'd felt in three days. We stopped in front of each other, popping bubbles of personal space. What I quickly associated as his signature smell, cigarettes and Dial soap, mixed with the sweetness of fall leaves. He wore a pair of dark jeans and a smart suit jacket, complete with white shirt and stripe-patterned tie.

"I'm sorry about your friend." His brow wrinkled with concern.

"Thanks. Thanks for coming." I wanted to touch him but wasn't sure about etiquette, given we were standing outside a funeral home.

Matt ducked his chin and looked up at me in a supposing way. Most people were shorter than me by a few inches, but Matt was my equal. He held out his arms, his eyes questioning mine, is this okay? I nodded once, twice. Hugs happened all the time, especially here. He came in closer and wrapped his arms around my waist and my arms fit around his shoulders.

While we embraced, the world stopped in a moment of perfect quiet. The electric hum from the funeral factory silenced. Traffic halted. Overhead, a V-shaped flock of geese froze midflight. With his chest against mine, our hearts were mere inches apart, pulsing their diagonal hellos.

Car doors slammed shut. Mom's heels clicked over the asphalt as she came near. A row of pigeons on a wire took flight, as another car pulled in near the staff spots. I backed away from Matt and turned to introduce him. I let my fingers brush against his.

Mom and Michael stood before us—a picture of every middle-aged couple in a modern version of American Gothic.

"Mom, Michael, this is Matt."

When Matt held his hand out to Mom, she swatted it away and put her arms around his neck. She whispered something in his ear, and he laughed his barky laugh that set Mom's eyes twinkling. She appreciated a person who knew how to laugh from the heart. She always told me to find those people.

Michael was formal but seemingly not bothered. He shook Matt's hand and grabbed his shoulder at the same time. "Good to meet you, Matt."

"We better get in there." Mom led us to the front of the building.

The funeral home was styled in the vein of a southern manor house, only without the architectural bones to support it. The one-story building boasted '80s tan bricks. In an obvious afterthought, pillars propped up the porch's overhang, and white rocking chairs and potted plants lined the area. I supposed it was quaint in a creepy mortuary way. Inside, everything was decorated in soft creamy colors. Prearranged communal spaces were staged with high-back chairs and well-used couches. Light bounced off brass chandeliers, and every side table had a lamp turned on.

The entrance hall was sectioned off by a set of wide hallways leading in different directions. The room directly in front of where we stood had its doors propped open. Rows of gray upholstered chairs filled the space leading up to a beautiful stained-glass window. The arched window was sectioned off into individual panes depicting a tree standing alone near a bright blue lake.

"Is that supposed to be the tree of life?" Matt whispered.

I shrugged. A thick velvet rope partitioned off the doors, and from one of them near the casket, a staff member in a somber suit emerged with a stack of programs. She brushed her hair behind her ears and set to work, laying one on each chair.

"This way, boys." Mom waved us toward another viewing room to the right.

A little black sign with white plastic letters spelled out: Olivia Vail. The velvet ropes near the doors had been pulled back, and we entered a less grand version of the great room we'd passed. The seats were the same, only less of them. There were no stained-glass windows, just regular ones lined with billowing gold curtains. We took programs from another staff member, who gave us his condolences, and seated ourselves in the front row. A portrait of a young Ms. V was propped on a tripod near a bronze urn. Minutes ticked by as classical music was piped through speakers I couldn't see. I let my knee brush against Matt's. He noticed, smiling as he scanned the program, nudging back. A jolt of electricity coursed through me. The greeter in the brown suit ushered others in, and I turned to find two older women taking places in the back.

Another woman with salt-and-pepper cropped hair stepped up to the podium. She wore a chain holding thick black frames around her neck and brought them up to her eyes as she began to organize her notes. The music quieted as it came time for her to speak.

"I had the pleasure of meeting Olivia Vail several years ago. She was not a regular parishioner, but came to my office hours and plunked a handwritten draft of this program on my desk." The clergywoman held up the slip of paper we all had folded or rolled in between our hands.

"When I asked her what this was, she said, 'It's my funeral service. All I need is an emcee.'" The six of us in the audience laughed at what sounded exactly like something Ms. V would say.

"We met several times to finalize planning, and a friendship grew out of those meetings. I even got her to attend a morning service here and there." A chuckled response chorused from the people who knew Ms. V best. "Before I step aside, I would like to take a moment and say that knowing Olivia was a great pleasure. I always left our meetings with some deeper understanding of myself, or something that was going on in my life. And I've thought on it many times—how does one do that? Because it wasn't like she'd lead me into these deep and heavy conversations every time we met."

The lady paused and looked up, removing her glasses. "My conclusion was that the secret was in her authenticity. Her ability to speak in a genuine manner lightened my daily burdens. And what a gift that was. I imagine she did the same for you." She cleared her throat and put her glasses back on. "Now, as I can see in my notes from Olivia here, she's written the words TICK, TOCK in all caps. So, without further ado, let us all enjoy the playlist of one, Ms. Olivia

Vail." The pastor stepped aside from the podium and gave a nod toward the back of the room.

Music started, the lyrics inviting us to do a new dance. It was Little Eva's version of Loco-Motion. I burst out laughing. We all did. Mom looked over at me. She'd known what Ms. V planned. Nothing sad and forlorn, but a true celebration of her life. Mom stood and held out her hand for Michael.

"She wanted us to dance," Mom said. "She wanted us to dance!" Mom shouted to the ladies in the back row. Their eyes were as big as moons. They'd probably never seen a funeral service like this.

Matt elbowed me. "Come on," he said.

"Oh god, no." I shook my head. "I don't dance."

"You're going to deny your friend's last wish? That's pretty cold, Samson."

"Fine." I let him drag me up from my seat. Was I embarrassed? Absolutely. Did it matter? Nope.

The four of us twisted and turned through the song. The pastor descended from the steps and joined us. The ladies in the back came forward and clapped offbeat. Michael busted out some sick moves and twirled my mom around the carpeted floor. We laughed at each other, and it was a beautiful thing.

Chapter Thirty-One

THE PASTOR INVITED the funeral attendees to our home for a meal. But the two ladies from the back row shook Mom's hand and said they already had lunch plans. Ms. V's graveyard ceremony was nonexistent. She'd chosen to be cremated, her name added to her husband's headstone out of tradition, and her final request was to be sprinkled over the Ohio River. Mom said we'd take care of it another day. As for now, the urn sat on our mantel above her boxed up things.

Matt flipped through the first Daredevil comic, lying diagonally across my bed.

"Told you, you looked like him."

Matt nodded but kept reading. I set my desk chair facing the window and put my feet up on the sill. The tree outside had changed to a vibrant red over the last few weeks.

"I see the resemblance." Matt slipped the magazine back into its plastic casing and pushed it toward the edge of the bed. He sat up. "You said in the car you thought you figured out your project for Charlie Wyatt. What is it?"

"It's, like, right on the tip of a fully formed idea. It has to do with Penny and letting things be how they are, and I wanna do something with interconnectivity."

"That sounds like a lot."

"It is. I can't figure out how to fit it all together."

"Why the comic though? I thought he wasn't impressed with it."

"It doesn't matter if he's impressed with it. It's mine, right. That was the requirement."

"Can I see it?"

"Not until it's done."

"I get it." He closed his eyes. "I don't like anyone looking at my work until it's complete either." A dreamy smile crept across his features. "Come here."

My bedroom door stood open. That had always been the rule. As much as I wanted a reenactment of our last encounter, my mom being in such close proximity killed all prospects of a boner. I dropped my feet from the windowsill though, and the mattress sank with my weight as I sat next to him. He turned on his side and grabbed my shirt in his fist. Definitely not death of a boner–style. He yanked on my shirt, pulling me near enough to kiss, and we did, sweetly at first, until our teeth clacked together and he bit my lower lip. That lit a groan from somewhere deep inside me. My whole body said "keep going," but my mouth said, "Not here."

Matt stopped, our faces still close, and he sighed. "What I get for dating a high schooler."

"You regret it?" I let go of the comforter gripped in my fist and swatted his stomach. It was flat and hard, even when he wasn't flexing.

"Not at all, Samson." Matt grabbed my hand and bit one of my fingers in a way that nearly sent me over the edge. He tossed my hand back at me. "If you can remain chaste, so can I."

I could barely form words. I wanted him. The only place offering privacy would be the woods out back. "Follow me."

I zipped a hoodie over my shirt and pulled the waistband down low. We walked past Mom and Michael, who were snuggled on the couch. Based on the dramatic music and soft focus, I assumed they were watching a Lifetime movie.

"I'm gonna show Matt around town."

"'Kay," Mom sounded sleepy, and her head was propped on Michael's chest.

We hit the parking lot pavement and sprinted for the tree line. The October air smelled apple crisp. Under the leaves, he pulled me toward him and kissed me again.

"There's—" (kiss, smash, teeth) "—a place—" (kiss, smash, tongue) "—not far." I pulled away and trekked farther into the woods. "Come on."

We took off over the rocky creek bed. I slowed down a bit. The path was familiar to me, but the last thing I wanted was for Matt to roll an ankle or something. "This way." I urged him onward, toward the tree stump with the dead cartoon smiley face.

"Cute. Did you tag that?"

"Me and my friend, Stu."

"Stu, huh? Should I be worried?"

I snorted. "God, no."

Camouflaged by the forest, the fort's dilapidated walls could barely be seen. What showed clearly was the bright red coat of a figure crouched near the firepit.

"Shh!" I stepped off the path, my back against the nearest tree, and Matt came up in front of me, distractingly close. "Someone's here."

"Let's go to another spot, then. It's a big wood." He ran his tongue over his teeth.

Hot damn.

Peeking around the tree, I recognized a clear plastic purse set on a log. "It's Kasey."

"So?" Matt shrugged.

"She's my friend."

"Okay." It was Matt's turn to glance. "Looks like she wants to be alone," he said, a hopeful note lingering in his tone.

"I'm sorry. I should check on her. She's got some stuff going on at home."

"That's fine." Matt moved back onto the worn trail heading toward the fort. I grabbed him by the front of his shirt and yanked him back to me.

"What are you doing? I thought you said you wanted to see if she was okay." He looked me over. "Oh, you want to do it. Not me. Got it." Matt crossed his arms.

"Who's there?" Kasey's shaky voice rang out. "I've got mace."

"See, that's why I wanted to go first. She'd mace you for sure," I whispered to Matt, with a quick kiss on his mouth. "It's me, Kase!" I called out from behind the tree.

"Jeremy?"

"And my friend Matt. Okay?"

"Sure. Come on out."

Matt and I made our way through the brush to the firepit. Kasey's backpack and duffel bag, propped against a log, were stuffed full. She went in the fort, opened a cooler filled with bottled water, and handed me one.

"I'd offer you one too. But I need them," Kasey said to Matt.

"It's okay. He can have mine." I handed him the bottle she'd given me. He twisted off the cap and took a sip. "You remember Matt, right?"

"Of course, I do." Kasey nodded at him and gave a sad little wave. Her lips disappeared in a rolled up smile. Her eyelids were red, and her cheeks were covered in little pinpoints. Petechiae. That was what she'd called them after spending a long drunken night puking and waking up with the red freckles dusting her face.

"What are you doing out here?" I asked.

Kasey opened her mouth to talk but turned and picked up her backpack instead. She balanced it on her knee and unzipped the front pocket. After digging around a bit, she handed me a pamphlet printed on smooth thick paper.

The front cover showed a picture of a cross on a hill. A line of backpackers climbed a rocky zigzagging route toward the sunset nestled in behind the cross. In tidy curvy white font, stood the title, Pathways.

"Pathways to what?"

Matt grabbed the brochure from my hand. "I've heard of this place. Look." He opened to the front page. Underneath a pair of rock-climbing teens having a grand old time, I scanned words like "same-sex attraction" and "God's promises."

"It's a conversion camp." Matt offered the paper back to Kasey. "You're not going, are you?"

"No. I left home before they got the chance to ship me off."

"What? Are you planning on sleeping out here?" I asked.

"For now."

"Why didn't you call me? You can stay with us."

"I didn't have time to call anyone, Jeremy." Her voice wavered with thickness. "And I already told you your place is where my parents would look first."

"Mom can cover for you. You can stay there until you have a better plan."

"I can't ask your mom to lie for me."

"You won't have to because I will."

Matt grabbed her cooler, and I picked up the extra duffel bag. Kasey hugged herself and sniffled the whole way back to our apartment, never leading the way, always staying a few steps behind Matt and me.

The three of us trudged up the steps. I swung open the front door and called out, "Mom, we need to talk!"

From the kitchen, Michael shooshed me. He mimed napping and pointed toward the couch, then turned back to the large stockpot on the stovetop. The smell of sautéed onions and peppers wafted through the apartment. He poured in a can of tomato sauce, and the whole thing sizzled wildly.

"I hope you guys like chili," Michael whispered, wrestling with a can opener. He poured a can of kidney beans over a strainer in the sink and turned on the faucet, letting the water run over them, rinsing away the gooey liquid.

"We need Mom." I set Kasey's duffel bag next to the couch.

Michael dumped the beans into the pot and turned to us. For the first time since we'd come in, he regarded us, taking in the bags and the crumpled girl behind Matt and me. His cheery eyes narrowed. "Connie!" he yelled.

Mom shot up from the couch. "What—what is it?"

"The kids need you." Michael stirred in a heaping tablespoon full of chili powder. The dry heat smell made it all the way to where I stood.

Mom rubbed her eyes and smoothed back her hair. "Hey, guys. I must've conked out after the funeral." She sniffed, took in the scene, and said slowly, "Hi, Kasey." A pillow crease lined her cheek.

"Kasey, let me see what you showed us in the woods," I said.

Without a peep, she ruffled through her backpack and handed me the same pamphlet. I gave it to Mom, pleading with my eyes.

"What is this?" Mom turned it over, opened it up.

"It's a conversion camp, Ms. Warsh," Matt said. "They want to pray her gay away." He finger quoted the phrase.

"I think we better have a talk, Kasey. Privately." Mom gave us her I-mean-business look.

Michael grabbed his keys from the counter. "I'll head over to the store and get corn bread." He leaned over the couch and pecked Mom on the cheek.

Mom eyed me and nodded toward the door.

"Guess we better go too," I said, and Kasey stepped forward as we turned to leave, staring only at the floor.

At the bottom of the stairs, Matt put his hands in his pockets and gave me a little shove with his hip.

"So... Nothing kills a mood like conversion camp," I said as we walked to the car.

Matt barked out a laugh. "Truth." He unlocked his car, but before getting in, he turned and asked, "Rain check?"

"Where did that saying come from?"

"I have no idea. But do I get one?"

"Yes, definitely." I tugged on his tie. We didn't kiss out in the open. I followed his lead on that. I took a step back, and he got into his car.

I knocked on his window. I needed to ask him something.

"What's up?"

"You're in the drama department with Anita, right? Do you have access to a projector?"

"Probably. Why?"

"Do you think you could borrow one?"

"Uh, that I don't know."

"Could you find out?"

"I can."

"Thanks." I checked if anyone was around. The streets were empty. School didn't let out for another thirty minutes.

I leaned into his car and pressed my mouth to his neck. It was stubbly from an uneven shave. "Rain check," I mumbled near his ear.

"Sure thing, Samson."

I walked circles around the apartment building for at least thirty minutes, wishing I'd grabbed a book or some homework. Eventually, Michael showed up with a little box of cornbread mix. He sat on the park bench next to me.

"Never a dull moment around here," he said, offering me a stick of gum.

"You can say that again." The hot cinnamon flavor overwhelmed my taste buds.

"Your mom will let your friend stay here."

"I know. That's why I brought her. Mom's good at helping people."

"She sure is."

I scratched the back of my neck as an awkward silence settled over our conversation.

"Your mom said your interview went well."

"Well enough. I should be up there working on my art project right now." My leg started doing that rabbit-hop thing.

"You know what you're gonna do?"

"I've barely got an idea. Hopefully, the rest will come once I put pencil to paper."

"Is that how it works?"

"Most of the time. If it doesn't work, usually means my brain needs to marinate more."

"Well, I'm looking forward to seeing what you come up with."

"Me too."

The door to my apartment opened, and Mom stepped out onto the landing. She waved us on up. Michael and I rose from the bench at the same time, and he motioned for me to go first.

"Go on in, honey," Mom said to me at the top of the stairs, but she stopped Michael before he could walk in. I closed the door behind me to give them privacy.

Kasey sat at the end of the couch with her arms wrapped around her knees.

"How'd it go?" I asked.

"She won't lie," Kasey said. "She made me call my parents and tell them where I was staying."

"It's probably better that way. Keeps the police out of the thing, ya know?"

Kasey wiped her cheek, and I sat next to her on the couch. There was a box of tissues on the end table, and I offered it to her. The paper whooshed from the box as she pulled out a few.

"I can't believe this is happening." Kasey blew her nose.

"I'm sorry. I can't either." I stared at the muted TV; a blonde chick got slapped. "Talk or distraction?"

"Oh, puh-lease distract me." She sounded stuffy, as though she had a bad cold.

I hit the volume button on the remote. When I held out my hand, Kasey took it, and we watched the end of the movie together.

Mom came in holding the box of cornbread mix.

"Is Michael not joining us?" I asked.

"He decided it would be better if he went on home." Mom grabbed a bowl and poured the contents of the box into it. She cracked an egg, threw in a splash of milk, and whipped it all together with a wooden spoon.

Kasey and I made eye contact, and I felt my mouth turn down in an "eek" position.

"I'll be out of your hair soon. I promise, Ms. Warsh."

"You'll stay as long as you need." Mom's lips tightened into a line I'd witnessed many times. She poured the batter into the cupcake pan and nearly dropped the whole thing when she banged it into the oven. She stirred the chili and excused herself for a minute. "Keep an ear out for the timer, 'kay, Jeremy?"

"Sure thing." I wondered what had happened on the landing between Michael and Mom.

Twenty minutes later, the oven timer beeped its finish. It was early for dinner, but Mom emerged from her room to set the table anyway. Kasey got up to help and grabbed glasses from the cabinet.

"How do they look?" Mom stood next to me. She poked a muffin top.

"Finished. Is everything okay?" I asked.

"Just fine," she said, overly loud.

We ate in silence except for spoons scraping the bottom of our bowls.

"You can take my bedroom, Kasey." I offered.

"I'll sleep on the couch," she countered.

"No, really, I don't mind."

"Jeremy, you need your space." Kasey ripped the cupcake wrapper off a muffin. "I'll be fine on the couch."

Mom finished her bowl of chili and set it aside. "I'll go into school with you in the morning and talk with the principal. You'll need to come with me, Kasey."

Kasey nodded, her mouth full of cornbread.

"So, with an extra person here, we'll need to work out a bathroom schedule."

"I can shower at night," I said.

"Me too," said Kasey.

"Great. I'll let you two work that out. I need to call my boss and let her know I'll be late tomorrow. Can you guys handle cleaning all this up?"

"Absolutely!" Kasey said. "Just show me where everything goes."

"I'll show you."

"There's extra blankets and pillows in the hall closet. Help her get set up, will you, Jeremy?"

"No problem, Mom."

Mom didn't come back out of her room the rest of the night. I wanted to call Matt but could hear her on the phone. Kase and I watched TV, and after a while, I went back to my room to try to get a little work done before bed.

I checked the clock. The homecoming meeting should have happened by now, and Stuart would know soon if his plan had worked. He'd try to call, but with Mom tying up the line, all he'd get would be a busy signal.

The project had been churning in the back of my mind ever since Charlie Wyatt brought up the notion of creating something real. Coming up with an idea was like looking at the sun though. I couldn't understand all of what I was supposed to create at once. If I perceived too much, it overwhelmed me—paralyzed me into not starting. Like a vampire caught in the dawn light, ideas vaporized as I desperately tried to grasp them. I'd had a glimpse of it at Union Terminal, and again at Ms. V's funeral. Then there were the moments in between, all of them smooshed together into their own beautiful quiet thing. No matter what I made for the assignment, if it came from the glittering place of almost understanding, then it should ring true.

Nothing was more intimidating than the blankness of a clean sheet of drawing paper. Blowing out a couple deep breaths, I flipped through Penny's gesture drawings. I needed to combine her looks of sadness and sass from earlier copies for her final chapter. Because what she'd been through was going to make her stronger.

"Whatcha doing?" Kasey asked. A towel wrapped in a beehive shape was balanced on her head, and she wore a pair of flannel pajama pants with an oversized plain white tee.

"I have to make an original piece for a chance at an internship with Mr. Wyatt."

Kasey uncoiled the towel and squeezed the wet strands of her hair. "You're gonna use Penny again?"

I shrugged. "Nothing about turning her into a zombie felt right to me."

"So, what's your plan?"

"I'm gonna turn her back."

"How? Bad stuff already happened to her. She's changed forever."

"In a way, yes, you're right. But nobody's ever completely changed."

"Debatable, at best. Good luck though."

"Thanks for the vote of confidence."

"I think *Dawson's Creek* is on." Kasey tossed her wet towel in my hamper and left.

"Let me know if you need anything!" I called after her.

Great. Now I was questioning everything I wanted to do for Penny. *Are people always the same? Or can they change? Is it both?* I looked back at Penny's face in episode one as she stared out at the reader. Her fierceness was undeniable. Would life events blunt that spirit? I checked my copy of the last episode. Penny was resigned to her fate, but I'd argue her ferocity had not been extinguished. In fact, I could still hear it in her voice. Just flickering. And like any flame, if it got enough oxygen, it would roar again.

I started drawing the chartreuse-tinged skin of her face, tilted toward the dance floor. As I drew, like always, she started whispering.

I AM ALWAYS ME...

Glitter lights from the disco ball twirl over Penny's shoulders.

I SAID, I AM ALWAYS ME!

Classmates stop dancing around her as they notice the zombie girl in a kilt shouting toward the outer limits of the page.

I'M ANSWERING YOUR QUESTION, YOU DUMB FUCK! I AM ALWAYS ME!

The DJ pulls the needle from the record with a screech. A boy standing next to her claps a slow steady beat. Behind him, a girl spits out the disgusting bit of shin she was munching on, vomits in a nearby trash can, and cheers along too. Soon, the whole room shakes with the voices of those who would not be ruined.

Penny raises her arms above her head, her eyes closed. Everyone falls silent...

I drew a long narrow frame and filled it in with a close-up of the tops of her round cheeks and her now open eyes. They were still the dead ones she'd commented on when I first drew them, their original hazel color worn and faded to a shabby tan.

I stopped for a minute and looked back at those eyes. I needed to give the reader more hope here. At this point, I wanted everyone to see that this girl could be true to herself even though she'd been through some shit. That, no matter what, she would always be Penny Kind, but I wasn't quite sure how to convey that yet.

It was dark outside. I listened for sounds in the house, but it had grown quiet. I never did hear from Stuart. I picked up the phone in my room, and there was finally a dial tone, so, I punched in his number.

Somebody picked up after the first ring, but they didn't say anything. Instead, I could hear yelling in the background. Damn. I hoped Stuart wasn't involved in this one.

"Hello?" I asked. A loud crackling swoosh made me hold the receiver away from my face. After a while, it stopped. "Jesus. Hello? Is Stu around?"

There was a thumping noise, and their dog barked. I could only imagine that one of the smaller kids had grabbed the phone and was dragging me all around the house. I'd give it a few minutes and then hang up.

More crackling, and then a distant voice.

"Hey, bud. Whatcha got there? Can I see?" It was Stuart. "Hello?"

"It's me, dude. What's going on over there?"

"The usual. I've got my headphones on, so I'm in my own world."

"Have you heard from Des? What's the word on homecoming?"

"It's a go."

"You did it!"

"We did it, man. Zombie Homecoming is officially a thing."

Chapter Thirty-Two

ZOMBIE HOMECOMING WAS in full effect. All four classes had designed and built their monster-themed floats. The parade had gone off per usual, when, on a brisk fall evening, two days before the dance, the whole town lined the sidewalks and cheered them on. I had to hand it to Landry. He'd executed the senior class float flawlessly. Des and Dani spent hours wallpapering the float's faux dining room walls, and Russ wired it for electricity and hung a janky chandelier. Four green painted mannequins, wearing our team's football jerseys, sat at a dining table with a slaughtered version of the opposing team's mascot. Along the sides of the float in a million tiny squares of balled up tissue paper were the words, "Devour the Panthers!"

The game was later tonight. All of us, save Stuart, were out by the track, lounging on the otherwise empty bleachers at the end of the school day. The cheerleading squad was busy hanging posters down by the field, and the student council kids had set up the carpeted walkway for homecoming court. All four floats were lined up near the end zone, along the other side of the football field's chain-link fence.

"What do they do with the floats afterward?" Kasey asked. She'd returned to school the day after we took her in, and if the administration, or her parents, had a problem with her staying with us, I wasn't aware.

"How can you be a senior and not know about the bonfire?" Des asked as she tore open a pack of candy-coated chocolates.

"They burn them?" Kasey put two and two together.

"Uh, yeah. Since, like, the beginning of time." Des crunched a handful of the sweets.

Each year, the bonfire was held after the football game. So, the floats were either scorched in effigy or victory. It was a toss-up each year.

"What a waste..." Kasey replied.

"Totally," I agreed. Having Kasey around the house the last two weeks had been awesome. It was like having a sibling.

"Do you have your dress?" Dani asked Kasey.

"No. I planned on hitting up the thrift store."

Getting her clothes had been difficult. We went together, in case her parents turned out to be home. They weren't, but maybe it would have been better if they had been. Drama would have been an easy distraction from the empty dark house with years of happy pictures attached to its walls. Kasey spent most of the time sitting on her daybed hugging an old stuffed giraffe while I zoomed around emptying drawers. I packed what I thought she needed because when I asked for her help, she snapped and started throwing things into the little wicker trash can near her vanity.

"What?" Des continued. "You better go soon. Homecoming is tomorrow. How are you planning on wearing your hair?"

"Honestly, I haven't given it much thought." Kasey tightened her long ponytail.

"Who are you going with, Dani?" I asked.

"Oh." She looked to her sister. "Um."

"Tyler Peterson asked her weeks ago." Des pursed her lips in a way that made me feel like I'd done something wrong.

"That's cool." Tyler was one of the nicest guys on campus. He was captain of the debate team and super active in school politics. Even though he was popular, he made time to say hello to everyone. Extremely cute in a preppy kind of way, I fully expected to find him mayor of Cincinnati one day. "He's a good guy."

Dani waved out to the field. Tyler was out there now, setting up the mic system for tonight's king and queen announcements. His voice rang through the speakers: "Check, check, check. Hey, girl." He smiled his winning smile.

Kasey gathered her stuff and walked off in a huff. Des and Dani looked at me with the same confused expression, but I just shrugged and followed Kasey. The bleachers rang out with our every step.

"Hey, wait up!"

Kasey reached the bottom of the bleachers before me and turned the corner without stopping.

"Kasey, stop!"

She passed the concession stand, and in one of those weird moments where you notice something's going to happen right before it does, I heard my shoelaces clack on the asphalt. I simultaneously looked down and stepped on the loose one, but my brain couldn't work the problem out fast enough. My other foot lurched upward, while the rest of my body toppled down. I got my hands in front of my face right before it skidded along the asphalt.

"Shit!" I rolled over unto my backpack, an overturned man-sized turtle.

Between Kasey's backpack, hard-cased plastic purse, and collection of key chains, she clacked and jangled wherever she went. All that noise ran toward the lump of me on the ground.

"Are you okay?"

"I think so." I sat up and investigated the scrapes and bit of rock stuck in my palms. "Why'd you walk off like that?"

Kasey let out a sigh. "Sometimes I get sick of the norm talk."

"The norm?" I flicked black pebbles from my hand.

"Dates, dresses, hairdos." She sat next to me cross-legged.

"Des and Dani don't mean anything by it."

"Exactly. It means nothing." She offered me a hand up. Together, we stood. She stumbled into the weight imbalance.

"It's high school, Kase. We'll have our whole lives to discuss more important things."

"You're right." She nodded, wrapping her arms around me and resting her cheek on my chest. "I'm glad I have you." Her words were muffled.

I gave her a squeeze and kissed the top of her head. She didn't smell like candy anymore. We'd left most of her toiletries at her house, so, instead, she smelled like the shampoo-conditioner combo my mom bought at Bern's store. She smelled like me. I leaned back, and she looked up at me. "Let's go get your dress, okay?"

"I wasn't gonna actually go."

"Are you kidding? You're my zombie date." That made her laugh, her eyes regaining a bit of the sparkle that used to always be there. I thought it would never fade and had taken it for granted.

"AHHHH! WHAT'S THAT smell, Jeremy?" Kasey asked.

We were walking under the fluorescent lights of our favorite consignment store, past the two register counters, and the glass cases filled with costume jewelry.

"It's whiff O'Thrift!" Kasey and I exclaimed.

"Mothballs, cigarettes, body odor, and detergent all mixing together to make the smell every thrift store reeks of." Her arms outspread, she twirled in the aisle.

"Don't forget death and pesticides," I said.

Kasey doubled over, laughing. "You're right." We strolled past the toys, and she picked up a rubbery puppet with the face of a monster. "Oh my god! Do you remember these?" She waggled the revolting thing in my face. "It's a Boglin!" she squealed.

"What was with the '80s? Was, like, hideously cute a thing?"

"You mean, like, a bunch of white business guys decided gross was the new charming?" She stretched the toy's elastic arm until it sprang backward.

"Exhibit A—Boglins"

"Okay, okay. Exhibit B—Garbage Pail Kids"

"Exhibit C—*Alf*." I grabbed a stuffed teddy bear and somersaulted it into the stale air.

"Alf wasn't ugly! He was adorable!"

"No, he wasn't." I caught the bear and put it back in its plastic bin.

"He was furry and had a great sense of humor!" Kasey removed the Boglin from her hand.

"He hunted cats and burped a lot."

"Point made." Kasey tossed the puppet in a random toy bin at the end of the aisle. "Speaking of the '80s! Loook." She skipped over to a circular rack filled with shiny dresses. The stand only held a few options due to all the lacy poofs around the bottoms and shoulders of each dress.

I selected a satin-sequined wedding dress from the bunch. "Just...why?" I picked up the fluff around one of the shoulders. "Why was it ever cool to make arms look like spools of cotton candy?"

Kasey laughed as the hangers scraped along the metal rail. She pulled a shimmering teal-green item off the rack. With the slightest hiccup of breath, she held the dress up against her frame. "What do you think?"

"Is it your size?"

"I don't know."

"Well, check."

Kasey fumbled with the hanger as she dug around inside the garment, practically turning the top half inside out. "There's no tag."

"Better try it on, then."

She nodded and made a beeline for the back of the store. The makeshift dressing rooms were two stalls with long dark curtains for privacy. They both had warped full-length mirrors and handwritten signs reminding patrons the space was not to be used for a toilet.

I waited nearby, until a row of suit coats called for my attention. I picked up one in dark black, made of a strange pilled fabric, and slipped it on. The jacket's lapel was made of a shiny satin material. Only one button fastened at my waist. I pushed up the sleeves. This would do.

Kasey pulled back the curtain, and her choice of dress fit perfectly. Her freckled shoulders were bare in the sleeveless teal number, and the color made her skin glow with warmth, even under the tubular lighting. She curtsied in her rainbow footie socks, and it was still totally charming.

"It suits you."

"I know. Check out the crinoline!" She picked the top skirt up and showed off gauzy underskirts in bright yellow.

"I love everything about this." Straightening her back, she smoothed her hands over slanting folds in the shiny bodice. "Even this." And she flicked the big bow positioned on her left hip.

"How much is it?"

"Not much. Like, twenty."

"You have to get it."

"I am. I don't know if I can zombie-it-up though. It's so pretty. Are you getting that jacket?" She twirled in front of a mirror at the end of the aisle.

"What do you think?" I slipped one hand in my jeans pocket and mugged for her.

"I like the silky collar."

"That's why I picked it."

"You'll need a very skinny tie though."

"Like a bolo?"

"Yes!" Kasey hopped up and down and clapped her hands. "Oh, I hope we can find one."

"I'll see if I can find one while you get changed."

In the tie section, I found an impressive array of bolos. With zero understanding of the actual function, I chose one with silver tips and an azure stone clasp to match the teal of Kasey's dress. It seemed just like a necklace, but really, so were all ties. I slipped it over the hanger handle of my jacket.

"Nice. Looks like we're ready to check out," Kasey said, her floofy dress draped over one arm.

We strolled through the near-vacant thrift store. An elderly couple in the book section had filled a basket with paperbacks. A college-aged kid was testing out a couple of old couches, stretching out on one, then another, and back again.

"What's Stu been up to lately?" Kasey asked.

"He got a new job."

"Oh yeah, where?"

"The Greenhouse off the highway."

"Is that why he's been MIA?"

"I think so. I talked to him last night. It keeps him busy after school, but he really likes it."

"Huh. I could've pictured him in that record store forever."

"So could he. That's why he quit." At the register, I motioned for Kasey to put her dress on top of my items.

"Fifty percent off day," The clerk mumbled as she checked for tags.

"Bonus!" Kasey and I fist-bumped. Total cost for decking out at the school dance: $15.50.

"Not bad." I waved away the option for a plastic grocery bag, and we picked up our stuff.

The cool fall breeze rustled dried leaves across the parking lot. Traffic whooshed by on the busy side street.

"Hey, I've been meaning to ask, have you talked with Anita lately?" I unlocked the passenger door.

"I mean, she knows I'm staying with you." Kasey got in the car.

"Any plans to see her?" I came around to the driver's side and sat down.

"Nope."

"Why not?" I put the key in the ignition and the engine rolled over. But I waited for an answer before shifting into gear.

"Because I'm leaving." Kasey inspected the seams of her new dress as if she hadn't dropped a bomb.

"You can't mean the camp?" I put the car in drive and punched the gas too hard. The tires squealed as I ripped out of the parking space.

"Gods, no. I'm talking about my brother. After the quarter's over, I'm transferring to a school in Columbus. He has his own apartment this year and a futon."

"Are you serious?"

"Deadly."

I clicked on the turn signal. The ticking filled the empty space of the car. I wasn't ready for her to go. "But—"

"I can't stay in this place, Jeremy." Her voice was true, unwavering, like a tree branch supporting all the withered leaves of fall.

I didn't say anything else. Kasey's mind was made up. Trying to talk her out of it would've been a giant waste of our time. What did I know anyway? My dad was a loser, but my mom was always on my side. Kasey had her brother. It made sense for her to be with a family member who wasn't trying to change whole parts of who she was.

"Guess we better make the most of this dance then." I stretched my arm over the console and held out my hand for her. She took it. Her skin was impossibly soft, elegant and fine, yet strong enough for flight.

"It won't be an easy thing." Kasey's sunglasses reflected the mowed-down cornfields.

"Probably not at first." I gave her hand a squeeze and then let go.

When we pulled into my apartment lot, I noticed Stuart sitting on the park bench in front. He had a terra-cotta planter in his lap and headphones on. His knees bounced up and down.

"What's he up to?" Kasey asked, waving at him as we passed.

"It's Stu. It could, literally, be anything." I parked the car, but before we got out, he was bounding toward us.

"Where you guys been?" he asked.

"We went shopping for dance gear, see?" Kasey held up her dress.

"Spiffy." Stuart snapped the gum he was chewing.

"What's up, buddy?" The three of us walked up the sidewalk.

"Got ya something." Stuart held up the terra-cotta planter. He grabbed a bag of soil he'd propped against the bench and a plastic grocery bag.

"A plant?" I asked.

"Not just any plant."

The keys jangled in my hand as we passed Ms. V's empty apartment. The door was propped open, and the whir of the carpet cleaner's big machine filled the stairwell.

"What happened to all her stuff?" Stuart asked as the three of us broached the stairs.

"She donated almost everything." I tried the doorknob—still locked. Mom was at one of her jobs. "We're not sure what to do with all the personal stuff though. Pictures, letters, that kind of thing."

"Jeez, is it a lot?"

"Couple of boxes worth." I unlocked the door and pointed out the stack along the wall of the living room. "It feels weird to throw them out."

Stuart put the planter and bag on the kitchen table and walked over to the boxes. He kneeled in front of them and poked through the top layer of one.

"Check out this old yearbook!" He pulled out a dusty book with shredded binding, laid it on the carpeting, and carefully turned the pages. "She was such a funny lady."

I'd ignored the stack of boxes after Mom and Michael brought them up here. The idea that someone's life fitted into cardboard slated for trash was too depressing. I left Kasey and Stuart to poke through the leftovers while I hung up our thrift store purchases in my closet. They were still at it when I got back to the kitchen. The grocery bag crinkled as I peeked inside and found a clear plastic baggie next to a roll of paper towels.

"What is all this, Stu?" I asked.

Stuart closed the yearbook and put it back where it belonged. He started toward the table, and Kasey followed. She grabbed the apple juice from the fridge and poured herself a glass. Holding out the bottle, she asked with her eyes if we wanted any. I shook my head, but Stuart nodded, so she took out another glass and filled it to the brim for Stuart.

"Thanks!" He took a long gulp, draining half his glass. "Apropos." He paused to stare at the golden juice before continuing. "Remember the other day out in the woods, when you started talking about apple trees?"

"Yeah, I remember."

"Well, it got me wondering what it would take to actually grow an apple tree from seeds. So, I got myself over to the Greenhouse and asked the manager."

"And got a new job. Congrats, by the way," Kasey added.

"Thanks. Surprisingly, I'm really into it. There's, like, a calmness around all those quiet plants. It's the only time I'm not burnin' to move." Stuart took a drink. "Anyway, Shelly, that's the manager, told me that to grow an actual tree from seeds there's a whole long process." Stuart reached into the grocery bag. His hand emerged with the clear plastic baggie containing a bunch of dark brown specks. "First, you need seeds from different kinds of apples. Then, you have to dry them out." He pulled out the paper towels. "After that, you have to simulate winter."

"You didn't dig up the ones we planted, did you?"

"God no, Jeremy. I'm not nearly as sentimental as you. I just grabbed a couple kinds from Bern's store and ate them. I've been drying the seeds out, but figure they won't be safe in my fridge for a simulated winter. There's too many people in my place. The seeds would be thrown out with the trash. So, to simulate winter, we need to wrap these in moist paper towels and keep them in the fridge."

"All winter long?"

"Yeah, we'll have to check them every couple days to make sure the towels are still wet. I can make sure it's done when I'm over here for dinner or whatever. Then in the spring, we plant the little germies in the pot."

"So, we won't actually need the pot or this dirt until spring?"

"Right. But they were on sale now, and with my employee discount, practically free."

"Yeah, but where can we keep this stuff?"

"You've got closets aplenty, Warsh."

"I have one. One closet."

"There's the hall one too," Kasey said.

"Give me the bag. I'll put it in my room." I took the dirt back, leaving Stuart and Kase looking through the lower cabinets.

"We need Tupperware, or even, like, a casserole dish, Jeremy," Stuart ordered.

When I came back, Stuart had pulled out a spray bottle and was spritzing the paper towels we'd laid on the table. I stood in the hallway and watched my friends. This was a weird little project Stuart had cooked up. All those times I'd planted a seed, I'd never once thought to go and figure out why they weren't growing. Stuart had though. He was making this happen, and as a result, the entire cosmos of an apple tree was getting its start right here in this big bang of a kitchen.

"This is cool of you, Stu."

"No biggie. Ya know, back in those woods the other day, I just really wanted that to happen."

"I get it, man." I folded a collection of seeds into its moist packet and placed them in the dish Kasey found under the sink.

"Do we need a lid?" Kasey asked, holding up a colorful assortment of options.

"Nah," Stuart said. He bit the cap off a Sharpie and wrote "Science Project. Do Not Trash!" on the side of the container. Then, he opened the fridge with a suctioned whoosh. After he closed it, he clapped his hands together like a magician completing a major trick. "So, what have you two been up to?"

"Not much."

"Jeremy's working on another Penny episode."

"You know about that?" I asked, and at the same time Stuart asked me, "What for?"

"I saw it." Kasey shrugged. "I'm living here."

"But why? We already got Zombie Homecoming." Stuart capped the Sharpie and put it in his back pocket. "What more could you want?"

"I'm gonna turn her back."

"Human?" he asked.

"She's not supposed to spend her life as a flesh-eating monster," I explained.

"Whatever, man. She's your creation." Stuart zipped up his hoodie. "What's your plan though? Are you doing another print run?"

"No. My friend Matt said he might be able to get a projector from his drama department. I was thinking about showing it at the dance."

"Do you know how to get your pictures from paper to the projector?" Kasey asked.

"No," I admitted.

Stuart blew out a big breath. "I've never done it either. I imagine you have to find a way to scan your drawings, save them to a computer, and then have the whole thing—computer plus projector—set up on the stage before the dance starts."

"A transparency machine would work though, right?" Kasey asked. She stood by the sink peeling a banana. "It's kind of old school, but it might be faster than trying to figure out how to use a projector. Every classroom at school has a transparency machine. Plus, the library has extras."

"She's right."

"Yeah, but then someone will have to stand near the projection and, in essence, turn the pages in front of the crowd."

"So?" Stuart and Kasey said together.

"So, who would do it?" I asked.

"You could."

I shook my head. Nope. I'd come a long way, but standing in front of a gymnasium full of clowns and showing them my work was still off limits.

"We could pay one of the prop crew from the drama department. They're used to being up on stage. They stand there, all dressed in black, and no one will notice them," Kasey said. She unzipped a pocket on her backpack and pulled out a wad of cash. "Ten bucks oughta do it."

"There should be music too! While it's all happening. I'll take care of it. I know just the thing," Stuart exclaimed.

"This is getting bigger than I expected. What should I do?"

"You finish telling Penny's story. We'll take care of everything else." Kasey and Stuart sat down and started planning, always my co-conspirators.

Chapter Thirty-Three

THE DAY OF the dance, Kasey bogarted the bathroom. I had time for a shower and a little extra hair fluffing before she knocked on the door again. Only wearing a towel, I sprinted for the privacy of my bedroom. The crisp white dress shirt Mom had picked out felt clean and light against my skin. My bolo tie clasp kept hanging crooked though. I checked it obsessively for a while and then gave up, letting the thing hang however it wanted to hang.

I rolled up my sleeves and picked up what I'd been working on for Mr. Wyatt. For a long time, I thought I'd submit Penny's Last Dance—that was what I'd been calling it. But as I worked on it, I realized I needed this project for Mr. Wyatt, the one that determined which way my future was headed, to be something new. I decided on a self-portrait. I went to the library and researched the most famous ones. Of course, there were the many variations of Van Gogh with thick impressionistic brush strokes of orange hair and light. And Picasso's 1901 portrait marking the beginning of his blue period was just plain hot. But what could I do? How could I show myself in a way that wasn't cliché or hadn't been done a million times?

Ms. V's ruby barrette still sat next to my desk lamp, where I'd put it weeks ago. The answer came to me the night I finished the transparencies for Penny. I picked up the barrette and held it. *Who am I?* Just a kid growing up with a love for drawing and comics. All my favorite comic books had superheroes. *What if I were one?* I side-swooped a section of my hair above my ear and pinned the glittering accessory in place, like it was a conduit for superhuman powers. *Boys never get to wear sparkle.*

And that's bullshit. Ms. V's repartee shattered the doubts in my head.

She's right, you know. That was Gramps. His voice always reminded me of percolating coffee. It had this anticipatory yet soothing feel, full of long-lived habits and sunrises.

The apartment was dark, and I crept to the bathroom, the only one awake. The exhaust fan still whirred, but a tinge of mildew persisted. Under the sink, Mom kept a light-up magnifying mirror. I grabbed it and headed back to my room. After wrangling the plug into the socket, I clicked on the light. There were three options of tinted lighting-bright white, yellowish, and light pink. I chose the last one and sat with a clean sheet of paper to sketch what I saw in the looking glass. The partial image of my face with a ruby-and-diamond barrette settled in among the mass of kinky hair above my ear stared back at me. I titled it Man with Superpower.

Now, the barrette wasn't going to be an everyday kind of thing, but I liked it for tonight, for homecoming. I counted the stones. There were four diamonds surrounding the center, larger ruby. It reminded me of the people around me. The ones who'd hung in there no matter what I did or didn't do. They'd always been there, part of the original setting. Contrasting the rubies' shine.

A knock at my door snapped me out of it.

"Hon, you still getting ready? Kasey's almost done," Mom's muffled voice called from the other side of the door.

I slipped my suit jacket on and went to the living room to wait. Sitting on the couch, next to Michael, I registered the Ohio State football game filling the TV screen.

"O-H," I mumbled with my thumb in my mouth, chewing away at a hangnail.

"I-O," he said with a smirk, matching my low-level enthusiasm.

Kasey and Mom had been working on "final touches" forever. For the zombie effects, we'd stocked up on Halloween face paint. I'd found a plastic severed hand at the grocery store and now had it tucked it in my suit pocket for pictures. Stuart had been extremely secretive about what he was wearing. I'd be lying if I said I wasn't excited to see what he'd pull off. I mean, he succeeded in creating an entire monster-themed dance. He could, literally, do anything.

"Here she comes!" Mom emerged from the hallway with her hands clasped under her chin.

Kasey glowed under the hallway lights. Walking like a princess, she daintily held the sides of her poofy turquoise skirt. She'd chosen a pair of black fishnets and combat boots. Her skin shone a pearly pale green, and her lips were painted blood red. Needless to say, she was a vision of zombie perfection.

"You look amazing." I got up off the couch, took her hand, and held it up high. She spun underneath our bridged arms and beamed. Mom had swooped Kasey's hair into a tangle of topknotted braids that sat like a crown on her head. "Who knew zombies could be so bangin'?"

She laughed and slapped my stomach. "Shut up, dork."

I feigned like she'd really hurt me.

"All right you two, time for pictures. Head outside before the light changes."

The sun was already setting behind the line of trees along the back of the property. Mom lined us up next to each other, giving very specific directions on where we should stand, so that the light was neither behind us nor directly in our eyes.

She snapped photos for a very long time, so Kasey and I started goofing until Mom started the countdown. Then we stopped and beamed out staged smiles.

"What's with the barrette?" Kasey asked through her teeth at one point.

I waited for the click of Mom's camera before answering. "Oh, it was Ms. V's. My neighbor."

"I like it."

"Me too."

"Okay, now for a silly one. Ready...one, two..."

Kasey lifted her skirt, showing off the bright yellow tulle underneath. She made the screaming punk-rock face I'd seen her make many times. I grabbed for the severed hand and chomped down on it. Then, I dropped to my knees and held out my hands, miming why, oh why, god? *Snap.*

"Is Stu coming over with his date?"

"I don't think so, Mom. He's planning some grand entrance."

"Okay then." Mom walked us to the sidewalk. She kissed me on the cheek. "Have fun tonight."

"We will," Kasey and I chorused.

She started to walk away. "Oh wait, what are your plans for afterward?"

I shrugged. I had no idea. We'd spent so much time getting to this point, we hadn't planned what came next.

"Well, no drinking and driving."

"Don't worry, Mom."

"I mean it. If you come back for the car, make sure to look out for each other and don't get back behind the wheel."

"We're aware."

I held my arm out for Kasey, and she looped hers around mine as we walked toward the high school. In the sky, purple-orange hues blended together while a few tiny points of starlight started to pop on.

"See that one?" Kasey pointed at one of the brighter stars. "You know, that one may not even exist anymore. It's so many light years away, it could already be dead."

"Stars live for billions of years. It's probably still alive." I put my hands in my pockets. "It's trippy to think about though. Space stuff makes me feel tiny."

"Really?" Kasey turned to look at me, her eyebrows gathered with consternation. "I'm the opposite. It makes me feel huge, connected to everything."

A line of cars waited at the stoplights we passed. Their windows were down, and music was blaring. Loud bursts of laughter and hoots filled the coming night air. The donut shop had several handmade posters up in the storefront—football player's jersey numbers in glittering print sparkled under the street lamp. Behind the display the shop was dark, and a neon sign flashed closed.

"So, you're really leaving all this behind?" I asked.

"I have to."

"I know. It'll just be weird not having you around. I got used to ya." I put my arm around her shoulder and tucked her in close.

"I'm only a Greyhound away." She wrapped her arms around my waist and hugged me. "Now, cut it out. You're gonna fuck up my hair."

I patted the braided bun on top of her head. It was stiff and crunchy. "Whoa, Mom really went hard on the hair spray."

"I think she used an entire can."

"I can smell it."

She shoved me with her hip as we turned toward the high school. The walkway was strung with twinkling lights. Fake tombstones with catchy phrases lined the sidewalk. As the front doors opened and closed, music from the gym accordioned into the evening air.

I'd expected the zombie theme to chill out everyone's evening wear, but that wasn't the case. Girls were dressed in slinky sequined numbers, and dudes were decked out in suits with matching shiny black shoes. The only difference from previous years was all the makeup. A lot of kids had gone for the pale green face paint, like Kasey. Others went for a light bluish tint. A common look was a trickle of fake blood running from the sides of people's mouths. Severed limbs protruded from purses and suit pockets.

We waited on the sidewalk to get in. I pulled our tickets from my wallet while the couple in front of us argued over who had their tickets. They'd obviously hit up one of the pop-up Halloween stores and were wearing costume contact lenses, their eyes creepily devoid of irises. Everyone's hair was a little more mussed up, tatty-looking, like how it usually looked the morning after homecoming instead of the night of.

Inside, the dance committee had recreated scenes from Penny's comic. Suspended from the ceiling near the stage was a massive papier-mâché airplane with streamers hanging down. It was the crop duster from episode two. It wouldn't last long though. Kids were already zigzagging their way through the streamers, tearing pieces off as they went. The airplane teetered with each movement, like a tightly strung piñata.

A disco ball hung in front of the plane and cast shimmering rainbows over the gym floor. The stage curtains were closed for now, and fake spiderwebs clung to its velvety surface. The DJ stood near the base of the stage, looking like DJ's do as he held one headphone up to his ear, his head bopping along to top 40. A few kids were already buzzed enough to be dancing.

Kasey spotted Dani with her date at a table nearby, and they did that girl bit where they squeal and hug like they hadn't seen each other yesterday. Tyler and I exchanged a typical bro greeting: the low-five handshake, shoulder bump, back pat combo. Then we all sat at the table.

"Where's Des and Stu?" Kasey asked.

Dani rolled her eyes. "Out back arguing. Stuart wants to come in late and alone." She tilted her head and gave Kasey a knowing look. "Desiree wants to come in now, together. It's just more of their stupid drama. I don't know why Stuart had to make this into a whole big thing anyway. Like, just come to the dance like a normal person."

"What's he got planned?" I asked.

"You don't know?" Dani's forehead wrinkled in an accusatory manner.

"He's been all mum." I pantomimed locking my lips shut and throwing away the key.

"You should go talk some sense into that boy." Dani sipped her punch. "I know my sister would appreciate it." She rested her hand on Tyler's thigh. His body reacted with a jolt—a jolt I remembered from the car with Matt. The DJ's jocular tone carried a few quick announcements through the speakers before he risked an early slow dance.

"Wanna dance?" Tyler asked. His eyes admired Dani's cleavage.

"I'd love to." The pair stood and hit the dance floor. Tyler's hand touched the small of Dani's back as the two came together under the decorations. Their foreheads touched.

"When did they become a thing?" I asked.

"Not sure." Kasey slipped a flask from her purse. "Want some?"

I grabbed the bottle and scanned for nearby chaperones. The adults stood in a group near the bleachers, looking bored and tired. I took a swig. It burned going down and made my tongue tingle. "Should we find Stu?"

"You go. I'll sit here and quietly judge everyone's choice of evening wear." Kasey nodded toward Bridget Foley in the middle of the dance floor, dazzling in an above-the-knee green sequined slip dress.

"She looks good."

"She looks like a leprechaun."

"You're such a bitch," I joked.

"Sometimes."

As I left the gymnasium, I looked back at Kasey sitting at the table, getting drunk alone. She shone like her own star. Both tiny and huge. I couldn't tell if the light years separating her from everyone else meant she was still alive or already burned out. But then I thought of Penny and how alike they were. Strong and feisty, and never settling, she'd be okay in Columbus.

Gravel scrunched under my feet as I walked to the back of the school building. Turning the corner, I picked up bits of the harried argument between Stuart and Des.

"Look, all I need you to do is take this CD to the DJ, please." That was Stuart's voice.

"No, I'm not going in there without my date."

"You don't get it."

"Oh, I get it. I helped you put all this together, and now you get to be the star."

"It's not like that at all, Des."

I frowned. Peeking around the corner, I could clearly make out Des in the light of the open locker-room door. She looked glamorous in a tight-fitting black velvet dress with matching gloves that covered her forearms. Her outfit didn't read zombie, but neither did Stuart's getup. In fact, I barely recognized his silhouette. His suit was all white, but somehow, his hair had grown impossibly long, reaching way past his shoulders. What looked like fur tufted at his sleeve cuffs. *What was going on?*

"Stu?" I asked.

"Shit. It's supposed to be a surprise," he whispered toward the night sky.

"Give me the goddamned CD." Des snatched the rainbow metal disc from his claws. *Claws?* "You two can escort each other in tonight." Des stomped off, narrowly missing my shoulder as she huffed past me.

"What's up, buddy?"

He turned around slowly. He wore a black shirt under his jacket. His face was barely visible under long scraggily strands of fur. He freeze-framed with his mouth open, revealing a set of gnarly fangs, and his claws extended as if in mid-attack.

"Oh my god. You're teen wolf from the prom scene." I cupped my hand over my mouth to stop from laughing. We had obsessively watched *Teen Wolf* on VHS in middle school. It'd definitely influenced parts of my first comic, *Pup Operatives.*

Stuart unfroze, shaking out the mane of his wig. "Technically, Homecoming. You can't have everything."

"Was this your plan all along?"

"No. It came to me later. The movie was on TBS a few weeks ago, and when it seemed likely the zombie thing was gonna happen, my brain started clicking."

"So, you get everyone to do one thing and then you do another."

"You gotta zig when people think you're gonna zag, Warsh. It's what makes life fun." Stuart pulled a black handkerchief from his jacket and folded it carefully into his breast pocket. "I'm either gonna make an ass out of myself tonight, or everyone's gonna go along with it." He flicked the triangle-shaped pocket square.

"You should have told me. I could have been your Stiles. Sold T-shirts and all that. What was the whole thing with the CD and Des though?"

"You know me well enough to figure this out.."

"Big Bad Wolf?"

"Hell, yeah, I am."

"All right, man. Let's get you in there."

Stuart took a deep breath, rubbed his hands together a few times, and hopped up and down. He popped his neck and then his knuckles.

"That's not how you pump up a wolf," I said.

"I'm nervous, that's all. Is that a barrette in your hair?"

"Uh-huh. You're a werewolf. Do you care?"

"No."

"Then what are you gonna do?"

"I'm gonna go in there and get this party started."

"That's right. If you're gonna be the wolf, be the motherfuckin' wolf, man. Howl, dude." I punched his arm and let her rip: "OW-OW-OOOOOOOW!"

"OW-OW-OW-OOOOOOOOOW!" Stuart's fists were balled up at his sides.

We stared at each other and, without saying another word, headed inside. We strolled through the lobby. A handful of kids were in line to have their pictures taken in the cafeteria. They gave Stuart strange looks. But they were all dressed like zombies, so what the hell could they say? I checked the double doors to the gym, and Stuart stood hidden behind me. Des sat at the table with her sister, and Dani's arm was draped around her shoulders. I hoped she wasn't crying. This was sure to be an epic moment. If Des knew the movie at all, the wolf would dance right over to the girl he was supposed to be with.

The DJ cut the song he was playing midway through. Moans rang out from the dance floor, but then the first few guitar riffs started in, quickly leading into the beep-bop beat of the song from the movie.

"This is it, Stu."

He rolled his shoulders and strutted in, seemingly confident as hell. People stared. *Did they not know the movie?* I caught Kasey's eye from across the room, and she was already dancing in her seat.

Our classmates finally chilled, and everyone started cheering and high-fiving Stuart as he swaggered over to Des's table. He held out his furry-clawed hand, and she took it. Together, they danced through the song. He'd done it.

I trotted over to Kasey, and we danced the last half of the song together. It was the most ridiculous, wonderful moment. Everyone in the gym would surely still be talking about this years from now—it was as memorable as Landry's game-saving touchdown last night. Maybe even more so.

The night wore on. We drank red fizzy punch by the gallon, mixing in shots of whatever Kasey packed. I knew halfway through, it would be one of those nights that ended when the birds started chattering in the predawn light. Where we all would laugh, talk, cry, and, eventually, puke. Glory days, as they say.

"It's time." Sweat had caused clumps of glued on hair to fall off Stuart's cheeks. It was coming off in patches, and he looked insane. He took me to a table near center stage and pushed on my shoulders until I sat. The curtains parted, revealing a lone transparency machine.

"And now for your entertainment, ladies and gentlemen, please bring your attention to the stage." The DJs voice sounded campy and radio-like. I wondered if he was born with a voice like that, or whether he'd learned it over the years. Anyway, what seemed like everyone gathered around.

A figure dressed all in black entered stage left without making a sound. She clicked on the big beige box of machinery. It whirred to life, shining its spotlight onto a large projection screen. The stagehand took out the first transparency and set it on the machine, and a blurry image filled the screen. She adjusted the knob for clarity.

"It's Penny," someone whispered nearby.

Slow strumming guitar notes played from the speaker next to me. I knew it before I heard the voice. Stuart had gotten a promo copy of *Orange Rhyming Dictionary* right before he left the record store. "Sweet Avenue" was hands down the best song I'd ever heard in my life. When Blake Schwarzenbach's scratchy tones lilted over light and sound, something inside me cracked open.

The next frame was placed on the screen. Penny stood on the dance floor, her miserable zombie-self. The line about always being herself appeared in her speech bubble. Finally, the green drained away from her skin except for a heart-shaped mark on her cheek. There, it had darkened. She was both the same and changed.

The last page was for me. A role of the credits, if you will. I checked the room for Russ Landry. I hadn't seen him all night, but I hadn't really been looking either. Over by the stage, he was very decked out in zombie gear; after all, this was supposed to be his idea. He'd stained a plain white shirt with fake blood around the collar, and a jelly brain poked out of his coat pocket. His skin was chalky, and he'd smeared black smudges under his eyes. The overall effect was a little more skeletal than zombie, save for the brains.

There on the big screen was a quick sketch of an extremely phallic tower, flanked by two rounded bushes.

"Unfortunate landscaping," Stuart murmured.

"Unfortunate architecture," Kasey whispered.

Underneath the phallic logo, in the same curly font I'd used on his car were the words:

D I C K B O R N

Productions

"Dickborn productions?" Dani giggled.

It caught on. Everyone started saying it out loud and eyeballing Russ's branding choice.

"I didn't draw that!"

"Come on, Russ. Everybody knows you're always drawing dicks everywhere." One of Landry's football buddies clapped him on the back.

"We can call you Dickborn if you want though!" Stuart yelled from the seat next to me. Everybody near me snickered.

"Shut up!" Russ was so flustered he took the gelatinous brain from his pocket and tossed it in the middle of the dance floor with a splat. He stormed out of the gym, his date running after him. Other kids threw the props they'd brought into the center of the room too. Some wiped the paint from their skin. Stuart took off his wig and mussed up his hair.

"Last dance?" Kasey nodded, and I took her hand. Near the trash heap of zombie gear, we swayed softly to the music.

"This is the most romantic song I've ever heard." Kasey sniffed in my shoulder. "I hope you won't always think of me when you hear this song, Jeremy."

"Kase, I don't."

When the lights came up, a collective groan emerged from the crowd.

Near the locker room hallway, stood a figure with a ball cap covering his hair. He'd told me he couldn't come, wouldn't be caught dead at a high school function, that he had other plans—a rally or something, but I knew it was him.

My very own Daredevil.

Epilogue

THE FIRST WEEK OF JUNE, 1999

I didn't get that internship with Charlie Wyatt. The news came right after Kasey left, around Thanksgiving, and it was like a kick to the sac. I had let a lot of hopes ride on scoring that internship. Mr. Wyatt did write me a pretty kick-ass recommendation letter, and Mom made me send him a thank-you note. With his reference and the rest of my portfolio, I applied to two art schools in Cincy and one in Columbus. I had a first choice, for sure, but it hadn't been that long ago that any of this was an option, so I convinced myself I'd be happy with whatever happened.

It seemed Mom and Michael had been a little worried after that rejection, so they presented me with my first computer at Christmas and ponied up for an AOL subscription. I set it up on my desk, which didn't leave as much room for drawing. I'd made do though, working on a continuation of Penny Kind in the leftover space. At the moment, she was busy beating back a gang of zombie zealots trying to recapture her and a new friend, Malone, who seemed like a promising sidekick. They shared those little green hearts on their cheeks; they'd both been to the other side and back.

The sound of a door opening squealed from the computer's tinny speaker. I wiggled the mouse to see who had logged online. It was Kasey.

ComiX_gI_720: Hey
snarkybUtterflieS1116: Hey yourself
ComiX_gI_720: How goes it in Columbus?
snarkybUtterflieS1116: Finishing up the last week of school and then graduating this Sunday. How's home?
ComiX_gI_720: Same ole...

I stopped typing because that wasn't really true anymore. Stuart and I graduated last week and nearly everything had changed over the course of the school year. A knock interrupted my thoughts, and Mom stood in the doorway, flipping through a stack of mail.

"This came for you." She placed a standard-sized envelope on my desk and squeezed my shoulder. The return address showed my first-choice college in the upper corner, but small envelopes were bad.

"Thanks," I whispered.

"Do you want me to stick around while you open it?"

"No, I can handle it."

"Okay." She rolled her lips together and looked around my room, stalling. But I'd picked up all the laundry and had been keeping up with the trash.

"Go!" I shooed her away. "I'll be all right. Promise." I picked up the letter containing all my prospects and tapped it against my knee. It was heavy. "Don't you have wedding stuff to do?"

"Don't remind me. How I let you and Michael talk me into an actual ceremony is beyond me." She kissed the top of my newly shorn head.

I'd cut my hair, mostly for graduation. Even though lots of stuff and people had shifted around me, I still craved a change for myself. Something I could see each time I looked in the mirror, but also, something that would grow back.

"I'll be in the kitchen if you need me." She turned to leave but then doubled back. "Oh, before I forget, I'm working on the seating arrangements, and I haven't gotten RSVPs back from your friends. Can you ask them if they're coming?"

"Matt will be there, for sure. Stu put in a request off from work but hasn't heard back yet. And I don't know about Kase."

"Make sure to tell her that she can stay here."

"I will, Mom."

She swung a dish towel over her shoulder and left. I ran my fingers over the university seal, a shining maroon foil paper pressed over the flap. The air was dense with the "before and after" feeling of the moment.

> snarkybUtterflieS1116: You still there?
> ComiX_gi_720: Yeah. A letter from one of the colleges I applied to just showed up.
> snarkybUtterflieS1116: Is it big?
> ComiX_gi_720: No.
> snarkybUtterflieS1116: OPEN IT!
> ComiX_gi_720: I don't know if I can.
> snarkybUtterflieS1116: Don't be a pussy. Open it.

Kasey had been accepted at three different universities but settled on staying near her brother in Columbus. I, on the other hand, couldn't escape the feeling that this whole college thing could just poof away.

> snarkybUtterflieS1116: Get out of your head, Jeremy, and open the damn letter.
> ComiX_gi_720: OK, ok. Hold on.

I slipped my thumb under the sealed lip and tore along the envelope's edge. The fancy paper was thick and stiff in my hands. An embossed imprint of the college logo centered the letter's header. I scanned for the word, "Unfortunately." My heart beat hard against my rib cage, and my sight blurred. I took a deep breath and refolded the letter, setting it aside for now.

> ComiX_gi_720: Mom wants to know if you're coming for the wedding. You can stay here.
> snarkybUtterflieS1116: I ALREADY BOUGHT MY BUS TICKET. NOW TELL ME WHAT THE LETTER SAYS.

An image of a future filled up my field of vision. There was that guy spread out on a hill overlooking the Cincinnati skyline with a giant sketchpad clipped to a drawing board on his lap. He was big and kind of lumbering and was letting his hair grow back in. A tiny chartreuse heart was tattooed on his drawing hand. With bold, sometimes confident strokes, he captured the shadows playing off the surface of the Ohio River.

> ComiX_gi_720: I got in.

Acknowledgements

If you've gotten this far, hi and thanks! Please know that I am grateful for you as a reader. Thank you to everyone at NineStar Press, but especially to my editor, Elizabetta, who saw past my participle phrasing and choppy-ass sentences to the heart of this book. A critique partnership was an integral part of this process. To everyone associated with AFW, I've learned so much from our work together. Kathy and Sarah, our meetings have forever pushed me forward as a writer. Thank you for the many hours you spent reading and discussing Jeremy and his friends. On the regular, I'm in awe of my amazing sisters and some special mama friends. I see how you navigate this world and/or motherhood; it's a beautiful thing. When I finally found the courage to tell people I was writing, my family believed in me, and it meant everything. To my husband, Josh, I love you. You changed my life in a million wonderful ways, and I never saw it coming. Thanks for going bowling that one night in February. And finally, to both my boys: I thought I knew everything about love, but then you were born.

About the Author

Jess Moore makes books and homemade pizza. Her past lives include careers in both teaching and social work. Currently, she resides in historic gold-mining California and writes novels in the very early morning while her family sometimes sleeps.

Email: itwasjess@gmail.com

Facebook: www.facebook.com/itwasjess

Twitter: @it_was_jess

Website: www.itwasjess.wordpress.com

Also Available from NineStar Press

Connect with NineStar Press

Website: NineStarPress.com

Facebook: NineStarPress

Facebook Reader Group: NineStarNiche

Twitter: @ninestarpress

Tumblr: NineStarPress

www.ingramcontent.com/pod-product-compliance
Lightning Source LLC
Chambersburg PA
CBHW032210180726
48284CB00001B/268